Praise for

Mrs. Mohr Goes Missing

Long-listed for the European Bank for Reconstruction and Development Literature Prize

"[An] exceptional debut and series launch . . . The translation showcases the novel's deliciously ironic voice. Fans who like colorful locales and tongue-in-cheek mysteries will eagerly await Zofia's next outing."

—*Publishers Weekly,* starred review

"A delightful debut whodunit written with abundant wit and flair. Pray for a series to follow."

—*Kirkus Reviews*

"*Mrs. Mohr Goes Missing* is an amazing Polish mystery—fascinating for its vivid portrayal of 1893 Crakow, its witty style, and for Zofia, its irrepressible sleuth. The *Daily Mail* called it ingenious—we call this new author 'marvelous!'"

—Charles Todd, *New York Times* best-selling author of the Inspector Ian Rutledge mysteries

"An ingenious marriage of comedy and crime."
—Olga Tokarczuk, Nobel laureate and author of
Man Booker International Prize winner *Flights*

"The unravelling of the mystery is ingenious and takes us through a social setting quivering with snobberies and dos and don'ts. It's fun and sparky, and the glimpse of turn-of-the-century Polish manners and mores is beguiling."
—*Daily Mail*

"Charming and moreish . . . Conjures up the delightful books of Dorothy L. Sayers . . . The perfect diversion for annoying commutes."
—*Stylist*

"While there is a strong whiff of Agatha Christie in this book, it is much more than a pastiche . . . The story fuses high comedy with an evocative portrayal of the period . . . Ably translated."
—*Sunday Express*

"Highly comical . . . An extremely absorbing novel."
—*Kurzojady* (Poland)

Karolina and the Torn Curtain

ALSO BY MARYLA SZYMICZKOWA

Mrs. Mohr Goes Missing

KAROLINA *and the* TORN CURTAIN

Maryla Szymiczkowa

TRANSLATED FROM THE POLISH BY

Antonia Lloyd-Jones

Mariner Books
Houghton Mifflin Harcourt
Boston New York 2021

First US edition

This translation is published by arrangement with
Społeczny Instytut Wydawniczy Znak Sp. z o.o., Kraków, Poland.

Originally published in Polish by Znak as *Rozdarta zasłona,* 2016.

This book has been published with the support of
The Copyright Poland Translation Program.

hmhbooks.com

Library of Congress Cataloging-in-Publication Data
Names: Szymiczkowa, Maryla, author. | Lloyd-Jones, Antonia, translator.
Title: Karolina and the torn curtain / Maryla Szymiczkowa ; translated by
Antonia Lloyd-Jones.
Other titles: Rozdarta Zasłona. English
Description: First U.S. edition. | Boston : Mariner Books/Houghton Mifflin
Harcourt, 2021. | Series: A Zofia Turbotynska mystery; 2
Identifiers: LCCN 2020033849 (print) | LCCN 2020033850 (ebook) |
ISBN 9780358157571 (trade paperback) | ISBN 9780358449478 (audiobook) |
ISBN 9780358449775 (audio cd) | ISBN 9780358150961 (ebook)
Subjects: GSAFD: Mystery fiction.
Classification: LCC PG7219.Z93 R6913 2021 (print) |
LCC PG7219.Z93 (ebook) | DDC 891.8/538—dc23
LC record available at https://lccn.loc.gov/2020033849
LC ebook record available at https://lccn.loc.gov/2020033850

Book design by Greta D. Sibley

Printed in the United States of America
DOC 10 9 8 7 6 5 4 3 2 1

For Martin Pollack,

not just for Emperor of America

CONTENTS

PROLOGUE

In which somebody's night of pleasure ends in a rather unpleasant way, and the platters have to wait awhile before returning to their place in the sideboard.

By the time Commissioner Stanisław Jednoróg had reached the beach below the Rożnowski Villa, the golden bugles had finished sounding the reveille at the Austrian barracks on Wawel Hill, visible above the river Vistula in the pale April sunlight that was breaking through the vestiges of mist. Two inquisitive housemaids were looking out of the second-floor windows of a neo-Gothic tower, marveling at all they saw: the policemen walking along the riverbank, the three soldiers standing slightly to one side, and above all, the corpse of a young woman stretched out on the wet sand.

She was lying on her back with her hair loose, covering her face and flowing in a wide chestnut wave across her breast. Her white linen blouse and thick navy-blue skirt, still damp, clung tightly to her young body; she couldn't have been more than twenty years old. If a student from the Academy of Fine Art had come this way he'd probably have thought of a Pre-Raphaelite Ophelia, but at this time of day in the Dębniki district the only people looking at the corpse were the housemaids, the police constables, the commissioner, and the soldiers — by their bright blue coats, red trousers, and caps they could be identified as dragoons from Archduke Carl's Third Galician Lancers — in short, none of them knew much about art. At a pinch, the wife of a local fisherman could have come this way, or an itinerant peddler, but as luck would have it, there was no art student on the scene. If there were, he could have stopped nearby, rested a foot on a stone, and recorded this moment in his sketchbook with a few swiftly drawn lines: daybreak on the seventeenth of April 1895, when the waters of the Vistula had tossed the girl's body onto the shore, with a brick-red stain of congealed blood on her blouse like a large, dark poppy, at the very spot where hours before her heart had been beating. The public liked a dramatic image, especially if there was a clear allegory painted in the background — a dour old man in a cape, symbolizing death, for instance. Or a broken lily. Two more policemen appeared from around a bend in the river, cadets with barely a shadow of blond down on their upper lips — the housemaids looking down from the tower took far more notice of them than of the venerable commissioner, who was more likely to appeal to an equally venerable matron. In his outstretched hands one of the young policemen was carrying a rag dripping with water; when they laid it on the sand beside the body, even the maids in the turret could see that it was a woman's jacket, found on the shore or in the riverside rushes, and made of the same navy-blue cloth as the skirt. Then they stood staring, now at the corpse, now at the ground, and now at the soldiers. The police doctor, Albin Schwarz, came up behind them; he must have been here earlier on to certify the death, but now he was getting rather bored waiting for the body to be transported to the mortuary, which might explain why he had gone off with the young policemen as if to search for clues, but actually to take a walk, though for mid-April it was still cold.

Someone called from inside the Rożnowski Villa, so the maids banged the little windows shut and ran to see to their duties. It was the Wednesday after Easter, the day for putting away the best dinner service in the cavernous sideboards, the celebration silver and the large platters on which the blessed sausage rings, garnished hams, mazurek tarts, and babkas made with five dozen eggs had lately been displayed. There was no time for gawking.

Part One

CHAPTER I

In which the story starts like a Hitchcock film, although he wasn't born until four years later, Zofia runs into her cousin and is affronted, and Ignacy goes on an unexpected outing.

It all began with the earthquake. On the evening of Easter Saturday, when the Turbotyńskis came home from Resurrection Mass at the cathedral, Zofia was already—to put it mildly—in a less than ideal mood. They had set off on the return journey from Wawel Hill in the company of Professor Rostafiński and his wife—he was a faculty secretary at the Academy of Learning, where Zofia wanted to obtain a post for Ignacy, while Mrs. Rostafińska was taking a rather active part in collecting money for the renovation of the cathedral, which lately had absorbed the attention of almost all the society ladies. Unfortunately, on All Saints' Square they ran into Zofia's cousin, Józefa Dutkiewicz and her children, who were also on their way home to Floriańska Street. Despite her best intentions, Zofia had never been able to rid herself of the principle instilled by her mother that "family, rest assured, are people too, despite being kin," so the encounter was not just limited to an exchange of bows, but led to both groups merging, and then heading at a brisk pace—the evening was cool—down Grodzka Street toward the Market Square.

What had promised to be a pleasant family walk in the greenish light of the gas lamps ended in an unpleasant quarrel of a spiritual nature. Much comment was always passed on the Resurrection Mass in Cracow; the usual debate included the relevance of the sermon, the singing of the choir, the appearance of the celebrants, and other such things of a not necessarily theological nature—but ultimately, as the history of the church tells us, these are not the sort of issues that lead to schisms or to people casting oaths at each other. But this time the quarrel was over a basic point, namely the superiority of the old bishop over the new one, as Mrs. Dutkiewicz insisted, or the new one over the old, as Mrs. Turbotyńska would have it.

To her cousin's cutting remark that the late, lamented Cardinal Dunajewski did not travel about in a carriage drawn by four horses and had no need to stress his own undeniable eminence at every step of the way, Zofia replied with the short but emphatic statement: "Józefa, this is Cracow!" as if that explained everything. Then, in case it didn't, and further elucidation was essential, she added: "The emperor has made Cracow's bishops into princes, so following the sudden death of the cardinal last year it seemed perfectly fit and proper for a representative of the ancient princely house of Puzyna to take his seat on the bishop's throne. In this city the miter is not to be placed on the head of the sons of railway workers, tradesmen, or I don't know what"—she waved the tip of her umbrella disdainfully—"junior officers."

"Zofia," said Mrs. Dutkiewicz, "I think you are speaking with the voice of local patriotism."

"No doubt," replied Zofia, and quoted a proverb as old as it was overused: "If it weren't for Cracow, Cracow would be Rome."

"Without question, but I was thinking of Przemyśl, my dear . . ." said her cousin in a sugary tone, needling her reviled relative with a smile; she knew Zofia was ashamed of the provincial city of her birth. "No wonder Bishop Puzyna is so dear to you—for many years he was a canon in your hometown, was he not?"

❧

So as Franciszka took her mistress's fur coat, Zofia was still quivering with rage at the memory of the affront inflicted on her by Mrs. Dutkiewicz in full view, and especially full hearing of, the Rostafińskis. Who could help where they were born?

"Where is Karolina?" she boomed at the cook, giving vent to the anger she'd been stifling for half the journey home. "Why isn't the girl doing her duty?"

And then, as confused as she was terrified, Franciszka informed her master and mistress that less than an hour ago Karolina had packed up her belongings and left Cracow, having previously "handed in her notice to *me.*" Before sinking onto the ottoman, Zofia Turbotyńska managed to utter just one sentence: "This is . . . this is worse than war."

Easter in Peacock House had been somewhat marred by the circumstances. Like it or not, Zofia had had to take some of Karolina's duties upon herself, while the rest had landed on Franciszka's shoulders. Fortunately, they had made most of the preparations in advance, but any resulting satisfaction Zofia might have felt was obscured by her rage at "that ungrateful hoyden who has vanished without a word of farewell," so the prevailing atmosphere in the Turbotyński house was far from joyful; all of a sudden Zofia would say into thin air: "So it has come to this—handing in one's notice to a servant!" and "What a decline in morals!" or simply a laconic: "The world is at an end." Nevertheless, or perhaps to dispel the dismal mood and occupy their thoughts with something else, on Easter Monday, like almost everyone else in Cracow, the Turbotyńskis went to the annual Emaus Fair.

It was their first trip beyond the city limits for several months. The weather was quite good, with a warm, by now unquestionably spring sun breaking through the clouds, so they planned to climb Kościuszko Mound to admire the view and survey the panorama of the city awakening from its winter lethargy. But these bold and ambitious plans were scotched when Ignacy was seized by a painful stitch ("I did ask you to refrain from a second helping of poppy-seed cake," hissed Zofia), and the outing ended with the purchase of a little clay bell and a tree of life that now stood on the sideboard.

Next day they stayed at home, and Franciszka set off for Lasota Hill alone, after being instructed by Zofia to watch out for young men who could be harboring ignoble intentions toward solitary young ladies taking part in the traditional egg-rolling event. Time passed slowly, measured out by the bugle call from the tower of St. Mary's, the striking of the grandfather clock in the drawing room, and the gradual dwindling of the Easter treats — mazurek tarts, cheesecake, and babkas.

Yet on the Wednesday after Easter, afternoon tea at Peacock House was to run an extremely unusual course, and would be remembered for a long time to come. It began with an apparently minor change. As soon as Ignacy noticed that, instead of the next instalment of Sienkiewicz's historical epic *Quo Vadis?*, "some English nonsense" had been published on the front page of the *Cracow Times*, he grumpily rose from his armchair and went over to the table to help himself to a slice of caramel mazurek. At this point Zofia did something she'd never have done in a better mood: almost instinctively she sat down in Ignacy's armchair and picked up the newspaper he'd left on the side table.

"*Strange Case of Dr. Jekyll and Mr. Hyde,*" snorted Ignacy. "That's a good one! Fancy a serious newspaper publishing such outlandish twaddle, I ask you! And instead of Sienkiewicz's latest novel, too! What is the world coming to?"

After casting an eye over the "English nonsense," which seemed to her very interesting, rather in the spirit of her beloved Poe, Zofia turned the newspaper over, with the aim of scanning the classified advertisements for servants printed on the back page. She knew they needed a new housemaid as soon as possible, but somehow she couldn't bring herself to deal with it. To put off the inevitable, she opened the newspaper, and starting from the end, began to read out the items that caught her eye in the lesser columns on the preceding pages.

"*During a bullfight in Barcelona one of the bulls jumped the barrier, causing indescribable panic,*" she read. "*A gendarme approached the frenzied animal and fired his gun . . .*"

"That's what the police are for, my dear, to protect people from dangers. Of whatever kind . . ."

"*The bullet killed the bull, but it also hit a spectator, who fell dead on the spot,*" concluded Zofia. This prompted no reply.

She turned the page.

"THE CHRONICLE. A tragic incident. On the 16th of this month at 8 a.m. at the Róża Hotel, in sight of two accidental witnesses, hotel guest Mr. José Silva, who had come to our city from Lemberg, and before that from faraway Brazil, took his own life with a shot from a revolver . . ."

"People have no shame — fancy killing oneself so close to Easter," remarked Ignacy, without looking up from his tea plate.

"But at least he did it far away from his family, who will always be able to say in company that he died of an aneurysm or shot himself while cleaning his gun," said Zofia for the defense.

On the opposite page she found a piece of news that made her sit up.

"Ignacy, there's been an earthquake!" she cried.

"You're exaggerating, Zofia. They do make the occasional threat, but the Prince of Windisch-Grätz's cabinet is sure to last for a long time to come — this is the dual monarchy, not the Kingdom of Italy. Of course, it is a long way from the prince to Viscount Taaffe, who headed the government from . . . How long was he prime minister for?" wondered Ignacy.

"Really, Ignacy, who cares about all that Viennese political maneuvering," snapped Zofia, but rather halfheartedly, absorbed as she was in scrutinizing the article. About an earthquake, a genuine cataclysm, in Slovenia and Carniola . . . with its epicenter in Laibach . . . *"The shocks were violent and long-lasting . . ."* she read. *"In some places they continued all night."*

"Tell me another," grunted Ignacy. "In Laibach!"

He was hurt by his wife's rebuff, on top of which she had assumed his role by reading him press reports.

"The shocks were also felt in Venice, Florence, and Rome . . ." she went on, unperturbed.

"Rome?" he muttered.

"Indeed. And Vienna too!"

"Good God!" Ignacy stood up abruptly, making the table shake. Cutlery jangled, cups, saucers, and tea plates trembled. "Is His Majesty safe? Read it, woman!" he cried, brushing cake crumbs off his waistcoat.

Just then the doorbell rang.

Soon after, Franciszka entered the drawing room—cautiously, in view of the shouts coming from inside. She stood in the doorway without speaking, counting on her master and mistress to notice her, but she had to wait awhile, because her presence did not prompt the interest of either Ignacy or Zofia, who was busy reassuring her husband that no harm had come to His Majesty. Neither of them thought anything the servant might have to say could matter as much as the news of an earthquake, even if it was in distant Laibach. How very wrong they were.

"What is it, Franciszka?" asked Zofia at last, reluctantly looking up from the newspaper. "Who was it? The coalman? I told you we wouldn't be needing any after Easter. It's getting warmer now, and at those prices . . ."

"It's for you . . . the police . . ." stammered the girl, nervously crumpling a dishcloth in her hands.

"The police?" Zofia leaped to her feet. *"Kyrie eleison!"*

For a split second Sister Alojza sprang to Zofia's mind, the amiable nun of unassuming appearance who overused that expression, and whom eighteen months ago she had helped to find the murderer who had been on the prowl at Helcel House.* But she soon focused her attention on things of far greater importance at this moment — such as the sudden arrival of the police at a respectable house.

"Calm down, Zofia, it's sure to be nothing serious," said Ignacy, trying to reassure her. He shook off the rest of the caramel mazurek crumbs and asked Franciszka to "show the gentlemen in."

There was only one, very thin, policeman, who looked like a starving rat. At first glance it was plain to see that this ginger youth in a rather baggy uniform was a very fresh recruit in the Imperial-Royal police. He bowed to the Turbotyńskis and introduced himself: "Cadet Jan Eclcr, at your service."

"To what do we owe this unexpected visit?" asked Zofia at once, sounding perhaps a little more perturbed than she intended. "Ours is a respectable home, Mister . . ." she

* See *Mrs. Mohr Goes Missing*, Mariner Books, 2020.

added hesitantly, realizing she had no idea how to address a policeman of such low rank, "Mr. Policeman."

"Forgive me," said Ecler with a bow, and clicked his heels, "but I have received an official order from the commissioner to speak to the head of this household. Do I have the honor of addressing Professor Turpentyński?" he said, turning to Ignacy.

"Turbotyński!" Zofia immediately corrected him. "Of *the* Turbotyńskis. Wadwicz coat of arms."

"I am most extremely sorry," said Ecler, blushing. "I've only been in service since last autumn . . . on probation."

"Indeed? I'd never have thought it . . ."

"Zofia, please," said her husband, casting her a beseeching look. "My dear sir, I am Ignacy Turbotyński, and I gather it is with me that you wish to speak. But we would both like to know what matter brings you here."

"I humbly beg to report that Commissioner Jednoróg sent me. I've been instructed to ask you to accompany me to Mikołajska Street . . . that's to say the police station, from where you and the commissioner are to proceed to the Forensic Medicine Unit."

"Aha, as you can see, my dear, there's nothing to be worried about," said Ignacy, smiling. "Our brave guardians of the law must be needing some, how shall I put it, expert advice. Professor Halban has been on sick leave since January, and Wachholz is in Lemberg, so . . . of course, I'm no expert . . ."

"What are you talking about, Ignacy? Of course you

are," said Zofia. "You are an eminent specialist. Go and do your academic and civic duty," she urged.

Once he had left with Ecler, it occurred to her that perhaps a new and unexpected career path was opening before her husband. Indeed, he hadn't become head of the regular anatomy department after Teichmann's departure, but maybe if he tried hard there'd be a chance for anatomical pathology? There was no great difference, after all. And then, who knows? Maybe the title of senior professor, maybe even, she mused, a chair at the Academy of Learning? As long as Rostafiński hadn't taken against the Turbotyńskis . . . And what's more, it would mean the opportunity to question him over lunch about the details of every crime committed in Cracow!

When Ignacy came home less than an hour later, he looked like a ghost: it was as if all the blood, lately in such vigorous circulation on account of the Easter cakes, had drained from his face. He sat in his armchair, sighed heavily, and in a graveyard tone announced: "Zofia, Franciszka, I have something very serious to tell you. Something dreadful has happened."

CHAPTER II

In which we learn why the walls of the former Jesuit college are so thick, where the lancers were returning from (from a nocturnal outing), what characterizes the ectodermal odor of a pure virgin, and the potential existence of waves not yet known to science.

Zofia Turbotyńska slept badly. Next morning she got up with a headache, and before she'd managed to dress, she'd already complained to Ignacy and to Franciszka that "my nerves did not allow me to close my eyes for as long as five minutes," though in fact there was a good deal of rhetorical exaggeration in that remark. But when in her drowsy state it occurred to her that she must be sure to tell Karolina about her sleepless night too, she felt something she wasn't expecting: real, acute grief. Not indignation at the decline in morals and the dangers of the modern world, which could be expressed in conversation to striking effect, not anger that she'd been deprived of an excellent servant, but genuine grief: something had happened, but Karolina would never, ever hear about it; from now on the whole world would carry on turning without Karolina, with no regard for her nonexistence.

For Zofia had to admit that in the long procession of housemaids that had woven its way through the Turbotyńskis' flat in Peacock House over the years, Karolina was the first girl since Franciszka to have stayed here for any length of time — more than that, she had gained the sincere sympathy of the householders. And now, thought Zofia with an affection she rarely felt, the poor girl was lying on a cold dissection table, or perhaps by now the postmortem was over, and she was resting in her final abode, very different from the servants' room on St. John's Street: in her coffin. Trying to move as quietly as possible, Zofia went to the bedroom door, turned the brass key in the lock, returned to her dressing table, sat down, and only then, knowing that nobody would disturb her, began to weep.

A few minutes later she got a grip on herself, washed her face, applied some Pompadour Milk to mask the evidence of lack of sleep and weeping, then added a little powder too for better effect, and finally tidied her hair, placing an elegant garnet-studded comb in it. Now she was ready to face the day.

❧

According to plan, Commissioner Jednoróg arrived at 10:00 a.m., and immediately installed himself in the drawing room, where specially for this purpose Franciszka had done some *extra* cleaning. Cadet Ecler, already familiar in this house, sat down to take the minutes, having first arranged a small portable writing set on the table, and some files containing documents and photographs—in short, police paraphernalia. Franciszka led two other trainee policemen to the servants' room, where they were to search Karolina's belongings for items that might help to explain the case.

The man appointed as investigating magistrate was Walenty Rozmarynowicz, a figure greatly respected in Cracow, and not just for his impressive gray beard. Yet his most celebrated successes had been in the days when the Turbotyńskis had tied the sacred knot of matrimony, in other words more than twenty years ago; nowadays in private conversations he was called "the great-grandsire of the Galician courts," and a blind eye was turned to the fact that he occasionally nodded off in the middle of a hearing, or mixed up a case involving the theft of a linen chest with a case involving the serious assault of a tailor's apprentice; there was always someone on hand to straighten things out, and Rozmarynowicz could continue to enjoy the reputation of the great Nestor of the judicial system. So it was in this case too: the commissioner had been delegated to conduct the inquiry, thanks to which Rozmarynowicz had no need to leave the courthouse. The thick walls of what had once been a Jesuit college stifled the rattle of the carriages rolling over the cobblestones on Grodzka Street, leaving him to doze for as long as he liked.

Each person was interviewed in the customary manner, in turn and separately. First Ignacy, because Zofia had stressed that her husband, as a Jagiellonian University professor and a great mind, was an extremely busy person, giving invaluable service to science, not just in Cracow but the entire empire, if not the whole of Europe, and so the police would have to accommodate themselves to his timetable. Which in fact did not prove particularly difficult, because as soon as Ecler asked him what time would be the most convenient, Ignacy replied without a second thought: "Really, whatever suits you! The tortoise is not a hare, I'll always have time to dissect it," and thus entirely defeated his wife's efforts to present him in the best possible light. So it was decided that the professor would be the first to make his statement, then the lady of the house, and finally the servant, and thus in order of importance. Though it occurred to Zofia that if she were organizing the interviews, she would naturally have started with Franciszka, who knew the victim best.

Now, as she waited her turn, she made an effort to organize her thoughts, and even fetched a notebook to jot down the individual facts. Karolina Szulc was seventeen years old, and had started working at St. John's Street in May . . . no, June of last year, because it was just after the death of Cardinal Dunajewski. Like all the other housemaids, she too had come from Mrs. Mikulska's licensed agency for the procurement of servants on Gołębia Street. But where was she from in the broader sense? Not from Cracow. Where was her mother? Aha, in Podgórze, yes, she was from the Podgórze district just across the Vistula, in other words—here again Zofia felt a sharp pang in her heart—from the riverside where she had been found lifeless, beneath the brick walls of the Rożnowski Villa. *Denomination: Roman Catholic. Character: impeccable, modest, industrious,* she wrote in the notebook, without knowing why, except perhaps to keep her hands and her mind busy. *Appearance: pleasant. Distinguishing marks: none.* Anyway, why would they want distinguishing marks? They didn't have to identify her, just find the killer.

The door from the drawing room into the dining room opened and there stood Ecler. He bowed and said: "The commissioner requests your presence, madam."

She rose from the armchair, rearranged the folds of her dress, and walked ahead; Ignacy had already left the drawing room by the other door, so without wasting time on needless ceremony in the form of conjugal farewells, she strode up to the commissioner, who adopted the right facial expression for offering condolences and said: "Mrs. Turbotyńska, please accept my deepest sympathy for the tragic death of your employee. I am convinced that she could not have chanced upon a better employer, so well known for her charitable nature."

Zofia adopted the right facial expression for receiving condolences, thanked him, and then took the seat offered her. Ecler sat opposite, with his nib suspended above some sheets of office paper.

"Professor Turbotyński is a scholar," Jednoróg began cautiously, "and so household matters . . ."

"Of course, my husband does not concern himself with such trifles as the servants, the cleaning, or the shopping. Tracking down the perpetrator of this outrageous crime is naturally a matter of the greatest importance to us both, yet, in truth, I have no idea how he could be of any help to you, or what he could have to tell you."

"We talked a lot about the Rożnowski Villa. The professor regards it as a scandalous example of interference in the shape of the city's former suburbs . . ."

". . . and that vulgar modern block acts as an unfortunate counterweight to the ancient walls of the Wawel Castle," she completed the sentence, as if reciting a lesson learned by heart. "Oh yes. And no doubt he told you that on this side of the river it couldn't have happened, but in Dębniki there is still . . ."

". . . a building act in force from the days of our ancestors, dating back to 1786. Yes, naturally the professor was good enough to mention it. He also joked that Mr. Rożnowski and his wife are cousins of the soap manufacturers . . ."

". . . so they shouldn't build so close to water. So now we have the matter straight."

Unlike Klossowitz, the magistrate who had conducted the inquiry at Helcel House, Commissioner Jednoróg was gifted with impeccable manners, and was generally well liked. An excellent dancer in his day, he had kept his dapper figure, though graced with a small paunch by now, but in the eyes of the ladies that simply added to the charm of a man in his prime. He had recently celebrated his fiftieth birthday, and to mark the occasion a letter of congratulation and a silver cross of merit with a crown had arrived from Vienna, which with a degree of gusto—as he wasn't free of vanity—he pinned to his chest at the slightest opportunity: any kind of festivity, procession, or masked ball hosted by the marksmen's fraternity at their headquarters, the Celestat.

Now Zofia was examining him closely: without his medal, his rifleman's fraternity robe, or his tailcoat he was simply a civil servant dutifully performing his function. He asked her the relevant questions: was Karolina a diligent employee, did she have any enemies, did she lead a life of virtue, was she free of melancholy and suicidal tendencies, and so on. And she took her time with her replies, doing her best to mention everything that could be relevant to the inquiry.

"Are you sure she led a life of virtue?"

"I have already given you my answer to that question," she said sharply. "It should be easy to find in the minutes."

The trainee raised his rather rat-like snout from his notes, stared vacantly at the previous page, and confirmed her words with a nod, but even so, nobody took any notice of him.

"Indeed, but you see, madam, the circumstances in which we found the body . . . the circumstances of the actual murder, or perhaps suicide, because . . ."

"Excuse me, but what circumstances?"

Jednoróg leaned back in his chair — a piece of furniture brought from Ignacy's family mansion after the division of the inheritance — twirled his slightly graying mustache, and cleared his throat.

"Well . . . in the middle of the night, a young girl walking about the city on her own . . . quite near the barracks. In a district where one might find a fair number of young persons of dubious reputation, persons — with respect for your ears, madam — employed in the world's oldest profession."

"Commissioner!"

"I don't wish to shock you," he said, raising his hands, "but you are sure to know that the police often see things from which, as good Christians, we would all prefer to avert our gaze. But then the Lord Jesus conversed with harlots . . ."

"How on earth could Karolina have been a harlot? She was a pretty girl, admittedly, but that's as far as it goes. She did have a young man, Franciszka may remember his name, a fisherman or rafter, who took her out in his boat from time to time, but as far as I know it was all quite innocent.

Surely you are not trying to suggest that a young woman might be employed in the respectable home of a professor whose personal conduct was dubious in the least respect?"

"Certainly not," Jednoróg assured her. "Yet one must bear in mind that the corpse was found by three soldiers . . . three lancers, who were on their way back from the . . . establishment."

"The establishment?"

"The facility."

"The facility?"

"The bawdy house," he finally gasped, distinctly embarrassed.

"Forgive me, but where the lancers go gadding about at night is a matter for their commanding officer and has nothing to do with where my housemaid spends her time. Or rather former housemaid, for as I have mentioned, on Saturday during the Resurrection Mass, she handed in her notice while I was out of the house and went off to points unknown. But while she was under this roof she had just one sweetheart, a rafter or fisherman, and behaved as a modest young woman should."

"I do not wish to insult the memory of your *former* housemaid," said Jednoróg after a pause, "so please regard this as a general statement, but there are girls who, while appearing to be the model of chastity, covertly abandon themselves to debauchery. Sometimes this is an innate tendency—after all, the deceased was born out of wedlock to"—he glanced at his documents—"Marianna Szulc, washerwoman and ironer—and sometimes it results from the influence of contemporaries or friends . . ."

"Franciszka is the perfect model for any housemaid."

"I was not suggesting otherwise. Sometimes it is simply an unfortunate set of circumstances that pushes the daughter of Eve into the embrace of sin."

"One can hardly speak of an unfortunate set of circumstances in this case—someone simply stabbed her with a knife . . . It's to do with that person's will, not the circumstances."

"With a sharp instrument," Jednoróg corrected her. "Yes, that is the possible cause of death, but not conclusively. I left the office early, before the postmortem report was issued. Let us hope that the inquiry will prove Miss Szulc's complete innocence. Please forgive me if I have offended you in any way—I had no such intention. We are all concerned about the truth, are we not? And the truth is sometimes painful, requiring us to pose painful questions. What about the sweetheart? Has he been in evidence lately?"

"If anyone knows, it will be Franciszka," replied Zofia, accepting the commissioner's apology with a gracious smile. "The romantic affairs of my housemaids are of no concern to me," she lied through her teeth; she didn't actually know much about Wacek or Felek, the fisherman or rafter, though not because it didn't interest her, but purely because the housemaid had been quite secretive. "In Karolina's final days it's not the sweetheart that puzzles me . . ."

"But you may be misguided! He is one of our suspects.

Of course there are the lancers, too, who found the body. They did inform the police . . ."

". . . but could have committed the murder themselves and then informed the police to evade suspicion."

"I see that you are in your element within an inquiry," he said, smiling. "Well, I have heard a thing or two. Cracow is a small place, and you have quite a reputation among the investigating magistrates. Of course," he reassured her, "our conversation will remain between us. I hope that with our combined forces we shall be able to solve this mystery."

Pleasantly flattered, Zofia returned his smile.

"Do you have any more questions for me? Or shall I call in Franciszka?"

"I wouldn't dream of disturbing you. Ecler!"

The cadet dutifully stood up, clicked his heels, bowed, and went to the door.

"The commissioner will see you now."

Franciszka entered the drawing room—not as one might have expected, with her gaze modestly lowered, but proudly, with her head held high. Zofia at once embraced the suspicion that someone had been listening at the door, and was not impressed by the insinuation about the bad influence on young women of their contemporaries.

"Good morning. If you please, madam, the other policemen have gone now, and I've cleaned the room."

"Thank you. We'll talk about lunch once the commissioner has finished his work."

And after closing the door behind her, Zofia heard the

shuffle of a chair being moved. She was itching to eavesdrop, but she was sure Franciszka had been listening at the keyhole shortly before, and following in her footsteps was quite beneath her.

❧

"I was coming home from some place at the end of the world, about three o'clock of a black winter morning, and my way lay through a part of town where there was literally nothing to be seen but lamps," Mr. Enfield told the lawyer, Mr. Utterson, in the novella that Zofia was now reading in yesterday's newspaper, found on the side table, in an attempt to stave off her negative thoughts and focus her mind elsewhere. *"Street after street, and all the folks asleep—street after street, all lighted up as if for a procession and all as empty as a church . . ."* As if out of spite, the gloomy shore of the Vistula and the brick walls of the Rożnowski Villa sprang to her memory again. *"Till at last I got into that state of mind when a man listens and listens and begins to long for the sight of a policeman. All at once, I saw two figures: one a little man who was stumping along eastwards at a good walk, and the other a girl of maybe eight or ten who was running as hard as she was able down a cross street. Well, sir, the two ran into one another naturally enough at the corner; and then came the horrible part of the thing; for the man trampled calmly over the child's body and left her screaming on the ground."*

What a fine thing, thought Zofia. *I wanted to read a nice novella, a story about conjugal life in the English provinces, but here we have crime, crime, nothing but crime!* She read on. *"It sounds nothing to hear, but it was hellish to see,"* the tale continued.

Zofia put down the *Cracow Times* in irritation. Ignacy was right; she would rather read Sienkiewicz's novel, *Quo Vadis?,* about the early Christians and Roman patricians in the days of Nero than about murders committed in London. As if there weren't enough terrifying stories about Jack the Ripper, a real murderer on the prowl at night—why did they have to think up additional scoundrels, too? But she went on reading, learning to her satisfaction that *"the child was not much the worse, more frightened, according to the Sawbones."* She liked the inquiring mind of Mr. Utterson, who wanted to know where the repulsive Mr. Hyde lived, whereas Mr. Enfield, who hadn't tracked Hyde down, annoyed her by saying: *"I feel very strongly about putting questions; it partakes too much of the style of the day of judgment. You start a question, and it's like starting a stone. You sit quietly on the top of a hill; and away the stone goes, starting others; and presently some bland old bird (the last you would have thought of) is knocked on the head in his own back-garden and the family have to change their name."* To tell the truth, the day of judgment, when everyone would have to confess their minor sins and shameful secrets, was for Zofia Turbotyńska a vague portent of the happiest moment in all eternity—assuming, as she hoped, that it was a universal confession, in which case, as it rose to heavenly heights, her immaterial soul would finally discover the whole truth about the earthly transgressions committed by the other immaterial souls of the entire Cracow bourgeoisie.

The door in the hall slammed, and she heard footsteps coming from the kitchen — it was Franciszka running to receive the professor's top hat and overcoat from him.

"Here is another lesson to say nothing," said he. "I am ashamed of my long tongue. Let us make a bargain never to refer to this again."

"With all my heart," said the lawyer. "I shake hands on that, Richard."

Continuation to follow, promised a note at the bottom of the column. She folded the newspaper and tossed it lightly onto the table, then leaned forward across the armrest of the sofa to reach for the bell pull.

"Franciszka, as the master has returned, you may lay the table."

❦

"The commissioner is a nice fellow," muttered Ignacy, helping himself to the last of the cold meats that were still left over from the Easter platters. "Though I'm afraid I couldn't be of much help to him."

"Yes, very nice . . ."

"But?"

"But somehow I felt hurt when he suggested that Karolina . . . that the cause of Karolina's death was immoral conduct, or at least some sort of . . . incident. You knew her in person, and we are both aware that she was the picture of honesty."

Ignacy looked up, while also trying to extract a thread of ham from between his teeth with his tongue.

"Well, perhaps there is a grain of truth in it. There are cases of love-induced brainstorms, even among the most modest of girls! It's to do with the physical difference between men and women, which is the main basis for the ensuing spiritual difference. This relationship," he said, leaning back in his chair, "is comparable, let us say, with the relationship that occurs between electricity and magnetism, which also supplement each other at right angles of ninety degrees, thus creating a new force, intensified by . . ."

"Indeed, it goes without saying that women are different from men . . ."

"Allow me to finish, Zofia," he said, and raised a finger. "The male and female soul are true opposites, which for this very reason inevitably belong to each other like two polar halves, and which mutually supplement each other, creating new forces only in the correct conditions. That also explains why there is such a great difference in the symptoms of love, since the woman feels not only with her nerve centers, but with every single nerve! That is the latest scientific opinion, based on the research of Dr. Czarnowski of Berlin."

Ignacy had his favorite topics, and as Zofia knew only

too well, he enjoyed giving lectures outside as much as inside the university.

"Meanwhile, here we have neither a budding young lass, nor a mature woman. Merely the ectodermal odor of such a chaste virgin is extremely pure and subtle, almost to a point of being odorless. When she falls in love, the odor changes, as in a flower when its bud unfurls. When inhaled by a man," he said heatedly, "this odor enters his bloodstream and has a direct effect on him, as an agent that stimulates rapture. Whereas his odor produces mixed emotions in the girl, on the one hand similar to the effect of the smell of a predatory animal upon its prey, an agent prompting alarm, and on the other the scent of the man whom the girl loves, perhaps in this case that rafter . . ."

"Or fisherman, I can't remember."

". . . or fisherman, is an agent prompting delight. With frequent contact the maidenly alarm recedes, and the purely blissful effect remains." He pushed away his plate, on which there was a half-eaten slice of ham and some horseradish sauce. "According to science, the spiritual shock acts on the nervous system in a way that breaks down protein, and thus unties the connection between emotion and smell. In the girl two sources of efflux predominate . . ." At this point he fixed his gaze on the table. "The sexual odor, which produces an emotion of innocence, and the cerebral current, which has a stimulating effect upon the man, like champagne. And he pounces on the girl as a hawk swoops on a dove!" Fervently waving a hand, he almost knocked over a plant pot filled with catkins. "Then, through the sudden and intense inhalation of the male odor, and as the result of short-term spiritual shock, the girl experiences plain overexcitement. The agent of alarm is released with such force that symptoms of paralysis take the upper hand, and the girl may become the passive prey of the man."

"Passive?" was Zofia's only interjection.

"Passive. That explains why even the most bashful, well-brought-up girls whom no one would suspect of such a thing still fall prey to seduction. Excessive inhalation of the male odor deprives the girl of her free will, rendering her cataleptic, as if magnetically hypnotized, and so she fully surrenders. She allows herself to be kissed, even though she remains cold and trembling—she is so far under the spell of the man that she would let her life be taken from her. But if she resists, then the angry ardor of her inflamed seducer causes his odor to intensify strongly, overpowering the girl entirely, with the same effect as chloroform!"

"I cannot believe that Karolina was in a cataleptic state at the time. She was a smart young woman with her feet firmly on the ground, and there is nothing to imply that the first Lothario to come along could have hypnotized her with the smell of brandy and cigars, or anything else for that matter."

"How many things we consider to be impossible, and yet science proves to us that they exist! Shakespeare may well have written that there are more things on earth than are dreamed of in philosophy, but there is none that hasn't been dreamed of in science!"

Having said this, he rang for Franciszka to ask her to serve the coffee, then fell back in his chair, clearly satisfied with his lecture.

❧

The learned talk at the lunch table would have been the final noteworthy event of the day, if not for the ten-minute episode that occurred that night, after Zofia had sat down at her dressing table, removed the garnet-studded comb from her high bun, and shaken her head to let down her hair. As she felt her tresses flow in a cool wave onto her shoulders, covered by her nightgown, Franciszka gently began to comb them—as in the past, before Karolina had taken this duty over from her.

Zofia often wondered why these moments in particular—and not just in her house, as she knew—were particularly conducive to confidences. Apparently, this wasn't the case among gentlemen; as she had often had occasion to see through the tall glass shopfronts, men's barbers and hairdressers generally worked in silence, their brows knitted, which made them look angry. It was a far cry from the tender, gentle way in which long hair is combed—perhaps the close contact between one woman's hands and another one's head somehow eases the flow of thoughts?

Who knows, perhaps in a year or two a scientist based in Paris, London, Vienna, or why not Cracow will discover the brainwaves that pass between the comber and the person being combed, like music that's inaudible to the human ear? After all, this was the age of progress, and not a year went by without a whole new set of extraordinary scientific revelations that prompted one to revise one's attitude to the surrounding world entirely.

And tonight would prove no exception to the rule of hair-combing, as a highly significant fact was about to fall from Franciszka's lips.

"If you please, madam . . ." she said, and paused. "I've been wondering . . ."

"Yes, Franciszka?"

"Are you allowed to break an oath? Even when you swore to God you wouldn't? If it would be a good thing for the person to whom you made that promise?"

"I think one should talk to that person and persuade them that . . ."

"But what if it's not possible . . . to talk to them?" interrupted Franciszka, trembling.

"Is there something you know?" said Zofia, turning to face her. "Do you know who killed Karolina?"

"No, I don't. But . . ."

"But?"

"But there was one thing she told me . . . except she made me promise to keep it secret. 'Not a word to anyone.'

And I swore to God. I swore on the picture of Saint John Cantius that's hanging in the servants' room. But now . . ."

"Now," said Zofia, alert as a hound that has caught the scent, "your oath does not count, because you swore it to Karolina when she was alive, and she is dead. The only thing you can do in memory of the unfortunate girl"—at this point she grabbed Franciszka's hand, not out of warm sympathy, but the certainty that this would be a better way to persuade her—"is to tell me everything she told you then. Come on, sit down and let's hear it," she said, holding out her other hand for the brush.

Franciszka obediently gave it to her, sat down on a chair that stood by the door into the bedroom, and sighed heavily.

"*Mater Dei!*" she cried out, and sighed again. "Karolina had a spark . . . a sweetheart," she corrected herself, because although she increasingly used the local Cracow slang, she still occasionally let slip a regional term from her hometown, especially in moments of stress.

"Yes, I know, the fisherman, or rafter."

"A sand miner, Felek—but I don't mean him. She had a new sweetheart. She said it wasn't serious with that Felek, just flirting. But a few weeks ago . . ." She broke off.

"A few weeks ago . . . ?"

"She kept being followed by this scruff, this old fellow. She even told me she was scared, because wherever she went she saw him there, disappearing behind a corner or the like. And Karolina was a bold lass—you knew her, madam—so one time she goes up to him and asks: 'Is there something you want? Is that why you keep trailing after me like a dog?' And then he was discer . . ."

"Disconcerted."

"Disconcerted, very much so, and he says he's sorry, but he's doing it for a gentleman, an engineer, who's eager to meet her. With a view to marriage. And he was checking to make sure she was an honest girl, because the engineer was delighted by her face, but he wanted to know if her heart was pure too, so that was why the old fellow had been trailing after her like that."

"And she met with him?"

"Oh yes, she did," sighed Franciszka. "He asked for them to meet as soon as possible, because he was in a hurry. He said they'd be summoning him any day and he'd be leaving. He took her to the Cloth Hall, to Rehman's for coffee and cakes, in style."

"Where would they be summoning him to?"

"To America. Because there's a mine in America and he's to be the engineer at that mine, a manager of some kind."

"What is his name?"

"I can't remember, just that he's an engineer."

"And what does he look like?"

Franciszka gazed around the room helplessly.

"How can I put it? He's young. Smart. Like a gentleman, he's got fingers as slender as lucifers—matches, I mean.

That's what Karolina told me, because I only saw him just the once, and that was from the window, when he was walking along with her, but just to the corner of the street. If I saw him, I might recognize him, but . . . well, he had hair, a mustache . . ."

"All right, it's all right now. You'll tell the police."

"The police?"

"Of course. You won't have to bother the magistrate, Mr. Rozmarynowicz, but first thing in the morning you can go and see Commissioner Jednoróg to tell him all this. What else?"

"The day Karolina left us . . ." said Franciszka, her voice faltering, and for a while Zofia thought she was going to start sobbing, and soon they'd both be in tears, but she got a grip on herself and continued. "She told me she was very happy, the engineer had a job in America, and they were going there as fast as they could. They'd get married on the way, without reading the banns, in Hamburk perhaps, because a priest friend lived there. A friend of the engineer's, not Karolina's. That's why she only took a few keepsakes, some photos of her ma. She wanted a holy picture but I didn't give her one, because the little Mary's mine, from home, and Saint John Cantius is mine too . . . nothing else. She didn't take no dresses or blouses, just put on her best clothes and said he'd promised to buy her everything anyway. He took her without a dowry!" The last phrase suddenly burst out of her in a different tone, as if she were complaining. "Without a dowry! She said he was going to buy her lots of much nicer dresses, hats, and gloves, because everything's cheap and beautiful in America, and he was rich. 'You can have my things,' she says, 'and if there's anything you don't want, you can give it to the poor, I won't be needing them anymore.' She was so happy. But now . . . now she definitely won't be needing them anymore . . . and I'll have to" — once again her voice faltered — "give them to the poor, just as she foretold!"

At this point she burst into tears, and to her shame, so did Zofia.

CHAPTER III

In which Ignacy prepares for a military expedition to Alwornia and Regulice, a sexlorist talks about sexlore, and the watering can pulls off an arm. The Turbotyńskis jointly participate in a sad event, and then separately suffer disappointment, each in a different field. We also learn who is not allowed to lie through, and who carried off Count Dzieduszycki's silver spoons.

As befitted a man, Professor Turbotyński tried not to show his feelings; restraint was one of the virtues he upheld most conscientiously, only rarely letting himself be carried away by social conviviality, patriotic emotions, or — as recently — fears for the health of His Imperial Majesty, shaken by the distant echoes of the earthquake in Laibach. Whereas he scrupulously hid his feelings of sorrow, grief, and despair. Yet Zofia knew that beneath his unruffled surface there was a vortex of wild emotions that found their outlet at the most unexpected moments.

Just as she was trying to occupy her mind by reading the novella in the *Cracow Times* or by tidying the wardrobes—though she'd done the spring cleaning shortly before Easter—so too Ignacy was devoting himself to the hobby of cycling with unprecedented vigor. He had actually been interested in it for quite a time, and had learned, not without mishap, how to ride a velocipede a couple of seasons ago; he'd even been in the old cycling club. When it had fallen foul of the apathy of most of its members (whose practice of the sport of cycling was impeded either by heavy falls or heavy dinners), he'd joined a new club, founded by those who were truly determined to promote the sport of cycling in the royal city. For the past half hour he'd been running about the flat trying to assemble his complete sporting outfit, just as his ancestors had gathered up their bucklers, saddles, and swords for battle. Zofia was sure the exaggerated exertion he was putting into it was his way of expressing his grief and helpless anger at the death of Karolina, for whom he had felt sincere affection.

"Where are my socks? Where are my cycling socks? Franciszka!" came the occasional loud call; meanwhile a pile of clothing grew on the bed, including a pair of plus fours, a cap, and a light jacket. With loving care he fetched out the enamel badge he hadn't pinned to his coat since the late autumn, used his sleeve to wipe the intertwined letters *CCC*, the city coat of arms, and the surrounding inscription: CRACOW CYCLING CLUB 1892, then tilted his head and once again bellowed for the servant, who was only just back from seeing Commissioner Jednoróg. She came running into the room, bearing in her right hand, like the precious greaves of a medieval knight, a pair of colorfully patterned wool knee-high socks.

"On Sunday, just two days from now, the club is organizing an outing to Alwernia and Regulice, and I am entirely unprepared! I'm as naked as the Lord God made me," he blustered, regardless of the blatant fact that he was fully dressed, all the way from his lace-up boots to his neatly knotted tie.

"Here they are . . . and there's this," said Franciszka, holding out the new silver-plated salver for visiting cards she'd brought in from the hall; in the fashionable Secession style, it had lately replaced the old one, which had been badly worn at the edges. On silver water lily leaves and flowers rising on silver waves lay a cream-colored visiting card inscribed: *Stanisław Teofil Kurkiewicz.*

"Kurkiewicz? So officially? Show him into my study, please."

Zofia went up to her husband, gently combed his hair, straightened his tie, and then said in a conspiratorial whisper: "Remember: no promises of patronage." On the whole, Zofia thought one shouldn't be overly selfless; one should reserve one's help for those who could return the favor somehow or other, but Kurkiewicz had little to offer. "You said yourself that he behaves oddly. Let him say what he wants, but don't go putting your foot in your mouth by agreeing to move heaven and earth for him."

Kurkiewicz was one of Ignacy's students, but unlike Tadeusz Żeleński, for instance, he was not among his favorites; he was said to be affected by a harmless mania, and spent his entire time conducting research into embarrassing topics, a discipline that he strangely termed "sexlore." He pestered everyone at the medical faculty, both students and professors alike, with his quirky vocabulary, which turned the generally accepted medical terminology on its head. Whenever the future physicians were shown a patient of either gender, he took no notice of the disease they displayed, which was the topic of the given tutorial, but always asked questions about whether the patient had "pleasured" himself or herself in childhood, or still did, whether it was a case of advanced scabies, delirium tremens, or consumption. He enjoyed nobody's sympathy; unlike the other students, who combined their studies with carousing, he spent most of his time at home, working on his lengthy survey, "a study on a scale of many years," as he liked to say, in which he aimed to include the sum whole of his findings: the findings—as he put it—of a "sexlorist." He was probably having trouble with one of the lecturers again, and wanted the professor to intercede; Zofia had seen him several times before, walking Ignacy home from the faculty or eating lunch at the soup kitchen on the corner of Wolska Street, and although it was to his credit that he was always exceedingly polite and impeccably dressed, somehow she couldn't summon up any affection for him.

"The watering can," she said to Franciszka under her breath.

"Beg your pardon, madam?"

"The wa-ter-ing can," she whispered, moving her lips in an exaggerated way so that the servant could read them.

Moments later she was at the study door, where since time immemorial a flowerpot holding a large geranium had been standing on a small mahogany table. As she pretended to water it, she put her ear against the door panel, trying to catch every word, to enter the room in case of need if she happened to overhear an attempt to beg a favor of Ignacy.

"I cannot say that this news leaves me indifferent . . . or unmoved," she heard him say. "Yet please tell me, did she . . . suffer greatly?"

"As for her death, it seems to have occurred quickly, by dint of a single well-aimed stab wound inflicted by a long, sharp instrument, most probably a knife, aimed toward the long axis, and so the tip . . ." At this point he lowered his voice, and she could only catch every other word: ". . . testifies . . . water in the lungs . . . I think . . . in short, she must have died almost instantaneously. The body was thrown into the Vistula."

For a while silence reigned. Then she heard Ignacy again.

"And . . . in your examination did you inspect the reproductive organs, too?"

"Yes. That is also why I hesitated when you asked about suffering. Because the deceased did suffer, in the sense that before her death she was ravished."

"Are we talking about loss of virginity?"

"If we examine this incidence of coupling, then thanks to the marks left on the body we can say a thing or two about it." Kurkiewicz had clearly grown animated, because he started to talk louder. "It's certain that the person beneath had not merely never given birth before the start of the sexual act, but her hymen was intact, not even slackened." Zofia mentally cursed Franciszka, who had filled the watering can almost to the top, forcing her to keep shifting it from one hand to the other, and even then it felt as if her arm were about to break. "So there is no question, as the police were asking, that she could have worked at a house of ill fame. And also . . ."

At this point Ignacy asked a question, but she couldn't hear it. Kurkiewicz answered him: "From the abrasions that resulted from the dryness of the entire sex, and also the tightness of the quim during the chafing inflicted on the person beneath . . . lasting injuries, from which it appears that the person on top did not climax quickly. We are more likely dealing with a case of retarded spending of the seed, because to cause damage of this kind his virile member must have been moving like a piston in her quim for a considerable time . . ."

"Mr. Kurkiewicz, indeed I admire your ingenuity, but"

— she couldn't hear — "some of the vocabulary that . . . after all, in the present day . . ."

"Professor, I started recording my investigations of sexual life long ago — mine is a study on a scale of many years, but please believe me . . . necessary, and also . . . the situation . . ." At this point there followed assurances and justifications on both sides, but the words and phrases piled on top of each other, rendering them incomprehensible. Only a little later did she hear Kurkiewicz's words again, surprisingly clear, though not fully understandable: "Nor did he use a fertilization barrier, for despite the action of the water we found the remains of male spend in the quim."

"Meaning seed?"

"Yes, seed. That is a term I also find preferable, as being derived from a native root."

The next part of the conversation was mostly uninteresting: the future doctor poured out his grudges against those who had allegedly put stumbling blocks in his way, by ignoring the fact that he was working on a significant study of sex that might extend to fill several volumes, so he asserted. But he wasn't seeking any favors, so finally Zofia watered the geranium and tiptoed back to the drawing room.

"Imagine what an extraordinary coincidence," said Ignacy half an hour later, when Franciszka had shown his guest to the door. "On Wednesday morning, when Mr. Kurkiewicz was assisting Dr. Schwarz at the forensic medicine unit, the body of an unidentified girl was brought in."

He took a handkerchief from his breast pocket and mopped his brow. "As soon as they laid her on the table he said: 'Unidentified? But this is Professor Turbotyński's maid, Karolina!' Because he had often walked me home. And I'll tell you, on almost every occasion he had said she was an extremely comely girl. It's hard not to agree with that," he added despondently.

"So he was the first to identify the body?"

"Yes! It was thanks to him that the police knew they should come to us, and it was only by following the lead from us that they discovered her name, address, and family."

"Well, I never. How very galling for him to have to use his scalpel on someone for whom he felt personal affection," said Zofia, and shuddered. "Especially for a postmortem, rather than a life-saving operation."

"For sure, for sure," replied Ignacy. "But then the doctor's profession . . ."

"Yes?"

". . . lends courage. You do not see a person, but a body, like any other, generally devoid of individual anomalies, of a uniform design. There is a sort of fortifying quality in the fact that when you open the rib cage, as a rule you find the liver where the liver should be, the pancreas where the pancreas should be, and so on." For a while he was pensive. "But it's very kind of him to have taken the trouble to tell me all about it."

"All about it?"

"Medical confidences." He raised a finger in a meaningful gesture, cutting off all further discussion. In any case, they had to get ready for Karolina's funeral.

❧

Zofia Turbotyńska was already at an age where she had heard the Ave Maria at a number of funerals, laid flowers on a number of graves, and walked in the cortege behind a number of coffins. She had particularly often been fated to perform this last function—what could one do, when the Cracovians, especially the more notable ones, were always dropping like flies? If it weren't Lenartowicz the sculptor, it was Matejko the painter, and if not Matejko, it was Hawełka the merchant, if not Hawełka, it was the cardinal; just as Fortune's wheel kept turning, so people kept dying. Ignacy had his own view on this topic, of course; suitably provoked, he could summon up a whole arsenal of arguments to support it, rolling out canon after canon of what he saw as irrefutable proof that the toxic Cracow water was to blame for this state of affairs, and until a waterworks was built, nothing would change. But deep down, Zofia did not entirely believe her husband's theories, and truly doubted whether an incidence of death could lead to any sort of fundamental change at all. People died in Vienna too, where the emperor had had some splendid aqueducts built, bringing in water from the Kaiserbrunnen source—Zofia remembered how, twenty-five years ago, His Majesty in person had stuck a spade into the ground with his own imperial foot, thus initiating the construction of the pipeline — and people died in Warsaw, where the British engineers, Lindley and Son, had built filter stations, so in Cracow, too, a modern sewerage system would fail to knock the scythe from the hand of the Grim Reaper. *For such is the order of things,* she thought; *people die to make room in this vale of tears for the younger ones.*

Yet as she gazed at the clods of earth landing on the simple coffin of seventeen-year-old Karolina Szulc, Zofia couldn't restrain her tears. Of course she accepted the laws of nature, but there was nothing natural about this death. Karolina, a slightly giddy but kindhearted girl, *her* Karolina, had fallen victim to a murderer, who had first shamelessly dishonored her, and then cut short her young life at its very start. Naturally, Zofia had been aware that the day would come when Karolina decided to leave — whether to care for her mother, or to marry and start a family — but not this way, for God's sake. Not this way.

"Look, my dear, they're widening the cemetery," said Ignacy, pointing his chin toward some workmen leveling the ground in the distance as they passed under the stone arch of the gateway. "Though Podgórze still won't escape building a new one."

Zofia didn't react. It was on the tip of her tongue to say "Not now!" or utter a reproachful "Indeed, Ignacy!," but she decided to pretend she hadn't heard his remark. She knew that at base he was simply trying to mask his grief by talking.

Outside the cemetery they found that the hackney coach which had brought them to the funeral had already left, despite having instructions to wait. Another one was standing there, but Zofia made a loud comment about the poor state, in her opinion, of the "miserable nag" harnessed to it, and then announced to all and sundry that she was certainly not going home with some "Podgórze cabby" who was sure to charge double purely because he'd have to drive across to the *right* side of the river, which — she added — certainly wouldn't be a bad deal for him. After almost twenty years of marriage, Ignacy knew that when Zofia was in this state he shouldn't argue, and even pleading colic would be of no use, so he dutifully offered his wife an arm.

They walked in silence, quite literally the silence of the grave. The professor and Zofia went in front, followed by Franciszka, her head lowered and her gaze fixed on the ground. Farther off, supported by two friends like Mary beneath the cross in medieval paintings, came Karolina's mother, half walking, half letting herself be dragged; shortly before, she had stared vacantly at the Turbotyńskis as they offered her their condolences. She was a couple of years younger than Zofia, but so ravaged by work and despair that it was hard to detect in her face the remains of the beauty she had passed down to her only daughter. As she recited the formulaic condolences, Zofia had thought of a phrase writers tended to overuse, that "the world has ended" for someone — it was plain to see from Marianna Szulc's appearance that with Karolina's death her entire world really had been snuffed out like a gas lamp. And deep in her heart Zofia felt an ever stronger desire to catch the snuffer in person.

The Podgórze district made a painful impression on her. The shabby houses, almost all squat and low, reminded her of Bochnia, the town she had been obliged to visit eighteen months ago—for the first and last time, she hoped. She looked at building after building, wondering which of these miserable little houses was the site of a brothel where women devoid of a moral backbone received youths intoxicated with . . . what did Ignacy call it? Oh yes, the "agent of rapture." She thought that in a district like *this* one, an establishment of the kind might easily exist in any of the houses.

They walked along Lemberg Road, passing Lasota Hill on their left, with the artillery fort of the Imperial-Royal army towering above it like a huge, gloomy castle topped with battlements. The silence was broken by the muffled shouts of soldiers audible from behind the machicolations on the bastion. Zofia remembered the lancers who had found Karolina—corrupt, dissolute fellows—and felt a stab of anger. At them, at what had happened, at this entire place, and finally at herself for having failed to protect the unfortunate girl.

At last they reached the open space known grandly in Podgórze as the Market Square, though goodness knows how it could possibly be compared with Cracow's Market Square, she thought. Instead of tall trees there were shriveled stalks, barely off the ground; instead of St. Mary's Basilica, which was good enough for Rome, there was a small church that looked like a barn with a bell tower tacked onto it; and instead of a square to rival Europe's most famous piazzas, there was a common parade ground. *Market Square indeed,* she thought irritably. *If* I *were mayor of this district, I would undoubtedly have more modesty!* Then almost immediately felt surprised at her own boldness — that was a preposterous idea too. A woman as mayor! What a thought.

They returned to their own side of the river via Franz Joseph's Bridge, where the tram was already waiting for Zofia and Franciszka, and a carriage for Ignacy, who had something to see to at St. Louis's Hospital. Naturally he had proposed that they should all travel together, but Zofia was adamant.

"You go on your own. It will be more convenient for us to take the tram to St. Florian's Gate."

"My dear Zofia, it is no cost at all . . ." Ignacy tried to protest.

"Ignacy," she firmly declared, "as a threesome we would have to travel by two-horse carriage, which would cost us the same as it did in this direction, meaning another eighty cents, but as we would have to drive the long way around, via the hospital, the driver would be sure to demand an entire crown . . . No, do not interrupt. From here you shall be at the hospital in fifteen minutes, and in an ordinary, one-horse cab . . . oh, like the one over here, for twenty cents, while Franciszka and I will pay eight cents each for our entire journey. So you see, that is a *substantial* saving."

Professor Turbotyński knew that his wife was excited by questions of logistics, and that for what she saw as prudent planning, saving time, effort, and money, she was sometimes ready to twist the facts, so he capitulated. He said farewell and boarded the cab; through the window he watched his modest, two-woman ménage heading toward the tram stop.

❧

Zofia knew from the newspapers that for some time there had been altercations with the Belgian firm that had built and operated the first line, who despite pressure from the city council were in no hurry to build a new one, but personally she had no reservations about the novelty represented in Cracow by the horse-drawn iron rail run by Tramways Autrichiens—Cracovie et Extensions. In fact, she was pleased that although there were steam-powered railcars on the streets of Vienna, and even electric ones in Lemberg, Cracow had not let itself be carried away by madness and was not slavishly adopting the latest achievements of technology. Zofia had the most atrocious memories of a journey by electric tram during Lemberg's National Exhibition, which she and her husband had visited last year. Although an ill-wisher might say that the reason was sheer envy of the larger, wealthier, and above all far more significant capital of the Kingdom of Galicia and Lodomeria, Zofia ascribed her dislike of electric trams to purely practical reasons.

"The Lemberg city council will very soon be forced to build a new hospital and a new institution for the mentally deranged," she explained, as if casually, to anyone willing to listen. "The former for those injured by this monster, racing along the streets at bewildering speed, and the latter for those who travel on it, who are bound to be driven mad by the frantic tram bells!"

To her satisfaction, the Cracow trams still moved at a rate that was not much faster than the horse-drawn omnibus which had run the same route in the past, and that she defined as "sensible."

Franciszka timidly sat down on a plush-upholstered couch in the first-class car. The liberality of her employer, after the sermon she had just preached on the virtue of economy, was a little surprising, but she knew the reason; the second-class car had been the first to leave, but as soon as the ticket selling began, the Orthodox Jews from the Kazimierz district (through which the tramline ran) began to board, shouting to each other in their own language, and to the conductor in rather lopsided Polish. Most of them looked quite ordinary, but there were *some* who, to Franciszka's eyes, looked extremely exotic.

Meanwhile, in the first-class car, apart from the residents of Peacock House there was only an elderly couple, and they were sitting on the other side of it. *They could be*

Jews, was Zofia's immediate thought. *Though in fact it is hard to tell,* she quickly reconsidered.

The conditions inside the first-class car were comfortable: instead of ten seats there were only six, and they were covered with cloth. The windows had no panes of glass (the management must recently have decided to change from the winter fleet to the summer one), but were shaded by gray-and-white drapes—in need of cleaning, as Zofia noticed at once with her good housekeeper's eye. The bell tinkled and the driver started up the pair of bay horses harnessed to the tram, at which Franciszka drew back the curtain; she rarely found herself in Kazimierz, and now, through sorrowful eyes, she gazed at the world outside.

Zofia sighed heavily.

"Oh, Franciszka, isn't it hard to believe that as recently as Good Friday, Karolina was helping us with the baking, but less than a week later we have escorted her to her eternal rest? By the by, our Karolina's funeral was held very promptly, wasn't it?"

"How do you mean, madam?" wondered Franciszka. "A dead man can't be left to lie through."

"Lie through?"

"Through Sunday. Or he'll drag someone after him, and death will remain in the house."

"Our great artist Matejko was buried on a Tuesday, but he died on a Wednesday—meanwhile Mrs. Matejko remains in excellent health," Zofia was quick to remark, though the term "in excellent health" was perhaps not entirely appropriate for this cantankerous woman of unsound mind. Yet at the same time it occurred to her that according to Franciszka's superstition, death would not take up residence at Karolina's mother's home in Podgórze, but at her own house on St. John's Street. And although she didn't believe in folk wisdom, a cold shiver ran down her spine.

"I don't know, madam, but so my mother told me. And so it says in *The Angel's Aid for Defense and Protection in Dire Need,*" added Franciszka for greater effect, though she knew that in the ears of her employer this would be no special recommendation. Indeed, Zofia let this last remark go unheeded.

"Tell me, Franciszka," she said, changing the subject, "I saw Karolina's young man, Felek, at the funeral, the fisherman or raf—"

"Sand miner."

"Or sand miner," agreed Zofia. "But I didn't spot anyone there who might have been that engineer of hers."

"I didn't see him neither," said Franciszka shaking her head, "but I did look around for him, if you please, madam, because if they were betrothed, he should have been there, shouldn't he?"

"Yes, you're right, Franciszka, he should have been. And tell me . . ."

She broke off, because at the stop on Józef Street a breathless woman of rather ample proportions had boarded the car, and was now looking around, plainly wondering which seat to occupy; when her gaze fell on Zofia, the dilemma resolved itself, she trudged to the other end of the car and sat beside the elderly couple.

"Tell me," Zofia continued, "what else do you know about this man, apart from the fact that he took her to Rehman's for cakes? Do you know how many times?"

"Twice, I think," said Franciszka pensively, but then suddenly brightened. "And . . . I know they went to Sidoli's circus together too!" she added. "I know, because I wanted to go on the same day, to see the new show." Franciszka's love of the circus did not appear to have waned. "But Karolina insisted that I stay behind, because *she* was going with the engineer. 'Let's go together,' says I, 'it'll be jolly. I'll meet your betrothed, and I can also make sure nothing improper should enter his head.' But to that she says there's no need, and she only wants to go with him. It made me rather sad, so out of spite I told her what my grandma used to say whenever I took her up to Cracow: 'Every maiden's weak and willin,' when she meets the proper villain.' And she says: 'Don't fret so, Franula,' because that's what she sometimes called me, 'the engineer is a very decent man, he went to all that trouble to find out if I was honest, so how could he have designs on my virtue? Not like Felek, who thinks of nothing but squeezing and cuddling.' If you'll pardon the expression, madam," added the cook as an afterthought, fearing she might have said too much.

"Don't worry, Franciszka," said Zofia, with a reassuring gesture.

"I know all too well what that sort of fellow wants," the

girl went on, "however noble he may be — the same thing as Felek! All boys have only one thing in mind. But she was young. Young and foolish," carped Franciszka from the heights of her twenty-six years.

Beyond Kazimierz, in Stradom the first section of the route ended, and the tram stopped for a little longer while one of the horses was unharnessed. Zofia tried to elicit more facts from the girl that might help her to get on the trail of the elusive — as she saw it — engineer; in any case, how could one be sure he really was an engineer? But while Franciszka had plenty to say about the dresses Karolina's fiancé had bought for her, and the loving words he had used to address her ("He called her 'my little pearl,' if you please, madam!"), despite her earnest efforts and her most ardent desire to please, it was impossible to draw anything out of her that would help to reveal his identity. She knew neither his surname nor his first name, nor the address at which he resided in Cracow, not to mention details such as the name of the overseas mining company for which he worked. Karolina may have been young and foolish, but she was plainly very good at keeping her admirer's secrets. And now, it seemed, she had taken them with her to the grave — that very grave in which barely half an hour ago the gravediggers from Podgórze Cemetery had buried her.

"Franciszka, why didn't you tell me all this before?" said Zofia, raising her voice in her frustration, causing the other passengers to cast her looks of silent reproach. But she knew the answer.

"Because I swore to God, madam." Franciszka dropped her gaze. "As I've told you. And if I'd broken my oath, what then? Saint John Cantius would soon have withdrawn his favor . . ."

"To tell the truth, I doubt that would have happened. Sometimes we have no choice but to commit a lesser sin in order to avoid a greater one, Franciszka. I am sure that as a learned scholar who strove his entire life to discover the truth, Saint John Cantius would have agreed with me," she declared confidently, though deep down she wasn't sure if the truth as she presented it would find support within the dogmas of the Catholic Church. "In any event, let this be the last time. From now on in my house . . . that's to say in Professor Turbotyński's house, nobody is to have *any* secrets from anyone else."

Meanwhile the tram had reached the Market Square at the top of Sienna Street, right by the spot where the ill-fated statue of Adam Mickiewicz was destined to stand, due to be erected for longer than anyone could remember. The plinth and four figures at the foot of it had been ready for ages; enclosed by wooden fencing that looked like a tool shed or, as others claimed, a Turkish camp, they sat waiting for the most important figure, but the monument committee had plagued Mr. Rygier, the sculptor, and argued with him so often that he had packed up his chisel and fled to Rome. Finally he had sent the statue of the Bard to Cracow, but the torso was bloated and the laurel leaves crowning his brilliant head were so sharply pointed that he looked like a pregnant Indian chief in a feather headdress. There was no end to the complaints, so finally both Mickiewicz and two of the figures from the plinth were sent back to Rome when the sculptor promised to do some more work on them. Meanwhile the wooden shack in the middle of the Market Square was a dreadful eyesore.

The conductor rang his bell and announced the end of the second section of the route.

"Well, Franciszka, our time has come. We're getting off, swiftly now," declared Zofia, leaping to her feet; they would have to squeeze their way through to the exit, because after stopping every few minutes on Grodzka Street, the tram was now full.

"But we're not at the Florian Gate yet, madam . . ." Franciszka shyly protested, and then dutifully alighted from the tram.

"My dear," announced Zofia, now standing on the cobblestones of the Market Square and setting about smoothing her mourning dress and straightening her hat with the black veil, "surely you do not imagine that, in a situation where for reasons beyond our control we were obliged to indulge in the luxury of the first-class car, I would pay for the entire route? I bought tickets for two sections in first class instead of three in second. I planned to spend eight cents per head, and that is what I did spend!" She spoke this final remark with sheer joy.

Just then, Dr. and Mrs. Iwaniec came walking toward them from the direction of Floriańska Street. Zofia returned first of all his greeting, and then hers. The short-sighted, if not half-blind Mrs. Iwaniec bowed whenever her husband, holding her by the arm, gave her a gentle nudge; this led to some comical incidents when he accidentally prodded her while tripping over a cobblestone, for instance, and she would bow to an advertising pillar or a lamppost. Luckily this time she aimed her nod in the right direction.

"And now," said Zofia, who didn't like what she defined as "aimless drifting," and always did her best to plan the route of all walks in the most economical way, "let us go into the Cloth Hall to buy the professor some cycling socks at Beyer's or Niesiołowski's, and then let us drop in at Maurizio's to buy biscuits for tea. Come along, Franciszka," she said briskly. And off went Franciszka, but realizing that Zofia hadn't moved at all, she stopped, and took two steps backward.

It was one of those moments that perhaps everyone knows: the plan that hatched deep down long ago suddenly jumps into focus, nullifying all lesser enterprises, which are instantly sacrificed to the higher cause. Thus Zofia Turbotyńska had finally stopped trying to persuade herself that Investigating Magistrate Rozmarynowicz and the Cracow police—albeit represented by the highly competent Commissioner Jednoróg—could conduct the inquiry into Karolina's murder unaided; as well as laborious procedures, postmortems, and inquiries, there was also such a thing as female intuition, so she told herself, which neither Rozmarynowicz, nor Jednoróg, nor Kurkiewicz possessed.

"Or maybe not," she said, reaching for the watch pinned to her chest, this time not the usual gold one, but a silver-gray niello inlay one, as the demands of funeral fashion dictated. "The professor has footwear for his impending cycle ride, and there is still plenty of time until the next one. You will go to Maurizio's alone and choose some candied fruits, chocolates . . . or simply a small basket of sweets. With restraint, of course," she said, wagging a finger. "And I will be home soon. If the professor returns before me, you will say I have gone to pray for Karolina's soul, but you don't know which church."

Passing the soaring towers of St. Mary's Basilica, she turned right, and at a brisk pace very soon reached the city police station on Mikołajska Street.

❧

The clerk's flustered response when she asked for the commissioner made her think Jednoróg must be getting ready to leave. It was almost three in the afternoon, and leaving for lunch at home, then coming back to the office for an hour of pleasant idleness was not so rare among Cracow's civil servants of a certain rank—even Ignacy occasionally did it. Yet the problem turned out to be of a completely different kind. The door to Jednoróg's office was wide-open; to be more precise there was no door there at all. Instead there were two carpenters by the entrance, cursing under their breath as they measured the doorway to fit a pair of new—and no doubt heavy—door leaves made of oak.

The confused clerk had no idea how to behave. It would be wrong to send Zofia away empty-handed—after all, she was a witness in an ongoing case—but the lack of a door seemed to him inappropriate in the presence of a lady, and it also meant no privacy for his boss, who was busy receiving a petitioner. After a brief hesitation the clerk showed Zofia to a bench in the corridor—at a suitable distance from the commissioner's office—and returned to his duties.

For a while Zofia watched the carpenters struggling with the hinges. Possibly disconcerted by the sight of an elegant lady in a hat, they stopped their work, carefully leaned the door against the wall, and disappeared around a bend in the corridor. Zofia looked around, and casually moved to the bench right beside the entrance to the commissioner's office, from where she could now hear everything. She was curious to know what other cases Jednoróg was dealing with—and how he behaved toward the people who came to see him.

"Please understand, Commissioner," she heard, "for me, being banned from plying my trade is quite simply fatal!"

"My dear sir, please don't get carried away," came Jednoróg's calm, dispassionate voice.

"How can I fail to be carried away, most honorable Commissioner, when my entire life, my entire existence is in the balance?" said the owner of a rather high, squeaky voice, shifting in tone from angry to plaintive, while Zofia moved to the very end of the bench. "I find myself in a desperate position!"

"I understand you, but what can I do about it?"

"What do you mean, Commissioner? I'll tell you what you can do! It was the honorable executive committee of the Imperial-Royal police that ordered me to vacate my facility between Dietl Street and Podbrzezie Street, where I have run my business, to the great satisfaction of all my clients, for the past five years. And yet the police health committee, delegated for this purpose, had acknowledged that the site was suited to purpose. You yourself were a member of that committee, and that is the reason why I have not gone to see anyone else, but have come to you in person, as a man who is favorably disposed!"

"Yeees, yes," said Jednoróg, humming and hawing, "but I do not think I can help you now, Mr. Brand."

"What can possibly have changed since then?" asked the man, ignoring the commissioner's reply. "I will tell you! It's all the fault of that new priest at Corpus Christi! We had no trouble with the old priest, oh, no, but no sooner had this new one arrived than he started sending out letters of complaint about me to the honorable police executive committee. He writes to say that my facility upsets the people who walk through Planty Park, and everything that lives and breathes is bound to go through it several times a day, including children. But that prompts me to ask how on earth can it disturb them? Do they walk down Podbrzezie

Street? A narrow, secluded alley? They never used to walk down it, and now suddenly they do? Nobody was worried about the children before, but now suddenly they are? Explain it to me, Commissioner, please."

She heard Jednoróg clearing his throat again, no doubt intending to reply, but the distraught petitioner refused to back down.

"He says my house is located too close to some churches, because as well as Corpus Christi in Stradom, there are the missionaries, and St. Catherine's nearby . . . But I ask you, weren't those churches there before? Forgive me for being so bold, but when the honorable committee issued its consent a few years ago, could it have failed to see the tower of Corpus Christi church? And besides, is this priest aware of any place in Cracow where there is no church, monastery, or holy figure within view? Wherever one may look in this city there's a consecrated site. I will have to move out to Grzegórzki, Commissioner! To Grzegórzki! Have pity on me, sir, driven to poverty and despair! I beg you most humbly, Your Honor . . ."

But before she could hear Jednoróg's answer, the carpenters came around the corner on their way back to work; with all haste she moved away from the doorway and sat at the other end of the bench. After all, she didn't want them to think her a busybody.

As soon as they had resumed the job, out of the commissioner's office came Mr. Brand, so ill-used by fate: he was a stout gentleman in a brown suit, with a face as sad and gray as Rakowicki Cemetery in January. He cast Zofia a glance—an acutely miserable one of course—and shambled down the corridor. In his wake Jednoróg emerged. He was clearly surprised to see Zofia, but immediately invited her to come inside; if he was getting ready to leave, he didn't let it show that her visit was an inconvenience, postponing his Friday lunch. On the contrary, he apologized for the fact that the office chairs were so uncomfortable, and even offered to open a window to rid the room of cigarette smoke. Zofia politely said no thank you—with the door missing there was sure to be a lethal draft!—but once again it occurred to her that Magistrate Klossowitz had much to learn from Jednoróg when it came to manners. And perhaps not just manners.

"I realize I may have come at a bad time . . ." she said, and paused.

"A visit from you is always at a good time, Mrs. Turbotyńska," he said, making the appropriate remark.

". . . yet the matter of Karolina's tragic death won't let me rest. As you can see, sir, I am just on my way home from her funeral. I am most eager to learn more about the lancers. Do you know what they were doing that night?"

Jednoróg frowned. He used a fingertip to raise the lid of a bronze inkwell, and immediately let it drop again with a loud clatter.

"Madam, you are aware that as an officer of the police I am duty-bound to observe the utmost discretion. Nonetheless, knowing your situation, and also your achievements, I cannot be a rigid authoritarian. But if I am going to betray one or another detail to you, I must bind you to a promise of total secrecy. Revealing the details of an inquiry to an outsider is not just nonchalance, but a violation, even if committed for the noblest reasons and with the aim of exposing the murderer."

"Your attitude can only be to your credit, Commissioner, and I am keen to assure you of my total discretion. Unfortunately it is a virtue that is hard to prove," she said, smiling, "because to give you a notion of the confidences that I keep for all manner of Cracow homes, I would have to betray them to you. And it would take a long time to tell them! Therefore mutual trust remains our only option."

"That is what I can provide, and I ask you to reciprocate."

She nodded—which, thanks to the imposing size of her hat and the solemnity of her black veil, may have appeared too ceremonial—to mark this covenant, a pact concluded between professional hunter and vocational huntress.

"All three of the lancers have . . . I would like to say an 'untarnished reputation,' but in their case that is impossible . . . and yet they do have verified alibis. They spent the night at a certain establishment, which they did not leave until dawn. Apparently the same thing happened the next night, when on leaving the place at a similar hour, their roving took them to the spot below the Rożnowski Villa where they found . . ."

"What's that?" Something didn't add up. "Can it be

that Karolina did not perish the night before her body was found?"

"No, she did not. The postmortem showed that the corpse was in the water for roughly twenty-four hours. Clearly the current must have tangled it in something first, then released it and cast it up on the shore."

This fact from Ignacy's conversation with Kurkiewicz that she had overheard had evidently escaped her. It may have been said at the beginning, before Franciszka had brought her the watering can.

"And did . . ."

"Death was almost instant. She was stabbed through the heart, a hemorrhage. I'm terribly sorry," he added, seeing the distress on Zofia's face.

"Thank you. So her death occurred on the night from Easter Monday to Tuesday the sixteenth of April . . ." She took a jotter from her jacket pocket, opened it, and made a note. "All three maintain the same version of events?"

"Yes, and so do the . . . incidental witnesses."

"Could they have put these persons off their guard?"

Jednoróg stopped himself from smiling, but there was a sparkle in his eye.

"Considering . . . their intimate proximity to those persons, I think that impossible. It would require a miracle. And not one of the divine kind, but rather a devilish one."

Zofia sighed.

"I know Franciszka has told you this and that, but it is still too little. I have tried to elicit more facts from her, because as we know, our memory has its secret drawers that sometimes become jammed, but if treated with the right question, posed at the right moment . . ."

"They spring open, as if freshly illuminated, revealing hidden treasures."

"Exactly so. This engineer, whom Franciszka has told you about, seems to me a most suspicious character. Even if we accept that she had in fact captured the heart of a young man from a good home, which is not impossible—take Mr. Tetmajer, for example . . ." She made a face. "Well, he is not an engineer, he is an artist, a hothead, but he married a peasant girl . . . It is unthinkable that he can have proposed to Karolina without asking for her parents' consent, in this case her mother's, and without informing us, her employers. It is totally inadmissible . . ."

"Totally!" agreed Jednoróg.

"Evidence of a complete lack of good breeding. I do not know of any engineer," she said, raising her chin slightly, "not even a young one, who would behave in this fashion. Nor do I believe that any technical college, within the empire or beyond its borders, would turn out a graduate with such scandalous manners."

"That is true, although the police cannot prosecute anyone for a lack of manners."

Time was passing, but to give him his due, the commissioner not only remained courteous, but could even amuse her with a bon mot. She smiled.

"That is true. However, I find it dubious to the highest

degree: an engineer comes out of the blue, then dissolves into thin air at the very moment when the girl loses her life. And does nothing? Doesn't ask anyone? Not even us, when he knows where she lived?"

Jednoróg twirled his mustache.

"All right, let's think about it. According to what your servant told me, the engineer had received an urgent message and had to take up his position as soon as possible. Let us assume the following situation: he bought tickets to Hamburg for himself and for Miss Szulc, sent a telegram to his acquaintance the priest who lives there, asking him to make arrangements for the wedding to take place there before they sailed for America . . . His fiancée did not arrive at the station. He is a young man, hot-blooded, full of bold plans. He can either look for the girl who"—at this point he raised his hands—"has turned his head, admittedly, and yet . . . he doesn't actually know her very well. When did they first meet?"

"A couple of weeks earlier," said Zofia.

"Meanwhile he has a great adventure ahead of him, probably his first serious job since college . . . a new continent, all the excitements of youth, when a new chapter in life opens before us. He can wave goodbye to the train ticket and the money he has already spent on the transatlantic voyage. But he can also . . ."

"Wave goodbye to the girl?"

"To his Dulcinea, in whom suddenly our unlucky Don Quixote sees just a pretty face and a flighty character, if she has failed to understand what a vital opportunity this is for him. Meanwhile his Dulcinea has not abandoned him at all . . ."

"But has been murdered."

"*Voilà.* By the jealous lad to whom she promised her heart earlier, but whom she dropped for a better match. If this is actually what happened, then without knowing his name, or anything else about him, we have no way of tracking him down abroad. Not even to tell him that the wretched girl did not make a fool of him at all," concluded the commissioner.

Zofia toyed with the black tassel attached to her umbrella.

"Yet you will admit that an engineer who arranges a hasty wedding to a housemaid is more like a character from a vaudeville or a cheap romantic novel than a real person of flesh and blood."

"The heart is capable of many things . . ." he said sententiously. She agreed, and he took up the theme again: "It might not merely overstep the social limits, but it might even kill. It is my belief that the sand miner found out the whole truth, and realizing that his paramour was slipping from his hands, he acted as his jealous heart dictated."

"But that is far too simple! The sand miner an Othello?" said Zofia, frowning. "Has he made a confession?"

"Naturally, we have interrogated him, twice. We know that Miss Szulc told him everything, and we know that he got drunk out of despair." He reached for a stone paperweight decorated with a brass eagle, from the same set as the inkwell, and took from under it a few sheets of paper resembling official documents, skimmed the text, and then continued: "For part of the night he was seen at a low tavern . . . first one, then another . . . though these are the statements of habitual drunkards who cannot tell the moon apart from a street lamp and are incapable of saying at exactly what time he arrived or left . . . or was thrown out, because that is what appears to have happened. We've got our eye on him. He's being tailed around the clock by two young policemen, Cadets Ecler and Pidłypczak. Sooner or later he'll give himself away somehow."

But his interlocutor was intransigent.

"You won't be pleased, Commissioner, but to my mind the phantom engineer is a far more interesting trail."

Jednoróg gave Zofia a look, cleared his throat, and then knotted his hands together—the large, solid hands of a genuine guardian of the law.

"I have the deepest respect for your opinion, Mrs. Turbotyńska, and I know how astutely you helped to solve the case at Helcel House," he began, and she waited for the word *but,* which soon followed of course, "but I would like to point out that murders are rarely the result of . . . how can I put it? Great criminal minds and elaborate plans. Most people are simple, and they act in a simple way. You are looking for a complex threshing machine where we usually find a flail," he said, smiling under his mustache. "In fact, there was a similar case in Lemberg only a month ago."

He reached for a smart document folder that was lying on the table: it was glossy, made of cherry-red leather with fancy patterns and the initials *SJ* embossed on it. *No doubt a gift from his underlings to mark his most recent promotion,* thought Zofia. He turned a little key in the lock and opened the folder, revealing a scarlet moire silk lining, and then took out a newspaper cutting.

"Naturally, I cannot show the police documents to you, as someone unauthorized," he justified himself, handing her the cutting, "but this piece of news is publicly available."

"Murder in Lemberg," she read in silence, knitting her brow and squinting because she refused to fetch out her lorgnette. *"Twenty-six-year-old washerwoman Marya Wajda was living at 10 Podlewski Street when Paweł Strzelecki, one of Count Stanisław Dzieduszycki's footmen, fell in love with her. Despite Strzelecki's ardent affection, and despite the numerous gifts he presented to her, Wajda did not return his feelings, but remained faithful to her betrothed, Szpaczyński, who was on military service for three years in Vienna. The day before yesterday Szpaczyński returned from Vienna, and Wajda informed Strzelecki that her marriage to him would take place soon. Distressed by this definitive statement, Strzelecki ran to his master's house, seized his firearm, ran back to Wajda's residence, and shot her from behind, in the back, as she was folding the linen."* "In the back," said Zofia aloud, "what a vile deed!" *"Having shot her, he dropped the firearm and went straight to the police to report the crime he had committed. The emergency am-*

bulance service was immediately summoned, but could only confirm Wajda's death. The culprit is being held in prison. When interviewed he stated that he had committed the murder 'out of despair and great love.'"

"Well, I never," she said aloud, "'out of despair and great love!' What a nerve!"

"Quite so. Further on it says that the gifts he brought her, silver spoons and rings, for instance, were stolen from his employers, and on top of that he had an unsavory appearance . . . In short, neither you nor I would wish to meet him. And yet"—the commissioner paused—"is it not true to say that even those of an unsavory appearance, not to say common thieves, have their feelings too? Surely, and I am not joking, they are capable of great and noble emotions, even, as this man said, of despair and great love?"

Here she had to admit—at least inwardly—that he was right; regardless of the opinions instilled in her in the past about people of lower status, or lower social class, as the socialists would say nowadays, experience prompted her to believe that people show greatness or pettiness regardless of their parents' station in life, the size of their dowry, or their heraldic shields.

"So it's an open-and-shut case. Jealousy," he said, knotting his fingers again, "*the green-eyed monster,* as Shakespeare put it. And not just a lover's jealousy, but something else, too. He is a simple laborer, who has spent years digging sand from the bottom of the Vistula, cutting out blocks of ice in the winter, toiling away in heat and frost, and yet he's poor as a church mouse, so what can he buy for his beloved? A cheap ring with a glass stone from the Emaus Fair? Then along comes a rich young gent, educated, with the whole world at his feet, and snatches this lovely girl from under the poor lad's nose — he finds her, woos her, captures her heart, and . . . snap!" — he waved his hand as if catching a fly in his fist. "In this harsh world, the world of raw emotions, rough deeds, and a curious, peasant sense of honor that is an insult for which one pays with blood."

"With blood? A fine idea," said Zofia, raising her voice. "But why the blood of a defenseless girl, why did he not attack the engineer with a knife? He would have been a more worthy adversary."

"Well, perhaps we shall get it out of him. But sometimes desperation and thoroughly inhumane envy are to be found in one and the same body as all too human cowardice and cold calculation."

For a while they were both silent, then Zofia thanked him for the conversation and prepared to leave.

"There's one thing you can be sure of," he said, escorting her into the corridor. "You will be the first to know who the murderer is."

Which would turn out to be true.

❧

She thought about this conversation right through lunch, all evening, and all the next day; it continued to occupy her mind on Sunday morning, during High Mass at St. Mary's Basilica and during afternoon coffee, which as an exception she did not take at Maurizio's, but at Rehman's in the Cloth Hall, guided by the naive idea that perhaps some detail would betray the name of the mysterious engineer who had brought Karolina here for cakes. For a while she toyed with the thought that he would come along with a photograph of her maid, and would ask the waiters whether they remembered them as a couple, but then she laughed at herself, sure she'd be taken for a madwoman for thinking like that.

Giving up, she went home and waited for Ignacy to return, which happened late that evening. He came back looking completely different from when he had gone out a few hours earlier. Then he had seemed robust, radiating good health, in well-brushed clothing, polished brown shoes, and variegated leggings, bringing to mind a knight's heraldic colors — he'd been a living testimonial for the sport of cycling. But now, dog-tired, sweaty, his hair in a mess, and his side whiskers matted, he was the image of misery and despair: there were splashes of mud on his shoes and socks and a cobweb on the sleeve of his jacket, brushed off the wayside bushes without him even noticing . . . He looked like a wild man! With Franciszka's help he managed to restore himself to a fairly tolerable state and came back into the drawing room refreshed, his side whiskers bristling jauntily. Yet Zofia could sense that something had gone wrong.

After supper, gloomily sunk in an armchair covered in dark red plush, Ignacy finally said: "How times have changed. In the past it would have been unthinkable for a vigorous young man who can see that a slightly older person is walking, or riding, it's all the same, at a lesser speed, not to slow down a little, out of common courtesy. Anyway, why be in a tearing hurry when there are such fine views to enjoy at this time of year, when one can see the ancient towers of Tyniec Monastery rising above the river . . . when there is something to look at, something to admire. Is it a ride or a race? But today's young men . . ." He sighed. "Bah, they're such hotheads, anything to be out in front, in front . . . goodness knows how it will all end."

They sat in silence. Zofia decided to cheer him up with his favorite treat, which was curious titbits from the *Cracow Times.* She picked up the newspaper and gave it a flick.

"At three in the morning the Rescue Association ambulance was summoned to Szewska Street to attend to twenty-three-year-old Marya Bylica, who with the aim of poisoning herself had swallowed part of a mercurial sublimate pill," she read aloud. *Part?* thought Zofia, *the very idea! If one's going to do something, one should do it properly. Surely she didn't intend to keep the rest of the pill for further use? Even thrift must have its limits!* She read on. *"Once the appropriate antidote had been applied, the emergency ambulance took the patient to St. Lazarus's Hospital.* Just a moment, this may be more interesting: *Berlin. Kaiser Wilhelm left for Weimar yesterday afternoon."*

"And?" was all Ignacy asked.

"And that's it. But there's news from Le Havre. *Yesterday the president of the Republic, Faure, visited hospitals and orphanages . . . he spoke to many of the patients . . . handed out toys to the children . . . and was received with cheers . . .* Nothing interesting."

Ignacy sighed.

"Oh, an earthquake!" she said, livening up, as she spotted the word out of the corner of her eye. *"Rome. As reported by Agenzia Stefani, the news of another earthquake in Sicily issued by the press and all the related reports about houses collapsing . . . are untrue."*

"Very good," observed Ignacy soberly, but in a tone that seemed to be saying "very bad."

At that she stopped reading. They sat awhile longer, listening to the ticking of the clock and the distant shouts coming from the street. Then they went to bed.

CHAPTER IV

In which Franciszka displays the skills of a detective, while Zofia refers to the Cracow townswoman's Bible and heads for the remote suburbs, almost all the way to Florence or Venice. There on the steps she meets an admirer of the Amazonian women and then becomes an Amazonian herself, by forcing a wall builder to capitulate once pinned to the wall. We also learn how much time it takes to send a very short letter, what Franek is useful for, and what a bare calf was doing at the Battle of Berezina.

Zofia felt as if the days were simultaneously passing and not passing, as if she were suspended in a timeless void. The usual daily tasks were going on around her: overseeing the meals, doing the shopping, one tea party, two visits, including one to Countess Żeleńska at Helcel House . . .

Naturally while she was there she remembered to drop in on Sister Alojza, who had been in poor health lately, and to offer her a sealed bottle of last year's raspberry juice, excellent for colds, and some of Dr. Pareński's famous cough pastilles; she had also exchanged a few words with the gardener and personally inspected the rhododendrons, which were branching out beautifully and were covered in buds — soon she would dazzle the public with them at the flower show. And yet . . . nothing was happening, because the most important news still hadn't come, announcing the arrest of the murderer. Somewhere out there Karolina's killer was blithely walking about Cracow, wearing a smart lancer's uniform, or a sand miner's laboring jacket. Or perhaps he was somewhere else entirely. Perhaps he had grabbed a suitcase full of clothes and his engineer's diploma, and was now in Hamburg, boarding the HAPAG ship, or in Bremen, getting on the Lloyd's ship, or else, who knows, maybe he was already blithely sailing across the Atlantic? Moving across water, as it was all written in water anyway . . .

Today, too, there was plenty to do, and yet she was squandering her time. Even if she used small patience cards, Potocki's solitaire did not fit on her writing desk — which was not large, a ladies' one, and thus designed for writing very short letters, notes to thank for hospitality, or invitations — and so she had to transfer her game to the dining table. She moved a silver sugar bowl (a wedding present from the Dutkiewiczes) from the tabletop to the dresser, folded the red plush tablecloth embroidered with gold flowers and hung it over the back of a chair, and now for the twenty-first time was dealing out four rows of cards on the polished wood. Six times it hadn't come out right, and the third, final deal of the seventh game wasn't inspiring optimism either. The eight of diamonds right behind a king . . .

"If you please, madam?"

. . . the ten can follow the nine, the seven can take its place, that provides a gap behind the king, so maybe . . .

"If you please, madam?"

Franciszka was standing in the dining room doorway, holding a small white object in her outstretched hands, but from this distance Zofia couldn't see what it was, at least not without reaching for her lorgnette. A pillbox? A small piece of card? The object may have been unobtrusive, but something about the servant's excited tone of voice, something about her triumphant gesture caused Zofia to abandon her thoughts about the fate of the eight of diamonds.

"What has happened, Franciszka?"

"You went on and on asking about Karolina, and about that engineer . . . so I thought to myself, we did live together, didn't we? We ate, slept, and did everything in each other's pocket, and when she got out of here she did it in a big rush, in and out in a flash. So I think to myself, something must have been left behind, a speck or a crumb. And as I can be certain Karolina won't be coming back, I might as well deal with all that mess. So I did some tidying up."

"And?"

"Weeell, I can't say I haven't worked hard. I pulled every

last sheaf of hay out of the mattresses and stuffed 'em back in again," she said eagerly, "and I didn't miss nothing. I took down the rugs hanging above the beds and gave 'em a good shake, I emptied the wardrobe of all Karolina's blouses, petticoats, and corsets, I turned 'em inside out, I peeped into every little pocket . . ."

"And?" repeated Zofia, but as Franciszka was carrying on with her monologue, she realized that it had to be recited in full, to bear witness to the vast amount of work she had done.

"I took a close look at her boots, and peeped into every crack in the floorboards. After all that I went up the walls, too, and decided to dust the picture of Saint John Cantius that the master gave me the Christmas before last, and take the opportunity to rehang it too. Because when Karolina came, I had both the Mother of God and Saint John, and she had nobody at all, so I said here you are, hang this above your bed, so you'll have someone to pray to. So I takes it down and dusts it, but something tells me to turn it over. And there, shoved behind the bottom of the frame I found this! The gentlemen from the police must have overlooked it."

She came up to the table and handed Zofia the white object, which close up turned out to be a visiting card.

"It's that engineer's card. I know because when she got it, she flashed it past my eyes and hid it away at once." Zofia reached nervously for her lorgnette lying on the tabletop and raised it to her eyes. "He had a whole case full of them, silver, like gentlemen have, and he gave her one so she'd know he wasn't just nobody. Well, there's not much on it, just his Christian name and surname, but that's good too."

"Marceli Bzowski?" she read, was momentarily dumbstruck, and then said in an agitated tone: "What on earth are you telling me? Engineer Bzowski cannot have proposed to Karolina, he has a wife and children. On top of which he is a mature and serious man, as old as the master. He would not pretend to be a bachelor in sight of the entire city, and he would never have taken an unmarried housemaid to Rehman's for ice cream!"

"For *cakes,*" replied Franciszka emphatically, which was proof that deep down she envied Karolina every slice of Pischinger she'd eaten. "Mature and serious? But I saw him. From a distance, to be fair, but he weren't more than twenty-five years old, not even standing on tiptoes! Dressed to the nines, dapper, with a walking cane, all lean and nimble."

Various adjectives could have been applied to Engineer Bzowski, but "lean" and "nimble" were not among them; he was a solid man, reminiscent of a large brick building, meaning a big, square barracks rather than a soaring water tower.

"Are you sure this visiting card came from Karolina's engineer? She could have gotten it from somewhere else, she could have found it in the street."

"As sure as eggs is eggs! She brought it home and

boasted to me. At the time she waved it about so's I couldn't see what was on it. But now I recognize it. It's his, his, I say!"

Zofia sighed. She turned the card over, but found nothing on the other side. It was blank. Decent paper, but without extravagance or undue elegance. The title *Eng.* in a simple font, and then the first name and surname. It occurred to her that perhaps it was one of the condolence cards that had been sent after Karolina's death—but it didn't have a bent-back corner or a crease from having been bent; in any case, so few of them had come that she would definitely have remembered being sent condolences by someone she hardly knew, when so many closer acquaintances hadn't bothered. Evidently, most people think of the death of a servant as something halfway between the death of a household member and the death of a dog or cat.

"Very good, Franciszka. You have acquitted yourself splendidly, I must say. Let us hope that this small thread will lead us to the heart of the matter."

Briefly she turned something over in her head and then, after firmly sweeping all the cards into a low pile, she addressed Franciszka again: "Please go to the kitchen and see if the vanilla custard has set properly."

Zofia was fond of saying that she never forgot anything. But what worked well as a self-confident remark did not necessarily tally with the truth—now she was racking her brains to remember where the Bzowskis had moved to. She couldn't ask Ignacy, nor would he be likely to know; the mundane business of sending cards with name day and holiday greetings was her responsibility, and all she could remember was that in the past year they had moved out of their flat on St. Anne's Street.

As all her efforts of memory were in vain, she decided to make use of a resource close to the heart of any self-respecting Cracow townswoman. Although she would undoubtedly have been outraged by this comparison, just as Franciszka had her *Angel's Aid,* so Zofia too had a sacred book that she may not have regarded with solemn reverence, but in which she sought the answers to her questions far more often than in the Bible. She went over to the bookshelf, and from a long row of fat tomes in red covers she pulled out the first to the right, *Józef Czech's Cracow Calendar for the year 1895,* which she opened at her favorite section: "The Cracow Who's Who," where, as in a register of good and evil, all the more notable citizens were listed: from councilors and city officials, via the managers of the Imperial-Royal tobacco factory, to members of the Lutnia Choral Society. There was no handier map for navigating the stormy seas of Cracow society.

Ignacy had featured in the Calendar for years, first as an ordinary doctor, then as Professor Teichmann's assistant and demonstrator, and now at last, in the section headed "Full and Associate University Professors" for the second year. But she hurriedly began to leaf through in search of engineers, and soon found the "List of Builders, Architects, and Engineers," where she read: *Bzowski, Marceli, 11 Studencka Street.* That meant she had an outing to the other side of Planty Park ahead of her.

She stood in the kitchen doorway, cast an approving glance at the vanilla custard, and then said to Franciszka: "There is still plenty of time until the master comes home . . . you shall see to the lunch on your own. I trust you will come up with something. If he comes home early and asks for me, then you do not know where I have gone."

Franciszka smiled to herself, remembering how only a couple of days ago her mistress had announced the introduction of a rule that in this house no one was to have any secrets from anyone else, but she dutifully bowed, wiping her hands on her apron.

Whereas Zofia went into the bedroom to sit at her dressing table for a while. As befitted a warrior woman, Zofia Turbotyńska never went out to fight without putting on her warpaint.

❧

Ignacy was constantly complaining about the "utterly uncontrolled expansion of Cracow, breaking all the bounds of common sense." Indeed, he liked the new public buildings, such as the fire service barracks, which brought to mind a large castle, the elegant Fine Arts School, and above all—

naturally—the new university buildings. "Truly imperial!" he said of them with satisfaction, which on his lips was an expression of the highest praise.

However, his response to the new residential buildings that were springing up like mushrooms after rain in places where not so long ago the wild wind had been blowing, was far less enthusiastic. He'd complain that "the suburbs," as he disdainfully called them, were being built without harmony and with too little space, generally breaking the rules in the process—and indeed, according to the government regulations a house could not be higher than the width of the street; meanwhile, if asked, any citizen would have little trouble pointing out streets that resembled canyons, where the sunlight appeared as rarely as a socialist at May mass.

Nevertheless, despite initially sharing her husband's opinion, after two or three social visits to friends who had decided to move beyond the confines of Planty Park, Zofia had started to form one of her own. More spacious rooms, more convenient kitchens, separate staircases for the servants—all this made an excellent impression on her, and even prompted envy. Yet on the question of moving house Ignacy was unshakeable; every attempt to broach the subject ruined the rest of the day at Peacock House.

Which certainly did not mean that Zofia intended to abandon further endeavors; she knew from experience that dripping water can drill through rock, and her husband—why hide the fact?—was not so much granite as marble:

noble and venerable indeed, but susceptible to the effect of external factors.

As she walked at a brisk pace along the springtime paths of Planty Park, where she could see nature coming back to life — the wrinkled young leaves of a chestnut tree, the dazzling white of cherry blossom, the beds of brightly colored primulas — there was one thing she did agree with her husband about: the decline in the number of parks filled her with grief. The Krzyżanowski Gardens in Wesoła had already gone under the axe, as had Jabłonowski Common opposite the university, and now the turn of the Wodzicki Gardens had come. No wonder; the ground here produced gold coins, just as in the town of Borysław it emitted equally valuable crude oil, so in places where there were orchards ten years ago, there was now construction work in progress: Rettinger, the lawyer, had erected a two-story house, and charted a new street right across the middle of the garden. A good thing General Kościuszko's Tower had survived, it suddenly occurred to her. She was afraid to think what sort of a fury Ignacy would fly into if this "priceless reminder of ages past, that hosted the commander himself under its roof" were to fall victim to the "vandals" he loathed so much. Though actually in Zofia's view it looked like a big ugly kennel.

She had now reached the residential building where — according to Czech's Calendar — the Bzowskis lived, and glanced up at it with a certain envy. The ground floor of the residential building was rusticated, as if clad in rough-hewn blocks of stone; above each window there was a head, either of Hercules in a lion skin, or a classical nymph; the two upper floors were faced with brick, with a balcony on each one at the corner and windows with wide Renaissance borders; and down the sides there were panoplies dated 1887. A real Florentine palazzo! She entered the gateway and was about to ask the watchman—another convenience that she missed at Peacock House—which floor was home to Engineer Bzowski, when a plump young woman appeared on the turn of the steps, wearing a snuff-colored dress from several seasons ago. Her dark hair was rather carelessly tied in a bun, hidden beneath a hat of a nondescript mouse-brown color. On her wide face ("strong and distinctive," said some, "coarse and crude," said Turbotyńska) her surprise showed; Zofia was equally amazed, but managed not to betray it.

"Mrs. Turbotyńska," the young woman greeted her.

"Mrs. Bujwid," replied Zofia, with a very slight nod: just enough for the movement to be noticed, but not a fraction of an inch lower.

"News has reached me of the tragedy that has befallen your house. Please accept my deepest sympathy. It is the most heartbreaking story." Zofia thanked her with another nod, this time slightly more distinct. "And further proof," Mrs. Bujwid continued, "of the importance of education for girls in our modern world. Very soon, in just a few weeks, we shall be opening our Women's Reading Room. I do hope you will come . . . in fact, I am on my way there now, as there is still the odd thing to be organized."

Zofia nodded a third time, trying to evade an unambiguous response. She had no intention of taking advantage of the invitation. All she needed was to get involved in *something like that!* Whenever she saw Mrs. Bujwid in the street she crossed to the other side in good time, to avoid encountering this destroyer of public order, this freethinker, not to say virtual socialist . . . *Or maybe she is an out-and-out socialist—with people like that one never knows!* she thought with alarm. Now that it had come to the misfortune of running into her, Zofia had to put a brave face on it. But the woman was relentless.

"What brings you to us?" she asked. "Have you come to see Odon about something?"

To us? thought Zofia. *What bad luck to head off to the suburbs and by sheer accident happen upon the very house where the Bujwids live!* Nor did she fail to notice the shockingly direct form used by Mrs. Bujwid to refer to her husband, Professor Bujwid; Zofia would never be so bold in conversation with a practical stranger to speak of Ignacy as "Ignacy," but the woman standing before her was known in Cracow for her ostentatious flouting of the rules.

"No, no," she said, feigning nonchalance, "I have come to see the Bzowskis . . . The engineer is a colleague of Professor Turbotyński's at the cycling club."

"Ah, Bzowski, our neighbor from the second floor . . ." said Mrs. Bujwid in a cool tone, as if the name had bad associations for her. "Yes, those cycling capers. Well, dear madam, when our husbands waste their time on fun, it falls upon us to take matters into our own hands, does it not?"

Zofia let this remark go unheeded. Not that she didn't agree with it, but she would never have said so aloud. And she refused to concur with Mrs. Bujwid at any price.

"Well, excuse me, but it's time I was off," she said, bidding Zofia farewell. She bowed, and skipped down the steps. On the bottom one she turned again and, with total neglect for good manners, shouted: "Perhaps you'll come to Dr. Trzaskowski's talk at the Lady Teachers' Association on Friday? Highly absorbing, I can vouch for it, on mythical and historical Amazonian women. Do come!" And then, without waiting for a reply, she vanished through the gateway.

Amazonian women, that's a fine one! thought Zofia. *As if I'd want to hear about those shameless creatures who take up male professions instead of seeing to their duty.*

❧

The study, into which the maid showed her, was located in the front part of the flat, roughly halfway down a corridor; there were a few of Bzowski's own designs hanging in large frames on the walls: here a small church in the Gothic style, there a townhouse with a playful turret, and over there the solemn block of a provincial courthouse or office building, crowned with a large heraldic crest. Below them were rows of bookcases, full of books about architecture, and some plan chests, not high but with deep drawers for storing designs. In the very middle of the spacious room stood a large desk scattered with papers, and behind it an armchair of a size to match the size of the part of the engineer that usually sat in it.

"Good morning, madam," she heard from the threshold after a brief wait, so she turned abruptly on her chair, cast Bzowski a glance from beneath her hat adorned with a raven's wing, and then returned his bow. "To what do I owe this unexpected pleasure?"

Zofia had realized in advance that instead of hesitantly starting with sweeteners, she should attack at once, making a tactical gain through the effect of surprise.

"Oh, it's just a trivial matter, Mr. Bzowski, but I didn't want to involve any of the . . . official authorities. As you may have heard, my housemaid has been murdered"—Bzowski made a face as if she had said something improper, but he mumbled his condolences—"and the police are trying to find a lead to identify the killer. It seems a particular man had been courting her . . ."

"Of course, it is very sad, but I fail to see any connection with my modest person," he replied, sitting down in the armchair, which under his modest person gave a loud creak.

"The fact is that this man beguiled my maid, took her to Rehman's for cakes, and, in my view, may then have contributed to her death. And by a strange coincidence he introduced himself to her by the name Bzowski. Engineer Marceli Bzowski."

Inside the real owner of this name something began to boil, just like in a steam kettle, and once it had turned his face red, it emerged in the form of a whistling sound, with words breaking through it.

"My dear lady . . . but that is . . . slander!" he said. "I, I never . . . I am a married man . . . the father of children! Madam, I . . . won't stand for it! A housemaid, well I never! I won't stand for it!"

"But under no circumstances am I claiming that it was you in person, sir, who made advances to my Karolina," said Zofia indignantly.

"I cannot imagine you could think otherwise! Anyone . . . anyone could have made dishonorable use of my name, dear lady. Anyone!" Bzowski ranted. "So I am astonished, truly astonished that, knowing me as you do, you have come to see me, as if it concerned me in any way at all that some dishonorable person . . ."

"Is making use of your name?" she interrupted him. "I believe it does concern you, because it could cast a shadow on your reputation. And that is something we would both wish to avoid. In any case, it is not just about your name . . ."

"About what else?" he growled.

"About this," she said, taking the visiting card from her purse and placing it on the desk.

Bzowski stretched out an arm and laid his mighty paw on the card, which next to it suddenly looked tiny; he slid the card across the surface all the way up to his belly, which was resting on the edge of the desk, then raised it to his eyes.

"What does this mean? It means nothing, dear madam," he said huffily. "A professional man of my standing hands out any number of calling cards on a daily basis. After all, I have a social life. I call on building material merchants at their firms and my clients at their private houses . . . Any butler, any chimney sweep's lad shown the way to the drawing room fireplace, any delivery boy could have stolen my card and used it for reprehensible purposes. It could even have been found in the street! And on the strength of that, you're trying to cast accusations at me? That is absurd!"

Zofia adopted the sincerest of her facial expressions and in a saccharine tone replied: "Accusations? At you, Mr. Bzowski? The very idea! My only concern is to find out who killed Karolina, but I haven't the faintest suspicion that it involves you. The point is to find out where the culprit could have gotten hold of your card."

"I have already said: from anywhere at all. From anyone at all. One calling card, what is that?"

"Oh yes, indeed," she said, smiling radiantly. "I had forgotten to mention the most important fact. He had an entire case full of your visiting cards."

Instantly all the air left Bzowski, as if the fire under the kettle had suddenly gone out and a bucket of icy water had been thrown over it. He stood up, went over to the window, returned to his desk, and finally spoke.

"Well, then, the mystery is solved. I have lost my card case, it's true. During Rękawka. I think it fell out of my pocket when I leaned forward to throw a few coins and roll an egg down the hill." Zofia had attended this eccentric Cracow Easter tradition before now, because Ignacy was strangely fond of it. "But who knows, perhaps a skillful pickpocket took it off me? I am sure you have heard of the Lemberg school of thieves, where they have real live *academic lecturers,* and the *students* practice on effigies festooned in little bells? All of them Jews, of course," he added in a tone that seemed to imply this last detail was obvious, then said nothing for a while. Zofia kept quiet too, and in an expectant manner, so eventually he finished his tale.

"So you see, it's hard for me to tell if a thief is to blame, or sheer carelessness. Suffice it to say, I came home and noticed that my card case had vanished without trace. As I'm sure you realize, that hardly provides a lead. Anyone could have picked it up from the ground or bought it from the pickpocket."

From under the raven's wing, Zofia cast him the sort of look that a cobra confers on a bird of paradise before devouring it.

"Yes . . . that changes the shape of things," she said. "I can see that the matter is far more serious, and will necessarily require police involvement after all, and of course the ensuing scandal. I'll also have to inform and question your wife, because I expect your alibi for the night of Karolina's murder is the alibi of a faithful spouse who spent the entire night in the marital bed, sleeping the sleep of the just . . ."

"Surely I misunderstand you, dear lady . . . ?"

"Surely not," she protested with a smile. "You are a man of lively intelligence and you understand me perfectly. You've just lied to my face"—at this point Zofia's eyes narrowed ominously—"which I know to be true even if you did adhere to that old nugget of conventional wisdom, that any good lie must remain as close to the truth as possible . . . Please do not interrupt!" She raised a hand. "That's why you brought up Rękawka, the Lemberg school for pickpockets, and even the egg you rolled: as a way of padding the untruth with various truths, to make it harder to detect the falsehood."

"My dear madam!" said Bzowski, boiling up again.

"Please do not interrupt!" she repeated, then rose to her feet and stepped toward him like the snake-haired head of Medusa in Rubens's painting. "I am just a weak woman, the modest wife of a university professor, but the police have their ways of investigating the truth, Mr. Bzowski! Of course, if asked, I would say that confessing to me what really happened would be your most convenient way out, because you can trust me to pass the matter on to Investigating Magistrate Rozmarynowicz and Police Commissioner Jednoróg as delicately as possible. But if"—here she leaned her hands on the desktop and suddenly came face-to-face with Bzowski, who had sat down again—"you prefer the magistrate, the commissioner, the stenographers, a search, interviews with every member of the household, a detailed report on your daily activities from sunrise to sunset and also from sunset to sunrise"—she held forth, terrified deep down that if she couldn't force him this way she'd never manage to do it, because Jednoróg wouldn't go quite so far to accommodate her—"in short, if you want to fight a battle, with that one feeble, pitiful lie about Rękawka as your entire arsenal, then please go ahead, do as you wish. But it so happens that previous statements provide convincing proof that your visiting cards were in the criminal's possession much earlier on, well before Easter, so either you will succeed in convincing the police that Engineer Bzowski organized a private Rękawka for himself in February, or else you have a hard time ahead of you, quite possibly a charge of murder . . . and a fair dose of shame in front of your wife, because"—at this point she went for broke—"it seems quite certain that you're hiding a good number of things from her, considering what a seasoned liar you are!"

Having gotten all that out she suddenly felt winded, so with her hands still resting on the desk, she took some deep breaths. Bzowski was silent too, with his head drooping, showing the small round bald patch on the crown of his head, which was glowing, as if sending a hesitant signal of surrender through the fog.

"Therefore . . . can I count on . . . your discretion?"

Therefore, she thought with satisfaction, *he's asking about the terms of capitulation.*

"Naturally, I don't mean the official authorities," he sighed, "though there too . . ."

"Though there, too, it is possible to submit information in a fairly discreet manner. I can promise you," she said, straightening up, "that I shall do it as delicately as possible."

"My card case was stolen from me along with its entire contents, and also my wallet, in mid-March. I cannot tell you the precise date . . . but it must have been a night from Friday to Saturday . . . and it happened at a certain establishment . . . in the Dębniki district."

"At which establishment?"

"Well, I would rather not . . ." He sighed again.

"So I shall have to summon the commissioner after all?" she asked.

The silence was so intense that she could hear a clock ticking in the next room.

"It is an establishment for gentlemen."

"That I have known ever since you started shying away from the truth," said Zofia derisively. "So please be more precise: tell me the date, the address, and the details."

"What details? The details are beside the point! I was fleeced by a thief who came in through the window. Or maybe through the door, if he's in league with them. Or perhaps it was the girl? I am not the first to be robbed there, apparently it has happened before, because Mister. . . ."

"Yes?"

"Never mind the name!" he snapped, in a gesture of male solidarity that concealed some pharmacist or city councilor. "Suffice it to say that I dozed off, and awoke poorer for the loss of a wallet and a card case. A small silver one with my initials engraved upon it, and a dedication inside . . . from my wife"—he cleared his throat—"on the occasion of our tenth wedding anniversary."

"The address?"

"Różana Street, but what's the number? I know the way by heart. It's a small house, just two stories, with a garret, set back from the street, a garden at the front, and jasmine, lots of jasmine. The place belongs to Madame Olesia . . ."

"Surname?"

"You evidently do not frequent such places!" he blurted.

"Regrettably, I cannot pay you the same compliment."

He sighed heavily, and then explained.

"One always refers to 'Madame Olesia,' and that is all, without further ado. Madame Olesia's establishment on Różana Street, any cabman will know."

Again she heard the clock ticking as clearly as if it were standing in Mr. Bzowski's study. Briefly she wondered whether to ask another question, but she let it rest; she merely took out her notebook and jotted down the most salient facts: *1st half Mar, night Fr/Sat, M. Olesia, Różana, Dębn.*

"If by some miracle you were to come upon my card case," said Bzowski, suddenly coming to, "then would you please . . ."

"Do give my regards to your wife" was all she said in parting.

❧

On returning home, Zofia hurriedly performed the most urgent tasks: she replaced her umbrella in the faience vase, removed the light cape from her shoulders, took off her gloves and put them away in the lacquer box that was kept beneath the mirror, then she took out her hatpins—one adorned with a butterfly, the other with a large carnelian—and stuck them into the little pillow that sat next to the glove box, and finally removed the hat and handed it to Franciszka; a fancy, cherry-red one, it was topped with five crêpe de Chine roses in full bloom and a raven's wing shimmering with every shade of black (an absolute masterpiece from Maryja Prauss's shop, apparently from Paris, though who knows if not conjured up by a milliner in a moldy basement in Grzegórzki, as Zofia suspected). Once she had made sure that the master was not yet home, and the lunch was almost ready, she raced to the telephone. She unhooked the receiver, stopped, and hung it up again. Although she was the one who had urged Ignacy to have the telephone installed, she was still mistrustful of conversations at a distance; they seemed rather peculiar, and definitely not as courteous as a note. So she headed for her writing desk.

She was not only an expert on etiquette, but also on

people; if Jednoróg had lately received her in such a friendly manner she was not going to impose on him by once again delaying his lunch. But at the same time she had to convey the morning's discoveries to him as soon as possible—she must send a short message, literally a few words. From a small drawer for stationery she took out an envelope and a sheet of writing paper, embossed with the initials *ZT*, then drew the inkwell closer, a trinket from the days when chinoiserie was in fashion: under a forked bush, with a silver penholder resting on its symmetrical branches, sat a portly Chinese figure. She used the tip of the penholder to nudge his head, which tipped back, exposing the vessel full of ink. She dipped her steel nib in it, as if jabbing it into the neck of a dead convict, beheaded at the command of a cruel Chinese emperor.

Honored Commissioner, she began, then swiftly, though trying to keep her handwriting legible, summarized the results of today's investigation. Then just a quick roll of the blotter, rather than wait for the ink to dry . . . and the envelope . . . She lit the single candle standing in a holder; then she held a stick of sealing wax over the flame, which began to sizzle; once a couple of bright red drops had dripped onto the envelope, Zofia took a small, slender die made of agate from the drawer, pressed her initials into the wax, and then wrote on the front: *Commissioner Stanisław Jednoróg Esq., personal, by hand,* and rang for Franciszka.

"I know you are about to serve the lunch and you have no time to run to Mikołajska Street. Send Franek, and tell him there's no need to wait for an answer," she said, handing her the letter and a coin.

Franek was the messenger boy at the wholesale depot just around the corner, on Pijarska Street, which was run by the Commercial Union of Farmers' Associations for the needs, as they always stressed, of Christian shops. There one could obtain imported foods, groceries, seeds, fertilizers, paraffin, items for sewing and writing, needles, buttons, insecticide powder for bedbugs and laundry blue—in short, everything that was then sold at a large markup in the villages and towns of Galicia. But most essentially for Zofia Turbotyńska, one could also find the said Franek there, a keen, bright, and above all trustworthy boy. He didn't have much to do at the depot, and it wasn't entirely clear why they kept him; perhaps for the splendor of the firm, because most of the customers came here from the provinces and ordered goods in wholesale quantities, which a skinny fourteen-year-old couldn't possibly have delivered single-handed, even if they only had to be taken to nearby Sławkowska Street, and not to Lanckorona, Biecz, or any other faraway town. But ever since he had first appeared on Pijarska Street a year ago, he had rendered the Turbotyńskis—and several other families in the neighborhood—countless services. And at extremely favorable prices.

Five minutes later Franciszka was back—arriving before Ignacy, who came home soon after. Fifteen minutes later the Turbotyńskis were facing each other at table, separated by a large tureen of French parmesan soup, in which, beneath a veil of steam, swam Ignacy's favorite veal and breadcrumb meatballs flavored with lobster butter.

Since Karolina's death, Ignacy and Zofia had both been having fits of depression; despite representing the stronger sex, it was he who seemed to be taking it worse. Now, as he sat in the light, with his back to the window, Zofia thought even his side whiskers, undeniably the object of his pride, were drooping. So she had decided to introduce a special culinary program to raise his spirits, and was systematically feeding him the dishes he liked best.

"What is the news at the university?" she asked in the interval between one spoonful of soup and the next.

"They say . . ." he began in a somber tone, then broke off, as if he hadn't the strength to finish his sentence.

"Yes?"

"They say that the chances of Professor Rydel surviving the recurrence of pneumonia are dwindling. Of course, Rydygier has long since performed his duties, but it would be an irreparable loss, irreparable. After all, he's not an old man; only recently we celebrated his sixtieth birthday. And this had to happen now, when the building work for the new clinic is just about to start! Apparently his son is a very able fellow, a pupil of Kostanecki's . . ."

"Aha, Kostanecki," snapped Zofia, who unlike her husband could not forgive him for taking over as head of the faculty after Teichmann.

"My dear Zofia . . ." said Ignacy, clearly losing patience; it was plain to see that at this particular moment his only concern in life was the meatballs swimming in his plate. "Adam really is very capable, and neuroanatomy appears to have a great future. His brother's situation is not so good; he may have a degree in law, but his head is filled with plays and poems! Poor Rydel, such an eminent doctor, is in danger of having his son become a . . . newspaper hack!"

"Surely not! Whereas I have heard that Pareński . . ."

"Is he sick too?"

"No, no, far from it. But now that they have moved to that"—patent envy was audible in her voice—"*palace*, yes, Ignacy, there is no other word for it but *palace*, he intends to move his practice there, too."

Pareński, a senior registrar at St. Lazarus's Hospital, was the object of envy of just about all the doctors in Cracow; not only had he made a brilliant career, he could also boast of a vast fortune. His father had been rather well off, and had married into a family in possession of a townhouse on the Market Square, right on the corner of St. John's Street; the son had then married a Miss Mühleisen, who may have been a Protestant, but a Protestant with a country estate in Kobierzyn. They lacked neither money, nor connections, nor children, and lately, as if out of malice, they had bought an authentic, two-story "palace" surrounded by a large garden on Wielopole Street.

"But who would want to go beyond Planty Park when they have a practice on the Market Square? A flight of fancy!"

And he began to elaborate in detail various cases where

a practice had been moved, and the financial consequences; it was extremely uninteresting, but as with the meals, Zofia was trying to choose topics of conversation that would raise her husband's spirits. Just then the next enticing course appeared on the table: a dish of vegetables served with a glorious rump steak, fried the English way, and thus swimming in bloody juices; on each piece lay a slice of lemon, and on each of those a pat of melting sardine butter.

"Rump steak!" said Ignacy, all but blushing. "Delicious! And have you heard about Fałat?" Everyone had heard about Fałat. Recently elected as director of the School of Fine Arts, he was due to arrive in Cracow soon, and was apparently intending to revolutionize the place. According to rumor, he wanted to replace the whole host of esteemed, traditional professors with new-fangled artists who were dubious at best. "And just imagine, he has quarreled with Kossak!"

"Indeed?" said Zofia, raising an eyebrow.

"Over their painting of the new panorama, featuring the Battle of Berezina. And so Kossak . . ." Just then Ignacy realized that he had heard this anecdote in male company, and it wasn't entirely suitable for repetition to his wife.

"Kossak?"

"The steak is superb! Superb," he said, trying to buy time.

"What about Berezina, Ignacy?"

Too bad, he would have to capitulate.

"Mr. Kossak has decided to paint something . . . indecent."

"It was probably a joint decision," she said. "It cannot be easy to paint thousands of people slaughtering each other without resorting to indecency." Zofia had quite categorical views on the so-called glory of arms.

"No, it's something much worse than that," he said, frowning. "You see, there weren't just soldiers on the scene, but also their . . . female companions . . . the *vivandières.* And a certain actress from the Comédie-Française was there, one Mademoiselle Mars. Kossak insisted he would paint her alighting from a carriage and . . ."

"And?"

"And he will display her naked calf!" said Ignacy, going purple, though it was unclear whether he was trying to suppress embarrassment or indignation. "Fałat may well be an artistic revolutionary and a rascal, but apparently his response to Kossak was that he wouldn't be taking the empress to see it. Anyway, it's not an isolated case. There was an entire letter in the *Lemberg Gazette* the other day from some concerned Catholics, complaining that the theaters show nothing but Parisian operettas and actresses in the roles of . . . *dames aux camélias*! Suffice it to say that Fałat and Kossak have had a frightful falling-out, and the whole Berezina project is up in the air!"

"What a pity Mademoiselle Mars's calf did not have such power a hundred years ago," said Zofia, "or it might have saved fifty thousand lives."

Summoned by the bell, Franciszka gathered up the plates and brought in the dessert: cups of vanilla custard, decorated with ruby-like wild strawberries in syrup. Even if the conversation had not turned out as the professor had intended, the vanilla custard after rump steak and soup with meatballs brought him to the verge of culinary ecstasy.

CHAPTER V

In which a fan confers with a newspaper and learns that it has solved a riddle, the socialists cruise around Cracow, destroying mementos of the past at the university, shooting firearms at the city's elite, and setting a match to a barrel of gunpowder at Peacock House, and a one-time opponent turns out to be an unexpected savior—but only for a while.

"No, too bright, too gaudy . . ." said Zofia, inspecting the dozen or more ties spread out on the counter by the obsequious, pomaded shop assistant. "My husband is a serious person, a university professor, he cannot appear in society dressed like a henpecked young newlywed or a dandy."

"We also have some splendid grosgrain articles, plain

colors, in very distinguished shades." He bowed, turned away from her, and reached for some more boxes from a shelf.

Zofia would have preferred to buy her husband ties imported from Vienna, Paris, or London, but she knew that *Janina, the first Polish national tie-making firm,* as the newspaper advertisements proclaimed, was supplying a rising number of society gentlemen, or rather society ladies buying ties for their husbands. The difference in price was major, while the difference in appearance was minor; there was also a guarantee that these were *French and English designs,* so both Mrs. Turbotyńska and members of the clergy (for whom there was a selection of special goods on sale here) were to be seen at the corner of the Market Square and Wiślna Street; Zofia knew several prelates and canons who were just as concerned about their apparel as the most ardent followers of fashion.

"Black grosgrain is always *à la mode,* or navy blue—very stylish with a pearl tiepin, or maroon . . ."

Box after box landed on the countertop, with a tie in each one, lying in wrinkled tissue paper like a butterfly stuck with a pin; or in view of the muted colors, a moth.

"While this good lady is deciding, may I please ask for your assistance?" she heard a commanding male voice to her right. "I would like to see that one, over there, in the corner, up above . . ."

Zofia irately turned and saw Commissioner Jednoróg,

who hissed at her softly: "I have some extremely urgent news for you."

"If you please, sir," said the shop assistant, placing a box in front of him.

"Close up it looks less appealing," muttered the commissioner, then tipped his hat and left the shop. A little later, when Zofia vacated the Janina factory store, after hastily buying two grosgrain ties—hideous, but to hand—she saw Jednoróg, shielded behind a slightly crumpled copy of the *Cracow Times,* standing outside the town hall, or to be more precise below the small tower at the corner of the new guardhouse, topped with brightly colored roof tiles. Naturally, she understood this stratagem—it wasn't appropriate for him to come to the Turbotyńskis' house and ask to see the professor's wife about the inquiry, rather than her husband; it would also have been difficult for him to summon her to Mikołajska Street. Whereas a chance encounter in a shop . . . *Aha, so he must have had me followed!* This thought filled her with truly childish joy. Zofia moved ahead and stopped two steps away from the commissioner, then looked around keenly, as if trying to spot someone among the passersby.

"You were right, of course—hats off to you," he said from behind his newspaper. "The sand miner had nothing to do with the murder. The culprit was the fellow you suspected from the start: the young man posing as Engineer Bzowski."

"Indeed," she said, taking a neat little fan from her handbag to shield her mouth from the sight of third parties. "Have you caught him already?"

"Yes and no," he began, and paused while a large carriage with wrought-iron wheels drove past over the cobblestones, making a dreadful rumbling noise; she wouldn't have heard a thing. "He was a seasoned criminal. Despite his youth he'd had numerous convictions . . . and during the manhunt he started shooting. He was killed on the spot."

"So he knew why the police had come for him," said the fan in response to the newspaper.

"Yes. I have no idea if he hoped to escape, or realized it was the end," said the newspaper, then paused. "But in any case, justice has been done. I promised you would be the first to know, and I have kept my word . . ."

"I appreciate it," said the fan.

". . . but you will learn all the details from the press the day after tomorrow at the latest. Until then, however, I would ask you . . ."

"To maintain discretion. Of course."

Commissioner Jednoróg folded yesterday's *Cracow Times,* tucked it under his arm, and strolled off in the direction of the Cloth Hall, then turned toward the top of Mikołajska Street, while Zofia, with her fan still unfolded, savored her success. So a woman's intuition is a woman's intuition—and no shiny buttons or tall shako could ever replace it.

In fact, her curiosity was not yet fully satisfied; she'd

have to find out why that thug had picked on Karolina of all people — was it just to do with base impulses, or something else? But these questions would come to light of their own accord: there'd be a fact or two in the press, some plainly stated, and as many to be read between the lines (it was Monday, and the papers would not appear today, so she'd have to arm herself with patience), then maybe she'd sniff out some more details in the places the criminal frequented, and perhaps she'd get something out of Mrs. Rozmarynowicz?

The main thing was that the good, cheerful, reliable Karolina could finally begin her eternal rest. For Zofia was sure that while the murderer was still walking the streets of Cracow, free as a lark, her unfortunate soul had been roaming around Podgórze Cemetery like a phantom in a Gothic novel, lamenting that her blood had not been avenged.

Her mind thus occupied, Zofia turned into St. John's Street — only just managing to avoid Mrs. Bujwid, whom she had seen out of the corner of her eye crossing the Market Square at the pace of a corporal — and then, passing Peacock House, she entered the Piarist church, where she lit a thanksgiving candle and said a prayer for the dear little soul set free.

✤

The conversation with Commissioner Jednoróg, so unexpected and so exciting, put Zofia into an excellent mood for the first time in a fortnight. To begin with, she thought it would be very hard to keep the secret, but she soon found that not revealing it to Ignacy gave her no trouble at all; what mattered was that Karolina had been avenged and evil punished; whether her husband learned about it a day later or a day sooner was actually of no great significance. She felt so cheerful that on Tuesday when she ran into her cousin Józefa Dutkiewicz in the Market Square she had a short but very polite conversation with her, devoid of spiteful or cutting remarks; she even praised her for collecting money toward the restoration of the Wawel Cathedral and heard out—though not without a touch of impatience—a detailed report on how Bishop Puzyna was planning to renovate the Silver Bell Tower.

But Zofia's upbeat mood clashed with Ignacy's dismal one. On Saturday, as foreseen, Professor Rydel died. They weren't such close colleagues that he had to say more than the standard "What an immense loss," and send the family condolences, but pondering the relatively young age of the deceased ("We were almost contemporaries, Zofia, just think!") was having a melancholy effect on Professor Turbotyński. Zofia could sense her own mild anxiety at the rapid approach of her forty-first birthday, which was making itself known if only through the ever more frequent need to pull white hairs from her head, but Ignacy too was affected—in his own way, of course—by the problem of transience. His troubles had not been helped by another

Sunday cycle ride, this time to Kalwaria via Skawina, which had done nothing to reinforce his sense of male prowess; on the contrary, it had cost him a pair of ripped breeches, stripped him of all his energy, and prompted a new wave of angry reproaches cast at "young men devoid of principles," the all-pervading dictatorship of youth and the decline of respect for one's elders. Monday evening ended in a quarrel. When Zofia tried to bring up the topic of moving house one day, perhaps, by casually praising the elegant apartment buildings on Studencka Street, she heard a familiar refrain: that only the other day a square yard of residential space on the streets running off the Market Square had cost eight crowns, but now it was as much as seventy; that on Studencka Street and thereabouts one used to pay two or three crowns in today's currency, but now one paid more than ten times as much; that it was a scandal, daylight robbery, and he, Ignacy Turbotyński of the Wadwicz coat of arms, senior professor at the Jagiellonian University, and Cracovian since birth, had absolutely no intention of taking part in this game of profiteering. On Tuesday he came home from Rydel's funeral looking grim, then took himself off on a solitary walk, from which he returned late, and retired for the night without a single word. Zofia felt as if the entire house were standing on a barrel of gunpowder, just waiting for a careless match to be tossed its way.

On the first of May, Ignacy came home from the university and angrily called from the threshold: "Eighteen!"

"Eighteen what, Ignacy?" she asked calmly, stopping in the doorway that led into the hall.

"Eighteen socialist posters on the way from my office to the house! For the love of God, eighteen of them!" he ranted, and then, in a slightly calmer, explanatory tone, he raised a finger and added: "I counted them."

The red posters heralding a workers' assembly to be held in the garden of the Hotel Londyński on Stradom Street had been on view for almost a week, but that day they really were to be found on every advertising pillar in the city.

"Oh yes, indeed, when I was out it caught my attention too," said Zofia unemotionally. "But are they really such oddities? Whenever Sidoli's circus is due to give a performance there are posters everywhere, but it doesn't seem to bother you. Franciszka is just about to serve the lunch. Don't fret, Ignacy, I have invited Mr. Żeleński to afternoon tea. We haven't seen him for ages. I am sure he will cheer you up a bit."

She was answered by a low grunt that could have meant anything at all.

After lunch, eaten in eloquent silence, Ignacy settled in his armchair and opened the newspaper. Not much time had passed before he suddenly exclaimed: "My God, Zofia! They've caught the villain, the man who murdered our Karolina!"

Zofia feigned surprise.

"Great heavens! Who on earth is he?"

"Police news," Ignacy began to read, his voice quivering with excitement. *"Late on Sunday night, sensational events occurred in our city, which we can only make public now. Commanded by Inspector Trzeciak, the police attempted to arrest Maciej Czarnota, aged 28, employed as a laborer at the State Tobacco Factory, and suspected of the rape and brutal murder of Karolina Szulc. Czarnota was well known to the Cracow police as a socialist troublemaker and rabble-rouser, as well as a habitual drunkard, as a result of which he had previously been detained at the city jail on more than one occasion. According to a police spokesman, Czarnota boasted of the crime in Cracow and Podgórze taverns, telling how he had beguiled Szulc by passing himself off as a more notable personage, but when the girl resisted his advances . . ."* At this point Ignacy broke off and muttered: "These are nonessential details . . . Ah, yes." He carried on: *"At nine o'clock in the evening, when the police unit tried to apprehend Czarnota at the room sublet to him in Grzegórzki, the criminal attempted to escape. When pursued, he pulled out a gun. Though his shots missed, the bullets fired by the guardians of the law did not. The police doctor who arrived on the scene had merely to confirm his death . . .* Zofia, justice has been done! Thanks be to God!"

God indeed, thought Zofia to herself, holding as she did a rather different opinion about who was owed thanks for the detection of the culprit—or at least for contributing to it. But being unable to say, despite her burning desire, that it was thanks to the combined efforts of Commissioner Jednoróg and Zofia Turbotyńska (with a small, truly minimal degree of help from Franciszka), she merely summoned up a curt: "Amen."

⁂

One would think the excellent news about the well-deserved fate of Karolina's murderer would calm Ignacy down, but—as it would soon appear—this was just a facade. The barrel of gunpowder did eventually explode, but the match was set to it by the socialist troublemakers, or to be precise, one of them in particular, who came to the Turbotyńskis' house by invitation.

At first there was nothing to presage discord; Tadeusz Żeleński was greeted warmly as ever, treated to sweets from Maurizio's, questioned about the progress of his studies, the health of his parents, and so on. But the mood changed abruptly when it turned out he had just come from the Labor Day festivity, or rather, as the professor would have it, "the so-called festivity."

"You don't mean to say, Mr. Żeleński," said Ignacy, glowering at him angrily, while energetically stirring his tea, "that you, the son of a professor at the conservatory, an eminent composer, took part in that workers' pantomime?!"

"Only as a spectator, Professor," said the young man, meekly nodding. "Out of interest."

"What on earth could be interesting about it? That entire 'festivity' is a foreign invention transplanted onto our terrain! Is it as if we lack important dates to commemorate in our own native history? I can think of a good two dozen of them myself, straight off. What about the anniversary of Stefan Batory's coronation and his wedding to Anna, the last of the Jagiellonians, for instance? It falls on this very day. But does anyone remember it? Do *you* remember it?" The professor raised an eyebrow meaningfully. "Mindless imitation of worthless examples, that's what it is! And only two days before a real festivity, too, May the third, Constitution Day, young man!"

An awkward silence fell.

"Well, then," Ignacy started up again, once he had calmed down a bit, "so what did you see there that was so interesting? Had a large number of people abandoned their work to attend the parade?"

"I'd say a couple of thousand, because the railway men were not there."

"Aha! Good lads!" rejoiced Turbotyński, though usually he was the first to disparage the state railway employees, whom he blamed for the virtually deliberate late running of the trains.

Zofia listened to all this without a word; she sat on the ottoman, like Hestia personified, using an embroidery hoop to sew her husband's coat of arms, with which she planned to decorate the bell pull for summoning the servants.

"But surely you will admit that their demands are not entirely absurd . . ."

"Mr. Żeleński," declared Ignacy in the tone he used for lectures, "the capitalists are sometimes guilty of misconduct and abuse, of course, for such is human nature. But in our national situation, so to speak, we should be taking care of more important things: we should be stirring lively activity in our sluggish nation, following the Western example by erecting factories, developing industry, and so forth. Only when that produces a result, when our lands are the jewel of the empire rather than a breeding ground for the worst poverty, then the time will have come for capital and labor to join forces on a healthy, so to speak, economic footing, to take care of the working man's living conditions and to ensure a piece of bread for his old age. But nowadays?"

"You said yourself, Professor, that we shouldn't be mindlessly imitating Western examples," replied Żeleński, smiling, "and besides, eight hours a day in a factory is more than one works at the university . . ."

"Don't nitpick with me, young man, and don't take excessive liberties!" said Ignacy, wagging a finger as he topped up his tea.

But Żeleński refused to be put off his stride.

"As for election reform, the government in Vienna has been working on it for ages."

"Yes, yes, yes, indeed, indeed," Ignacy rattled away like

a barrel organ. "But the idea that any whippersnapper, devoid of education, could vote in an election on an equal footing with . . . who shall I say . . . Count Tarnowski, is entirely at odds with reason. If we were to introduce universal suffrage, what then? Perhaps we'll give women the right to vote? Can you imagine, Zofia?" he said, turning to his wife. "Of course, you, my dear, would have all the necessary competence . . ." he added in a defensive tone.

"What an idea! I simply can't imagine it, Ignacy. You know perfectly well that I have no knowledge of political affairs," said the goddess of the hearth, without raising her eyes from her embroidery.

"What hope can there be for the *benighted masses*?" said Ignacy, pleased with his wife's support. "A tradeswoman from the Kleparz market? A washerwoman? What can they possibly know about the subtleties of politics or the intricacies of legal affairs? How on earth can they know whether one prime minister or another will be better for the entire empire, or simply for Galicia and Lodomeria? Some of the cabbage heads they sell or the dolly tubs they use would be better at choosing members of parliament than they would!"

Though she still didn't look up, it occurred to Zofia that on the other hand, her Franciszka would be sure to vote more sensibly than a number of Ignacy's grumpy old colleagues. But she kept this remark to herself. As she carefully inspected her embroidery, she could see perfectly well that if Tadeusz had gone on the defensive it was only to avoid a more serious quarrel with his professor, and not at all for lack of cogent arguments; but it was inappropriate to bring matters to a head, and this was the exact point where Hestia should come into play, as the soother of quarrels.

"Gentlemen, your remarks are certainly extremely interesting, but please don't forget that not everyone is concerned about matters of government and voting." Here she reached for the cake stand, on which Franciszka had set out the chocolates from Maurizio's in just the right way: neither too sparsely, to avoid offending the visitor by being miserly, nor too lavishly, to avoid excessive expense. "Meanwhile events have occurred, may I venture to say, of an extremely dramatic kind."

"Excuse me for having bored you, Mrs. Turbotyńska," said Żeleński, taking the blame, "but as for dramatic events, I am not quite sure what you mean."

"Events that have touched this very house! With the finger of death!" added Ignacy in the tone generally adopted by actors of the old school in scenes that terrify the audience.

"The finger of death?" repeated Tadeusz hesitantly.

"Aha, I see that thanks to your fun and games at the Hotel Londyński, you haven't had a *decent* newspaper in your hand today." The professor stood up from his armchair and handed their guest the *Cracow Times*, pointing at an article. "Read that."

Żeleński swiftly ran an eye down the text and exclaimed: "Oh, how extraordinary!"

"What is extraordinary about it, my dear sir?" said Zofia, coming to life and finally putting aside her sewing. "We placed our trust in the police from the start, and they have brought the result we expected . . ."

"It's an amazing coincidence! This man's death was briefly mentioned from the tribune today, but I did not realize he had anything to do with the tragic events that took place in your house!"

Zofia remembered that Żeleński had been one of the few people who had sent a note expressing their condolences. Perhaps, in view of his youth, Karolina's charms had worked on him with the same force as on that other medical student, Kurkiewicz.

"Is that so? What exactly was said about it?"

"Mr. Daszyński made a speech on the topic . . ."

"Daszyński!" The professor went red all over, virtually assuming the color of the socialist poster. "Ha, yes, I remember that barbarian all too well—he was the instigator of the outrageous, *extremely* outrageous events at the university. It's a disgrace to mention it . . . You do not remember that, of course, you were not yet a student at our university, it is the right of youth to have a distorted view. Things that I remember from barely the day before yesterday are prehistory from your perspective. Yes, yes," he said, waving a hand, "there's no need to deny it. You students treat us like archaeological figures, ancient mastodons! But I will tell you what it was like in those distant times, actually just a couple of years ago. When Vice Chancellor Korczyński criticized a certain student association known as the Academic Reading Room . . . not without reason, I might add, not without reason . . . a crowd of radically disposed students forced their way into the Theatrum Anatomicum, where with his own hands that Jacobin Daszyński" — by now Ignacy's voice was all but quivering — "hurled the commemorative bust of Professor Korczyński to the floor and smashed it to pieces! Donated just a few years earlier by his grateful students! So what on earth might one expect of such a gross iconoclast?"

"I am not able to express an opinion on the topic of Mr. Daszyński's iconoclasm, Professor," said Żeleński, finding it hard to suppress a smile. "All I know is that he talked about the fatal beating of a man named Rotter, inflicted on him by some policemen a couple of years ago at the jail on Kanonicza Street, and then about the trial of a socialist activist who had publicized the whole matter in *Forward*! . . . That is the name of the socialists' weekly," he explained. "And now Mr. Daszyński claims that the shooting of this Czarnecki . . ."

"Czarnota," Zofia corrected him.

"Czarnota, is nothing more than another police assassination of an innocent man."

"Innocent?" exclaimed Zofia, who had instantly lost her Olympian calm, so strenuously maintained until now. "Mr. Żeleński, that evil scoundrel first dishonored and then stabbed my Karolina to death! Our Karolina! If he were innocent, would he have fired at the policemen? Oh, no, excuse me, but the police certainly knew what they were doing."

"Sacred words, my dear," her husband supported her. "The truth, sir, is that he was a nasty type devoid of any moral principles. A socialist, that's what. And a drunkard to boot, because every drunkard is a socialist!"

Views may be views, but a guest for tea is a guest for tea; Zofia too may have raised her voice a short time ago, but she had to salvage the appearance of hospitality at the very least.

"Now, please tell me instead, how do you regard your future?" she asked out of the blue. "Rumors have reached us that following the example of your cousin, Tetmajer, you have been trying your strengths as a poet."

Ignacy understood at once, and made the same adjustment.

"Indeed! My wife mentioned to me that several of your sonnets have been published in *The World.*"

Żeleński was distinctly put out, dropped his gaze, and muttered that they were "just some youthful exercises."

"And perhaps you'll be attending the evening devoted to the Constitution the day after tomorrow? There will be polonaises by Chopin," said Zofia encouragingly, though she realized that neither she nor Tadeusz the student was unduly excited by Chopin.

"It is sure to be a splendid event," replied Żeleński evasively, then moved a hand, as if to reach for one more chocolate, but exercised self-control. A well-brought-up young person does not drive his hosts to unnecessary expense.

✤

She saw him from the very doorway of the Celestat, home to the marksmen's fraternity, standing beneath one of the columns supporting the arches across the center of the ceremonial Shooting Gallery, smiling as he entertained a circle of ladies with conversation (one of them was undoubtedly the wife of Dr. Pareński, easy to recognize even from a distance by her white powdered hair which made her look like a French marquise of the Ancien Régime). Indeed, Investigating Magistrate Rajmund Klossowitz, for he was the man in question, had eventually accepted Mrs. Turbotyńska's help in solving the mystery of the murders at Helcel House a year and a half ago, but their first few encounters had not been pleasant ones, and the scars in Zofia's heart had not yet entirely healed. Zofia was not inclined to forgive the affronts she suffered easily and she nursed her injuries just as carefully as the rhododendrons that the Sisters of Charity kindly allowed her to grow in their garden. Even more carefully perhaps.

The crowd was more colorful than usual on similar occasions, and that was because not only were the ladies dressed in a wide range of hues, but among the gentlemen, too, apart from the black of frock coats and tailcoats and the white of shirt fronts, the crimsons, sapphire blues, and bottle greens of the traditional aristocratic *kontusz* coats were on display — long, flowing, and full-skirted with buttons at the front, loose, slashed sleeves, and wide silk sashes; under each one shone a bright *żupan* — the long gown worn as part of the same national costume, some pure silver, some pure gold in color. On Constitution Day, not only the fraternal marksmen — such as Commissioner Jednoróg — came in their festive attire, but many of the other gentlemen chose to dress up in their old-fashioned Polish outfits, too. Some had done up the buttons that, according to family legend, had been torn from Turkish enemy clothing in the past, and had dug out of the wardrobe their ornate Słutsk sashes dating from the Republic; while others had wrapped their bellies in brand-new, shiny sashes woven at Count Potocki's "Persian" workshop at Buchach, which had been a huge success at the Lemberg Exhibition.

Ignacy too had a Buchach sash, brought back from Lemberg. In fact he would rather have donned more comfortable attire, but the solemnity of the moment demanded special measures, and although Zofia would have been perfectly happy to see him in a tailcoat or an academic gown, she categorically demanded that he put on his *kontusz,* which had been fetched out of the wardrobe the day before and aired to rid it of the smell of clothes-moth deterrent. Franciszka had had to help the professor to wrap himself in the five yards of material woven with gold thread — several times over, because the knot kept refusing to come out as it should; the *kontusz,* navy blue, with slit sleeves lined in raspberry-red silk, had been made two decades ago for the Turbotyńskis' wedding—luckily a few pounds more here or there did not make much difference to the wearing of a *kontusz,* and the *żupan* could always be widened from the back, which had already been done several years ago.

Zofia looked around, urgently checking to see if they had jointly made the right impression, nodded to a few familiar people, then sat down on a chair and tidied the flounces of her dress. When Ignacy opened his copy of the program, adorned with the coats of arms of the old Polish-Lithuanian Commonwealth, he noted with some amusement that almost nobody but women were responsible for the musical setting of the evening.

"Miss Kohn will sing . . ." he began to read aloud, "Mrs. Stengel-Tabor on the piano . . . Mrs. Poselta on the violin . . ."

"And where is Hock?" someone joked from the row behind him. "I did not think there could be a musical celebration in this city without Kapellmeister Hock's concert band!"

"Fear not, Counselor," replied another voice, "tomorrow he's accompanying Mrs. Strzelecka, who is to sing arias from *William Tell* and *The Marriage of Figaro* at the Hotel Saski. As long as she's not drowned out by the trumpets and kettledrums, of course."

The concert was as patriotic as it was dull: Chopin's polonaises performed by the Lutnia Choir, billed as *the jewel of the evening,* proved rather monotonous, and twice Zofia had to give Ignacy a discreet poke in the side when his head began to nod; she too came close to falling asleep, and shielded her mouth with a hand several times when she couldn't stifle a yawn. She had been awoken extremely early today by the dawn, or to be precise, the mazurka "Welcome, Bright Dawn of May" played directly below the Turbotyńskis' windows by the Harmonia Musical Society. However, this was not a distinction — the band had been trawling the streets of Cracow since five o'clock, waking all social strata without exception. To tell the truth, Zofia had heard enough music for one day, and she wasn't particularly eager for socializing, conversing with the same people on the same topics as always; as it was, she saw them all time and again — now at mass in St. Mary's, now in Planty Park, now on the Market Square, which was impossible to cross without bumping into someone she knew. She had actually wondered whether to wriggle out of this event by pleading laryngitis and staying at home, but ultimately a sense of patriotic duty had prevailed, in other words a desire to show off her new dress, and to hear any new gossip that might leak out between the rounded phrases during an exchange of courtesies.

But there was nothing of the kind. During the banquet most of the talk was about perfectly familiar matters: the ongoing preparations for a fete and a lottery on behalf of those injured by the earthquake in Laibach; some entertainments for children and young people in Dr. Jordan's park (co-organized, and how, by Mrs. Bujwid); the imminent arrival of the great Shakespearean actress, Helena Modjeska; and the approaching political crisis in Vienna — because it seemed that despite Ignacy's assurances, the Prince of Windisch-Grätz's cabinet would not last long.

However, the main topic of interest among the audience gathered at the Marksmen's Garden was not the session of the Academy of Learning that had been held that afternoon, but the failed attempt on the life of Judge Dąbrowiecki, though the information about it was still fragmentary and uncertain. Indeed, ceremonial sessions of the academy, graced by the arrival of the governor, only took place once a year, but guns being fired in the courthouse happened incomparably less often in Cracow, so this incident had caused an understandable sensation.

"The culprit was caught immediately," Commissioner Jednoróg was assuring a small group of listeners. "You have nothing to fear."

But every few minutes someone else bleated that there was a madman with a gun at large in the city, and perhaps it would be worth employing the entire marksmen's fraternity to catch him, at which the commissioner had to repeat his assurances. Much surprise was prompted by the revelation that the culprit was not a socialist, as had been instantly assumed, but a local citizen, the owner of two butcher's shops. This news stirred some consternation among the assembled company — more than one of them had had occasion in life to rail against the indolence of officialdom, or the unjust verdict reached in one or another case affecting him, but to fire a revolver at a judge for that sort of reason? It was inconceivable. Could an entrepreneur really sink to such an act? And a local citizen, too? Virtually one of them! That was not just unthinkable — first and foremost it was unspeakable. So they soon shifted their focus to a safer topic: the railway accident at Bochnia station, where a standing train that had arrived from Cracow had been run into by another.

"Ah, yes, of course, the railway men!" said Ignacy. "No good can be expected of them, as I always say."

"How fortunate that no one was killed," said a woman in a red dress.

"But plenty of people suffered serious injury! Maybe not physical harm, but they certainly had a dreadful fright!" added a stout man.

"The impudence of the railway surpasses human understanding," quipped Ignacy.

"Indeed, indeed, perhaps you will have read in the newspaper the day before yesterday how Countess Starzeńska was traveling with three children on the northern railway when she was treated by the conductor in a truly barbaric way."

"What are you trying to say? Did he speak to her in a vulgar manner?"

"Worse than that. When she had bought her ticket and boarded the train, the conductor informed her that there were no seats left for four in first class, and despite the countess's protests he separated the family. Two of the daughters had to make the journey in a different carriage! With complete strangers!"

"I hope the count lodged a complaint with the director general . . ."

The commissioner, having greeted Zofia very warmly earlier on, was now standing nearby, occasionally flashing his silver cross of merit as he tried to break free of a man subjecting him to a tedious diatribe about the historical significance of the cut and color of individual *kontusz* coats.

Zofia suddenly felt breathless, and was trying to go outside for some fresh air when her hand was seized by Mrs. Jakubowska, renowned throughout the city as a busybody, a good friend of Mrs. Zaremba, and—however hard to believe—an even bigger bore than she was. Mrs. Jakubowska was famous for constantly latching on to someone, assailing her victim with tale after tale about who was suffering from what ailment, and on what day a particularly virulent attack of it had struck them. Naturally, there were times when Zofia valued that sort of information, but there was a limit to what she could endure. Like Jednoróg with his devotee of historical curiosities, she too tried to get away, but she had chanced upon a worthy adversary; Jakubowska took no prisoners, and soon, nodding almost mechanically and praying not to have a yawning fit, Zofia was having to hear her stories about the shingles affecting her husband's cousin that had been very painful on Wednesday. Or on Thursday.

"Don't you think it's a pity our last connection with the past did not live to see this happy day, Mrs. Turbotyńska?" said Mrs. Jakubowska, smoothly changing the subject, though not greatly, merely passing from illnesses to demises.

"Our last connection?"

"Mrs. Kotarbina, haven't you heard of her? A little old lady born in 1791, the year the May the Third Constitution was enacted, can you imagine? I wouldn't mind living to such an age!"

God forbid, thought Zofia to herself. *And if God in his infinite wisdom were to make it so, then let him kindly remove me from this world before this chatterbox to spare me from this burden . . .*

"Yes, it is a great loss," she replied with resignation. "And what a fine age."

"She lived near Tarnów, in Zakliczyn . . . No, not in Zakliczyn. In Czchów . . . Well, not exactly in Czchów, but not far off . . . Have you ever been there? Very fine scenery, Tropsztyn Castle on the Dunajec, very picturesque . . . Not in Czchów but further west, toward Nowy Sącz, or rather to the north, Wi . . . Wy . . . Not Witowice . . . Wytrzyszczka!"

Zofia was considering feigning a mild faint, when suddenly Klossowitz sprang up beside her.

"Mrs. Turbotyńska, Mrs. Jakubowska," he said, bowing low to the ladies.

"Mr. Klossowitz," said Zofia with a nod. She would never

have expected salvation from this quarter, but in the present situation she'd have accepted anybody's help.

"Forgive me for interrupting your fascinating conversation," he said to Mrs. Jakubowska, "but I must briefly abduct Mrs. Turbotyńska on a matter of some urgency . . ."

The woman muttered a few words of assurance that of course she understood perfectly, turned on her own axis, and, without moving from the spot, collared her next victim, picking up the recitation of her chronicle of ailments and expirations at exactly the same point where it had been interrupted.

They went outside into the Marksmen's Garden, where there was hardly a soul apart from two young couples and a chaperone following one of them at a distance; from the bushes rose the scent of the first lilac blossom. With some distress, Zofia had to admit to herself that the investigating magistrate made an extremely good impression in a *kontusz.* Tall, but not a beanpole, slender but not skinny; despite having been born a couple of years after Ignacy, he looked far younger. When he took her hand and kissed it, she cast her savior a more favorable glance.

"What is this matter of some urgency?"

"Does it not seem to you that a *certain affair*"—he stressed these words with great care—"ended rather too . . ." He paused, trying to find the right word. "Straightforwardly?"

"Surely you're not trying to tell me you believe that

troublemaker Daszyński's version of events? I have heard some highly alarming things about him." She raised a finger. "Perhaps you are not aware, but in his time that man once smashed a bust of Professor Korczyński."

"Well, madam, there are things on earth the philosophers never dreamed of, including truthful socialists. Or at least socialists who sometimes tell the truth, if only unwittingly," he said, raising his eyebrows meaningfully.

"To be sure, I have no idea what you are talking about," replied Zofia indignantly, irritated by the fact that Klossowitz, no doubt envious of her achievements, because after all it was she who had set Commissioner Jednoróg on the trail of the fake Bzowski, was once again trying to belittle her skills in the field of investigation. And just as she had been ready to forgive him his past misdemeanors.

"Please do not be angry," he said. "We all care about catching the culprit."

"The culprit has not only been caught but also shot dead while attempting to escape, certainly prompted to do so . . . Good evening, sir," she said, bowing to Professor Kostanecki, ". . . by a guilty conscience."

Klossowitz twirled his mustache. It occurred to her that every single man, the moment he donned a *kontusz,* was instantly imbued with old-fashioned Polish manners, as if at the touch of a magic wand.

"The fact that Rozmarynowicz has let himself be caught out does not surprise me—he should have retired long ago, because he cannot distinguish between dream and reality. The fact that Commissioner Jednoróg was fooled, who thinks of nothing but promotion and medals, and for whom every case solved means another feather in his cap, is no surprise to me either. But that you, so astute in your inquiries . . ."

So that's how he wants to play me, she thought, raising her lorgnette to her eyes. *He cannot forgive Jednoróg his medal or for making a faster career than he has, so he's using flattery to try to steer me into a new investigation that will undermine the commissioner's conclusions . . . Regardless of whether or not he looks good in his* kontusz *he is incapable of rising to true heights of magnanimity. Ach, men! They think of nothing but their petty wars!*

"What can I possibly do? I am just a woman. You gentlemen are there to establish the facts and catch the miscreants. And this miscreant has been caught, and has paid for his hideous crime as in the Old Testament: an eye for an eye, a tooth for a tooth, a life for a life."

"If of course we accept that it was the verdict of divine justice and not of some kangaroo court," replied the magistrate, "because I'd like to point out that . . ."

"Ah, here you are," she heard her husband's flustered voice behind her. "I've been looking for you everywhere. Good evening . . . Mr. Sebald has finished setting up his machinery."

She bowed to Klossowitz, took Ignacy by the arm, and

went back into the Celestat building. Indeed, where not long ago the Lutnia Choir had been singing lyrics written to Chopin's music, the photographer's two assistants had hung up some painted backdrops. In front of an ancient forest, a misty rural landscape, or a vast, half-ruined ancient castle (perhaps it was Tropsztyn, as mentioned by Mrs. Jakubowska), the ladies and gentlemen were adopting various poses. The tireless Fikalski, who to mark the national holiday had come rushing in with a large red-and-white rosette pinned to his chest, was most spiritedly arranging tableaux vivants, mainly—in view of the attractive costumes—from Mr. Sienkiewicz's historical trilogy published a couple of years ago. Needless to say, he avoided Zofia's gaze like wildfire. Then came the turn for some more run-of-the-mill pictures, in which all the heroes of those novels changed back into the meek husbands of their wives, weighed down by their flounced dresses and several decades of conjugal life. In due course, two days hence the Turbotyńskis were to collect some photographs printed as cabinet cards; one showed Ignacy on his own, with his kalpak hat pulled down slightly too low; another one featured Zofia with her gaze blurred by blinking; and a third showed the two of them with Commissioner Jednoróg—they'd decided to gift him a print as thanks for the swift resolution of the murder inquiry. Meanwhile the guests, especially the tipsy ones, were dispersing to their nearby homes or getting into hackney coaches parked outside. There was loud hooting and shouting coming from the garden, followed by snippets of song, sung in a none too coherent manner:

The bottle's run dry . . . the revelry ends!
Long live . . . all our company of friends!
Long live the brothers . . . in chorus we chime!
Brothers, we're brothers to the end of time!

And then in unison:

Brothers, we're brothers to the end of time!

Like children, thought Zofia, *just like children!*

CHAPTER VI

A thankfully brief interlude, in which throughout May and for almost all of June nothing happens, although in fact a lot happens, Mrs. Bujwid is on the rampage, Zofia's cousin praises her flowerpots, and on Midsummer Eve a young lass sees a phantom in the candlelight.

Zofia Turbotyńska had her own opinion on the wisdom of Solomon, and found little more irritating than the maxim, repeated to a point of tedium in Cracow, that "pride comes before a fall"; first, because, like most biblical adages, sometimes it was true and sometimes not, and secondly because by a strange coincidence jealous tongues often said it about her. Yet it was true that since prompting the detection of Karolina's killer, she now saw a wonderful, bright springtime ahead of her, a season that would bring her a string of social triumphs. Unfortunately, the reality was to prove entirely different.

Above all, there seemed to be a deluge of Mrs. Bujwid—wherever one turned, there was Mrs. Bujwid, and Mrs. Bujwid again, if not a lecture, then an opening, if not an opening, then a fundraiser. She was so mercilessly active, in the company of two fellow Furies, on behalf of the Society for People's Schools, that people had taken to calling them "three taxation screws crushing all of Cracovian society"—they had their ways of extracting money from every wallet, every purse, from even the most tightly sealed drawer. The education of the common folk may be a useful thing, indeed, but it seemed—and not to Zofia alone—that the task of covering all Galicia in a network of schools was now to rest on the shoulders of Cracow's bourgeoisie alone. In drawing room conversations it was agreed that the mania for educating women was worst of all.

"Cracow is failing to put up any sort of defense against modernity," said one of Ignacy's colleagues. "If some morbidly liberal parents wish to destroy their daughters' brains with learning, then they're free to do so! Those *Higher Courses for Women*"—he sneered—"have been up and running for almost thirty years."

"Our *Ass-enaeum!*" added someone from behind him; the joke had been repeated for at least twenty-five years, but it still amused the gentlemen.

"That is where the degeneracy of young women begins

—anyone will agree that one worthy mother or one decent wife is of more value to society than a mediocre doctor."

"If there is a place for him at all," put in one of the doctors.

"Wise words. Instead of searching for a job, the young filly should look around her, for broad fields lie fallow, not try to grab a piece of bread that a man is holding in his hand."

"Millions and millions of groschen are going abroad on those trifles and trinkets of theirs that they cannot live without," another man pontificated, raising his glass, "paper figurines, little fans, painted knickknacks, and patchwork! Foreigners are taking the bread, the butter, and meat from our mouths, as if doing trade with savages, swapping our money for baubles for women."

"As soon as a girl learns to read and write a bit, she starts to complain," Ignacy agreed with him. "Who cares if the talents for writing novellas are multiplying when one has to look abroad for capable and industrious seamstresses and cloth cutters?"

"Some of today's men are intent on erasing the natural differences between the sexes and establishing their absolute equality! Can you imagine anything more preposterous? Within the body alone one can see the completely different tasks assigned to us! Take facial hair, for instance," said an academic, stroking his sparse beard. "It is the proof of nature itself that dignity is inherent in the male. Women do not have beards . . . or at least, the majority do not" — at this point they all snickered — "simply because they do not have to be as dignified. It is a known fact — Aristotle wrote about it."

"Yet he could not have known what the scientists have discovered in faraway America," added another gentleman, "which is that facial hair attracts electrical elements, and thus it is an attribute of life force, of *élan vital*!"

A murmur of approval ran through the company.

"The figure of a man is erect and solidly compact," one of the anatomists began to explain, "whereas the female figure is not as evenly balanced, with wide hips and prominent curves on the breast, belly, and pelvis. While the male figure seems in search of . . . how can I put it? . . . activity, physical activity, the female figure easily enters a state of repose and seems to find satisfaction in a mildly forward-inclining attitude" — at this point he leaned over, pushing out his puny rib cage — "in a pose of submission, as it were . . ."

"But bodily posture is of no significance in matters of education . . ." a younger man interrupted him.

"The connection between gender and the nervous system is of significance," explained the anatomist, "to be specific: the link between the cerebellum and the embryonal glands! When we put one-sided pressure on the brain in our girls, when by doing so we steer all the blood to one single pole, as is constantly happening in present-day schooling, I'm sorry to say, the functions of the nervous system are bound to atrophy, entailing weaker activity of the stomach"—he bent back a finger—"the gut"—he bent a second finger—"the liver"—a third—"the spleen"—a fourth—"and also the degeneracy of the embryonal glands, leading, my dear colleague, to in-fer-til-ity!"

Catching these words out of the roar of conversation from her seat on a bergère chair in the neighboring circle, where the ladies were discussing their own affairs, Zofia would rather have believed the anatomist to be mistaken, but her own case seemed to confirm his views. In her youth, emphasis had indeed been placed on her education; it had been of particular concern to her father, a pharmacist who always regretted not having completed his own medical studies; if he had had a son, he'd have sent him to university, but in this situation . . . And now what? It was hard to deny that the Turbotyńskis' marriage had not been blessed by progeny. Could that have been because of one-sided pressure on little Zofia's brain? But surely not: whatever one might think of her, Mrs. Bujwid was no fool, yet she had borne her husband child after child. According to the latest gossip—from a good source, though—she was carrying the next little Bujwid now.

Whether with child or not, she was an extremely shrewd operator; not only was she insisting on founding high schools for girls, at the teachers' congress in Lemberg she had identified a legal loophole in the university statutes to do with allowing student teachers to attend lectures, and had so successfully entangled the entire, mostly male assembly ("Though naturally," the spiteful tongues had remarked, "she did not entangle them with beauty!") that they had voted through the admission of women as silent attendants at higher educational establishments. Then she had put it into the heads of various lasses from the Congress Kingdom—the Russian partition of Poland—that they were to apply in Cracow and Vienna for acceptance at the Jagiellonian University, until more than fifty of them had done so. And to make matters worse, after various refusals, dodges, and efforts, three had been accepted. "Once the first woman gets her sweet little soft-slippered foot in the door it'll be the end!" the professors said gloomily; in fact most of the applications had been rejected. Only the philosophy faculty was involved and three female pharmacists had been admitted, though they had no right to take tests or sit exams, and each of them had to obtain individual permission from each professor to attend his classes—but the breach had been made. Now they were just waiting for the capture of further redoubts and trenches.

Zofia took no part in any of these Bujwid Follies. Ostentatiously. Just as she had ostentatiously not gone to the lecture on Amazonian women, so on May the fifth she did not go to Dr. Jordan's park for the entertainments for schoolboys and girls from the people's schools, where *naturally* Mrs. Bujwid was on the committee; nearly two thousand of that brood, almost as many girls as boys, came running in, clearly a bad portent for the future fertility of Cracow's women; what's more, Dr. Jordan himself was feted, a man whom Zofia had disliked for years. On the same day Ignacy had not distinguished himself in the bicycle race, and had come home feeling bitter, so both of them, each in their own separate rooms, had had to suppress their anger. On May the eighth she had ostentatiously not appeared on Poselska Street at the opening of the Women's Reading Room, eagerly attended by all the dangerous emancipationists, a real pit of vipers!

Deep down, Zofia was aware that no one was likely to have noticed her ostentation. But she consoled herself that there would be further opportunities to get even and to mark out her place in Cracow's higher spheres, a place that, as she knew well, was never permanent and demanded constant confirmation. Unfortunately Ignacy, who was in a foul mood lately, perhaps because of losing yet another race, had made no effort to get invitations for the banquet in honor of the actress Helena Modejska, making the excuse that it was an entertainment for members of the Artistic and Literary Circle, and thus almost exclusively actors and writers. So the poet Asnyk was there, but the Turbotyńskis were not. What a fine kettle of fish. All they had left was to watch Modejska's performance as Viola in *Twelfth Night*, but that was not the same as spending an evening at table with her, especially, as Zofia jealously read in the newspaper, when *the lively chat had continued until two in the morning.*

She had one source of hope: the exhibition of rhododendrons, roses, and strawberries being held at the Marksmen's Garden. Thanks to her scheming with Sister Alojza she had secured the help of a gardener at Helcel House, and for quite a time had been tending to three beautiful specimens: white, pink, and purple, expertly nurtured in a small flower bed against a stone wall, which duly shielded them from the wind. They were showing splendid promise, their sprigs well showered in swollen buds; every effort was made to protect them from being frost nipped by the Ice Saints or the cold on St. Sophia's Day. Early on Saturday morning Franciszka and two boys hired to help went to fetch the bushes, which had been replanted in some extremely pretty flowerpots, and carried them to the show ground; the cook made sure the boys were careful not to snap off any of the sprigs.

The Turbotyńskis arrived punctually at one, stood a short while in the queue to enter, paid twenty cents each, greeted several familiar couples, and hurried to the rhododendron section. The conversations were about nothing but the flowers.

"Apparently an entire carriage full of roses has been sent from one of the provincial gardens . . ."

"Two carriages. Roses in bloom. In flowerpots."

"I heard that it was sent by Princess Lubomirska, from the nursery at Mieżyniec."

"The rose is the queen of flowers!"

"Lots of good things are said about Kudasiewicz of Prądnik," said a man with a white beard, whom for a while Zofia took for the magistrate, Rozmarynowicz.

"Indeed, especially the polyantha variety."

"I prefer La France and Viscountess Folkestone."

"Well, I rate Canon Drohojowski's roses above them. First-rate specimens."

"And Mrs. Kossak is showing some beautiful strawberries."

"But they're not in competition. There are only three exhibitors in the cultivated and wild strawberry section," said a lady with a parrot on her hat disdainfully. "In Lemberg that would be unthinkable."

Finally they came to the rhododendrons. They looked splendid, and the sign saying MRS. PROFESSOR IGNACY TURBOTYŃSKI was neither too small nor too large.

"What lovely flowerpots!" she heard her cousin's voice behind her.

Though in her inevitable mourning dress, Józefa Dutkiewicz smiled radiantly. No wonder—it turned out she was publicly showing off her rhododendrons too, though goodness knows where she grew them, certainly not in her apartment on Floriańska Street. When asked, she evasively replied that every woman has her ways and means of cultivating beauty.

They met again on Sunday, when the public voted for the most beautiful specimens. The ladies and gentlemen strolled about the garden paths, between the restaurant building and the orchestral pavilion, to the tune of trombones, drums, and clarinets; at three o'clock a concert of military music began, and a small, jaunty bandmaster enthusiastically conducted march after march, commemorating a wide range of the Austro-Hungarian army's mostly rather ancient triumphs. Almost all the competitions turned out to have been won by the Freege brothers, who were professionals; they took the gold medal for rhododendrons, too. The silver went to the Josephite Fathers. *Which is no great surprise,* concluded Zofia, *because they have little else in life to occupy them.* But she found it hardest to come to terms with the bronze medal, which as if to spite her was awarded to Józefa Dutkiewicz.

As if that were not enough, Mrs. Dutkiewicz and Professor and Mrs. Bujwid—especially her, that taxation screw! —outstripped Zofia in collecting contributions for the renovation of the cathedral. How much everything in Cracow had changed! Not long ago the only fundraising was for orphans, the old, the lame, or the victims of a whole range of diseases. But these days? Now it was people's schools, the renovation of various buildings—there was no end to the charitable acts. Day after day the newspapers were publishing information on the contents of each collection tin when its time came to be opened, and Zofia's tin had had its turn, too. Thirty-one zlotys and twelve cents—a considerable sum, strenuously extracted using a whole arsenal of methods perfected over the years—but what of it, when a week later it turned out her cousin had collected almost twice as much? Ha, she had all those acquaintances from the insurance company where her late husband had been employed. And as for the contents of Mrs. Bujwid's tin, that was best not mentioned.

The Turbotyńskis were in perfect agreement about one

thing: that this year was a real *annus horribilis,* so they were doing their best to support each other in these difficult times. He urged her not to be upset about minor failures and to turn a deaf ear to the emancipationists' silly statements, and said that her rhododendrons had been the finest in the entire exhibition; in her turn she told him he was sure to do well on the last day of June in the six-mile race to Liszki, in which the senior members of the Cracow Cycling Club were to compete, meaning men of thirty-three and over. And when he came in second to last in that race too, she said: "Ignacy, say what you like, but I see it as follows: fourteen cyclists put their names forward, seven competed, therefore with regard to masculine prowess you are sixth in the entire club. And what about the university? Of the entire university you are in first place, Ignacy!"

But before it came to that, before Professor Turbotyński had gritted his teeth to compete in the race, something happened that was enough of a shock to prompt Zofia to go straight around to Commissioner Jednoróg's office.

❧

"I had reached the gateway before I remembered that our joint portrait is still lying on my desk, in the letter rack—the photograph taken at the Celestat," she said as she sailed into his office. "I will send it via my servant or the post. But never mind about that. I would not dream of taking up your valuable time if not for a matter of extreme urgency.

Commissioner, I am afraid our investigation"—on hearing the pronoun "our" Jednoróg almost invisibly smiled—"will have to be reviewed, perhaps even repeated. Just imagine" —at this point she sank, as if her legs had been pulled from under her, into the armchair he offered—"yesterday my servant, Franciszka, went to a Midsummer Eve celebration."

"Yes?"

"And whom do you think she saw in the crowd? The man who passed himself off as Engineer Bzowski."

"My dear madam," said Jednoróg, laughing. "Call me a skeptic if you wish, but I refuse to believe in the phantom apparition of a bandit who was shot dead. Even on Midsummer Eve."

"But what if it wasn't he who perished? Surely this is of vital significance to your inquiry?"

The commissioner sighed, gazed out of the window at the sun-drenched facade of the building opposite, then turned to Zofia again.

"Indeed, there is nothing on earth that might not appear to a female servant. Especially a young one. These girls are overexcited, day after day nothing ever happens in their lives but making the fire, cleaning, cooking, beating the rugs . . . Every housemaid lives on a diet of sensation: neighborhood gossip, their master's and mistress's affairs, old wives' tales, and if they are in the least bit literate, nonsense from the penny dreadfuls. No wonder they think up fantastic stories. I wouldn't be unduly worried about it. She saw something there, took fright, and that's the entire mystery."

"She says she saw him distinctly . . . and recognized him at once."

"At night? In a crowd? By candlelight?"

"There is the afterglow of the sun, too, it sets so late that in the evening light . . ."

"In the evening light Miss Franciszka managed to recognize a man whom she was unable to describe, apart from the fact that he was young and had a mustache?"

The question hung in the smoke-filled air, where it remained for some time.

"One thing I am sure of," Zofia slowly began, weighing each word, "is that my Franciszka is not an excitable young person — on the contrary, she is unusually conscientious; her feet are firmly on the ground. If she came to me with this matter, she has certainly given it due consideration. She was trembling with nerves!"

"She was trembling because she was impassioned. Overexcitement, exactly what I'm talking about. Perhaps boosted by a shot of drink; there's always someone offering wine or a bottle of beer in places like that. Especially to a pretty girl."

"Commissioner Jednoróg, anyone would be shaken if they came eye to eye with a friend's killer. That is the most natural reaction in the world."

Jednoróg locked his fingers on the desktop, leaned his solid, hefty body forward, those shoulders that neatly filled his uniform jacket, and said: "Am I to understand that in your view my men have killed an innocent man? That

Inspector Trzeciak who commanded the operation is incompetent? Is that the accusation you are making?"

Zofia was somewhat taken aback, and needed time to answer him, so she complained of the stuffiness in the room.

"Perhaps I should open a window?" he said.

"No, thank you, I feel better now . . . I certainly do not intend to accuse anyone of anything. Czarnota may well have had something on his conscience anyway, possibly a murder, and tried to escape for those other reasons. You said yourself that he was well known to the police."

"Dear madam, I do not dispatch armed men to Grzegórzki to fetch the first citizen to hand on whom a shadow of suspicion has fallen! In such a case Ecler or Pidłypczak would have gone to see him and would have politely invited him here for an interview . . . No, my dear Mrs. Turbotyńska, we knew he'd been boasting in the taverns about the murder of Miss Szulc."

"What is meant by 'boasting'?" said Zofia. "Did he stand in the middle of the room at the tavern and say: 'I have committed a murder. I took a girl prisoner and stabbed her through the heart?' That doesn't sound very credible."

"My dear madam . . ." said Jednoróg, leaning back in his chair. "That's not how it happens. Almost every criminal, even the most depraved, eventually feels the need to admit his guilt, or at least to show off his deed. He doesn't make an announcement; he merely whispers something to someone, or drops a hint . . . How very often I've seen it happen!

Do you know the Grimm fairy tale about the spots of light on the wall? No? It's a very short one. A man kills his associate, or a stranger with whom he's traveling, I can't remember which, and seizes a large sum of money. But his victim curses him, saying: 'The spots of light on the wall will betray you!' The murderer takes no notice; he buys a large house and some land, and lives in peace for years on end. He has children and grandchildren . . . and one day, by which time he's an old man, he looks at the wall and starts to laugh. To laugh. When he's asked why, he says: 'I once killed a man who cursed me, saying the spots of light on the wall would betray me. But here I am, I've lived to a ripe old age, I'm looking at those spots quite calmly, and no harm has come to me!' Yet on hearing this, some righteous people take him before a judge who sentences him to be executed. But do you know what? There's one mistake in that fairy tale."

"Which is?"

"They never wait a lifetime. A day or two, five at most. Then they give the game away, when not entirely sober, to a drinking companion, he repeats it, naturally in the greatest confidence, to another one, and two days later the whole of Podgórze knows. And we have our people for that, to bring us that sort of gossip."

"And did they?"

"Yes, yes, they did. It was a report from a secret informer."

"Could I . . ."

"Read it? Unfortunately, those are documents that I never show to anyone," he said, unfolding his hands, "because a good informer is worth his weight in gold. In their profession reputation is of crucial value. The ones with a reputation for never betraying a confidence discover the most. It's hard to win men like that over, and once you have, you must guard them with your life. But yes, we had a report of this kind, two in fact, from different sources. So Czarnota spilled the beans without waiting for old age. It's a pity he didn't appear before a court, but his escape attempt is perfect proof that . . ."

"That he knew why they had come for him."

"Quite so. I am sorry, of course I am," he continued, sighing, "because the whole business of the fake identity and the calling cards was intriguing, and might well have betrayed some curious secret of the human soul. But if there really was more to it than rampant masculine urges, the dead man took his secret with him to the grave. And he certainly won't be coming back from there to watch housemaids floating garlands down the Vistula."

Zofia looked up and saw the blue eyes of His Imperial Majesty gazing from a large portrait on the opposite wall; he was casting her a benevolent look, as if his calm repose guaranteed the verdicts of the courts, the efficiency of the police, and the wisdom of the officials of every rank.

"However, in view of the very special services that you have rendered to this investigation," said Jednoróg, smiling, "I solemnly promise to reexamine the case. I shall read the reports a second time. I might even summon the informers again, and discreetly question the policemen who took part in the action in Grzegórzki, to make sure their statements are consistent. If, God forbid, something were to catch my attention, I shall let you know without delay, but please believe me: every sign in heaven and on earth points to the fact that this is just the fantasy of a little woman weary of everyday life."

Two days later a shop boy brought a paper cornet filled with bitter almonds, which apparently had been ordered. Admitted by the kitchen door, he spent so long arguing with Franciszka that he had instructions to hand the item to no one but the lady of the house in person that finally he won—he was led to Zofia, who found out that the delivery had been paid for in advance.

She turned back the gray paper, and inside the cornet she found a small card, resting on some appetizing-looking pralines. Above the initials *SJ* there was a message that said:

Everything is in perfect order. Either a spiritualist with a whirling table appeared on Midsummer Eve and conjured up a ghost, or else it was a common-or-garden delusion.

Part Two

CHAPTER VII

In which a plague of Egypt rains down on Cracow, Zofia shows professionalism, and Franciszka shows a good memory and a smart mind, thanks to which a wolf is identified as The Wolf. In spite of which Zofia is obliged to go to her Canossa, on Grodzka Street.

Fourteen months had gone by. The end of August 1896 was an auspicious time — crowned heads were hovering in the vicinity, or actually stopping off in Cracow. On the twenty-ninth, at exactly 8:37 in the evening (according to the press), the enormous imperial train of the Russian tsar and tsarina, on their way home from Vienna, drove into the station at Szczakowa, some forty miles west of Cracow, where under a wooden railway shed festooned with lanterns, an entire delegation awaited them: the head of the Cracow police, Counselor Korotkiewicz and several of his underlings, Mr. Rogoyski, the local mayor, and the station manager — a man unused to encountering the great and the good, but who for the four solid minutes while the train was at his station could barely keep upright. A rumor spread all the way to the Cloth Hall that as soon as their majesties had gone the station manager fainted, and was brought around by the owner of the station buffet; apparently his shirt was so wet with nervous sweat that it had to be wrung out. Although to tell the truth, there hadn't been much to see; all the train windows were curtained except for one, by which the tsarina was sitting, busy with some writing. Only when the train moved off did the tsar come and stand beside her; he bowed to bid the delegation farewell, and then they both rode off toward the brilliantly illuminated, flower-bedecked station at Granica, where they were to transfer to a wider, Russian carriage. Two days later, at four in the morning, His Imperial Majesty traveled through Cracow on his way to maneuvers near Lemberg; two weeks after, he was to stop in Przemyśl where the local nobility and clergy would pay homage (it was one of those rare moments when Zofia Turbotyńska felt proud to admit that she was a daughter of Przemyśl), and then on the return journey, he was to stop in Cracow, which demanded innumerable preparations, in which almost all the citizens took part.

But as when a comet flashes across the horizon, disturbing the usual way of the world, so too — perhaps because of the sudden increase in the number of monarchs in Galicia, as well as some other, more mysterious forces at work in the Turbotyńskis' apartment and all over the city—some strange things started to occur.

On September the first, when Franciszka, so stalwart in any unfortunate situation, just happened to have finagled a day off, the roofs, towers, and cobblestones of Cracow were bombarded with hailstones of a size not even the late Mrs. Kotarbina, born in the same year as the Third of May Constitution, could ever have seen. Huge balls of ice thudded against the stone walls, whacked into the ancient sculptures on the facades, mercilessly hammered at the metal-coated roofs, and smashed roof tiles and windowpanes. Those who were caught outside in the storm ran screaming into gateways, under market stalls, and into hurriedly closing churches; in the restaurants everyone abandoned their food, and moving back from the windows for safety, they watched this plague in dumb horror—the cabbies trying to curb their startled horses, the stout gentleman leaping out of a hackney coach in panic when the hail tore a hole in its hood and fell inside, the stall holders saving whatever produce they could and dashing for cover beneath the Cloth Hall arcades, like an army under artillery fire. In Planty Park lots of chestnut branches heavy with leaves and fruit came crashing down, and soon it would come to light that in the western suburbs the same storm had uprooted some large, old trees; in the city center it was not as bad, but even so the occasional violent crash of breaking windowpanes was audible through the deafening roar, showering glass down the fronts of houses. As soon as the clouds of hail had raced onward, or had discharged their entire load, sudden silence reigned, and from all the gateways, cafés, and inns people came pouring into the streets and the Market Square to find the biggest hailstones. Ice had blocked the storm drains, and at the western end of the Market Square a lake had formed, in which the Cracovians were now splashing around, raking through heaps of hail; lumps the size of peas or cherries, normally regarded as fine specimens, didn't attract the least attention, but now and then someone shouted: "A pigeon's egg!" or "A walnut!" until finally the victors showed each other some rapidly melting balls of ice the size of hen's eggs.

Ignacy preserved stoical calm throughout; first he watched the storm from behind the courtyard windows at Hawełka's restaurant, where he and his colleagues were finishing their "late breakfast" in a break between lectures, and later he just as blithely ignored the search for the largest hailstone and the people racing to Hawełka's shop scales, putting lumps of ice on it, and then exclaiming, "Twenty ounces!" "Thirty ounces!"

"What an extraordinary business" was all he said, after reading out an item from the *Cracow Times,* to which his colleague replied: "Indeed it is, indeed it is. And how dangerous! We think we could be killed by a bullet from a revolver, or a bomb, but meanwhile . . . Which reminds me of the story of Dr. Pasteur's duel."

"Pasteur fought a duel? That's an absurd idea!"

"You would think so! In those days there was a trouble-maker in France, you see, a man who loved fighting duels, and who was extremely skilled at it, whether with firearms or cold steel, so he deliberately provoked anyone he chose to insult him, and then beat them in a duel. But he met his match in Pasteur."

"Pasteur wasn't a brilliant swordsman, was he?"

"No. But when . . . er, the man's seconds came to his laboratory—and you can imagine what it was like in there—ah yes, his name was Cassagnac! . . . when Cassagnac's seconds came, Pasteur said: 'So you've come to challenge me, gentlemen? As the man being challenged I may choose the weapons.' And he handed them two sausages"—at these words Turbotyński frowned—"and then he said: 'One of these sausages contains perfectly good meat, but the other contains trichinella, though outwardly they look exactly the same. Let Mr. Cassagnac choose and eat one of them, and I shall be obliged to eat the other.'"

"And?"

"They took the two sausages and the proposal to Cassagnac, who dropped his challenge."

"Splendid, how splendid . . ." said Ignacy, ignoring the fact that it was raining again and crowds of people were racing for the nearest shelter. "And that in turn reminds me . . ."

❧

Meanwhile on St. John's Street the house was in a state of panic. Józia, by now the second replacement for Karolina, murdered over a year ago, and constantly compared with her — to her detriment, needless to add — was kneeling on the floor, gathering onto an unfolded newspaper the triangular pieces of a shattered pane, earth from some overturned and smashed flowerpots, and some slowly melting lumps of ice, while Zofia, fearful of drafts, was hanging thick pieces of material over the broken windows: a kilim, a hefty plush tablecloth, and a wool rug. But the heat was still escaping, and waves of ice-cold air were pouring in.

"Madam! Madam!" cried Franciszka from the threshold when, soaked through by the downpour, she finally got home.

"Help!" called back Zofia, feeling like a deckhand in a sea storm, trying with all her might to save a large galleon from sinking. "Quickly!"

Still dripping wet, still wearing her rain-sodden bonnet, Franciszka came rushing into the drawing room, but instead of hurrying to help either Zofia or Józia, she stopped in the middle of the room as if arrested by a magic force. And she was such a picture of despair that even in the general confusion, even in her frenzy to defend the house against drafts, Zofia understood that something serious was up. So she simply cried: "The windows!," tossed Józia the rug to shield the broken pane, ran over to the cook, grabbed her by the elbow, and marched her to the servants' room.

"Get out of those wet clothes this instant or you'll catch

the flu or worse," she fussed, fetching some dry clothes from Franciszka's wardrobe, while the girl, standing in a puddle of water, burst into loud sobs.

"If you please, madam . . . I . . . I can't . . . I can't bear it! It was him . . . It was him again!"

"Whom?"

"That man who . . . who str . . . strung Ka . . . Karolina along!"

Zofia froze. With hands outstretched to pass Franciszka a dry frock, she looked like a figure from a Christmas crib, a king bearing gifts, a shepherd, or an angel with a harp perhaps, with truly naive nativity play surprise in her eyes.

"What do you mean, again? You saw him again? Where?"

"At the opening . . ." she said, calming down a little, "at the opening of the tramline. Before . . . before the hailstorm."

Then, hidden behind a small screen, she obediently removed each item of wet clothing, dried herself with a towel handed her by Zofia, and put on the dry things, while at the same time describing rather incoherently who had spoken at the opening of the new tramline, what they had said, what sort of garlands, wreaths, and messages had adorned the tram stop, and so on, while constantly returning to the same thing: a young man with a little black mustache.

"And he was walking about, this way and that . . . looking over here, then there, now at the horses, now at the tram, now at the . . . official gentlemen . . . as if very taken by it all . . ." By now she was pulling the frock over her head, with her upraised arms sticking out above the screen. "He wasn't doing anything, just walking about in the crowd. But when I sees him the blood rushes to my face . . . as if his gaze were burning me . . ."

"Did he notice you looking at him?"

"Oh, no, madam, he was too nervous for that, it was as if he was looking at everything, but without seeing it. But I definitely saw what I saw. It was him, I swear it, madam, I'd swear it by the Virgin Mary, by my own dear mammy!"

"I believe you, Franciszka, I do," muttered Zofia hesitantly. From the depths of the flat came a loud clatter: it was Józia dropping the pieces of glass, earth, and snapped flower stems into the rubbish bin; meanwhile a last, delayed clap of thunder sounded in the distance.

"Well, I shall have to go and see the commissioner again."

❧

"Your servant will be asked to examine an album of photographs of detainees that we have been collecting in our register of criminals for many years," explained Commissioner Jednoróg, watching Pidłypczak as he brought some files in cardboard covers and put them down on a battered tabletop at the far end of the room. "Naturally, Miss Gawęda won't have to look through all of them. As she saw a young man of at most thirty, there is no need to show her the pictures of those arrested almost twenty years ago. In any case, if one of them was rearrested later, his updated likeness will have gone into the files. We have the photographs taken facing forward and in profile, just as they do in Paris, as recommended by Mr. Bertillon in his book *La photographie judiciaire.*"

"Bertillon? *The* Mr. Bertillon?" said Zofia, livening up.

"What's this?" said Jednoróg, smiling. "Is your interest in crime more than just an amateur pursuit?"

"My dear sir, who has not heard of the famous case of Ravachol!" said Zofia indignantly, who for years had not missed a single article about crime, and eagerly watched out for spectacular information about renowned villains such as the anarchist who had planted bombs all over Paris. "I read something about it in the newspapers."

"So you are sure to remember that the most invaluable tool for identifying the culprit in this case was the method devised by Mr. Bertillon known as anthropometry."

"Yes, of course. Thanks to his system, the infamous terrorist Ravachol and a recidivist named Koënigstein, a grave robber, turned out to be one and the same person."

"As ever, your memory does not mislead you," said Jednoróg, nodding. "In that case *bertillonage,* as this method is known, proved a truly revolutionary instrument. Measurements of the skull, hand, fingers, and other unchanging parts of the human skeleton, also the width of the cheeks, the length of the ear and several other elements form a unique *portrait parlé* for each of us. A talking portrait," he added in an explanatory way.

Zofia raised her chin a touch.

"I have a command of French, Commissioner."

"Naturally, *madame,* please forgive me," said the policeman in embarrassment, nervously tugging at his mustache. "You are sure to know that for some years this method has allowed the French police to carry off some undeniable successes, but you may not yet have heard that for some months it has been used in several places within the German Empire . . . Counselor Koettig is very active in this field in Dresden, for instance, and they are considering applying the system in Hamburg and Berlin as well. One can hope that Vienna will soon take a decision to introduce it to the Imperial-Royal police. Though our crime service still cherishes an admirable fondness for . . . more traditional methods," the commissioner calmly stated, but Zofia could hear a note of regret in his voice.

"Yet Mr. Gross is in favor of the new method, is he not?" she said, deciding to impress him. It worked.

"Mrs. Turbotyńska, you never cease to amaze me." There was a look of genuine astonishment on his face. "Am I to understand that you have read his *Handbuch für Untersuchungsrichter*?"

Zofia's heart skipped a beat. Even Ignacy, to whom she had made marriage vows before God, had never been let into the secret that she was the one who had solved the mystery at Helcel House, or that she had made a vital contribution to the discovery of Karolina's murderer—though considering the present situation, that was no longer a certainty. But for some time the need for a confidant had been maturing in her. She had Franciszka at her side, of course, truly invaluable in matters demanding female sagacity or contacts with . . . ahem . . . the lower classes, but Zofia had no one to appreciate her properly. What had Jednoróg said to her last year? That every criminal actually wants to show off his wrongdoings? Well, she felt exactly the same way: she wanted someone to know her secret, someone to view the sedate Mrs. Jekyll with appreciation for the hidden Mrs. Hyde, the fearless stalker of criminals. And she had a rising feeling that Commissioner Stanisław Jednoróg was the man who deserved to be her confidant.

"Indeed I have," she said at last, slowly, as if she herself were confessing to a dreadful crime, "his textbook for criminal investigators has come into my possession."

"I am highly impressed, and not just by your fluency in the German language. I know of guardians of the law in our city . . . I would rather not name names, but some of them may be familiar to you, who have never even picked up that publication," he said, raising an eyebrow meaningfully, and then cleared his throat. "But we were talking about photographs. Although we do not use the anthropometrical system for identification, there is nothing to stop us from applying Mr. Bertillon's other shrewd ideas, for example the method he recommends for cataloguing the photographs of criminals."

He opened a solid filing cabinet and used both hands to fetch out a large, heavy album in brown canvas covers.

It was quite tattered, evidence of the fact that it was in frequent use. He put it down on the table and opened it at random. Numerous faces appeared before Zofia's eyes, a veritable rogues' gallery for the Cracow region.

"May I?" she asked shyly, taking the corner of a page in two fingers to indicate her wish to turn it over. "This is truly fascinating."

The inspector smiled and answered with a nod. There, staring out at Zofia were dozens of thieves, drunkards, troublemakers, and surely murderers, too. They were old and young, some with long years of experience in the criminal profession, others still wet behind the ears, still childlike, with large, terrified eyes and puffy lips; most of them looked weary, some full of anger, and some wore a rather amused expression, perhaps more for display than in reality. A down-and-out with a furrowed, drink-sodden face featured beside a fop in a patterned tie fastened with a jeweled tiepin, and next to the fop was a respectable-looking Orthodox Jew. And here among this company the man connected with Karolina's murder might be lurking.

"We caption each photograph with nothing but a catalogue number, which corresponds to the relevant entry in the register where we record not just the offender's first name and surname," continued Jednoróg, amused by Zofia's all too visible excitement, "but also his profession and workplace, his religious denomination, age, and other identifying data — sixteen items in all. And naturally the crime for which he was arrested, too."

"I cannot see many women," observed Zofia, without interrupting her browsing.

"Dear lady, the female sex, by God's will, is less inclined to delinquency."

"I would not dare question your experience, Inspector, but my *own* experience in the matter prompts me to have doubts," she firmly stated. Perhaps a little too firmly. She didn't want to damage the thread of understanding that had developed between them, so in a milder tone she added: "What about the criminal professions in which women have . . . er . . . the majority? Not to say a monopoly."

Jednoróg practically blushed.

"Indeed, dear madam . . ."

"Inspector, there can be no one for whom the location of facilities of this kind in our city are a mystery. Near the railway station, for example. And there is one woman of loose morals who stands in the street behind St. Thomas's church, where she accosts men in the nocturnal hours. In a respectable district, I might add! While we're on the topic, maybe you could keep from intervening in that case?"

"Allow me to remind you," said the commissioner, spreading his hands, "that plying the oldest profession in the world is not a crime in our empire. Which, speaking for myself, is a cause for regret. A lack of moral constraint may be suitable for the French Republic, as the heiress to a libertine revolution, but I agree with you that in our Catholic empire there should be greater circumspection in this regard. However, prostitution is governed by medical and police supervision; since 1877 we have kept a register of women of loose morals, and I must say that many of them are still working in the profession to this day. If the harlot whom you mentioned is registered, has a health booklet, and submits twice a week to the relevant medical inspection, then unfortunately I can take no action in the matter."

It occurred to Zofia that in spite of it all, Jednoróg was sometimes surprisingly naive. Experience — above all many years of marriage to Ignacy — had taught her that although one could try to restrain human nature, or force it into a certain framework, it couldn't be changed entirely. As history and the Holy Gospel taught us, women of ill repute had existed since the dawn of time, a known fact if only from the Bible story of Rahab, the harlot of Jericho. Zofia doubted a statutory ban on running bawdy houses could make any difference at all; any blatant prostitute would simply try to avoid persecution by going in for illicit harlotry.

"I did not mean that you should arrest the woman," she calmly explained, "but perhaps she could be encouraged to relocate her . . . business a little farther off. Best of all beyond Planty Park, but if not, then perhaps to the other side of the Market Square?"

In reply to her inquiring look Jednoróg spread his hands helplessly again.

"May we call in Miss Gawęda now?" he asked after a pause.

After leafing through the bulky photograph album for almost an hour Franciszka must have been tired, but she didn't let it show, and with a grim expression she kept on turning the pages, carefully examining each picture. Zofia had nothing to do — it was all up to the cook and her memory now. Jednoróg should have gone back to his work, but Zofia's presence changed the official task of showing the album into a social encounter. So he was bumbling about, receiving the occasional documents brought by his underlings or issuing instructions in a hushed tone; he fetched the registry books from the cupboard and lined them up on the same table as the album of photographs; but all this time, as a man of good breeding, he did his best to keep up the social chitchat with his guest.

"It is hard to imagine a better method for identifying criminals," he said, coughing. "Although an even newer means of identification has appeared, still at an experimental stage. It is hard to tell if it will ever be of any use, but the initial results are very promising. It involves making a print of the right index and middle finger, one could call it a stamp . . ."

"A stamp?"

"Yes, apparently the whorl of wrinkles that each of us has on his fingertip" — at this point he must have realized that the word "wrinkles" was inappropriate in front of a lady — "or we could call them lines — they're not related to age after all . . . nor do they alter with age . . . but apparently the pattern those whorls make on our fingers is unique, the body's signature, so to speak. It's a method that's been introduced in the New World, Argentina of all places."

"Who would have thought something could come to us from the other side of the ocean," said Zofia. "Generally the traffic flows in the opposite direction — so many citizens of our monarchy are moving to both Americas nowadays."

"Yes, the United States, Brazil, Argentina as mentioned . . ."

"I've got him," they heard Franciszka calling. "Please, madam, please, sir, I've got him!" They leaped up and hurried to the window, where the girl was sitting over the album. "That's him!" She tapped a finger on a photograph stuck to the thick paper. "That's definitely him!"

The picture showed a young man in urban attire, slender, swarthy, squinting scornfully into the police photographer's lens, but his clenched lips implied that he had not taken his arrest lightly. There was nothing distinct about his shirt, tie, and jacket; they were neither shabby nor excessively smart, just the decent clothes of a student, a young tradesman, or, indeed, an engineer who had only just emerged from college.

"Are you sure that's him, Franciszka?"

"Please, madam, I'm more than sure, because on the day I saw him with Karolina he was wearing exactly the same clothes! The other times he was in different ones, both on Midsummer Eve and at the tramline opening, but the first time that's exactly how he was dressed!"

The commissioner leaned over the registry books in

search of the one where the features and personal data of the swarthy young man in the photograph were listed in sixteen different categories.

Zofia noticed that Franciszka had abruptly lost interest in the case; she was looking out of the window—not a very clean one—at Mikołajska Street, where an ordinary Cracow day was in progress: people walking about, an indigent tradesman carrying a box on a string around his neck, a portable stall selling trash, cheap trinkets perhaps, or possibly shoelaces and boot blacking.

Meanwhile Jednoróg picked up a file labelled *216-308,* opened the cover, and began to go through the list.

"Fortunately here we have . . . criminals . . . not just from Cracow itself," he said, breaking off now and then, "but also . . . from the villages in the neighboring area . . . Podgórze . . . and even . . . here he is!" He frowned. "Yes, this is the one. You have done beautifully, Miss Gawęda," he said to Franciszka. "Your concern for finding your coworker's murderer does you praise, even if we have every reason to believe the killer has been dead for over a year. The main thing is that you are a good girl, and you have good intentions. Thanks be to God. Ecler," he roared, "take Miss Gawęda into the corridor! And wait by the door for Mrs. Turbotyńska. She and I must have a chat."

Franciszka nodded in silence, took her cape from the coat stand, and politely let herself be led to the door by the scrawny cadet, Ecler.

Jednoróg sat down at his desk, knotted his fingers, and

spoke in a low, sincere tone, though betraying a touch of impatience.

"Mrs. Turbotyńska, I doubt anyone is quite as impressed as I am by your knowledge of things and your unusual investigative intuition. I would like that to be clearly expressed. Unfortunately, my capacities are not boundless," he said, sighing heavily, "and I must be frank with you. There is no option for me to send my men after the man identified by Miss Gawęda. I won't deny that he's a criminal, his name is recorded in our files, but I can assure you he's not there for coercing and murdering women. All his crimes are of a far lighter caliber. And even if she has identified him correctly, even if he did make advances to your housemaid, we have no reason to suspect him of murder. It could just be a case of common human similarity . . ."

"If she says she recognizes him . . ."

"I can assure you that anyone who had only ever seen me once, fleetingly, could easily find someone in the album who could be my double; they could be certain that it was definitely me, without a doubt, without the slightest hesitation. Human memory is deceptive and often plays tricks on us, but the problem is when the tricks . . ."

". . . end in the conviction of an innocent man," agreed Zofia, feeling dejected.

"Exactly so."

"But surely one can make inquiries about him, seek him out, follow him, perhaps interview him?"

"In what connection? For a case that is already closed,

that was crowned with a success trumpeted in the newspapers? Perhaps I should also be handing Mr. Daszyński Inspector Trzeciak's head on a plate?" He was clearly enervated, and evidently his conscience was shaken, too. "Miss Szulc's murderer was shot dead while resisting arrest. And that is that."

Zofia said nothing for a while, then struck a note of pathos, imagining it would work on Jednoróg, fond as he was of high-flown words.

"What about justice? You are not just a man who enforces the law, but a man who respects the law. Surely the mere shadow of suspicion that the real murderer is at liberty . . ."

"Mrs. Turbotyńska," he interrupted her, "with the greatest of respect: I would remind you that the investigating magistrate in this case is Mr. Rozmarynowicz, who wanted to arrest the sand miner and put him behind bars. It was you who took notice of the alleged Engineer Bzowski, whom thanks to intelligence obtained from our informers we managed to identify and catch. I have stuck my neck out in this case once already, though as God is my witness, Rozmarynowicz wanted to settle it quickly and without a fuss, so he tore a strip off me for believing in 'female hysteria.' Am I now to go and tell him that I have damaged his and my own reputation? That there is more female hysteria, and now we are to pursue someone else entirely, because a serving girl has pointed her shapely little finger at a photograph in an album?"

Following this rhetorical question he paused, but of course Zofia had no idea how to respond, so after a while he picked up the thread again, speaking laboriously, as if explaining something to a child, but perhaps also in an effort to assuage his own conscience.

"We do not live on a desert island, dear lady. There is Cracow, and all our local interconnections, then there's Lemberg, the capital of Galicia, and further off, Vienna." He turned and pointed to the portrait of the emperor. "And each of us can only do as much as he is allowed by the limits set above us. On official matters there are bureaucratic rules in force, complex systems of dependency rather like the delta of a river. At the source of power stands His Imperial Majesty, and to reach him one has to sail against the current. The farther upriver, the higher into the rushing streams, the stronger the flow, and the harder it is to sail," he said, sighing. "So however much I would like to help you, I must give you an honest account of my limitations. I know how to navigate that river — suffice it to say, I have advanced quite rapidly, I have been decorated . . ."

". . . for your undeniable merits," she offered in desperation, hoping to gain at least something through flattery.

"There are many people of merit, Mrs. Turbotyńska, but not all of them are promoted, and Vienna does not award medals to everyone. It is about finding the right balance between active and passive, defiant and dutiful. One cannot sit like a mouse in the corner, or nobody will take any notice, but nor can one make too much noise. And I am just a man," he said, spreading his hands. "A small cog in the large machine of imperial-royal justice."

Gazing benevolently from his portrait, the emperor silently confirmed every word spoken by Commissioner Stanisław Jednoróg.

❧

Franciszka was sitting cozily in the corridor, with her hands folded in her lap, gazing blankly at a wall, the very picture of indifference. Only when they reached the Market Square did she look around conspiratorially and say: "Please, madam, when I recognized him, I didn't speak up at once, but found his name in the register for myself."

Zofia was amazed.

"What? It will fade from your mind at once!" she stopped and said, then reached into her bag and instantly brought out her notebook bound in purple morocco leather.

"Wolf alas . . ."

"Alias."

". . . alias Zeev Szyfryn . . ." said Franciszka, chewing her lip ". . . alias Sztycer."

Zofia wrote down: *Wolf/Zeev. Szyfryn/Sztycer.*

"Good. And the address?"

"There was something else, as for all of them, height, eye color, and so on, but the commissioner could have turned around at any moment and caught me looking at his registers, so I couldn't read it all—it's hard to read that quickly . . ."

"You have done well anyway!"

"Besides, I think . . ."

"Yes?"

The girl cast her a hesitant look.

"Perhaps Mr. Kurkiewicz and that Sztycer . . . were up to something together? He always talked to Karolina, he always had something sweet to say to her. Though she said one time he talked nothing but smut, and made her angry."

Zofia blushed, then looked at Franciszka with genuine respect.

"I shall think about this, I shall." Then, as if something had suddenly caused a change in her, she adopted a more restrained expression and said: "The professor has almost run out of shaving alum. We must call at the pharmacy. Though in fact," she said, smiling roguishly, "let us go straight home. We have both done our work for today. And Józia will be sent for the alum."

❧

When the Holy Roman Emperor Henry IV decided to do penance before Pope Gregory VII, he stood below the castle at Canossa barefoot, wearing sackcloth, and with ashes scattered in his hair. Rather than ashes, as usual Zofia Turbotyńska applied Dr. Rix's Pompadour Milk Substitute for Powder, and put on a dress of lavender satin with subtle sprays of violets printed on it. Emperor Henry was welcome to walk about the mountains barefoot, but she chose a pair of purple glacé leather boots; she was halfway across the Market Square before she realized that purple was the color of repentance.

Magistrate Klossowitz did not keep her waiting for very long. His study, paneled with dark wood, was smaller than the room where Jednoróg worked, but far more elegant, though the portrait of the emperor — this time in a dove-gray, rather than a white uniform — was more modest in size and a bit less conspicuous.

"To what do I owe your visit to this dangerous building?"

"Dangerous?" she said in surprise as she sat in the armchair offered her.

"The last time we spoke, a year ago, at the Constitution Day concert, the shooting incident was in the news. I thought that was why you never came to see me. Out of fear."

"I have had no reason to come and see you until now, Mr. Klossowitz," she said, a little indignantly.

"Allow me to put it another way. You thought you had no reason to come and see me. I understand the situation has changed?"

"Oh — so that means . . ."

"Yes, I was expecting you to come sooner or later." He scratched his cheek. "We've known each other for a while, and I was sure that sooner or later . . ."

"Later, I am afraid."

"I hope it is not too late," he said, then energetically opened a notebook. "So what new facts have we discovered?"

She had been expecting him to wreak his malice on her for longer; clearly he regarded her as a rival of a high caliber, and the fact that she had had to admit her mistake was enough for him.

"Franciszka Gawęda, my servant, as you may remember, spotted the man who had been making up to Karolina."

"And who passed himself off as Engineer . . ."

"Bzowski."

"And who was apparently shot dead by Inspector Trzeciak. Was Miss Gawęda shown the corpse?"

"No. He was pointed out by police informers. He ran off, tried to defend himself . . . There was plenty to imply that he was Karolina's murderer. In fact his face was severely disfigured by one of the shots. There was no point in exposing her to such a sight, when she had only seen him fleetingly and was not entirely sure what he looked like. But later on . . ."

"Yes?"

"Later on she saw him in the crowd. Twice. What is more, she has identified him in a police album. But now Commissioner Jednoróg who, I must say, has been extremely helpful to me, has his hands tied."

Klossowitz smiled triumphantly.

"He does not wish . . ." she broke off.

"He does not wish to risk his career, obviously. He may have been helpful, but only as long as it caused him no obstruction — on the contrary, it may have brought him a step closer to promotion. The gentleman and I have known each other for quite a while."

There was a knock at the door, but Klossowitz ignored it.

"Yes, but you could force him to do it by putting pressure on Mr. Rozmarynowicz . . ."

"Rozmarynowicz!" he said, waving a hand. "There is no chance of that. He's been in a world all his own for a very long time — such things are just unwanted bother as far as he is concerned. And the fact that he is the oldest one of us . . . What else did the commissioner say about the man your servant identified?"

"Not much. That he is a common pickpocket . . ."

"Not now!" bellowed Klossowitz in reply to another knock at the door.

"But we do know his name. It is . . ." She took her notebook from her reticule. "Either Wolf or Zeev Szyfryn, or else Sztycer."

"Wolf Szyfryn," muttered Klossowitz, "that rings a bell . . . I've never conducted a case involving him, but somehow that name is familiar . . . Just a moment."

He left the room, berated someone in the corridor, saying he was too busy to see any clients at the moment, then disappeared for a while. Zofia gazed at the cupola of Saints Peter and Paul, lit by the warm September sun, looking as if it had been brought here straight from Rome as it rose above a thoroughly Cracovian wall of bare brick sinking into the shadows.

"Wolf Sztycer," said Klossowitz from the threshold, "is a common good-for-nothing, no great king of crime, it's true. A pickpocket, which explains why your servant always saw him in a reasonably big crowd. He was there to do his usual job. He has no regular source of income, he is known to work at a . . . er . . ." Klossowitz was on the point of sitting down at his desk, but the problematic word interrupted not just the flow of his speech but his movements, too, so he stood suspended over his armchair.

"At a . . . ?"

"At a brothel," he finally said, and simultaneously sat down.

Zofia pretended not to be remotely shocked by this word, although it occurred to her that with time she really was finding it less and less shocking, and asked: "At a brothel, I see. But which one?"

Mildly surprised at such lack of ceremony in a society lady, Klossowitz cast her a searching glance.

"In Dębniki, on Różana Street, the house of a Mrs. Dunin. At liberty for the past two years, apart from two brief periods in custody, in the first half of last October and toward the end of December. Do those dates . . ."

"No, they do not coincide, either with Karolina's murder or the sightings. Franciszka saw him last year on Midsummer Eve, and again on the first of this month, at the opening of the new tramline."

"Well, we shall have to keep watch on him. Perhaps . . ."

"Różana Street?" Zofia suddenly exclaimed. "Różana? At Olesia's? Is there jasmine in the garden?"

Klossowitz was quite confused. Could the wife of a university professor really have been to a brothel in Dębniki, where she was on first-name terms with the madame, Mrs. Dunin?

"Yes . . . I'm not sure about the jasmine—I've never been much of a botanist—but *that person* is known by the diminutive Olesia, short for Aleksandra."

"I must entrust you with some confidential information. Engineer Bzowski's calling card was stolen, along with the entire card case, while Mr. Bzowski . . ."

"Was having a nice time at a house bordered by jasmine?"

Fortunately, the emperor could not hear all these obscenities, and continued to gaze down as serenely as ever.

CHAPTER VIII

In which Franciszka is subjected to moral torture, Zofia is ashamed to ask the price, Ignacy sticks his neck out entirely unnecessarily, and Planty Park bears silent witness to a conversation between a veil and a vegetable.

The peal of the servants' bell surged across the room in a wide wave, passed through the door into the passage, flowed over the coat rack (where at this time of day neither Ignacy's bowler hat nor his overcoat were to be found because they were quietly hanging in the cloakroom at the university), then finally poured into the kitchen and summoned the relevant person.

"Is Józia not at home?" asked Zofia moments later when Franciszka stood before her in the drawing room.

"I sent her to the colonial store for anchovies, as instructed."

For a while Zofia watched her closely, as if still in two minds about whether to bring up a highly sensitive topic.

"Franciszka, I shall have a task for you to perform," she finally declared in a mournful tone. "It might prompt fears of a moral nature. Entirely justifiably, I might add, because it breaks God's commandments . . ."

"Oh, no," said Franciszka, almost raising her voice, "I will not cook meat on a Friday, madam."

"I am afraid the request I wish to make is far more serious than that," said Zofia, sighing heavily, and offered the girl a chair. "You had better sit down, my dear."

The response was a hesitant, rather horrified look.

"It is a very delicate matter demanding absolute . . . I stress: *absolute* discretion. But I am sure that once you overcome your perfectly understandable reluctance, you will make a splendid job of the task."

Franciszka was all but biting her lip with nerves, while her hands crumpled her apron, freshly stained with the beets she had just been chopping to make into soup. But seeing that her mistress was feeling awkward too, she said nothing.

"You must go to St. Thomas's Street. Late in the evening—at night, when there is nobody there, because no one must see you, do you understand? No one," said Zofia, lowering her voice, though there was nobody at home except the two of them. "When you leave the house you are to walk down Sławkowska Street to the Market Square, go along its northern side to Floriańska Street, and from there into Kącik Lane without anyone seeing that you have come from the direction of Peacock House. There you will meet a certain person. Once you have finished, you are to walk to Szpitalna Street, pass in front of the theater, and from there you are to come home via Planty Park. Have you memorized that?"

"Yes, madam," stammered Franciszka at last. "Sławkowska Street, the Market Square, then down Floriańska to Kącik Lane, then back along Szpitalna and through the park. But who am I to go and see, madam? There's no one there at night except, if you'll pardon the expression, that old prostitute who waylays young lads, like a vampire . . ." She glanced at Zofia's face, her meaningfully raised eyebrow and her sad but piercing look. "Mother of God! Please, madam, but why would I have to do that? What on earth for? It's most improper!" she said, crossing herself.

"Franciszka, I know I am asking you to do something bordering on indecency, but believe me, I am acting in a noble cause. My aim is to find the man whom you saw, the man who shares the blame for our Karolina's murder. Perhaps you will agree that this justifies . . . the minor transgression I am asking you to perform?"

The girl hesitated, but finally nodded, though with her entire being she made it plain that she did not like the idea. Zofia toyed nervously with the chain of her lorgnette.

"Besides, I think that if the Lord Jesus allowed a harlot to wash his feet, I too shall suffer no disgrace if I merely exchange a few words with her in a rightful cause. But I need your help to arrange to meet her. I am sure that she will agree to devote a quarter of an hour to me or even half an hour, if in my name you offer her a crown."

Franciszka frowned even more fiercely, but nodded.

"And if she resists," added Zofia after a pause, "but *only* then, remember, only then you can offer her a crown and a half. But not a penny more!"

The evening before Zofia had suffered torment trying to extract information from Ignacy on how much the "services" of a meretrix might cost. Naturally, she was not expecting him to know this at first hand, but perhaps in exclusively male company, at a late breakfast at Hawełka's, one of his colleagues from the university may have mentioned something on the topic. But how was she to ask him about it without prompting his amazement? In theory she could have asked Engineer Bzowski, who was surely still terrified of his marital indiscretions coming to light, but it was not the sort of question you could pose informally in a note, and she was not going to make another expedition to Studencka Street, or risk running into Mrs. Bujwid again. For a while she considered consulting young Tadeusz, who as a student might know this sort of information; though she liked Żeleński, she generally had an extremely low opinion of Cracow's students, who to her mind were interested in everything but their studies: getting drunk, brawling, gambling, and carousing in the company of wanton women, of course. But how was she to question her husband's student in a casual way, without arousing astonishment, about something that as a woman, a wife, and a representative of her class, she should not even know existed? So she abandoned this idea too; it was all down to Ignacy, whom she decided to approach by relating her inquiry to philanthropy.

"Sometimes it feels as if Cracow is a bottomless well for charity. Prince Lubomirski has only just built a house for fallen girls to be run by the Sisters of Charity in Łagiewniki, designed to take one hundred charges, but sometimes there are one hundred and thirty, sometimes one hundred and sixty of them living there—they simply cannot meet the demand."

"For sure, for sure," muttered Ignacy, who was busy sticking newspaper cuttings in his album.

"Well, I suppose it is a garrison town. And a university one. Soldiers, students, corruption everywhere, the whole place is filled with the . . . stale odor of squalor."

"That odor won't go away until the waterworks is built!" mumbled Ignacy in reply.

"Ignacy! I am not talking of impurity in the sense of hygiene, but the moral sense. Tell me, do you not find it astonishing in the present day that so many women choose to follow the path of sin?"

"Yes indeed, I do," he replied; this time he put down the glue and scissors, and looked up at her.

"Are they so sorely tempted by Mammon?"

"Truly, Zofia, I have no idea."

As if casually, Zofia opened her book and began to leaf through it. A tall column lamp standing beside her cast soft light on the pages.

"How much can work of that kind possibly earn anyway?" she cast into space a minute later. "More or less than a washerwoman, a charwoman, a market stall holder, or other honest tradeswoman? How much are they paid to dishonor themselves?"

The scissors clattered against the tabletop again, then there was a sound of disconcerted throat clearing. She waited, but nothing else was forthcoming.

"Half a crown?" she ventured.

"I really have no idea, after all . . . Zofia, how should I know?"

Now Zofia closed her book and adopted the most indulgent tone imaginable.

"Oh, I know you took me as a wife when I was a young girl, and sometimes you still think of me as one, but I am not a child, and I presume that as a doctor at the university you sometimes encounter things that neither you nor all the more I would ever wish to hear or see. It is"—here she paused meaningfully, then at once continued with a deep sigh—"a service to mankind. Yes, nothing else. A service to mankind. So I know that you come across things that are shameful, painful, and sinful . . . do not deny it! But it does you no discredit at all. On the contrary, it ennobles you!"

Ignacy sat at the table with a queer look on his face,

since his main occupation for years had been the study and dissection of animals, especially reptiles and amphibians; any connection with prostitution was highly doubtful, nor had he ever had any special interest either in venereology or forensic medicine. But he knew that if his wife praised him, it was a bad idea to interrupt her or argue with her.

"Half a crown?" she suddenly repeated at the end of her disquisition.

"More like a crown," he let slip automatically this time, because he did in fact know a thing or two; then he added uncertainly: "At least so I have heard . . . from other doctors."

"A crown. For the loss of one's soul," exclaimed Zofia dramatically, and then, regarding the matter as settled, she turned up the lamp and opened her book again.

So now it was this quote, that is, a crown, or at most one and a half, that she bid Franciszka offer to the *harlot,* with the stipulation that the sum would only be paid upon meeting. Finally she made sure the servant had precisely memorized the route she was to take to Kącik Lane and back again.

That night, when Ignacy was snoring away in his gloomy Gothic bed like a sleeping medieval knight, in her twin bed she was wide awake, intent on the softest sounds audible from the house as well as from the city outside: occasionally one of the ancient joists creaked, or the brief yowl of two fighting tomcats rang out; on St. Mary's tower the one o'clock trumpet call was played, and then an aging reveler, a long-retired lyric tenor, let forth a clumsy *La donna è mobile.* Only then did Zofia's sensitized ear hear Franciszka's soft tread as she almost noiselessly crept along the passage to the door, turned the key in the lock and—here there was a single creak—went down the stairs. Shortly after, Zofia heard her footsteps outside: as she approached Pijarska Street they faded, and once she had turned the corner toward Sławkowska Street the sound vanished into the dark night as if into a veil of black velvet.

Next morning, as Franciszka dressed Zofia's hair, they discussed it all in a conspiratorial whisper. The good news was that *that woman* had agreed to a meeting with the mysterious lady. The bad news was that she had insisted on a crown and a half, and not without some grumbling. The place and time had been fixed, so now Zofia would have to consider how to remain incognito. She sat on the sofa with her needlework, mentally devising a detailed plan for effective protection from the prying eyes of her fellow Cracovians.

Meanwhile Ignacy was immersed in other events entirely. Doomsday had come, the fourth of September, meaning that first, with great pomp, Father Chromecki had said mass at the Piarist church, and then the company had walked down St. John's Street, right below the windows of Peacock House, to the Wodzicki Palace at number eleven, where with equal pomp Cracow's first high school for girls was being inaugurated, founded through the efforts of both Bujwids, Napoleon Cybulski, dean of the medical faculty, and the linguist Bronisław Trzaskowski, who was to be headmaster of the new school. If it had been the work of some barmy emancipationists, or some eternal students, who instead of passing their exams had spent years on end drifting around cafés and fantasizing about women's education, never mind. But as many as three university professors, men of distinction, men of serious standing, with achievements to their names?

So Ignacy was sitting right by the window, pretending to be reading yesterday's *Cracow Times,* but in reality casting occasional glances at the procession below, the end of which was still emerging from the church, while the front had already disappeared into the palace gateway. He was reading items of news aloud, breaking off now and again to make a gibe.

"According to a report from St. Moritz in Switzerland the patients at the local sanatoria like to amuse themselves by throwing snowballs, sledging, and other winter entertainments, since snow is lying a foot deep . . . A mass! As if they didn't know what effect learning will have on those poor girls' bodies! It's tantamount to murdering the children who might have been born from them. Zofia, it is murder on a grand scale, and there are the clerics, setting their hands to it . . . and Trzaskowski too! He is a former Jesuit who cast

off his monk's habit. But then the *Jesuits* . . ." he said, stressing the word, "we know what they are like . . ."

The only response was silence. He glanced out of the window, saw Mrs. Bujwid's nice round hat from above and Cybulski's black mop of hair, then started reading again, and suddenly exclaimed joyfully:

"Here you are, this is what scholarship does for you! The scholarly confirmation of what I've just been saying. Listen to this: *At the medical congress in London, Mr. Forbes Winslow presented a fascinating work on suicide. This study, based on 7,083 cases*—that's no small study, you see—*sets out the reasons that led to each suicide, as follows: 905 men and 511 women were driven to take their lives by poverty; 728 men and 524 women by domestic troubles; 322 men and 233 women by financial losses; 287 men and 208 women by drunkenness and addiction; 155 men and 141 women by gaming losses . . .* Who'd have suspected so many women could fall into the abyss of gambling? *. . . 100 men and 410 women by disappointed ambition*—as many as 410 women! —*97 men and 157 women by romantic troubles; 53 men and 53 women by inflated amour propre*—an equal tally—*49 men and 57 women by pangs of conscience; 16 men and one woman by fanaticism; 3 men and 3 women by misanthropy; and 1,381 men and 667 women by unknown causes. As one can see from these figures, the various causes have a roughly similar effect on both sexes* . . . Zofia, are you listening to me?"

"Of course, Ignacy," she replied, this time in keeping with the truth.

"*. . . with the exception of love and disappointed ambition, which drive far more women than men to suicide. As regards the first of these two causes, it is quite natural*— indeed, we know a thing or two about female hysteria— *whereas the second is a revelation, showing that women are much more ambitious than men.* But not by nature, they aren't; it's all because of this disastrous idea of educating them. It stirs unhealthy desires, and it all ends in a handwoven noose, a leap in front of a train, or an overdose of laudanum! Does it not surprise you that . . ."

"It surprises me, in the first place, that if I have counted correctly, an unequal number of male and female suicides has been chosen for the study. And in the second, no one has taken notice of the greatest disproportion: sixteen male fanatics and only one female," replied Zofia coldly.

Ignacy tried adding up the numbers mentally, came to the conclusion that there were indeed more men, and went back to his reading without another word, though now and then he glanced out of the window.

"Yesterday the emperor returned to Lemberg from maneuvers at three o'clock in the afternoon. In the evening Komarno was once again illuminated. Today the weather is delightful . . ."

There was silence again, broken only by the ticking of the clock and the voices of the last few people entering Wodzicki Palace.

"Inconceivable," said Ignacy furiously, "and right under our noses! Practically in our dining room." He leaned heavily on the windowsill and fixed his gaze on the small crowd being swallowed up by the baroque gateway. "One has only to lean out of the window to see it all as clear as day!"

"Then do not lean out."

"You rang, madam?" asked Franciszka, entering the room.

Zofia looked up from her novel, which in any case she hadn't been reading for quite some time.

"No. You must have misheard. And if I were to ring, you should send Józia."

"Should I make some tea, perhaps?"

As a well-trained servant she was not in the habit of suggesting such things off her own bat, so Zofia realized something was up and agreed to the proposition.

"And make some lime blossom tea for the master to calm his nerves," she added. Ignacy said nothing, but to give him his due he had stopped glancing out of the window.

Soon after, Franciszka brought in a Japanese lacquered tray, bearing a cup made of fine porcelain, also Japanese, for the mistress and a faience mug with a mustache guard for Ignacy. The corner of a folded slip of paper was poking out from under Zofia's saucer. Could Jednoróg have changed his mind and sent her something via a courier?

But no, the message was from Klossowitz and was typically laconic.

"No trace of Wolf. He is not in Cracow. Am checking other possibilities. Among informers too. R.K."

❧

Come what may, styles of headwear were capable of stirring strong emotions in Cracow. Nobody had forgotten the time when the wife of the noted artist Wojciech Kossak took a stroll along the north side of the Market Square wearing a hat from Paris of a rather original style; two days later the *Cracow Times* had reported in indignation that here was a veritable horror, purple at the front and green at the back, what Parisian extravagance, and so on. Rumor had it that after this article she dared not leave the house for the rest of the week, not even for a walk along the suburban Rudawa river. True or not, it was a fact that she had never appeared in public in that hat again. On the other hand, thought Zofia, old Countess Potocka had turned up at the theater with a complete tropical garden on her head, everything bar the parrot, and she hadn't met with a single word of censure. Well, different rules had always applied to countesses and duchesses than to mere mortals—such was the established order of affairs.

Believing adamantly, though perhaps erroneously, that her own hats were familiar to the entire city, Zofia had decided to borrow one of Franciszka's—an unassuming little felt hat of a dull green shade (the girl, despite some resistance, did not dare protest). Now, after carefully positioning a thick funereal veil, fixed to the hat with a simple hatpin, to make sure that her face was concealed and nobody would recognize her, Zofia made ready to leave the house.

She had specially arranged for her meeting to take place in the "inferior" part of Planty Park, bordering Szczepański Square, a site known for the fact that mainly youth of the male sex frequented it, to smoke cigarettes and accost the young ladies who passed that way. In fact, the park keepers chased the young men away, but not very effectively; they preferred to tackle easier disruptors of public order, such as boys who played football in places where it was prohibited. By a strange coincidence, one of the twelve park keepers always appeared when they did—in full uniform, including the special cap—wielding a long, pointed stick designed for gathering fallen leaves. Suddenly, with a swift lunge he would pierce the scallywags' football and stride off without a word, leaving the despondent urchins on the spot. The children knew they should limit their games to the area surrounding the Barbican, but they were holding on to a stretch along Podwale Street. As in all Cracow, within Planty Park, too, everything had its fixed place.

Meanwhile, Zofia was now in a place entirely wrong for her. Instead of walking along Cracow's answer to the Corso, past the university buildings, nodding to the society ladies, returning the gentlemen's bows, and making an impression with a fine hat from Lemberg or Vienna, she was sitting on a bench in her cook's miserable little bonnet, wearing a dress unearthed from the back of the wardrobe that dated from many seasons ago (here and there it was a little tight, so she was hiding the creases under a puffed jacket), and waiting for her appointment. The disguise was clearly performing its task, because nobody paid her the least attention.

In the distance she could hear the trumpeter sounding the hour. She looked around her, but the person whom she was expecting did not appear to be in sight. A young man sat on the bench opposite, smoking a cigarette and reading a newspaper—if her sight was not deceiving her, it was the socialist journal *Forward.* Hidden by the curtain of her veil, Zofia rolled her eyes. Behind her, on Szczepański Square, the market trading was now coming to an end, the peasants from the suburban villages were folding up their stalls and loading sacks of unsold cabbages, potatoes, and carrots onto their carts. *Perhaps* that person *has had a change of mind?* thought Zofia.

A woman in a dull gray outfit, undoubtedly one of the stall holders, tired from her long day's work, decided to rest awhile. She sat down on Zofia's bench and let her head droop. She breathed noisily, coughing now and then. There they sat in silence for a good few minutes. Zofia was starting to feel anxious. What if the person she had arranged to meet, approaching from a distance, were to see this other figure on the bench beside her, have second thoughts, and not come any nearer? The whole subterfuge would be in vain!

"I think you're waiting for me," said the woman in the dull gray clothes, in a low, hoarse voice.

"I think not, madam," replied Zofia quietly but firmly.

The woman gave no reply, but fixed her gaze across the gravel-coated path on a bed of dahlias, which thanks to the assiduous care of the park keepers flowered abundantly even in the inferior parts of the city gardens.

"But you have a veil," replied the woman, "and I was to meet a lady in a black veil. Is it not you, madam?"

Zofia narrowed her eyes and finally took a close look at the woman; her entire knowledge of the topic of prostitution came from literature, so she was expecting to see La Dame aux Camélias—a wanton Jezebel in challenging makeup, a decidedly too-revealing costume, endowed with vulgar yet undeniable allure. Was that not after all the quintessence of the profession? Meanwhile, beside her sat a person whose appearance was no different from that of a seamstress from the Grzegórzki district. Indeed, she was coughing in a somewhat consumptive manner, but there the similarity to the courtesan Violetta came to an end. She looked considerably older than Zofia; from under her headgear, greatly inferior in quality to Franciszka's little hat, strands of mouse-colored hair protruded, damaged by curling and coated in the remains of auburn dye; her dress, of the most wretched type, with patches here and there, was not in its first youth. But worst of all was her face: the clumsily applied powder was incapable of concealing its horrifying red, if not purple color. It was as bloated as a balloon from the church fete in Emaus.

"The lassie promised me a crown and a half," the pitiful woman said.

Zofia was speechless. Was this what a fallen woman was like? She had expected to see moral decline, but here before her eyes was the image of misery and despair. Were men really prepared to . . . ?

"Please pay in advance, madam, or there won't be nothing doing," said the woman firmly.

Still dumbfounded, without a word Zofia reached for her purse.

"I already told the young miss, I don't do *those* things. If that's what you're after, madam, there is one girl, Mela, she's called, she lives in Grzegórzki. I can give you the address. But *I* don't never touch *that.* I only do it in God's honest way."

She uttered the words "those" and "that" in a tone that Zofia found surprising, though she had no intention of asking what "those things" were, or why they went beyond the traditional repertoire of services offered by the woman sitting beside her. The reference to God seemed to her inappropriate, but she wasn't going to argue. *There are more things in heaven and on earth than the philosophers have dreamed of,* she thought to herself, *but even I do not need to know about all of them.*

"The business I have with you is not of a . . . professional nature," she said. "Or at least, not entirely."

"So what do you want?" said the prostitute. "No one ever wants anything else from me but you know what."

"I would like to talk to you."

"Talk to me?" Despite the veil, Zofia could see that in her

puffy face the prostitute's eyes widened. The woman could not have been more surprised if Zofia had declared that she was expecting her to perform the dance of the seven veils at a solemn assembly of the Archbrotherhood of Mercy charitable society.

"Indeed. And I am sure that the sum I have handed you will entirely suffice for us to be able to exchange a few words," Zofia declared firmly, having finally recovered her equilibrium. "Have you ever met a woman who goes by the name of Dunin? According to my information she runs a . . ."

"Brothel in Dębniki! Of course I know that!" said the woman, livening up, which brought on a fit of coughing. Zofia shuddered, thanking God (and herself) for the veil. "But she never wanted me there, oh, no! She's got her young lasses, comely and healthy the lot them, not without the clap or the pox, mind, but without consumption, without nothing, smooth faces, palates intact. Not a common shambles but a luxury place. They might even have unplucked cherries there, you know."

Zofia did not know, but she nodded affirmatively.

"You see, there was three of us. Faiga Blum, Olesia, who you're concerned with, and me. Now they call me Beetroot Mary, you can guess why . . ." She coughed violently. "But back then I was still known as Flame-haired Maria. I dyed my hair red; I had hair like Mary Magdalene herself, very beautiful it was. My bubbies weren't bad neither, but everyone in Cracow used to say: 'Nobody's got flaming-red hair like Maria, go to her,' they did . . ." Then she added sadly: "I were famous."

Zofia waited in silence for the continuation. And once her companion had finished reminiscing about her glory days, it came.

"Back then we used to stand out in Planty Park, near the station. We received our clients in a run-down place on Pawia Street that one of us hired there. It was a room like any other, there was just a shakedown and a basin, but it was enough. Faiga didn't fancy standing out in Kazimierz, she said they pay better in Cracow, and besides, if some young gentleman fancied himself a Jewish girl, he needn't traipse off to Kazimierz. That was her notion. She were smart, it has to be said. But not smart enough, because she ended up with the syph, the pox that is. She took a cure, but in vain, and after that no one wanted her . . . She couldn't work, legally anyway, because the doctor refused to stamp her booklet when she went for the police health check. In the end she lost her wits, and a couple of years ago the poor thing died. And I took to the drink."

Zofia didn't interrupt. She wanted to get away from here as fast as possible, and to get home without anyone seeing her or recognizing her, but she realized she must let the woman tell her story in its entirety, with all the details and digressions, the whole painful truth. So she learned about the mother who had sent her out into the street to earn their keep, about the siblings who had died in succession of illness after illness, about the bullying policemen who didn't hesitate to help themselves to an "official fee" paid in kind, about her fading hopes of ever breaking free of "the game," about all the things she had probably never had the opportunity to share with anyone, and that no one had ever heard out in full. Beetroot Mary's life was laid open like a black, bottomless pit into which Zofia felt herself falling deeper and deeper.

"But you wanted to know about Olesia, not me," the woman finally said. "She met a fancy man. He wasn't bothered about her being a professional, perhaps he thought it'd work out cheaper for him that way. And she wasn't the type to be fussy neither . . . which of the girls is, anyway? And this Dunin, because that's who he was, vouched for her at the police and had them remove her . . ."

"Remove her?"

"From the register of prostitutes. If a fiancé vouches for her, they cross the girl's name off and she doesn't have to report for health checks and all that no more. She's free. For a while she stopped working, settled in Dębniki . . ."

"On Różana Street?"

"Ee, no," said Mary, shaking her head, and her body was racked by spasms of coughing again. "She only went there when she met that Jew."

"A Jew?"

"I don't know much about him. A big shot. They must have come to terms, she became his floozy, his lover, because Dunin was put out to grass, then he got a knife between the ribs in Podgórze anyway so that was the end of him, and that Jew stayed on with her as her ponce."

"Who did you say?" asked Zofia.

"Her ponce, like I said. Pander. He bought her an 'ouse; he started the brothel and set her up in business. Now she's a great lady, she's the madame, she's forgotten her old friends, turns her nose up at us, the devil take her . . ."

"Mr. Pander, did you say? Do you recall his full name?" Zofia quickly asked, wishing to avoid the litany of oaths she was expecting to hear.

"Somehow it's slipped my mind. I can't remember what he's called."

"What do you mean? You said his name is Pander . . ."

The woman shook her head, and something resembling a smile appeared on her lips.

"You ladies in hats, you don't understand a thing. That's what the keepers are called, panders. I don't know nothing about that Jew."

They sat awhile in silence, until finally she remembered something else.

"Oh, but the doctor might be able to tell you more about him. He knows his way around the business, who's who and what's what, and he's a good man. Whenever a girl's in trouble she goes to him, no matter if she's Jewish or Christian. He tried to cure Faiga, but it didn't work—it must have been her destiny," she said, shrugging.

"The doctor? My husband . . ." said Zofia, and bit her lip. "That is, my late husband . . . I am a widow, as you can see . . . kept company with doctors, so perhaps his name will mean something to me."

"Dr. Roth," said the prostitute, striking a note of genuine respect. "On Skawińska Street, at the Israelite hospital."

"The Israelite hospital? No, my husband definitely did not know him!" said Zofia, slightly dismayed. But she made a note of the name. Then she coldly said goodbye to Beetroot Mary, too coldly perhaps, and taking a roundabout route, frequently looking back to be sure no one was following her, she finally reached home.

Franciszka was standing in the window, as if to wash the newly fitted panes of glass, which were still covered in the glazier's fingerprints, but actually to send Zofia a signal to say that neither Józia nor Ignacy was at home. She solemnly nodded, and then an oddly dressed, slightly bizarre figure passed through the gateway of Peacock House before running at top speed into the flat and retreating into the bedroom, where she finally restored herself to her proper, dignified shape.

CHAPTER IX

In which Zofia Turbotyńska sets out for exotic lands in the company of a brave squire, learns the difference between a mother-of-pearl casket and a sack of potatoes, and is persecuted by a duck.

From the gateway of Dębno House, directly below the bastions of the Royal Castle, an ancient woman had just emerged in widow's weeds, crowned with an old-fashioned bonnet that looked like a crow's nest; she was leaning on the arm of an equally ancient servant in a rather faded, tatty frock coat. Judging by the little leather-bound prayer book tightly gripped in the lady's arthritic fingers, they were on their way to mass at one of the nearby churches. Zofia strode past them, then past two slow-moving nuns, a young officer leaning over to stuff his pipe, and many other people too. She was in a hurry. On the right, the wide facade of the Bernardine church flashed by, on the left, the Church of the Missionaries, and finally the former St. Jadwiga's, rebuilt a century ago by the Austrians to be offices of some kind, and then the post office; a couple of years ago when the new post office building was erected on Wielopole Street—"worthy of Lemberg or Vienna," as people rather extravagantly said—one of the numerous military institutions, the garrison command, had taken up residence on Stradom Street, and now as she passed the windows she saw the figures of army pencil pushers sitting at their desks.

In the distance she could see a green strip of young trees in the stretch of Planty Park along Dietl Street, and at the corner, between the facade of the Jacobsohns' grand mansion, with its huge terrace, and a wooden kiosk, she spotted a figure, tiny from this perspective, but gradually growing: it was a thin, slightly stooping young man with a head of black hair, Tadeusz Kamil Marcjan Żeleński, medical student.

"Ah, Mrs. Turbotyńska," he said, bowing, "what a surprise!"

"Mr. Żeleński, how nice to see you."

"Which way are you going?" he asked.

She looked to either side.

"To the hospital . . . the Jewish hospital, on Skawińska Street."

He offered her his arm. The laconic note she had sent to him via Franek, the invaluable messenger boy from the

Commercial Union of Farmers' Associations, lay safely in his jacket pocket.

My dear sir! I should be most obliged to you if you would kindly meet me on an important matter tomorrow, at noon precisely, in Planty Park on the corner of Dietl and Stradom Streets, and then grant me an hour or two of your time. May chance observers regard this meeting as accidental.

"I did not telephone to avoid cause for gossip. Servants are not always discreet. The matters of which you shall learn must remain between us," she explained in a hushed tone, as they walked along crowded Krakowska Street. "It seems Karolina's murderer has not been punished at all. But we can discover him with the help of a certain doctor, whom, however . . . I do not know personally . . . nor would I wish to call on him alone. Especially as to reach him one is obliged to go through . . . this district."

A small wagon loaded with baskets of apples rumbled past them, harnessed to a brisk young carthorse. As they were now *on a walk,* the right thing to do was to hold a conversation.

"How are your dear parents?"

"Oh, they are extremely busy . . . as you know, Cracow is hosting . . ."

"Mr. Paderewski, of course."

"Yes, his pupil Miss Szumowska has just married Mr.

Adamowski, the cellist, who is a good friend of Paderewski, and the maestro came specially for their wedding. As apparently did Mr. Górski, first violin at the Paris Opera. On Wednesday my parents are giving a farewell party for them at our house on St. Sebastian's Street."

"It is sure to be a splendid occasion!" said Zofia enthusiastically, counting on being invited; she hadn't succeeded with Modejska, but perhaps with Paderewski she might?

"There will be no one but musicians," he said, shattering her illusions, "or people connected with music in one way or another, if only through family, such as the maestro's sister . . . or Mrs. Stojowska, who runs a musical salon. In any case, she is the mother of the pianist and composer, Zygmunt . . ." He dodged to avoid a generously built lady. "Either way, you can easily imagine that the whole house is in a state of preparation. My mother is busy planning what to serve and how to cook it, while my father is drafting a different menu — of the music to be played, because once they all get together, each one will put on a show . . . the latest idea is to play a few new songs and excerpts from the opera *Goplana*, but it is hard to say if that is the final version."

"No doubt a true musical feast is in store," replied Zofia, this time without enthusiasm, now that she knew this celebration would pass her by too.

"Fortunately it will have a set limit," he said sarcastically, "because Paderewski and Górski have to catch a train, and will need to be taken to the station."

Meanwhile the scenery had changed: crowded, shabby Krakowska Street had none of the grand sweep of Dietl Street. At every point there were clusters of men in long, almost floor-length overcoats, loudly debating matters that seemed to Zofia mysterious, because they were immersed in a strange, unfamiliar jargon, with only a slight resemblance to German; but she was amused to think that in reality they were probably just as prosaic as the things discussed on Szczepański Square, or at the stalls in the Kleparz market. Here and there she could see an old man with a long white beard, some of them in round fur hats, elsewhere old women in embroidered bonnets and patterned aprons. Next to the shop names in Polish and German, such as *Anna Rubinstein—MIDWIFE—HEBAMME,* there were twisting, fiery letters that looked as if they were announcing something grand and sacred, though if one were to believe their Polish equivalents, they only meant: *KOSHER MEATS FACTORY, Fresh Sausages Daily,* or *Victuals Sold Here.*

Now they were deep inside a world of other words, other physiognomies, and other smells; even the culinary odors wafting from the low, dark gateways were different here from in the poor Christian districts. They walked along streets with low-rise, dirty little houses, maybe just as ancient as Peacock House, but undoubtedly much poorer. The damp, lichen-coated walls looking as if they should be taken to a dermatological clinic suddenly came to an end, giving way to a low fence consisting of a brick base topped with simple little posts and railings, past which some spindly trees were visible, and beyond them, in a large, empty plot, there was a two-story building slightly set back from Skawińska Street. This was the Jewish hospital. How miserable it looked compared with the impressive, newly built Collegium Medicum building, a veritable palace with a rusticated base course and slender Corinthian columns!

"It looks like a provincial railway halt," said Zofia.

"Or the barracks in a small town," agreed Tadeusz.

"At least there is some decoration around the windows, otherwise a person would be afraid to go inside," she said, passing through a gate, politely set open, "for fear of ending up in an abattoir, not a hospital."

Informed in advance, Dr. Roth was waiting for them in his consulting room; he opened the door to them in person, and showed them to two scuffed wooden stools, while he sat down in an armchair that must have known better days. The room was very narrow, but it had a high ceiling with some tawny stains on it, forming the map of a land no one would wish to go to. The suite of furniture, simple and incomplete, may have been bought from a wealthier hospital or clinic. There was an odor of wet rags and illness.

"We have very modest conditions here, I'm afraid," said the doctor apologetically.

"So I have noticed. Even the building is . . . restrained," said Zofia. "I was expecting something smarter, more up-to-date."

Roth laughed.

"Oh, Mrs. Turbotyńska, you must be one of those people who mistakenly thinks the Jews like extravagance."

"I have heard it said . . ." she replied, awkwardly trying to extricate herself.

"Our hospital was built thirty years ago, when different tastes were in fashion. In any case, the community has never been well off, not then and not now. It was built by Mr. Stacherski, a Catholic. He designed churches, too, but unfortunately he died young. I do not think he lived to the age of thirty."

"Ah, that is a curious fact. So a Catholic built a Jewish hospital, and meanwhile Mr. Sare, who has only just completed his work on the Collegium Medicum, is, after all . . . descended from an Orthodox family."

"Yes, he is a Jew," said the doctor, putting it more precisely.

An awkward silence fell. And here Żeleński, as a student at the medical faculty, turned to professional language, clearly to dilute the odium of a shameful topic.

"We have taken the liberty of disturbing you because Mrs. Turbotyńska, a well-known philanthropist, wishes to become familiar with the medical and social aspects of prostitution. Rumor has it that by token of your practice at this hospital, among . . . the more indigent classes . . . you have gained great experience, and may be able to help us with your knowledge . . ." At this point he paused, then suddenly completed his speech, as if recognizing that it sufficed, ". . . in this field."

"Ah, philanthropy, a fine thing," he replied, though it wasn't clear if he meant to be courteous or sarcastic. "Collecting money for noble causes . . . very nice, very nice. But on this question, I am afraid that fine ideas and noble efforts are not enough — what we need here is to rebuild . . . the whole of society. Not just in our country, but worldwide, I would say. And that is a task requiring years, decades, centuries perhaps."

For a while he stared at the desktop in silence, as if hoping to find some advice or help there.

"Who recommended me to you?" he suddenly asked. "I did not know that any of the doctors outside Kazimierz were in the least bit aware of my existence. I lead a modest life, as you can see, moving to and fro between home and the hospital, but I do not attend meetings at important institutions, I do not go to mass, or frequent drawing rooms, and I rarely venture beyond Planty Park. How kind of someone to have . . ."

"It was not in fact a doctor," said Zofia cautiously, "but one of the ladies who cares about the welfare of women."

Roth nodded.

"A good thing too," he said. "It is nice to meet a kindred spirit, and I am pleased that more and more society ladies, like you, are showing a socially caring attitude by championing the rights of women. This is exactly what I mean," he continued enthusiastically. "Without a fundamental change in the female role, without casting off the corset confining modern woman, without subjectifying women, without giving them the right to vote and making them equal to men, we shall never eradicate the disgrace of our century known as 'paid love.' Ha, love! Simply placing that word alongside 'payment' tarnishes it. But surely that needs no explanation."

Zofia put a brave face on it, and said nothing to betray the fact that she was far from being a supporter of women's equality, while Żeleński sat with a stony face, evidently doubled up with laughter inside at the idea that whether she liked it or not, the professor's wife had become a militant emancipationist. Meanwhile Roth was silent, weighing something in his mind; a small man, clad in a rather threadbare jacket, he looked like a draft animal with a large, heavy head, coarse features, and a furrowed brow.

"I would not wish to be misunderstood," he said at last, "but the issue in question cannot be expounded in a manner suitable for repetition at the tea table or . . . at a charitable reception. We are talking of a descent into Dantean darkness, into the inner circles of hell. I realize that the demands of courtesy forbid one to discuss such matters with the ladies. But I also know that there are some women who have broken free of the false limitations of their sex, and that one can talk to them on equal terms. Because community workers . . ." At this point his brow wrinkled even more. "Community workers have no gender. They are above gender. They take life and the world as they are, and do their best to change them, to shape them with their own strength, they do their best . . ."

Żeleński had taken a cigarette case from his pocket and had fixed his gaze on it, whereas Zofia focused her attention on the doctor, and then interrupted him.

"Dr. Roth, these things are perfectly understandable. Please do not spare my blushes. We have greater concerns."

Recognition flashed in the doctor's eyes: here he had found one of his own kind.

"I take it you have read Engineer Szczepanowski's *The Poverty of Galicia in Figures*?" he asked.

He had miscalculated. Zofia remembered Ignacy dipping into it, and then railing against the defamation of Galicia and Lodomeria, "after all, one only has to walk about Cracow to see for oneself that nobody here is dying of hunger."

"Ah, I understand," said Roth. "Well then, let us start from the beginning. Our country is one of the most densely populated in Europe—three-quarters, if not four-fifths of the population are employed in agriculture, and each square mile has to nourish far more people than elsewhere, except perhaps for China and parts of India. But our agriculture is backward—each Englishman produces six times as much meat and milk and over three times as much agricultural produce as our peasant. All our combined industry, mining, and handicrafts bring less income per head than in the Congress Kingdom, for example, and on top of that a large part of the money goes toward repaying foreign capital. Of all the countries in the world, labor in Galicia is the least productive! But at the same time, if the same worker is transferred to America, or Westphalia, let us say, to better conditions, where he is treated like a human being, he works far more productively and is valued for his diligence. Why is that?"

"It is all to do with malnourishment," said Żeleński. "The Galician is badly nourished, in fact he's starving, so he hasn't the strength to work. He works badly, so he reaps a poor harvest. And then he has to sell most of it in order to pay taxes, buy shoes or an apron for his wife. He also has to pay up for the ever growing nonproductive classes: the army and the bureaucracy."

"Quite so. Our entire population eats far less than England's paupers, who are supported at public expense, and the food here is not adequate to maintain existence. That is why the people here are becoming stunted, we have"—at this point he struck his open palm against the desktop —"the highest percentage of men who are unfit for military service in all Europe. The average male life expectancy is twenty-seven years. In England it is forty. Each year we lose more than fifty thousand people to death by starvation, and twice as many again to common illnesses that attack their weakened organisms. One hundred thousand have died of cholera alone in the past two years!"

"But that is more than the entire population of Cracow!" said Zofia in surprise.

"Quite so, quite so. On the face of it, all this might seem inessential. But I am telling you this because moralists of every stripe, priests preaching sermons from the pulpit . . .

You smiled. Well, perhaps it amuses you to hear a Jew complaining about Catholic priests, but the moralists are the same everywhere—the rabbis are hardly different ... In any case, all these people claim that prostitution is a matter of morality." At this point Zofia felt like asking: "But is that not so?" but she bit her tongue. "When in fact it is a matter of economy. Purely and simply economy. We can only talk of ethical choice when we are dealing with genuine choice. Please forgive the example, but can a woman who is forced to do something by a man who has put a gun to her head be said to be acting immorally?"

"And those women may not have a gun to their heads," said Żeleński, "but are facing death by starvation, a far longer and more painful end."

"One's own death is not so bad, for one can sacrifice one's own life on the altar of virtue, as they say," said Roth, adopting a derisively lofty tone. "Although it is a heroism that we should never demand of anyone. But what about the life of a child that day by day is slowly fading away before its mother's eyes? Instead of railing against the 'licentiousness of women,' which of those moralists would have the courage to condemn our entire social outlook?"

Zofia and Żeleński nodded in mute agreement.

"In the Galician countryside it is plain to see that prostitution seems to be the only path for these girls, who lack even the most basic education, who suffer from poverty and are treated at home like farm animals, in some cases like slaves, forced to satisfy the base needs of their male neighbors, fathers, uncles, and cousins, because it is in those dark cottages that the worst degeneracy occurs . . . and a girl has only to fall pregnant for the very men who have defiled her to become strict moralists: either they make her get rid of the fetus with the help of a village abortionist, otherwise known as an 'angel maker,' who often sends the girl off to the next world in the process, too; or else they drive her out of the family village. And a girl of this kind, who has seen nothing beyond her own parish, beyond a small patch of land with a Catholic or Orthodox church, or a synagogue, must suddenly survive as a vagabond. Surely you are aware of the institution known as the 'servants' fair'? Every Thursday, at the Market Square, on the western side of the Cloth Hall?"

"I always hire my maids from Mrs. Mikulska's employment agency on Gołębia Street. A licensed agency," declared Zofia with pride. "But of course I know about the fair, everyone does."

"But does everyone know what is really going on there? I promise you, the girls standing outside the Cloth Hall are not just of interest to Cracow's respectable townswomen. A girl of that sort, who has only just arrived in the big city full of lights, imposing buildings, and crowds of people"—in Roth's account Cracow suddenly took on the role of a great city, Paris, London, or New York—"is, as I have said, naive. And lets herself be tricked by the first 'kind lady' she meets, who says she will 'take care' of her, lends her money for a new dress and a corner to live in, and thus slyly drives her into alleged debts, from which she won't be able to extricate herself and which she can only pay back in one way. Or else she falls for the persuasions of an amiable gentleman who offers her a well-paid job as a home help or childminder, which turns out on the spot to be common prostitution. It is nothing else but modern slavery," said Roth, going completely red. "The peasant has been freed from serfdom, but the woman has been pushed into an even more dreadful form of it."

"But there are cases," said Żeleński, "of women who go into this . . . profession without being cheated or forced by anyone. I remember an item in the newspaper a few years ago about a girl from the countryside who ended up in somewhere like Rio de Janeiro, made fabulous money there, died prematurely, and left her father a fortune. And when the whole story became known in that village or small town, the young women began to vie with each other to buy tickets to go to . . ."

"My dear sir, my dear sir," Roth interrupted him, "I know what you are talking about. It is the story of Jelena . . . I cannot remember her surname, from near Śniatyn, a famous case. No one knows how she bought her way out of that, er, industry. Suffice it to say that she died in Havana, Cuba, because the place in question was Havana, not Rio, as the wealthy owner of a brothel and left her entire fortune to her old father, who in any case soon squandered it all and died in even greater poverty than he had suffered before. But did anyone actually see those thousands of guldens of hers? Indeed, it was in the press, and at once the procurers were ready and waiting for those young ladies who suddenly dreamed of bringing boxes of gold home to the peasant cottage . . . I would not be surprised if the whole story was made up in one of the taverns by a council of old pimps and then passed to the press. Well, as ever, what's really to blame is poverty, poverty and lack of education," he said, sadly shaking his head. "Am I to understand," he said, addressing Zofia, "that your interest in this matter arises from working with the Society for People's Schools?"

Until now Zofia had been listening to the doctor's discourse patiently, although for a while she'd been feeling as if she'd somehow ended up at a socialist rally, listening to that "golden-tongued Ignacy" Daszyński making a speech. In other words, she could make many allowances, but she refused to be associated with Mrs. Bujwid.

"Oh, no!" she vehemently protested. "The reason is one particular dramatic incident. My maid"—here she took a deep breath—"has been murdered. Abducted and murdered."

The doctor sat up in his chair.

"By sex trade touts? People traffickers?"

"That had not occurred to me," gasped Zofia in amazement. "Nor did the police follow a lead of that kind. But I do know that a certain young man, posing as an engineer, beguiled her with an offer of marriage. I also know that he worked at a . . . *maison de convenance.* She handed in her notice, intending to be married to him and then leave for America."

"Oh, that is a very typical *modus operandi,* and unfortunately is especially common with the Jewish criminal set." At this point he paused, as if considering something. "I think, madam, by now you have, by now you have both realized . . ." he went on, addressing Żeleński too, "that I am a man who speaks his mind, and will not moderate his words merely to avoid offending anyone's self-esteem. And that is why in many circles I am a veritable pariah, an untouchable who is not welcome at meetings, either social or academic. By a strange coincidence, invitations from the Medical Society fail to reach me, though that is less surprising—after all, racial prejudices are very much alive in Cracow. But the Jewish philanthropic organizations do not invite me either. Why is that? I can boldly say that, to my great regret, it's because much of the blame for human trafficking lies at the feet of our ethnicity."

"But that is grist for the mill of every anti-Semite, of course," said Żeleński.

"Unfortunately, I must agree with you. There are people who are happy to spout the sort of vile nonsense that says 'prostitution involves an active male, a passive female, and a catalyzing Jew.' In fact, while the oppressors include Jews, so do the victims. Not only do most of the traffickers happen to be Jews (who also pay large bribes to Polish and Austrian policemen and officials of all ranks), but most of their victims are, too. Far more Jewish girls go off to the brothels of Turkey, the United States, and Argentina than Polish or Ruthenian girls. One could say it is a crime committed within the family. And of course, there is plenty to be said about the reasons for this state of affairs, about the unfairly inferior place of Jews within Polish society, within the entire empire, about the centuries of neglect and prejudice, but still . . ."

"You spoke of a *modus operandi,*" Żeleński reminded him.

Meanwhile the afternoon clouds had thickly coated the entire sky, and it was even gloomier in the consulting room than before. Wherever the polish had worn off, the desktop was entirely black, and wherever the raw wood had already gone smooth and shiny, there was a livid glow, like the skin of a corpse.

"Yes, there seems to be one. Usually a good match appears: an engineer, a banker, or a merchant, on a brief trip from America, to which he emigrated a few years ago and where he has made a rapid career, of course. He is young, handsome, well dressed; he spares no cost to buy expensive gifts. He has come back to the old country to find a girl from a decent Jewish home, devout and pure. The measure of a virgin hymen"—here he cleared his throat, and Zofia dropped her gaze—"is purely financial; it is a tangible, valuable piece of merchandise for which one can demand the relevant rate, especially if the girl is particularly pretty. A matchmaker, male or female, presses her, saying that the young man must return to America quickly to see to his flourishing business, so the wedding ceremony is performed in a rush by a supplied rabbi. The couple leaves at high speed, and after a while the same young man comes back, as a bachelor again, to seek a wife not in Borysław this time, but in Rovno or the Drohobycz area."

"Almost all of it tallies," replied Zofia, "except for the crucial detail that my maid was a Catholic. She was to be married in Hamburg, by a local priest, supposedly a personal friend of the engineer."

"What counts is the girl, not her denomination," said Roth, shrugging. "Despite the prejudices common among the hoi polloi, a Jewish girl is not anatomically different from a Ruthenian or a Polish girl. Excuse me for asking such a question, but was your maid a virgin?"

"That we do know with certainty. A postmortem was performed, her death was caused by a single thrust of a sharp instrument into the heart, but Dr. Kurkiewicz discovered that shortly before her demise, the victim"—it felt strange to be talking about Karolina in such an impersonal way—"had been violated."

"Dr. Kurkiewicz," said Roth, livening up, "ah, yes, an odd fellow. I have come across him several times. I cannot say that I feel any great sympathy for him."

"I suspect every doctor and every medical student in this city could say the same thing," said Żeleński, laughing.

"Why didn't Schwarz do the postmortem?"

"Kurkiewicz was assisting him that day," explained Zofia, "and he recognized the body, because he had been to our house a few times when escorting my husband home from the university."

"What an extraordinary coincidence."

"Are you trying to make an insinuation?" asked Żeleński, who plainly had a strong interest in the investigation too.

"No, of course not. But surely you will agree that it is an odd concurrence of fate. Especially as Mr. Kurkiewicz has had a long-term interest in questions concerning sex, and that, I would say, in a somewhat pathological manner."

Could it have been him? thought Zofia feverishly. *But that is absurd; after all, if he had wanted to win her over, he would not have had to imitate Bzowski, nor hire someone to pose as him . . . But on the other hand, his attitude to Karolina was always more than just courteous. Apparently every time he saw her, he paid her a compliment.*

"But never mind about that, something else entirely is worrying me," muttered Roth. "If he had already abducted her, violating her on the spot would have been totally unprofitable. Was she attractive?"

"Yes, she was, I can bear witness to that," said Żeleński. "She was a very attractive young person."

"The dealers have their own criminal jargon, in which they call the ugly girls 'sacks of potatoes.' The pretty ones, especially the virgins, are sold as 'carpets from Smyrna' or 'bales of silk,' and the most beautiful as 'diamond crosses' and 'mother-of-pearl caskets.' And indeed, they often fetch staggering prices on the black market. They could have beaten her if she resisted, but not mutilated her, or left any permanent marks—during the journey to Turkey or Argentina the bruises would have faded. But why kill her?"

"What if she tried to escape? Then somebody might have shot at her," thought Zofia aloud. "But as he stabbed her, he could just as well have grabbed hold of her and dragged her back to a hiding place where she could have been kept until she was dispatched abroad."

"There are sometimes quarrels among the captive girls. I have come across a case of this kind," added Roth, "but death by a single knife thrust is the work of a professional, not a desperate seventeen- or eighteen-year-old girl who might at most scratch her fellow victim, or tear out a clump of her hair. I can't see the sense in it, nothing here tallies with business, and white slave trafficking is above all a business. A dreadful one, but calculated, counting every cent. Who would botch the job like that? Do we know at which establishment this alleged engineer was employed?"

"We even know his name. Wolf Sztycer, otherwise Zeev Szyfryn."

"I have not come across him," said the doctor, spreading his hands, "but I am mainly occupied with sick and suffering women, not their oppressors."

"And his workplace is on Różana Street. The owner is a woman named Dunin."

"Oh yes, I know the place. A minor footnote: Dunin is not the owner, just the figurehead. The establishment belongs to a man named Lewicki, or Loewenstein. You are sure to have heard of him."

"But we do not know people from that sphere," said Zofia indignantly.

"The Lemberg trial? Surely you remember it. Three or four years ago a fairly large group of traffickers was convicted in Lemberg, including this man Loewenstein. Just like the others, he was given a short sentence. I cannot remember the exact length of time, but they were all sent down for three months, six months, or a year at most. He served his time, and once he was at liberty again, naturally he put the remains of his former wealth to use. He had not lost the brothel in the course of the trial, because he had entrusted it, and his other dubious enterprises, to his most reliable associates. Such as the aforementioned Mrs. Dunin, who on her own would immediately have fallen victim to the competition, if not for the discreet care of her patron. He changed his name officially, and now he has various businesses as Szymon Lewicki: a timber firm here, a tavern there, a colonial store somewhere else, so he's a respectable Podgórze tradesman. But on the side he reaps a profit from the place in Dębniki. And that is how it all works."

"So he is the procurer for that woman . . . her . . . *pander*?" As Zofia said this word, Żeleński's eyes opened wide. "And no one puts a stop to it?" she continued in outrage, because suddenly she could see that prostitution was a more serious matter than just the disagreeable sight of a tired old harlot in an alley off St. Thomas's Street. "Such a vast extent of human injustice goes virtually unpunished?"

Resting his wrinkled forehead on his long waxy fingers, the doctor scowled at her.

"Who do you think cares? Who cares about some simple village girls or some skinny little misses from damp basements? Once they were here and now they're gone, they may have died of consumption, or rickets, but at least they're out of our sight. Madam, if you only knew, if you both knew how often I have been accused of looking after trollops and strumpets instead of lavishing my care on no one but respectable matrons in wigs and young wives giving birth to legal offspring, sanctified by a wedding under a canopy . . . As if the one were in contradiction to the other! If you had seen some of the cases, some of the cases . . ." He fixed his gaze on the dark desktop, and it looked as if he were staring deep inside himself, once again seeing all those genital sores and syphilitic ulcers, those emaciated, bruised bodies that had ceased to give anyone pleasure and had been thrown out like old rags, those twenty- and thirty-year-old women who looked like their own mothers, bent double, utterly destroyed. "But of course the progressive doctors, such as I, are always the greatest enemies of the religious doctors, who think a physician should be the punishing hand of God . . . Very Christian, isn't it? But it's an attitude that's widespread among Jews as well. Meanwhile I swore an oath to save human life unconditionally, not to treat only those whom some self-appointed committee has issued with a certificate of morality . . . Oh dear," he said, smiling in resignation, "here in this forgotten corner of the city, we are far more backward than the Cracovians on the other side of Dietl Street!"

"You are too severe," replied Żeleński. "Nowadays, when the emir of Afghanistan's doctor is a woman . . ."

"Miss Hamilton," said Zofia; for some reason the name had stuck in her memory.

"Miss Hamilton, thank you, who in that half-savage Asian country has been introducing inoculations to protect against smallpox, and who is jointly establishing a truly European pharmacy there, in short, these days, when even in a Muslim country the health of the entire nation has been entrusted to a woman, our medical faculty is still going to great lengths not to admit women as students. And Professor Bujwid is called all sorts of names purely because he wants to provide female doctors for a society that is suffering from an acute lack of male ones!"

Dr. Roth glanced at the window, then said: "And what good is it to me if everything at other hospitals and at the university is old, rotten, and soulless too . . ." This made Zofia feel quite indignant, but she didn't say a word. "A community worker," he paused, "a community worker sees the whole world before him, and finds no consolation in the fact that somewhere else it is equally bad or even worse. He should always devote himself entirely to making things slightly better at some place on earth. So he spends his whole life on this task, and then lies down in his grave with a sense of having tirelessly performed, but never completed his duty, a lonely, exhausted, totally embittered corpse," he concluded, in a surprisingly joyful tone, and it occurred to Zofia that in spite of all this misery Dr. Roth was not devoid of a singular sense of humor.

When they left, the clouds were still hanging low over Kazimierz, as if trying to press the crooked little houses even more firmly to the ground; there wasn't a storm on the horizon, it was just dark and gloomy; even if they had visited Corpus Christi church, in this dull gray murk its soaring nave shimmering with gold would have lost the honeyed tone emanating from the old gilding and the warm tinge of the wood.

Zofia was grateful to young Tadeusz for his help and would have been happy to return to their casual conversation, to the gossip about Paderewski and the musical evening, but they were both too crushed by Dr. Roth's words, so they walked in virtual silence, just uttering a few words now and then for the sake of appearances, until finally they parted where earlier they had met—on the corner of Stradom Street, below the terrace of the Jacobsohn house. Naturally, Żeleński offered to escort her all the way home to St. John's Street, yet she thanked him politely, but firmly; she wanted to be alone.

From there she walked more slowly, pondering everything she had heard today. Could it be true that in Cracow, a city of eminent professors, splendid foundations, countless churches and monasteries, reverent processions carrying the relics of saintly patrons, so much squalor lay hidden? Now the city was revealing a completely different face to her: dark, brutal, and incomprehensible. Hypocritical fathers, little houses on the outskirts, ruthless people traffickers, and young village girls transformed in just a few short years into worn-out wrecks consumed by vile diseases. Could Beetroot Mary once have been attractive? Zofia tried to remember her round, red face, to find a reflection of that former beauty in it. Would the same fate have befallen Karolina? If so, perhaps it was better to have died at once from a single thrust of the knife, or other sharp instrument.

But what if . . . she thought feverishly, so preoccupied that she failed to notice the assistant from Maurizio's bowing to her with a smile, on his way to one of the wealthy houses with a stack of chocolate boxes. *What if she was not abducted at all? What if, earlier on, she was already . . . after all, she brought those dresses home, those trinkets, and hid them from her employers . . . But her virginity is a clear sign, her virginity is, one might say, Karolina's medically certified moral alibi.*

She could breathe easily. But at once she felt tight in the chest again, and was forced to stop at the top of Grodzka Street when an entirely new thought occurred: *What if, as in the past, a medical error has been made? No, it is impossible. Kurkiewicz would have to have lied on purpose, what is more he was assisting police doctor Schwarz. But who could prove they checked everything together? What if Schwarz left the room for a while, what if he left the entire postmortem to Kurkiewicz? Or let us suppose . . . all this is written in the wind, but then . . . let us suppose he did not find any signs of injury at all. What would that mean? What suspicion, and against whom, would he be trying to distance by certifying this particular falsehood? What if this "sexlorist," obsessed with matters of the flesh, who so often complimented Karolina's beauty, was her secret lover, posing as Bzowski? Nonsense, Franciszka would have recognized him!*

At last she moved on, but crossed the Market Square slowly, as if wading through thick, viscous tar, as if a countercurrent were pushing her back the whole time, never giving her a moment's relief; she felt beads of perspiration erupt on her brow, which in spite of her face powder, gathered and trickled down her cheeks. Something was telling her that the unappealing young Kurkiewicz knew decidedly too much. Her intuitive dislike of him had now become clear and understandable: she had simply perceived the darkness that lurked inside him long ago. The mere thought that she would have to have an encounter with him sent an icy shiver down her back, from her frilly collar to the edge of her bustle.

That night she was tormented by bad dreams, which she put down to an overgenerous supper the next morning, though she knew that her sleeping imagination had come up with some terrifying scenes based on scraps of knowledge, images, and forebodings. Kurkiewicz had been standing in a sort of old-fashioned anatomical theater, explaining that his work had to be on a grand scale, and thus it included experiments and research on living organisms. On a stone table before him lay Karolina, with a red bloodstain on her chest, her body blue as if she were dead, and yet she was entirely conscious, with her eyes wide-open, blinking every few seconds. On each tier of the theater stood naked men; one had thrown on a coat, a second wore just a top hat, another had nothing but leather gloves. They were watching Kurkiewicz, who was preparing his scalpels to perform the dissection, but he was taking his time, carefully choosing the right instrument, which turned out to be a costly dagger studded with precious gemstones. Gradually the men were descending from the upper to the lower tiers, and from those to the very bottom, until they were closely surrounding the stone tabletop and the corpse, or rather non-corpse lying on it, which awoke their unrestrained desire . . .

"I shall never have stuffed duck for supper again," she said to herself in the morning, as she pulled sweat-soaked strands of hair from under her nightcap, "never again!"

CHAPTER X

In which a hot week starts with an encounter with a jingling rat, a bearded librarian shows off his knowledge of argot, and the press tears aside a curtain of appearances. We encounter Job again, who claims children should not spend time in Cracow's parks; we also find out that a certain medical student is neglecting his customary habits, and Zofia Turbotyńska pushes her way alone into the cave of a red lion marked by the emblem of a lamb.

On Friday 7 September 1896, Zofia Turbotyńska went to the university. No, she did not go to visit Ignacy at the anatomy department, as she occasionally did—she would use the excuse of being on her way to a tea party, or an outing to Strzelecki Park or to the palm house to carry out a merciless inspection of his study, repositioning ("tidying," as she put it) the papers on his desk and cutting short all attempts at protest with a categorical: "It is purely for your convenience, Ignacy." So no, this time Zofia made her way to the university's fount of knowledge, the Jagiellonian Library, to find some information on the Lemberg trial that Dr. Roth had mentioned, and thus about the mysterious Loewenstein-Lewicki, keeper of Mrs. Dunin, the employer in her turn of Wolf Sztycer.

Following the rainstorms of the day before, the Market Square had rarely been as clean; the next day was the feast of the Nativity of Mary, less noisily celebrated in the city, but important for the peasants, for whom it was the day when the priest would bless their seeds for sowing, so most of them were at home in their villages, apart from a few stragglers who had come to town at the last minute to buy something essential for the holiday but unavailable elsewhere. So most of the people Zofia could see in her vicinity were from the higher classes, plus a few workmen, errand boys, and flower girls. Zofia set sail into the broad expanse of the main square and glided across it like the flagship of the Cracow bourgeoisie, bedecked with frills, hooks and eyes, and buttons, and flying as her ensign a large crimson plume on her hat.

As she walked, she pondered the mysterious Lemberg case. Of course she had heard of the Wadowice trial—no one in Cracow, probably no one in the whole Kingdom of Galicia and Lodomeria could have failed to follow the news from that sleepy, Godforsaken local town some seven years ago; no one imagined anything of interest could ever emerge from Wadowice, and suddenly the whole world had turned its gaze on it. Everyone remembered the horde of foreign journalists who came down to Cracow and took rooms at almost all the better hotels; as well as the usual Polish and German, one could hear French and English at the cafés and restaurants, and suddenly the city had gained a truly international sheen. Along the way, most of the citizens tried to ignore the unpalatable fact that the foreign reporters were not drawn there by the beauty of royal Cracow or its splendid monuments to the majestic past, but by a criminal scandal on an extraordinary scale — in, God help us, Wadowice.

Representatives of the Oświęcim branch of the Hamburg emigration agency were almost entirely in control of voyages to the west. But their agents turned out to have been recruiting emigrants through bribery, blackmail, even violence, physically forcing peasants to buy tickets for ships to America. On top of that, it appeared that dozens of people had been breaking the law for almost a decade, while the state officials did not just leave them in peace, but were in close collaboration with them: a customs inspector was mixed up in it all, and so was the local mayor. According to Cousin Dutkiewicz — a fact the newspapers hadn't mentioned at all — the hotel where the whole practice had taken place belonged to Count Potocki, but somehow Zofia, along with almost all of Cracow, could not believe it. The city preferred to turn a blind eye to a scandal that cast a shadow on the imperial administration, so there were just some loud complaints about the so-called "rapacious Jews," meaning the main defendants, Klausner and Herz, who became household names in Cracow, the main topic of conversation over coffee, tea, Pischinger cake, and Tafelspitz.

The Lemberg trial was quite another matter. Young Żeleński seemed familiar with the case, but Zofia had never heard of it, although she read the *Cracow Times*—perhaps not as carefully as Ignacy, but fairly regularly, only omitting the "Political Review" section, which was filled with endless speculation on the subject of cabinet crises, analyses of elections to the Prague city council, and accounts of visits paid to the Russian tsar by the Ottoman envoy. Evidently, reports of the trial must have slipped her notice and she would have to study the news again.

Ignacy was in the habit of keeping back numbers of the *Times,* but rising piles of "wastepaper" drove Zofia spare, and she had long since been waging an underhand war on them. Sometimes she would shift a pile from here to there, or else she would pretend to have tripped over one; but mainly, with merciless regularity, she rolled her eyes dramatically, while uttering the immortal words: "Ignacy, for the love of God, when will you *finally* deal with it all? It's impossible to live like this." Until at last it happened—a few months ago, Ignacy stopped collecting cuttings on the more interesting events in Europe and the world (with special regard for the peregrinations of members of the ruling houses), and capitulated.

Some of the newspapers had ended up in the kitchen as kindling, but the rest had been given to an itinerant rag-and-bone man who had knocked at the Turbotyńskis' door asking for "any old rubbish." He had been given several pots too worn out for the tinkers, a broken mousetrap, and the remaining issues of the *Cracow Times,* stuffed into a disintegrating wicker basket. If Zofia had been in less of a hurry to get rid of items she regarded as "redundant," she could have done this research in the privacy of her own home; meanwhile she was faced with a trip to the only real library in the city that was open to the general public. She kept telling herself a higher force was compelling her, but—as she refused to admit to herself—it was her own obsession with tidiness that had brought about this obligation.

Not only was the Collegium Maius building medieval, not only did the library's vaulted ceiling date back to the fifteenth century, but the whole interior design bore witness to the antiquity of the place: the armchairs for readers were like bishops' thrones, each bookcase bristled with pinnacles and crenellations like a soaring castle, and down the center of the hall stood long tables of dark oak, with some large folio volumes with gold embossed patterns glowing on their covers on top; each piece of furniture was like a burial tomb from a cathedral, in which, instead of the body of a nobleman, lay the knowledge of countless generations. Zofia was reminded of one of Ignacy's favorite sayings: that although the university was centuries old, the Gothic halls, like this one, were only built in the year Columbus discovered America, when the House of the Cracow Councilors, now known as Peacock House, had already been standing for some time. But in fact their bedroom was furnished in a similar style, so she might have felt at home here, if not for one detail: the smell, the most ancient thing in here, that heavy odor of old sheets of paper, crumbling parchment, and dust—not an odor of sanctity like the incense-imbued aroma of a church, but equally august.

When she sat down at one of the tables in the reading room, a library assistant glanced at her in surprise, unaccustomed to the presence of women within the walls of the Collegium Maius; minutes later he silently set a pile of gray cloth-bound *Cracow Times* annuals from the past few years in front of her, just as she had requested.

She had imagined she'd make short work of this task, but she had been poring over the newspapers for almost two hours without finding anything at all. She was ready to give in, when all of a sudden she heard a strange noise coming from a distance, like the tinkling of a little bell. She raised her head from the desk; the sound was getting closer, but to her amazement none of the other people in the reading room was taking any notice. Then from behind a bookcase something small and white came scuttling out, tinkling implacably.

"A rat!" screamed Zofia, clutching her heart, terrified by the sight of the creature and by the fact that she had broken the silence in this grand temple of knowledge. Several of the students sitting at the tables looked up; some indignantly, others plainly amused.

"But my dear lady," said a deep and benevolent voice, "please do not be afraid, it is just Jimmy."

"Jimmy?" asked the astonished Zofia, not yet over the shock.

"My whippet," replied an elderly man with a smile on his face, who had emerged from behind the bookcase. Of average height, stooping slightly, he had an unruly storm of white hair and a tousled beard, between which his lively, dark eyes were shining merrily. "I used to have a pair of parrots, smart little birds, I can safely say. Unfortunately, I myself was the cause of their doom: when we installed gas lighting in the library, they came to a tragic end . . ." Then, in reply to Zofia's inquiring look, he added sadly: "They burned to death, the poor little things. Who'd have expected them to fly like moths into the flames? I was given Jimmy as a consolation."

As if he knew he was being talked about, the little dog pressed close to his master's feet and wagged his tail happily, while casting mistrustful glances at the flagship of the Cracow bourgeoisie, moored at not its usual jetty.

Karol Estreicher had held his post as head of the Jagiellonian Library for longer than the Turbotyńskis had been married. He ruled his kingdom just as His Majesty reigned over the Habsburg monarchy: he managed his subjects with a gentle but steady hand, while seeking with all his might to enlarge his sovereign empire. As the budget assigned to the library by the university and the Ministry of Religions and Education was modest, Estreicher relied above all on humanitarian generosity. He procured numerous volumes, sometimes entire archives, from publishers, authors, editors, and collectors—he was said to be as good at extracting collections of books as the most determined charitable countesses were at extracting donations from the pockets of Cracow society.

"What brings you to our humble abode?" he asked with a smile, but before Zofia had had time to utter a single word, he supplied his own answer: "I am always pleased by visits from people outside the university, especially ladies thirsty for knowledge, for whom the education that society chooses to offer them is not enough . . ."

Zofia swallowed, trying to reply to Estreicher's smile by the same token. Although she felt a pang of regret that he hadn't recognized her—they had never in fact been formally introduced, but had crossed paths many times at the theater or at university ceremonies, so he should have remembered her—she realized that it would be better not to introduce herself. The topics she intended to explore at the library were not suitable for a university professor's wife. In any other circumstances she would have been the first to express the view that a woman of irreproachable reputation could only be looking for *decent information* here, but the situation was exceptional.

"You see, madam," Estreicher went on, "my granddaughter, for example, will be finishing at teaching training school this year, and if the Senate undertakes the right steps, in a few years from now she will start her studies at our university."

She did not know which granddaughter he meant. The director took just as much care to expand his dynasty as he did the library collections; Mrs. Estreicher, herself the daughter of a great Cracow family, the Grabowskis, had had seven children, all grown up long ago. Ever since the emperor had conferred on Estreicher the title "Ritter," his descendants could choose, just like the archdukes, from among the best Cracow clans. Why on earth would his granddaughter risk her chance of a good marriage by taking such an outrageous step? That, Zofia was unable to understand. She was equally baffled by Estreicher's enthusiasm for it, but she decided not to share her thoughts with him.

"And so how may I help you?" asked Estreicher. "As you can see, there is plenty to choose from in the journals section. When I took on the management of the library, the journals barely filled a single case, would you believe it? But these days . . ." He drew a circle with his hand. "The *Illustrated Weekly*? Or maybe the women's magazine, *Ivy*? They are sent to us regularly from Warsaw. Or perhaps one of the Parisian journals?"

"Most willingly another time, sir," said Zofia, finally recovering her composure. “I am looking for information about a particular criminal trial that took place a few years ago before a court in Lemberg.”

“How intriguing! Well, I must admit that I was once fascinated by criminal cases myself! In my youth, many, many years ago, in the closing days of the Cracow Republic, I trained as a legal apprentice at the Court of Appeal, and as the occupation did not overburden me with work, I decided to make use of the opportunity to collect ‘cant,’ which means prison argot, thieves’ ditties, and songs. I was going to publish my dictionary in some of the newspapers, but I wonder whether to supplement it and have it printed . . . How did it go?” He scratched his beard and raffishly declaimed:

Understand, if you please, I’m a traveling thief,
The gonophs all call me the gypsy;
By the rattler I ride when I’ve taken my brief,
And I sling on my back an old kipsey.

“Ha, who knows, maybe I’d have become an investigating magistrate if my literary activities hadn’t damaged my career . . . But never mind, fate had other plans for me.”

“I am sure it would have been an irretrievable loss for Cracow, sir,” said Zofia, smiling as sweetly as she could. “The whole city knows there is nobody who could possibly rival you in knowledge or replace you at the library.”

“You are very kind,” he said, thanking her with a bow,

"but that's enough about me. Which trial is it that interests you? Which 'gonophs' are you after?"

Although they were speaking softly, as one should in a library, Zofia lowered her voice even more.

"The Lemberg trial of traffickers in women," she whispered. Estreicher raised an eyebrow, and she added: "It is a matter of the highest importance and the greatest discretion, I cannot say more, but you can be sure of that. I have looked through the archive editions of the *Cracow Times* . . ."

"I'm afraid you won't find much about it in the *Cracow Times*," he interrupted her. "If my memory serves me right, the editors regarded that case as too . . . unpleasant for its readers and decided not to publish any reports. I would advise you to look in the Lemberg periodicals: the *National News*, or the *Lemberg Courier*. On our terrain, if I am not mistaken, Mr. Asnyk's *New Reform* wrote about it. I will go and fetch you the relevant annuals right away," he said, and disappeared behind the bookcase. Jimmy trotted after him, giving a wide berth to one of the waist-high globes positioned here and there the length of the room, perhaps only to stop people from bumping into them.

Zofia shuddered at the thought of the task ahead of her but, she told herself, the end justifies the means. Or at least the end she had set herself.

In fact, in the journals brought by Estreicher she quickly found the news the *Cracow Times* had not reported. *The community is going to learn some dreadful things*, the *Na-*

tional News solemnly warned. *It is going to watch its own vivisection, as they lance a repulsive, foul-smelling ulcer right before its eyes. If it can, it shall weep for the poor victims, those white lilies thrown into feces—the young girls deceitfully snatched from their mothers and abandoned in foreign lands to public debauchery.*

As she read, she took note of the names: Blima Zinader from Lemberg, Itta Seif from Drohobycz, Betta Kiesler from Żółkiew. They all seemed to be Jewish girls, but no, there were Ruthenian and Polish names among them too: Antonina Peczeniuk from Złoczów, Julia Buczak from Przemyśl . . . Przemyśl! She all but shuddered.

She came upon a list of those accused of "the crime of public violation." Twenty-seven people. The more she read, the more of the gang's *modus operandi* was revealed to her. The traffickers were divided into "*gebers*"—also known as the "transmitters," who seduced and won the girls over, beguiling them with the vision of well-paid jobs as nursemaids or cooks, the "*fahrers*," or "travelers," who escorted them to the Turkish brothels, and finally the "*herren*," or "gentlemen," who resided in Constantinople and belonged to a "*bund*," or union, responsible for controlling the prices and bribing Ottoman officials to keep their distance from the "trade." All this implied that Wolf Sztycer was one of the "*gebers*," and in this role had managed to fool poor Karolina. Did this mean that his boss's keeper, Loewenstein-Lewicki, had gone back to trading in "carpets from Smyrna"?

The court had only acquitted five of the defendants,

and several others had managed to run off abroad: Yankiel Herschdorfer from Lemberg, Ruchla Weiss from Kołomyja, and Józef Silberberg from Cracow. But Zofia couldn't understand why the rest of the defendants had been given such low sentences. She read that despite great efforts by the police—including her old friend Jednoróg—and the investigating magistrates, the ringleader, Izaak Schaefferstein, a Lemberg jewelry dealer, had only been sentenced to one year's hard labor. Aggravated by a Lenten diet and the dark cell, true, but only a year? It seemed to Zofia quite absurd. She read in disbelief that the other defendants had been given even lower sentences: Chaya Ehrensdorf—three months' prison on a Lenten diet; Isla Bucholz—six months of ordinary prison regime. Compared with the rest—apart from the ringleader—Solomon Loewenstein from Cracow, the intermediary for the gang's operations in Western Galicia, was given the harshest sentence: nine months' hard labor on a Lenten diet.

Estreicher, who was clearly fond of women, and who for obvious reasons rarely encountered them at the university, came up to Zofia several times, burdened with large albums in brown covers; he gabbled away, making sure she had everything she needed, then went off, lugging his treasures, obtained with great effort from the cavernous cupboards of manor houses and monasteries, escorted the whole time by Jimmy's tinkling. She thanked him, then returned to the newspapers.

Jack the Ripper, whose crimes fill everyone with disgust,

only took his victims' lives, but these degenerate individuals delivered them into harsh and shameful slavery, worse than death or any torture. They sold these women for a handful of gold, thundered the *Lemberg Courier.* But Zofia couldn't think about either the victims or the criminals; here the game was being played for a completely different stake. Evil did not surprise her: ever since Eve plucked the apple, ever since Cain killed Abel, some people had harmed others, breaking divine and human laws. But within the empire they had not just the Ten Commandments and the legal codes against them, but the entire state apparatus, a towering succession of official ranks, all the way up to the foot of the throne, from where His Majesty cast his china-blue gaze upon the countless lands of his monarchy, bestowing kindly looks on the good and severe ones on the bad. Those looks of his were passed down the ladder, from official to official, to lower and lower ranks, until they reached his subjects in the form of punishment or reward.

Zofia was not a child, and did not harbor the naive belief that all state officials were law-abiding, decent people, but the scale of the corruption exposed in the trial was shocking. With growing incredulity she read that representatives of all sorts of professions had played their part in smuggling the girls abroad: the doctors who examined them before the "*fahrers*" took them on their way, the customs inspectors who issued the relevant documents, the policemen who turned a blind eye to the whole practice . . . And presumably the criminals' tentacles reached even further . . .

Doctors? Could Dr. Kurkiewicz have two different personalities? she suddenly thought. The rather eccentric young scientist, like Dr. Jekyll, and the traffickers' ruthless assistant, Cracow's Mr. Hyde? That could change the shape of things. When Jednoróg interviewed her, she had rejected his suggestion that Karolina could have had a secret immoral side to her as absurd, and the postmortem, as she soon learned, had confirmed her virginity. On the other hand, experience had taught her not to trust any scrap of paper, because there was always a person behind it. Could Kurkiewicz have faked the notes in the postmortem report? If so, then to what end? What was his role in it all?

She wasn't sure if it was the muggy atmosphere in the library or her own anxiety, but she felt a weight on her chest; the same sentence from one of the articles kept coming into her mind: *When the curtain of appearances is torn aside, the sight of a murky pool confronts us.* When she noticed that after a few hours of leafing through the papers her fingers had gone black, it occurred to her that it wasn't dust and printer's ink but the filth that had pervaded the imperial and royal Austro-Hungarian monarchy.

She was roused from her reverie by a sudden clatter: a few yards away a portly old man had fallen asleep over a bound volume of a scientific journal, and had almost sprawled to the floor; he had come to fast enough to grab hold of the tabletop, but in the process had knocked several large books off it; the thumps had echoed off the high Gothic ceiling, and from the next room Estreicher could be heard muttering muffled curses, and the previously silent Jimmy barked a few times to say that certain things simply weren't done in the library. Zofia glanced at her watch; it was coming up to eleven thirty. She knew that if she were to accomplish all her plans for the day, she must say goodbye to the friendly librarian and hurry off to the courthouse.

✤

"Unfortunately, if you do not have an appointment," said a low-ranking court official in a weary monotone, "the magistrate will not receive you . . ."

"If you would please ask him . . ."

"No one's going to ask the magistrate," the clerk interrupted her, then in an equally dreary tone, without looking up from the papers he was examining, he continued, "when the magistrate is busy."

"In that case, perhaps . . ."

"No."

"Please, sir, I . . ."

"No," he replied, still not looking up; all she could see were some thin strands of hair, combed from right to left to cover an advancing bald patch, despite his relatively young age.

And so she sat down on a small bench; there was still an hour and a quarter to go before one o'clock, and if Klossowitz was in court, then presumably . . . And indeed, at almost that very instant he emerged from one of the offices, cast her a knowing look, and hurried onward. Ten minutes went by, then fifteen. In the corridor, usually a noisier place than this, there was hardly a soul, not counting a dismal old man sitting by the window and the lawyers and magistrates who flashed past now and then.

She took out her notebook to review everything she knew about the case by now, but her gaze kept wandering above the top of the page in search of Klossowitz. Instead of him, she caught sight of someone else, clambering up the stairs with an effort. It crossed Zofia's mind that she had seen this portly little man with the perspiring brow before, but she couldn't think where. Evidently looking for someone, he glanced at her, frowned, and then out of the blue he spoke to her.

"Madam," he exclaimed, "I have heard it said in the city that you have taken up prostitution!"

Everything went dark before Zofia's eyes. She managed to shield her mouth with a hand and cry: "Holy Mother of God!"

"I know all about it, madam!" said the little man who had cast this outrageous slur in the middle of the courthouse corridor.

"I beg your pardon, sir, but I believe you have mistaken me for someone else," she muttered. "What on earth are you saying? I do not know you. How dare you . . ."

"I have my connections, I know what I am saying!" he said, waving impatiently, and then struck a beseeching tone. "Please help me, madam. You have taken up helping girls who've gone down the wrong path, you've been to see Dr. Roth about it; I know everything! You alone can save me, madam! Dear countess of philanthropy, help me!"

Being addressed as "countess" definitely helped Zofia to recover her composure. She peered down the corridor to make sure nobody had heard the shocking remark that had been aimed at her, but it was just as empty as before, and in the meantime the old man by the window had dozed off. Once she had calmed down a bit, it once again occurred to her that the little man's acutely mournful face seemed familiar, but she still couldn't ascribe it to a specific individual. As his little mustache twitched nervously from side to side, his dark eyes, with real desperation visible in them, were closely fixed on her.

"What are you talking about, Mister. . . . ? I demand an explanation!" she declared in a tone that brooked no argument.

"Noble countess, I fall at your feet and beg for mercy! My name is Brand, Leon Brand, at your service," he said, bowing low, if not excessively. "I am appealing to you in this unexpected, no doubt incorrect manner because I find myself in such a tragic position that I don't know where to seek help and salvation anymore, and you are an exquisitely well-connected person . . . you have the best possible associations, not just with Dr. Roth but also with Mr. Klossowitz, whom I have come to see today, and Commissioner Jednoróg. I beg you to intercede for me!"

Zofia rested her umbrella against the dark wooden

bench, sat down, brushing off the flounce of her dress, placed her handbag beside her, and then said in the most businesslike tone possible: "Would you please be so kind as to outline the situation a little? You plainly know me, but I must confess that I do not know you, or the nature of your concerns."

"Of course, naturally, I shall explain . . . please forgive the incoherence of my speech, the surfeit of words, and the lack of clarity in my reasoning . . . It is the result of nervous vexation, yes, vexation, I have fallen into a pit of nervousness. A surfeit of misfortunes has landed on my shoulders." Though standing in front of her, he couldn't stop moving, making all manner of superfluous gestures. "Last spring the venerable police authorities ordered me to vacate my house, where I maintained a lupanar . . ."

"You are the owner of a house of debauchery?!" said Zofia in horror; in the past few days little had been capable of shocking her, and yet actually coming face-to-face with the owner of a brothel was bound to make a staggering impression on any university professor's wife, even Zofia Turbotyńska. Brand spread his hands helplessly, and adopted an even sadder expression.

"I admit, such houses are indeed commonly described as places of debauchery, but I can promise you that my facility is a quiet house, and the clientele are from the best circles, the very best! They drive up quietly at night in cabs and leave in the same way. At night outside my house there is silence, because the girls are asleep; at most they go for an afternoon outing in closed cabs. Would you please tell me how"—by this point Zofia was afraid the apologetic Brand was about to resort to extreme measures by bursting into sobs—"in this state of affairs one can call my modest lupanar a house of debauchery? What debauchery is there to speak of here?"

Suddenly she remembered. It was his conversation with Commissioner Jednoróg that she had heard through the door more than a year earlier! At the time she had not realized he was talking about a house of ill repute. She thought he was talking about a Jewish institution that was impeding the parish priest at Corpus Christi in some way. It involved evicting the facility from . . . which street was it?

"On Podbrzezie Street?" she said, remembering that too.

"Aha, so I see you are familiar with my case!" Something vaguely resembling a smile appeared on Brand's face. "When I was driven out of there, I found a new place on Joselewicz Street, off Starowiślna Street, a secluded spot, which, following a site visit, the police health committee deemed suitable. On one side there is a train track and land belonging to the state railway, opposite there are some empty plots, and the street is quiet and peaceful, a site destined for this very purpose, as nobody can deny!"

"I shall take your word for it, sir," said Zofia snidely, but Brand didn't notice. Or preferred not to. He hastily returned to his tone of lament.

"I acquired the house at exorbitant cost because, knowing what I needed it for, the seller charged a steep price, and as a result I paid ten thousand crowns above its real value, investing more than six thousand. However, just a year on, human envy is ousting me from there! You see, madam, my neighbor, at one time the proprietress of a lupanar herself, suddenly declared that she feels affronted by my proximity! I stress"—here he raised a finger—"she used to run a lupanar herself! The regulations issued by the most excellent governorship states that brothels may be located in any district within the city, except for the neighborhood of major academic institutions, churches, and monasteries. So you may well ask, whence the opposition, when there are no places of worship in the vicinity of Joselewicz Street?"

Zofia had not in fact asked anything of the kind, and was not terribly sure where all this was heading, but she decided to hear out Brand's tale. After all, the topic of his stories was one that she had, as the brothel keeper so awkwardly put it, "taken up" of late, so she came to the conclusion that she might learn something useful from this conversation.

"Just imagine, my neighbor has persuaded the head of a school on Starowiślna Street to exercise a veto! Meanwhile I wonder what danger my establishment could possibly pose to the young people?" He spread his hands helplessly. "First of all, they are children, who do not even know what a *maison close* is! Secondly, walking to school along Starowiślna Street cannot have a demoralizing effect on them, otherwise it might be necessary to forbid young people from entering pedestrian areas or public gardens, which on warm summer evenings are the site of countless amorous trysts that could have an alluring influence on the sensitive minds of young people!" Zofia was reminded of salacious snickers in the bushes at Strzelecki Park. "There are other districts where the young people walk straight past lupanars . . . I will give you an example. Mrs. Korkuczkowa has run a brothel for some years on St. Lawrence's Street, a stone's throw from the city gasworks and Corpus Christi church. And what happens? Nothing! By a strange twist of fate the parish priest is not disturbed by this particular brothel, although it is almost right by the church gates, but mine, out of the way on a sheltered little side street, incommoded him. It is a mystery. By another extraordinary twist of fate the committee issued Mrs. Korkuczkowa with a positive testimonial. It is baffling, truly baffling. But I would not dare to accuse the most excellent police authorities of bribe taking!" He raised his hands. "As if such an idea were to cross my mind!"

"Why on earth should I intercede on your behalf, Mr. Brand?" Zofia finally asked. "Forgive me, please, but your debts are no concern of mine, and I must say, I find your means of earning a living quite atrocious . . ."

Brand took a deep breath, gathered his strength, considered his next move, and began again from a different tack.

"I understand your outrage at the sort of activity that I conduct, but please bear in mind, dear lady, that I must support my wife, my old mother, and my six children — yes, six of them!"

Seeing that Zofia's face was as stony as ever, he added: "I also do my best to be of service to science! Yes, please do not be surprised, dear lady, to *science*. And I do not just mean to say that the clientele at our house sometimes includes students of the medical faculty, and even the occasional professor!" Zofia knitted her brow, half in anger, half anguish, which Brand took as an expression of doubt. "But it is true, please believe me! Professors, too! Indeed, in keeping with police regulations, I cannot give any names, but I can assure you that some of our guests enjoy international fame. And as I wish to be of service to science, I enable the medical students to gain knowledge essential for their profession. For instance, there is one student who comes to see me, in fact he's a doctor by now, who is most enthusiastically exploring the mysteries of something that he calls 'sexlore.' He's a somewhat bizarre fellow, but always very polite, so on quieter days I allow him to talk to the girls during working hours, when they are not occupied, of course. And for this alone I do not demand a single kreutzer! But I could!"

"Are you referring to Dr. Kurkiewicz?" she asked cautiously.

"Yes! The very same. You can see for yourself, you are familiar with everyone! What excellent connections, what superb acquaintances!"

"Forgive me, sir," she interrupted him, "but as a social volunteer"—for the second time in the past few days she was convincingly playing the role of another Mrs. Bujwid

—“my paramount concern is the fate of those unfortunate girls, and not their oppressors; I care about the fate of fallen women, not of their . . . their . . . panders!” she berated him.

That prompted him to play his trump card.

“Well, I can see that you are not concerned that if I am evicted, not just I, but my small children are at risk of poverty and starvation . . .” He shook his head sadly. “That house, for which I paid a handsome price, as I have already said, will be hard to sell, because anyone who knows my situation will offer me far less than its actual value. But I realize that the fate of *my* children, my *poor* children cannot move your heart,” he said, refusing to give up. “But are you not touched by the fate of a widow with four little ones, who is also facing the grim specter of bankruptcy?”

“What do you mean?” wondered Zofia.

“If you please, madam, the widow of whom I speak is a very generous soul, for it was she who lent me the extra ten thousand crowns to buy my property, but if ruined, I would not be able to repay the debt, and so my creditor and her innocent children, yes, her children too, would also be in danger of financial catastrophe. Yes, madam, the fate of two families lies in your merciful hands! But if your main concern is the fortune of the girls who work for me, then please read this!”

He pulled a sheet of paper from his inside jacket pocket, but instead of handing it to Zofia, he began to read it out:

“*In talking of ruin, we are not casting words to the wind, but regrettably we are voicing the saddest truth. We are all in debt, because that is what our life entails. If we were evicted today without making preparations, we would have to leave in the clothes we stand up in, because our belongings have been pawned . . .* Can you hear the pleas of these daughters of Corinth?" he desperately added, then continued to read aloud: "*We are overwhelmed by despair at the thought of what will become of us. Despite living in the shadow of the world's disdain we have not so utterly lost our sense of shame as to sell our bodies in the street . . .* It is true, they have not; they are decent girls! *Why do people despise us? Why does the world spurn us?* Noble lady, if the fate of my innocent children does not move you, then perhaps these sad pleas will? They compiled this letter of their own free will, without being forced to do so, and have asked me to submit it to the police and to the court! Of their own accord! Please consider that the girls at my house have a safe place to ply their trade, by which, in view of their situation, and their lack of familiarity with any other profession, they would earn their living anyway. Would it be better for them to sell their bodies in the street? I have no other place for them. If the police authorities evict me again, the street will have to be their shelter, the street will have to feed them! Please take pity, please implore the commissioner, the magistrate, the governor himself in Lemberg, please beg them, for humanitarian reasons—let us not be afraid of this word: *humanitarian*—to take pity on me, a poor, veritable Job, innocently driven to despair, and to accede to my humble request! Let them agree to appoint another committee to consider my arguments and put a stop to my dislodgement."

Luckily at this point a sound came down the corridor, at first low, muffled by the thick walls, then ever brisker — the footsteps of Investigating Magistrate Klossowitz. Brand, still in the full flow of his monologue of the Job of the Cracow pimps, broke off in midsentence, turned to Klossowitz and began: "Most excellent magistrate . . ."

To which he heard merely a brusque: "Not now, Mr. Brand."

". . . I make so bold as to . . ."

"Please make so bold in office hours. Goodbye, Mr. Brand."

The owner of the unfortunate first-class lupanar now stood there like a bedraggled hen. He automatically pressed his hand to his hat a few times, then bowed humbly and began to descend the stairs, one step at a time, as if he were going to be guillotined on the ground floor. Meanwhile, rescued from the impudent little man, Zofia cast Klossowitz a look full of gratitude, as if to say "My knight on a white horse!" then rose from the bench and headed toward his office.

"I am obliged to beg your pardon," he said, lowering his voice; he did not offer her a chair or take his place at the desk, but just stopped in the middle of the room, "but I am right in the middle of a case, so my time is extremely limited . . . I merely broke free for a moment. And I hasten to tell you that our search for Sztycer has brought nothing. Sunk without trace, none of our informers . . ."

"One word," she interrupted him, "one name: Loewenstein."

"It rings a bell . . ."

"The Lemberg trial."

"Of course, convicted at the Lemberg trial. Now named Lewicki, a former pimp . . ."

"A current pimp."

Klossowitz raised an eyebrow.

"Well, prostitution is not the main field of my interests. That is, I meant to say . . ."

"Oh, I am aware of that."

"However, I can ask Commissioner Swolkień about Loewenstein. No one in the Cracow, maybe the entire Galician police is as well versed in these matters as Swolkień — he exposed the gang of traffickers convicted at the Lemberg trial. What is it that interests us?" Here with as discreet a gesture as possible he took a watch from his waistcoat pocket and glanced at its face.

"Loewenstein, alias Lewicki, is the real owner of the establishment on Różana Street. The Dunin woman is merely the administrator; they are united, as I understand it," she said, hesitantly, "by a *long-term alliance.*"

"Oh, in that case it will be worth taking a look at Mr. Lewicki . . . Please forgive me, but now I must . . ."

"Naturally."

They emerged into the corridor together, where Klossowitz bowed and rapidly headed for the courtroom, where he was about to pass sentence on a receiver of stolen goods; but halfway there he stopped, turned back, ran up to Zofia, who had already laid her hand on the stair rail, and whispered:

"I have just remembered something. Daszyński. Loewenstein spent quite a long time in the same cell as Daszyński. Perhaps he knows something."

She nodded, then began to descend the staircase—not as clean as it might be, as she noticed to her distaste—at the majestic pace appropriate to a Cracow professor's wife. In fifteen minutes' time an apparently chance encounter lay ahead of her. And in light of what she had read in the newspapers and learned from Brand, she had every reason to expect it to be very interesting.

❧

Some time ago Zofia had realized that with age her mind had started to work in a completely different way from other people's, but she had never attached any weight to this fact; she thought it was just a personal quirk, something rather embarrassing that no one need know about. It was that she couldn't not think; her brain was like a fire that incessantly needed fuel of some kind. If she wasn't occupied by reading a book, considering complicated social relationships, reducing gossip to its elements, and exploring which bits of it contained a grain of truth and which were entirely fabricated, if she did not set it the complex task of planning all the meals for the coming week, she had to throw it something else to chew on. While waiting in a shop, she automatically read all the labels; while talking to a boring person she would count something — the buttons on their cape, the pleats on their collar, the stones in their brooch, the windows of the house on the opposite facade of the Market Square. When out walking with Ignacy, who did not always offer a major conversational challenge, she was in the habit of counting too — she counted their steps, and as a result for several years now she had known exactly how many steps would lead her to various points in the city. She couldn't have summoned up a figure on cue, but somehow her mind took note of them and filed them away, giving her an intuitive sense of distance.

Thanks to this particular mental skill, she knew that if she wanted to talk to Stanisław Teofil Kurkiewicz she needed to be just outside the Collegium Novum at two minutes past one precisely. So many times in the past few years she had returned his bow as she chanced to run into him at exactly this hour that her mind had grasped and noted this regularity, just as it had noted hundreds of equally nonessential facts. The reason for this consistent timing was simple — like all great scientists, or rather, like all those with an obsessive desire to become great scientists, Kurkiewicz had imposed an absurd, truly monastic regime on himself, which had its own particular *canonical hours.* Six months ago he had been awarded the title of doctor of medical sciences—not without controversy, as she remembered from Ignacy's account—and yet he still stuck to his student habits. He would complete his engagements at one o'clock, and at five past he would always occupy the same table by the window at a cheap chophouse located in a shabby two-story building on the corner of Wolska Street.

She sat down on a bench and, as if lost in thought, furtively kept a lookout. But Kurkiewicz did not appear at two minutes past one, or at five minutes past, or ten; so she got up, slowly crossed the street to the hostelry and casually walked past the door, but just around the corner she stopped and pretended to be looking for something in her reticule, while at the same time casting careful glances through the grimy windowpane. There was a scruffy old man sitting at Kurkiewicz's table, leaning low over his bowl and slurping his soup. Clearly the student's life did not run quite as regularly as she had supposed. Could the chaos of Hyde have infiltrated the order of Jekyll?

It was early afternoon, and the September sun was still high in the sky, illuminating the elegant face of the Collegium Novum and reflecting off the soaring windows. She could go home and occupy herself with *something useful*, but her investigative work for the day was not yet over; as she had not managed to pin down Kurkiewicz, she would try her luck elsewhere.

Half an hour later Zofia emerged from the gates of the police building on Mikołajska Street in a state of agitation. Now the flagship of the Cracow bourgeoisie was sweeping across the smooth cobblestones like the Flying Dutchman, driven not by the wind, but anger at the endless obstacles she kept running into in the course of her inquiry.

Now, as she had two new pieces of information, about the connection between Sztycer and Loewenstein and the fact that Daszyński had shared a cell with Loewenstein, she had decided to question Jednoróg. But it was like running into a brick wall—whatever she asked, he rebuffed her. Of course, he kept up his good manners, he received her politely, if not genially, but he had clearly quelled any pangs of conscience he may have had about causing the death of the innocent Czarnota. To her first question he replied firmly: "My dear lady, I did indeed try to bring up the topic with Magistrate Rozmarynowicz, but the answer I heard was that he categorically refuses to discuss a case that is closed. Please believe me: even if I wanted to investigate your servant's hallucinations, the final word on the matter belongs to the magistrate. And I do not intend to expose my position any further for the sake of somebody's illusions." They had promptly said goodbye, preserving decorum, but now without the cordiality. She had taken him for a confidant and an ally, but meanwhile he had turned out to be fainthearted, focused only on his own career as an official. How disappointing.

However, Zofia Turbotyńska was not discouraged by

this sort of adversity; on the contrary, it made her even more determined. She stopped on the pavement, leaned her gloved hand against a wooden shop display case, took a few deep breaths, and then steeled herself for the far harder task that now lay ahead of her. She walked down Mikołajska Street, around St. Mary's Basilica, across the Market Square, and soon reached Szewska Street; she headed for number seven, where above the arched entrance there was an emblem just as old as the one at Peacock House—a fine stone-carved ram.

❧

Known as Little Lamb House—a name that was the source of endless jokes among the conservative readers of the *Cracow Times*—it was home to the editorial office of the socialist journal *Forward,* and thus it was the lair of one of Cracow's worst rabble-rousers, probably worse than Mrs. Bujwid herself: Ignacy Daszyński.

Zofia was in no doubt at all that he was a scoundrel—and the smashed plaster bust that Ignacy had lamented was nothing compared with the rest of it! The rest of it was more than enough! Not only had this man established a socialist party, incited the populace at rallies, complained about every national anniversary, and accused the contributors to the *Cracow Times* of having their snouts in the trough, but as casually as can be he had served time in Russian, German, and Austrian prisons for his political troublemaking!

A real live criminal, although, as Zofia was capable of admitting deep down, of a very different kind from the one she was after.

But for that very reason, convinced she was stepping into a lion's den, or worse, straight into the lion's jaws, she had decided to proceed in a different way from the approach she would have taken if she had encountered him by chance on social ground. She was going to lie through her teeth from start to finish—and the idea excited her, rather like going to a costume ball. Like any intelligent person, at bottom Zofia quite enjoyed telling lies, but scruples of a moral nature spoiled the pleasure for her. Now, justifying herself with a noble purpose, she let herself fib without a care in the world, further given wings by the fact that a man like Daszyński, a socialist newspaper editor, was separated from her life by as thick a wall as a tinker from the suburbs; he would spend his whole life penning subversive little articles and fulminating at workers' rallies, but no one would ever admit him to the sort of drawing rooms where they might run into each other again. So Zofia was going to take a gamble.

In the journal's first room there was a skinny boy sitting at a little desk. His swollen face was wrapped in a checked scarf. As one would expect of a person suffering from gingivitis, he could only mumble his words with patent effort.

"Ow may I 'elp you?" he said.

"'Ofia 'Urbo-yńska," she gabbled just as unclearly. "Is Mr. Daszyński here?"

"On what 'atter?"

"One of the highest political importance," she said in a tone that left no room for argument.

"Co'rade 'Aszyński's in 'is 'oom. Jus' a mo'ent." He cast daggers at her, but got up and disappeared behind a door, then came straight back and, without another word, pointed her toward the same door.

Golden sunlight shone through the windows of Daszyński's office overlooking the street, picking out all the shabbiness of the interior; Zofia had never been to an editorial office before, but she had always imagined the *Cracow Times* office, within the Kirchmayer mansion, as a series of elegant rooms, where graying gentlemen sat at carved oak desks, covering sheets of paper with their graceful handwriting, and the articles and columns produced in this way were then conveyed to the printer's on silver trays by messenger boys. She had thought the *Forward* office would be similar, but less affluent, perhaps a little grimier. She certainly hadn't expected such an important man, the editor-in-chief of the journal, to work in a room as unremarkable as that of a common clerk. There was no carpet on the floor, not even a rug, but there was a small desk with turned legs, covered in papers, two cabinets full of documents and a few books on a well-used etagere. And behind the desk Ignacy Daszyński, the devil incarnate, who was just getting up to greet her.

"I have come to see you," she began from the threshold, "in the hope that I shall not occupy too much of your valuable time. I was emboldened by a dear colleague, Mrs. Bujwid, whose acquaintance I made the other day . . ." For a moment she was lost for words, but at once found them in a recess of her memory. "At a most interesting lecture on Amazonian women. It is thanks to her that I know you are well versed, by reason of your heroic, not to say dramatic political struggle . . ."

"Dear madam, I merely do my duty." He bowed slightly, twirling his mustache.

"You do not have to explain yourself, we are all, *all*"—she repeated, because she didn't think the first "all" had sounded sincere enough—"immensely grateful to you for your . . . first-rate, honest . . . labor."

Daszyński looked at her from under the ridge of his dark eyebrows; she had been expecting various things, going into this devil's cave, but not that the devil would be devilishly handsome. Just thirty years old, tall, and slender, with sharp features that could have been carved by Veit Stoss, he had what are known as smoldering good looks, the sort of man whom women fell for by the dozen. He had pitch-black hair, swept back to form a sort of lion's mane, in the same style as Paderewski, his eyes were dark and deep set, but from under those thick eyebrows they shone—as she reluctantly had to admit—with intelligence; on top of that he had an impressive mustache, perhaps not as majestic as that of Umberto, king of Italy, but testifying to masculine vigor.

"As I have already mentioned, I know that you are well

versed in all sorts of shadowy affairs that happen here in Galicia" — at this point Daszyński made a face that implied he did indeed know something about some shadowy affairs, but might not necessarily talk about them — "but I am concerned about one issue in particular: the great scandal destroying our working class, to wit, trafficking in women."

"A burning question, to be sure. In the forthcoming issue . . ." he said, and began to look for something on the desk. "Oh, here, if you please, in the forthcoming issue we shall be writing about it once again. Above all Constantinople, in the Galata district in Pera, where there are masses of girls who have been tempted by offers of marriage or positions as governesses. Merely in the house of a man named . . . oh, here it is," he went on, reading from the page, "Scharfman, *Abraham Scharfman, who was wanted for murder by the Bulgarian government, some forty girls were to be found in 'better times'!*"

"I know that you were once put in jail on some excuse, and were imprisoned with a loathsome individual . . ."

"Ah, dear madam," he said, waving a hand, "what do they not do to denigrate me. Sharing a cell with a villain is nothing. Just imagine, one time a young legal trainee came to see me here at the editorial office, sat down where you are sitting, and told me that at the state prosecution service they were overjoyed, the policemen were celebrating, and Commissioner Wolaniecki was saying that I was finally going to be charged with an extremely nasty crime, namely seducing a minor . . ." Zofia shuddered, not at the thought of seducing a minor, so much as the fact that Daszyński had made no attempt to put it more delicately than that. "At first I had no idea what to do about it, but then it occurred to me that my flat is being spied on around the clock!"

"Is that so?" she said, just to say something.

"And I realized what was behind it. Not long before, some friends of mine had been going on a trip out of town, and had sent their thirteen-year-old daughter to get me to join them without fail. But I had a headache."

"Migraine is a nightmare," Zofia said automatically, just as she would have remarked on hearing the same thing from one of her female acquaintances.

"I think it was a migraine," he said, smiling faintly. "Suffice it to say that although I had promised to come, I could not, and so poor Stacha, my friends' daughter, burst into floods of tears. She happens to be very fond of me. The secret agent standing on the stairs must have noticed her coming down them weeping, and at once reported to the commissioner that I was trifling with little girls!"

"And how did you cope with it?"

"I immediately raced off to see Korotkiewicz, the chief of police, explained my case, and said that if I did not receive satisfaction, first I would write to the minister of the interior to tell him all about it, and second, at the next public meeting where Commissioner Wolaniecki appeared as a representative of the authorities, I would slap him in the face, and tell the assembled company why I had done it!" At this, Zofia imagined a similar scandal happening, at the dull Third of May concert at the Celestat, for instance, and almost blushed at the thought of how splendidly it would liven up the entire evening. "Trust me, that Korotkiewicz fellow squirmed like a rat in a trap," Daszyński went on, clearly in his element — he obviously enjoyed telling anecdotes. "He promised to summon and question Wolaniecki."

"And then of course he said nothing of the sort had occurred and it was merely gossip?"

"Just as if you were there, madam! But I made it plain to him that my information about the commissioner's bragging was true. But if it's not one denunciation, it's another, if it's not one lie, it's another. On a different occasion I was woken up at dawn by a young laborer. At first I couldn't understand what he was on about, but once I'd fully come around, can you guess what I heard him say? Apparently a Jesuit working for a clerical magazine had hired a man, for something like forty gulden, to denounce me by testifying in public that during a lecture at the tailors' association I had insulted the Virgin Mary."

"A Jesuit!" hissed Zofia convincingly, and once again felt like the actress, Modejska. Then patiently heard out his convoluted story.

"What sly creatures!" exclaimed Zofia in the middle of it, wondering whether she was overacting.

"Sly in the extreme! That is how venerable old Cracow defends itself against me, though it would do better to guard against someone like Count Starzeński, for example — the man is devoid of self-respect!" To hear this said of any count at all, Zofia was mildly shocked. "You probably know what he's like, eh? He's a real scoundrel! He lives off supplying hay for the army and profiteering, and rakes in a fortune by lending money at a scandalously high interest rate. Frankly, he's a common-or-garden usurer. No, not a 'Jew in a gaberdine,' as the ignorant and prejudiced would like to imagine, but a Polish count with a coat of arms on his carriage door. But no, it's toward *me* that people who don't know me"—as his speech grew more heated his face went redder—"officials, policemen, Bishop Puzyna, and his cohort of priests, none of whom has ever seen me in his life, commit villainy upon villainy . . ." Throughout this tirade, Zofia maintained a stony facial expression, and even went further, physically forcing herself to give a tiny nod of agreement. "Purely in order to trample and obliterate, yes, obliterate the 'socialist' from the face of the earth for ever, for stirring up and agitating ancient Cracow, city of fifty churches and convents, Cracow, stronghold of bigots and bureaucrats, who . . . who . . ."

Here Daszyński broke off his rant, because his nose was itchy and he was about to sneeze; he said the word "who" twice more, while fumbling in his pockets in search of a handkerchief, then finally sneezed, and did so in great style, thunderously, violently, in defiance of the bureaucrats, bigots, and Bishop Puzyna himself.

"Prison must have been the worst thing," said Zofia, taking advantage of this heaven-sent interval. "I have heard that you were once locked up with a procurer . . ."

"Oh yes," he said, putting his handkerchief back in his pocket, then frowning to restore his solemnity after the sneeze. "I was in prison with a procurer, a man named Loewenstein. But with whom have I not served time—with Father Stojałowski, for example!" he said, smiling broadly.

Internally, Zofia was fuming at this torrent of pointless anecdotes; of course she had heard of the subversive priest whose superiors had first of all sequestered his income, then suspended him, and finally condemned him from every pulpit in the country. Only last year, just before Karolina's death, in fact, or maybe just after, a letter from as many as three bishops had been read out in the churches, ordering the congregation not to read not only *Forward* but also Stojałowski's magazines, *The Wreath* and *The Little Bee.*

"And we met in St. Michael's prison, three years ago, when we wrote about the murder by the police of a man named . . ."

"Mr. Rotter, who was killed by the police at the custody jail next to the telegraph office!" said Zofia, sounding extremely well informed, the moment she came upon something in this stream of words that interested her.

"That's the one!" he replied, with patent appreciation. "The prosecutor's office filed a case against the editor Englisch for slander, and his witnesses were charged with perjury and put in jail, where they were terrified. That is the sort of method they apply in Cracow to combat socialism. And as at the time I had been issued with a fine of twenty-five gulden, exchangeable for five days in the jug, I prompted the judge to lock me up, and be quick about it, so that I could see the witnesses," he said, smiling roguishly, with a twinkle in his eye. "In fact the judge was duty-bound to have the fine collected by the bailiffs, but I made it very clear to him that all my furniture combined was worth less than a fifth of the value of the fine." Zofia calculated what sort of furniture one would have to have at home for it to be worth only five gulden, and virtually shuddered. "And Father Stojałowski was in that prison at the same time, commanding great respect from the prison guards. They took me to see him, and he embraced and kissed me, offered me some excellent brandy, and started telling me the details of his political life. Have you had the pleasure of making his acquaintance?"

"No, unfortunately," she managed to say. "But perhaps one day there will be an opportunity. I have heard that he is a remarkable man. And I know that you were also in prison with a proc—"

"Remarkable, yes he is! I have been thinking about him a lot in the past few days, because he's stuck in prison again and is on hunger strike in protest. But you really should see him! He's solidly built, with a pale face, an aquiline nose, a high forehead . . . it's a curious thing, but in conversation he has two main tones: one is derisory, almost clownish, and the other is noble and powerful. He told me how the authorities took away his rich parish outside Lemberg, and then incriminated him, making it look as if he had embezzled the contributions toward a lamp to stand before the Holy Sepulcher in Jerusalem."

"It beggars belief!" exclaimed Zofia, who really did refuse to believe it.

"Then he told me how the court sentenced him to lose his civic rights to prevent him from being elected a member of parliament. Have you heard the bishop's curses?"

"Who has not?"

"All Galicia has heard them! His reverence and I laughed about it! *Through the bowels of God's mercy we implore you not to read these journals, nor to support them either verbally or financially, on pain of sin*—that was how it went! We repeated it so often when we were in good spirits that it's carved on my memory. I had *Forward* sent to Bishop Puzyna for the whole year free of charge for giving us such excellent advertising."

Zofia acted out some sincere laughter, with which she infected Daszyński, and then she launched a counterattack.

"What about that man Loewenstein? Because the reason for my call . . ." she began.

"Loewenstein? Well, yes," said Daszyński, lacing his fingers. "He's a notorious character—in his youth he was an extremely artful pickpocket, then he became a white slave trafficker. He amused me splendidly in prison, splendidly! We were together on Corridor Four, familiar to our comrades twenty years ago, right up to the most recent history of socialists locked in the clink in Galicia. Even there he had style, in his black frock coat and snow-white shirt front, but with the face of a gallows bird. We had lots of conversations—he explained the entire theory, ethics, and practice of trafficking girls, which he saw as the function of a true benefactor of humanity."

"How on earth?" she asked, with evident indignation, this time genuine, at which Daszyński frowned, unsure if he could go into detail. By now she was gradually losing patience for explaining to every man that although she was a woman, she was able to bear even the most immoral stories from the demimonde, if it would lead her to solving the mystery. "Mr. Daszyński, there is no need for undue delicacy. On the pages of your journal you write without mincing your words, so please do not spare me either. If I were a timid young lady, I would not be involved in such tragic matters."

"Well, of course, your friendship with Mrs. Bujwid proves that you are ready to declare war on Cracow's narrow-minded reactionaries," he said, laughing. "All right then, without mincing my words. 'Just you think about it,' Loewenstein said to me, 'usually this sort of stupid trollop hasn't a piece of black bread to her name, and goes about in filthy rags. But if I wash and bathe her, dress her up in diamonds and silk, and take her to Buenos Aires, the little minx will get drunk, not on champagne, but on the steam from champagne!'"

"The steam from champagne? I do not understand," said Zofia, cocking her head like a guinea fowl.

"I asked exactly the same question! To which he replied: 'Just so, because when the Englishmen who are building railways in the mountains arrive, they have a bathtub filled with champagne and want to see the tart bathing in it. In champagne!'"

"Allow me to comment that most of these girls do not end up bathing in champagne, but dying in hospital corridors," said Zofia.

"You do not have to convince me," he replied, raising his hands in a defensive gesture. "I am perfectly well aware that the man is ruthless, rotten to the core. Though even such ruthlessness has its lights and shades. He is capable of inflicting the most atrocious villainy on an enemy, merely to save a comrade in adversity. Even such a chance acquaintance as I was. Just imagine," he said, lowering his voice, "he was burning with such fury toward Prosecutor Tarłowski that he wanted to sell his daughter to a brothel in Buenos Aires!"

"The poor girl!"

"If she ever existed, because I am not sure if Mr. Tarłowski has a daughter, but of course I calmed him down as best I could—he was always coming up with one plan or another with the aim of abducting her, or at least sending someone to . . . dishonor her. He boasted that it wouldn't be the first revenge of the kind he had taken."

"Outrageous! And now he is pretending to be an ordinary Podgórze entrepreneur."

"Indeed, so I have heard. Suffice it to say that he treats his employees, especially the female ones, the same way as any other capitalist."

"While we're on the subject, do you happen to know anything about Wolf Sztycer?"

"Sztycer? I do not recall the name. Is that an associate of his?"

"One of his employees, low-ranking. And I have reason to believe, which might interest you, that he may have a connection with the police shooting of a man named Czarnota . . ."

"Comrade Maciej Czarnota? From the tobacco factory!" said Daszyński animatedly. "Yes, of course I'm familiar with the case!"

"I know, I heard your speech during the Labor Day festivity."

"Then you are sure to have heard about the latest incidents of this kind. Four policemen and a sergeant came rushing into Majerka's restaurant in Podgórze and threw two perfectly innocent workers down the steps, so they landed on the cobbles. And when one of them pointed out that they shouldn't beat him up, he was hit about the head with the flat of a saber, causing him to lose consciousness."

Zofia had it on the tip of her tongue to say that they cannot have been innocent if the police had come for them, but she checked herself in time. Bah, she even felt the same way as in the library when she had read about the torn curtain of appearances, but she quickly pushed it to the back of her mind.

"But that is nothing compared with the case of a worker named Stolarczyk, from only a couple of weeks ago. He took some policemen to task for arresting a small boy, barely knee high, and marching him off like a prisoner, so they arrested him too. He gave them the slip, was caught again and hauled off to the cells. He was released the next morning, went home, and a few hours later he gave up the ghost. He had large black bruises on his back and sides. Twenty-seven years old. He left a wife and child, in poverty of course. But what's this about Czarnota?"

"Did you know him?"

"He was recommended to me several times as a capable comrade. But I don't think I ever spoke to him in person."

"Could he have been cooperating with white slave traffickers?"

"Czarnota?" said Daszyński, bridling. "No, it's out of the question! I won't deny that we do have people among us who make . . . various deals, let's put it like that. But no, not him, definitely not. What was the name of the man you mentioned earlier? Sztucer?"

"Sztycer."

And so they chatted away for another quarter of an hour or more, like two ardent socialists fulminating against the villainous authorities and the prince bishop, the ruthless white slave traffickers, and the sufferings of the working class, until the boy with gingivitis brought in an urgent piece of work; Daszyński very humbly apologized to Zofia, saying he must bid her farewell.

"Do forgive me, please," he said finally, "but what is your name again? I didn't quite catch it."

"'O-ia 'Urbo-yńska," she muttered once again, then, bestowing a radiant smile on him, she turned on her heel and left.

CHAPTER XI

A long and substantial chapter, in which Zofia Turbotyńska holds two conversations, though only one of them proves important, and Franciszka holds just one, but perhaps more important, while the rhinoceros's horn rips open the soft underbelly of the elephant.

Professor Ignacy Turbotyński had only just emerged from the gateway of Peacock House and was walking slowly toward the university, when two women came out of the same gateway—one a bit older and smarter, in a royal-blue dress with wide puffed sleeves and a hat adorned with a bird's wing (this time a magpie's), the other younger, in a simple but not entirely inelegant suit with large horn buttons. Anyone inattentive—the pale little girl with freckles, for example, who was staring at them from the windows of the new women's high school, but instantly stopped when called on to answer the question "In which year did Duke Mieszko marry the Bohemian princess Doubravka?" — might have thought the professor's wife and her servant were off to do the shopping, as they were in the habit of doing, and were sure to turn toward Szczepański Square or the Small Marketplace. Nothing could be more wrong, for in that case Franciszka would have been dressed for work, not for an outing. So did she have the day off? No — she was going on a mission.

Together they reached the main Market Square where, after a short farewell, they finally parted ways: the servant went to wait at a tram stop, while the mistress walked onward, following her husband in the direction of the medical faculty buildings on Kopernik Street. She didn't want him to see her, so she kept at a suitable distance — close enough to see his silhouette, the swing of the cane in his right hand and his steadily bobbing bowler hat — but at the same time far enough away for him, should he look back, to fail to recognize her. At first she found it quite comical that here she was, following Ignacy like a jealous wife who suspects her husband of sneaking out of the house for a secret tryst on the pretext of work. Meanwhile, in this case if either of them was hiding something from the other, if either of them was sneaking out and telling lies about their doings — or at any rate not telling the whole truth — it was she. She felt sad. Did that make her a faithless wife? After all, she had sworn not just to be loyal to Ignacy — an oath she had never broken, not even in thought ("at least not conscious thought," she added mentally, "who can be responsible for their dreams?")—but to be honest too. Yet recently things had been rather flimsy on that front, to say the very least.

She felt a stab of guilt for leading her second life not just in parallel to the conjugal one but instead of it. The life that should have sufficed her, as a woman—a good husband, a successful home, activity in the charitable sphere, the spiritual care of the church—had decidedly been pushed into the background. The excitement she gained from her daring quest for the murderer was far greater than the joy of sedately caring for the domestic hearth; leafing through the periodicals in the library had been far more enjoyable than studying prayer books, and collecting donations for the restoration of the cathedral couldn't compare with gathering clues and trying to piece them together to solve the mystery of Karolina's death. Bah, lately she had had much more excitement from her conversation with the wrong Ignacy—Daszyński, not Turbotyński. It was frightening to think what the latter would have said if he knew that his sober, solid spouse had been to the hotbed of those socialist destroyers of public order.

Oblivious to his wife's musings, the professor increased his pace, but was then obscured by a passing carriage. All Zofia could see now was his bowler hat, after which he disappeared completely.

She stopped, sighed heavily, then vigorously walked ahead. Her aim was to turn her sense of guilt toward her husband into action, to achieve her purpose and prove to herself that the task to which she had devoted the past few days made sense. She felt she was hard on the heels of the murderer.

After passing the main post office she speeded up, wanting to get past a large, lavish building that prompted the envy of almost every doctor in Cracow. Medicine was not an unprofitable occupation here, of course, yet no one else in the entire city could afford such a grand mansion as the one Dr. Pareński and his wife had bought themselves. Zofia couldn't stop herself from peeking through the fence. The yellowing leaves on the trees concealed the facade of the residence, but beyond some bushes in the distance she spotted a nursemaid, trying to control the Pareńskis' riotous flock of children. "Mid-September already and just look at that! The bases of the rhododendrons have not been surrounded by straw or bark chips," she snorted to herself. "How unprofessional! All their plants will be destroyed by frost," she thought to her satisfaction.

She stopped just a few houses farther on. Right beside this palace of the Cracow medical aristocracy, in an unobtrusive little house, there lived a completely different physician in a rented apartment. He was not a professor, or a head doctor, and had only been qualified for about six months, but a conversation with him might give Zofia the answers to most of the questions that were bothering her: Could he possibly have been in league with Loewenstein, providing him with girls? If Karolina led another sort of life entirely, then why had he confirmed her violent loss of virginity in the postmortem report—what suspicions was he trying to avert? This time she wasn't going to play a subtle game by posing an accidental encounter—she meant to put her cards on the table.

❧

"Mrs. Turbotyńska, how pleased I am to be honored by a visit from you!" said Kurkiewicz, bowing low as he opened the door.

"Dr. Kurkiewicz," declared Zofia firmly, "we must have a serious talk."

"But of course, come in, come in." He gestured toward the door leading into his small subtenant's room. "I was not expecting you to seek my medical assistance, but I cannot say I am surprised. Indeed, I am a young doctor, admittedly, but I am sure that in our entire city there is no specialist to rival my experience . . ."

"I must warn you," said Zofia, sitting down on the wobbly chair he offered her, "that, as God is my witness, I shall show no restraint."

"But we can talk freely, Mrs. Turbotyńska!" he twittered, desperately trying to tidy up the mess in the rather modest interior without dropping his hesitant gaze from Zofia. "What matter brings you to me? I admit that I am more willing to work on the problems of people who are . . . do forgive me . . . younger, but issues of concern to long-married couples are not entirely alien to me either. In men in their prime the weight gain that I must say I have observed in the professor is sometimes to do with exhaustion . . . And then difficulties appear with the service of Venus . . . Is it that the professor is an anorgasmic?"

"No!" shrieked Zofia. "No! Good grief, what on earth are you saying?"

"Dear Mrs. Turbotyńska," said Kurkiewicz in dismay, while deftly kicking two books under the bed, "I cannot understand your indignation. The concepts of morality prevalent in all quarters tell us to have nothing to do with the realm of sex, calling it if not sinful, then at least immoral, but meanwhile everyday life, even as observed on a crowded city street, presents a sea of unavoidable sexual phenomena that are of interest to all and demand explanation . . . Madam, it is my dream to introduce a sexual theme into the everyday course of our speech and thought, but always"—here he raised a finger—"always in a scientific way."

Zofia was all but speechless with horror. Once she had taken in the scale of Kurkiewicz's impertinence, she lost her voice entirely. Trying to catch her breath, she began to choke.

"Water . . ." she finally managed to gasp, at which Kurkiewicz leaped from his chair and rushed toward a shabby sideboard, then, without interrupting his oration, he poured her a glass of soda water from a siphon.

"All so that even in company one might be able to conduct a sober-minded conversation in the sexual sphere without offending the ear with coarse expressions, and especially in conversation with a sexlore doctor, a person competent in every respect," he said, striking his chest, as if anyone might have doubts that he was talking about himself.

"Enough! Enough of this! I implore you!" Zofia finally cried in a hoarse voice, internally rejoicing that Ignacy had different scientific interests and that their life was filled with *marital duties,* rather than "sexlore." "The questions I have for you are to do with matters of a . . . let us not be afraid of the word—fundamental nature."

"But yes, quite so, Mrs. Turbotyńska!" said Kurkiewicz, beaming. "How happy I am that you understand, that you appreciate how vital it is to fight against sexual obscurity, against the lack of real knowledge about the wellness and illness of sexual relations. I wish to contribute at least one small, but very laboriously produced brick for the general good, and that is what I am striving toward, madam!"

"And I, Doctor, am striving toward the truth. The truth about the death of Karolina Szulc, my young maid who was well known to you, and who in April of last year was murdered and thrown into the river. And whose postmortem was carried out by none other than you in person."

"Indeed, so it was," said the doctor in embarrassment. "But the professor is familiar with the results of Miss Szulc's postmortem, and the culprit, as I know from the press, was soon caught by the police . . . I really don't know how I can help you."

"You can tell me the whole truth about your relationship with the deceased."

"My relationship? I don't understand."

"On the contrary, you understand perfectly. Will you deny that you secretly made advances to her? Whenever you have visited our home, you have always been received as a . . . good friend, in fact there is no denying it, like a member of the family! Is this how you have repaid us for the kindness we have offered, for the patronage that my husband Professor Turbotyński has shown you without the slightest hesitation, whatever the need?"

"Mrs. Turbotyńska, I cannot deny that Miss Szulc's beauty may have stimulated an agent of rapture in me on more than one occasion," said Kurkiewicz, confusion writ large on his face, "but I am not one to lead a roistering sex life, and not for an instant did it ever cross my mind to seduce Miss Szulc."

"Is that so? In medical circles you are to some degree famous, not to say infamous. Your interest in sexual matters is defined as *pa-tho-lo-gi-cal,*" she hissed.

"Human envy knows no bounds, madam!" he exclaimed plaintively, but quickly changed his tone. "And to think I assumed you had come on a scientific matter, wishing to improve the service of Venus within your own conjugal life, when in fact you too want to grind me down! All sorts of difficulties have already been inflicted on me at the university, but they have not succeeded in destroying me! Now, when by truly superhuman effort I have managed to defend my doctoral dissertation, the city is once again warning off my patients, spreading ugly rumors about me, and coming up with charges that are not just indecent but an affront to common sense!"

It occurred to Zofia that she had had quite enough of all these self-pitying men by now, blaming everyone but themselves for their problems. It was usual to say that women become hysterical—a topic that always prompted vast amusement among Ignacy's colleagues—but meanwhile Zofia found that it was chiefly the men in her environment who were prone to this affliction. Without holding back, she threw the facts in Kurkiewicz's face.

"Enough of these games, sir. I know everything. Your contact with the world of prostitution is familiar to me. You frequent a house of ill fame belonging to a man named Brand, supposedly for 'scientific' purposes . . ."

"Not supposedly, madam!" said Kurkiewicz indignantly. "I research the agents of sexual arousal in both women and men, so it is natural for me to seek knowledge on that topic in a place as obvious as a whorehouse, and Mr. Brand is good enough to allow me to conduct my research. I talk to the girls who work there, I question them on the said topic . . . naturally, while maintaining the greatest discretion, without asking about their clients' identity. Moreover, as you may know, the regulations for the conduct of prostitutes forbid them from revealing names on pain of imprisonment. As you yourself can see, my interest in the facility on Joselewicz Street is of a purely scientific nature."

"Am I to understand that your contact with Madame Dunin is also purely of the same nature?"

"Madame Dunin?" said Kurkiewicz.

"Please do not pretend. Her, as you put it, 'whorehouse' is on Różana Street in Dębniki. A small house, with jasmine growing in the garden—you know the place very well."

"I do not understand, truly . . . I have never been there, I do not know that establishment, please believe me!"

Certain until now that she had identified a suspect, Zofia began to have doubts. The amazement on Kurkiewicz's face seemed sincere. Could the young doctor really be such a skilled actor? Or perhaps, like the hero of Stevenson's novel, he was horrified by his own evil deeds, and sought atonement in charity work, or at least the sort of work that is regarded as charitable? She decided to go for broke, and regardless of the consequences, to try to call forth Mr. Hyde from inside Dr. Jekyll. If the worst occurred, she could always defend herself with her umbrella.

"Are you really trying to persuade me that you do not belong to the despicable company involved in trafficking young women? That you do not help Mr. Loewenstein, or Lewicki, to sell innocent virgins to houses of ill fame in Constantinople and Buenos Aires? That you do not exploit your medical knowledge for dishonorable purposes, thus breaking the Hippocratic oath?" Rising from the creaking chair, she almost screamed the final sentence, and towered above Kurkiewicz, who cowered in his armchair as she leaned over him like the goddess of revenge in a royal-blue dress. Just in case, she kept a tight grip on her umbrella handle, shaped like the beak of a bird of prey. The magpie's wing on her hat quivered menacingly, like the wing of an enraged Fury.

"Mrs. Turbotyńska, I don't know what you are talking about!" She could see genuine terror in Kurkiewicz's eyes. "I don't know anyone called Loewenstein, or Lewicki, I . . . I could never . . . I am disgusted by whorehouses, those dens of female degradation . . . It is sexual obscurity to which . . . I am opposed, which I would gladly fight . . . I swear to God! I swear on my dear old mother's life!"

Instead of a terrifying Mr. Hyde, a rascal devoid of all moral restraint at the service of Loewenstein, what Zofia had extracted from Dr. Jekyll-Kurkiewicz was the Tartuffe of the medical world.

"And so," she said, sinking onto the chair in resignation, "if you were not in league with Loewenstein, and you were not out to seduce my Karolina, why did you try to ingratiate yourself with her?"

"I did no such thing! I tried to persuade Miss Szulc to help me with my work!"

"What kind of work, for goodness' sake?"

"Scientific, of course!"

"Dr. Kurkiewicz, from what I understand, the sphere of your scientific interests . . ." said Zofia, pausing to clear her throat, "concerns intimate matters, and yet the late, lamented Karolina had not the least experience of anything of the kind. You yourself confirmed it when you conducted the postmortem on her unfortunate remains. What possible use could you have had for her? Unless"—she raised an eyebrow—"you lied in your police report."

"How can you say that, Mrs. Turbotyńska? I wrote the truth. Miss Szulc was in a virginal state until almost the final hours of her life."

"Then why were you so interested in her? What help with your work are you talking about?"

"Please forgive me when I tell you that you are wrong to think a lack of physical experience in sexual matters is the same thing as sexual obscurity. One can be a dissolute person but have little idea about sexual matters, and vice versa, one can be a very modest person and understand everything perfectly. A modest, sheltered virgin who spends her life in seclusion is not necessarily a sexually immaculate person . . ."

"How can you make such insinuations?! Have you no shame?"

"It's not a matter of shame, madam," he briskly replied, "when in everyday life shame is a demand of obscurity, shame prompted by the mere thought of 'indecent' parts of the body and its capabilities. Indeed, it is hard for a doctor specializing in sexlore to conduct such conversations, especially with women, who are unaccustomed to talking openly to men about sexual themes, and regard them as obscene. Meanwhile everyday life presents multiple, unavoidable sexual phenomena. We grow up, we mature, the developmental changes to do with reaching sexual maturity take place in us, which is a shock to our entire system; we observe the sex life of dogs, poultry, and other domestic animals." Kurkiewicz spoke faster and faster, with ever greater and more patent excitement. "Sharpening our curiosity and awakening our imagination push our thoughts onto lecherous tracks. Female servants, young, but still in a maidenly state, offer particularly valuable research material here. They are being sexually aroused, whether while operating a foot-treadle sewing machine, or riding a bicycle, or performing particular dances . . . in fact all dances, because they are essentially a sexual amusement, when bodies come close together during the moves, especially when heated by liquor . . ."

"Dr. Kurkiewicz, please come to the point."

"I am just about to. I was interested in Miss Szulc's experiences. I tried . . . in vain, unfortunately, to question her about her experiences of pleasuring herself."

"Pleasuring herself?" Zofia frowned, not entirely sure what exactly the man had in mind. Though nor was she sure she really wanted to know. As the wife of a professor of anatomy she was not someone in a state of—how had Kurkiewicz put it?—sexual obscurity, and yet she maintained the attitude that some topics were quite simply indecent, even on the lips of a doctor.

"Oh yes, madam. From the research I have conducted to date, still incomplete, I should add, but already capable of providing a certain basis for some general statements, pleasuring oneself is an extremely common phenomenon.

One schoolboy admitted to me that he and a large group of other pupils sat down on several benches in Planty Park and committed self-pleasuring."

Zofia was finding it all increasingly uninteresting, so she began to look around the modest room; if it stank of anything in here, it was definitely not money. The furniture was cheap and shabby, the armchairs with worn-through covers must have seated many a tenant in this lodging and there was a row of chipped plates on the sideboard. In short, every detail of the place implied poverty, not to mention general neglect; someone was definitely saving on the cost of a maidservant here.

Meanwhile, Kurkiewicz did not stop talking.

"Only a few days ago there was a farmhand selling cucumbers on a cart in Szczepański Square, lying on his belly on top of them with his appendage out! In the Cloth Hall, a young high-school pupil was ogling a shop display of postcards showing the likenesses of naked women, while pleasuring himself through his trousers!"

"That is quite enough! I refuse to hear another word!" Zofia was sure by now that the doctor had nothing to do with the abduction and murder of Karolina. He was completely insane—no bandit in his right mind would have employed someone like that in the role of his subordinate. This man had no restraint, he spouted whatever nonsense sprang to mind, and he'd have exposed the criminal gang's entire clandestine operation at the first opportunity. Quite apart from the fact that any underhand income gained from supporting the criminals would have found reflection in this miserable interior. "The things you are saying are shocking! I am not surprised Karolina refused to talk to you about such matters! She was little more than a child!"

"Shocking, yes! Cracow is like Babylon, dear Mrs. Turbotyńska! Debauchery is rife, the sexlorists' waiting rooms are always filled with patients, where one can even see school uniforms, and yet there's never a squeak about introducing sex education in our schools! Everywhere there's talk of all the depravity, but lewd etchings continue to circulate among the youth, lewd journals lie calmly beside their pillows, girls bring each other such literature, 'from one young lady to another.' And what is done about it? Nothing! There should be no place for a feast of the imagination, or furtive conversations among friends both male and female, but there should be a place for facts, for reliable information. We should be promoting genuine sex education, on a large scale, especially among women . . . then they would be more level-headed, more resistant to the threats lying in wait for them from all directions. We must dispel the darkness that is causing the defective state of sexual affairs! And that is the task I have set myself, madam, I, Stanisław Teofil Kurkiewicz! I guarantee that my name shall be famous yet! Not just in this city, not just within the empire, but throughout Europe. It shall undoubtedly be so when I publish my work, my *opus magnum,* which not only sums up the state of present sexloric knowledge, 'sexological' knowledge, but also, let us openly declare, considerably expands it!"

But Zofia refused to listen any longer to the doctor so obsessed with "sexlore" that he sounded as if he himself were in need of medical help. She stood up, straightened her hat with the magpie's wing and muttered a few words in farewell. Once in the doorway she turned on her heel and said: "Why have I not seen you at the eating-house on Wolska Street of late?"

Kurkiewicz shot her a pitiful look and said just one phrase: "The schnitzels."

"The schnitzels?"

"Veritable hemlock. Three days of food poisoning, while my scientific work lay fallow. I cannot risk such a long interruption a second time. Now I dine near the medical faculty. I do have to pay a tiny bit more, but . . . you are sure to understand."

❧

While her employer was navigating the streets off the Market Square, Franciszka had ventured into a far remoter part of town.

If Zofia had alighted the tram now, if it were she who was now passing the eccentric, rippled facade of the church of the Brothers Hospitallers, she would certainly have thought the city was at an end, with nothing but a bridge separating her from the countryside — in fact, the Podgórze district. Franciszka had a different gauge for these things; if she could see more hackney coaches around her than farm animals roaming free, she had to do with the city, and that was all.

A washerwoman was emerging from the penultimate house before the river, carrying the large wicker basket in which she had just delivered some clean laundry; she placed the basket, now light, or at least lighter, on the cobblestones and reached into her pocket to count, or most likely recount, her payment — a few small coins. To make sure, Franciszka glanced at her in case it was Karolina's mother, then turned into Podgórska Street, which ran along the riverbank, passed a painter with a ladder slung over his shoulder (carefully, to avoid catching her puffed sleeve on it), then two ragamuffin boys heatedly arguing over nothing, and finally reached the solid stone bridge named after the Emperor Franz Joseph I, which led her to the triangular Podgórze marketplace.

Izdebnicki Road, the oldest in the city, bore no comparison at all with its more prominent streets; the houses were not built here to be decorative, or to show off their turrets and frills, but to provide a roof overhead, sheltering countless little chambers, the workrooms of brush makers, leatherworkers, rope makers, seamstresses, milliner's assistants, glove makers, etcetera, etcetera, the worker bees of the Cracow hive, supplying the city on the other side of the Vistula with first-rate goods and—very occasionally—third-rate, haggard faces.

Such places and such people were not unfamiliar to Franciszka; she herself had been brought up in the countryside near Bielsko, and in Cracow had gone straight to the home of the Dutkiewicz family, may the master rest in peace; but unlike Zofia, she had come to know the darker—though luckily not the darkest—parts of the city. So she was not at all surprised by the strong, sweetish odor, a mixture of the smell of boiled cabbage, cat piss, mildew, and sewage pits hidden in courtyards, nor was she amazed by the dark gateways, gloomy hallways, damp basements, and creaking wooden steps that threatened to collapse underfoot at any moment as in a nightmare.

Karolina's mother lived in one of these houses—definitely not at the front, because even in Podgórze, launderers and washerwomen couldn't have afforded rooms looking onto the street. Finally, Franciszka learned from a bony old woman, resting her elbows on a cushion in the window of a small two-story house, that Miss Szulc Senior lived two gateways farther down, in the annex. Franciszka thanked her and, quickening her pace, walked onward.

The courtyard was no uglier or prettier than the rest; it was dull and dirty, with a puddle shining here and there, and the miserable foliage of the occasional weed. At the far end, in the shade of a gallery suspended from the first floor, she could see a door into the annex—the blue and red panes of glass set into it provided the only splashes of color in this desert of brown and gray. Her signpost was a window to the right of the entrance, the only one set ajar, and that was belching out a damp, pungent smell of soapsuds. She pushed open the door with the colored glass and went into a hallway.

She knocked once, waited awhile, then tried again. Finally she heard a shuffling noise and a lock grating.

"Jesus Christ be praised."

"Forever and ever, amen," replied the wreck of a woman whom Franciszka remembered from the funeral a year ago; the woman clearly recognized her, too, because at once tears sprang to her eyes; with a hand as red as a piece of meat, she reached for her apron and wiped her face. "Come in, missy, come in."

Despite the open window, the room was so full of steam that it was hard to make anything out beyond the shape of a holy picture on the wall, surrounded by stains of black mold, a few miserable sticks of furniture in the corners, and above all some large, steaming washtubs.

"Take that basin off the fire, Mother. It's a pity to waste it; we must have a talk."

For a while the washerwoman said nothing, looking at her hesitantly, but then she wiped her hands and said: "I were just getting close to breathless. I'll take off me smock, let's 'ave a sit and rest a wee while."

Franciszka sat down on the small stool offered to her,

while Karolina's mother fetched another from behind the tubs, put it in the middle of the room, and sat with her legs wide apart. She rested her elbows on her knees, propped her head on her hands, and asked: "So what's there to gab about? 'E killed my little girl; there ain't nothing will bring 'er back."

"So he did."

"But the police tracked 'im and killed 'im. Revenge for the wrong 'e done me."

"They didn't kill the bloke as killed her."

The woman crossed herself, then said reproachfully: "What's this yarn you're spinning? It were in the papers, the sacristan 'imself read it to me."

"May lightning strike me on the spot if I'm not telling the truth," said Franciszka.

"You're gabbling nonsense. When's the lightning ever indoors?" She waved dismissively, then fixed her gaze on the floor. "Oh my, the whole floor's wet. I've slopped water on me shoes . . ."

"I'm telling you," Franciszka repeated emphatically, "the man who killed her goes free. And we've got to find out who he is. And for that" — she took a deep breath — "you have to tell me whose child your daughter was."

The washerwoman cast her a mistrustful glance, then shook her head.

"It's all the same to me now. Soon enough I'll be a goner, and I tell you, that's all I'm waiting for. All I'm waiting for is to die soon, and then I'll see my Karolina. And we'll look down together from on 'igh as the devil in 'ell sticks splinters in 'is eyes."

"But what if he's alive? What if he goes on living for a long time?"

The washerwoman raised her tired eyes to her, blinked, and sniffed.

"I've all eternity to wait, so I can wait a few years."

"Tell me whose child Karolina was, and I'll make sure that . . ."

The washerwoman put her hands on her hips.

"'Oose child? She were mine! Mine alone."

"And you won't say who else's?"

"No, I won't."

"You won't say?"

"I won't."

"Even if that would mean they caught him?"

She hesitated, but for the third time she snapped: "I won't."

"So that's the kind of mother you are," said Franciszka. "Don't you care if the man who took her life goes free?"

"What kind of a mother am I? What kind of a mother am I?" She leaped to her feet. "What sort of a life 'as it been? What sort of a life 'ave I 'ad, what sort of a life would she 'ave 'ad? Launder and iron, iron and launder. Coughing over the tub's the least of it, but it makes you spit out your guts . . . sweltering 'eat or freezing cold, trailing to the city on foot, lugging all that weight, pushing that laundry basket . . . 'ear-ing out the whining of all those ladies, this ain't ironed well enough, that stain ain't come out . . . feeling scared there'll be nothing to put in our mouths, or we'll 'ave to eat peelings like animals again?" she almost screamed. "Cramped in this room, with rats and weevils running about it? When she were so 'igh" — she raised her hand less than a yard from the floor — "a little tot, she were already grabbing the 'em of my smock, wanting to 'elp. A golden child, golden . . ." At this point she was overcome by grief. Franciszka waited, while nothing but disjointed syllables broke through her sobs, impossible to decipher.

"By the mother of God, you must understand: it all depends on you alone whether or not they find him! And for that to happen you have to tell me whose child Karolina was."

"Noo, nooo . . . he's a b . . . a b . . . bad man!"

"I thought as much, seeing he abandoned you," said Franciszka, looking around for a piece of rag, then finally reached for the apron the washerwoman had removed and began to wipe her tears for her. "All right now, it's all right, have a good cry."

And she cried and cried, but more and more quietly, until she fell silent and just lay in the girl's arms, suddenly seeming even smaller and scrawnier than before.

"What's there to gab about? There's nothing to gab about. Karolina were born out of wedlock."

"That I know."

She shook herself free of Franciszka like a dog shaking

off water, sat upright on her stool, and smoothed down her skirt.

"'E were a liar, 'e spoke fine words to me. And I were young and foolish. At first 'e took me for 'oney, 'e dressed like a lord, 'e were good-looking . . . And 'e were a fighter, 'e'd smash anyone in the mug. 'E 'ad plenty of respect 'round 'ere."

"Strong, eh? So was he a sand miner? Or a porter, perhaps?" asked Franciszka, but in vain.

"Why are you so eager to know? We 'ad a good time. 'E did what 'e did, the main thing were 'e came 'ome and 'eld me in 'is arms. But when I swelled up 'e turned savage; 'e spoke to me quite different from before. Things changed mighty quick. Every day 'e yelled at me, and 'e took to thumping me, too. One time I 'ad a bump on me 'ead for a fortnight."

"But what's his name?"

"I won't say," she replied through clenched teeth. "Go and ask an old tattletale; she'll spin you plenty of yarns, she will. So I gave birth to Karolina, and I were on me own with 'er, 'cos me ma denied me, too. And she were a lovely child! Well, you know how lovely she were. And I . . . I could see . . . she were starting to cough, spluttering in the corners, sometimes she coughed all winter, 'cos everyone's throat sickens from the soapsuds. Soon she'd stop growing, out of poverty . . . My golden child . . ." And she began to weep again, but this time it was brief. "When it pinched really bad I even went over there to see 'im, I knew what 'e were doing, 'oo 'e were biding with . . . I knew that for 'im taking five gulden out of 'is wallet was like nothing . . . but not a chance."

"He didn't give you anything?"

"Not a penny." She spat on the floor. "'E didn't value me or Karolina."

"A fighter or not, he sounds like a dirty cur!"

"A dirty bastard!" agreed the washerwoman.

"Mother, what are you hiding it for? Why can't I go and tell the world about it?"

The washerwoman shrugged.

"'Ow the 'eck do I know? These days 'e's the lord and master, 'e goes to faraway lands, they say. Years on end I ain't seen 'im. But 'e's a bad man, bad. 'E'll find out I've yapped and 'e'll crush me like a bedbug."

"But the police . . ."

"The police are worst of all," she said, and spat. "'E 'as policemen like dogs on tethers."

For a while Franciszka examined her closely; it wasn't a matter of fear, or at least not just fear.

"Are you ashamed?"

"What do you think? Should I be proud of a child out of wedlock?"

"No . . . don't be ashamed that she was born out of wedlock."

The washerwoman got up, turned her back on Franciszka, plunged her hands into the washtub, and started doing the laundry. But the girl felt she was on the right track now, and wasn't going to let it drop.

"A priest? Was she a priest's child?"

The only answer was a giggle and a splash of water.

"Was he married?"

Silence.

"A Jew?" asked Franciszka, though it seemed to her very unlikely; different kinds of people kept to themselves.

The washerwoman blushed to the tips of her ears. She stopped doing the laundry and turned to face Franciszka.

"'E was a Jew, but you'd never guess. 'E ate 'am, and 'e never went to the synagogue. Never dressed like other Jews neither, but in city style . . ."

"Oh, Mother, Mother . . . you've told me everything now. So just tell me his name."

She fixed her gaze on the floor again and said nothing. She raised her large, wet hands, folded her arms, and then finally spat it out.

"Józef. Józef Silberberg. But now go. And God be with you."

Then she swiftly turned, plunged her hands into the water, and began violently washing someone's shirt or tablecloth. Through the splashing, intermittent choked sobbing could be heard.

☙

Franciszka served at table, instead of Józia, who had the day off—and if Ignacy had been less absorbed in consuming his lunch, he might have spotted the constant stream of meaningful glances running between his wife and the cook. But there was mushroom soup with cream, then veal cutlets *à la Maintenon,* spread with goose liver pâté in Madeira aspic, followed by crêpes with cherry jam, dishes that were not just among his favorites, but heavy too, forcing him to take a solid nap. The moment the first tentative snores resounded from the ottoman, Zofia was already halfway down the stairs; moments later she was at the top of St. John's Street entering the Market Square, and then on her way to Grodzka Street.

At the courthouse most of the cases were over by now, the defendants and their accusers, the plaintiffs and witnesses, lawyers and members of the public were all gone from the corridors, at any rate today, when no particularly interesting cases had come up for trial, only a few of the regular attendees had appeared, who were ready out of boredom to watch anything, even someone's boundary dispute. At this hour, afternoon repose was gradually pervading the thick walls of the venerable building.

When Zofia entered the hall, Klossowitz was just lowering his brightly polished shoe to the bottom stair; he had finished work and, a little preoccupied, with the afternoon newspaper — plainly brought by the court usher — under his arm, he was heading off to an unknown destination, which in any other situation would certainly have been of great interest to her. But today, excited by Franciszka's discovery, she didn't care if the investigating magistrate was on his way home for lunch, to join a friend for a game of chess or to see his lover, or even if he actually had one at all.

"Good day, Mr. Klossowitz!" she exclaimed with slightly exaggerated warmth, watching from the corner of her eye as the usher trudged out of his wooden lodge and came to a stop, like a puppet. "I was just crossing Grodzka Street, so I thought I would take the liberty of dropping in on you with a small invitation. We are organizing a tea party . . ." She noticed to her satisfaction that the usher had lost interest in her person and had now fixed his watery eyes, red from conjunctivitis, on the opposite wall.

"Ah, Mrs. Turbotyńska," replied Klossowitz, "how very kind, I would love to take tea at your house! In that case let us not stand in the hall — may I invite you into my office for a moment?"

And without waiting for affirmation, he turned on his heel, and with swift, vigorous strides of his shining shoes, he climbed the stairs to the first floor, heedless of whether Zofia was keeping up with him. He stopped outside a dark brown door, took a key from his pocket, and turned it in the lock, which probably dated back to the days of the Cracow Republic.

"So what is the matter?" He showed her to an armchair, and walked around his massive desk. "Have you come upon something interesting?"

"This and that." She shrugged, hiding her minor triumph for the time being. "I have made some inquiries here and there; in truth I have approached a wide variety of people, with whom you would never suspect me of being in communication."

He didn't say a word, just quietly muttered to himself.

"And so," she began, "today I sent my servant to Podgórze, and thanks to her sterling efforts she has extracted some information. An astonishing piece of information. It is that Karolina had a father."

"Everyone has a father of some kind."

A fly buzzed, trapped between two panes of glass.

"Indeed. And yet not everyone knows his father's identity."

"Mrs. Turbotyńska, I can assure you that this is not news to me. I even have experience of cases where the mother was not so much unwilling as unable to say who had brought about her . . . er . . . in this situation one hesitates to call it 'blessed,' but so be it, blessed condition."

"That cannot be said of Karolina's mother. She was involved with the girl's father for some time before he abandoned her and refused to acknowledge his daughter. He never provided for her or supported her in any way—he did not care. He took himself off to distant countries on business."

"And presumably she never set eyes on him again?"

The magpie's wing gently quivered along with the rest of the hat.

"That I do not know. But I would like to find out, because it seems his identity is not without significance. In fact Karolina should have been named Miss Silberberg."

Klossowitz's eyebrows shot up.

"That Silberberg?"

"Józef Silberberg, who trafficked young women in league with Loewenstein, then eluded the police before the Lemberg trial and vanished like a dream at break of day."

She watched as with a semiautomatic gesture Klossowitz slid an index finger under his buttoned-down collar and scratched pensively; but soon remembering that opposite him sat a lady, he hid his hands under the desk in embarrassment, like a small boy caught behaving indecently.

"He vanished, then reappeared."

"Aha, I can tell you know something else about him," said Zofia.

Silence fell. His Majesty looked down with the same imperturbable, china-blue gaze at the odd couple sitting on either side of the desk, quietly pondering the problems affecting his large empire. In this silence the buzzing of the trapped fly became ever more furious and desperate.

"Well," said Klossowitz, sighing, "I know this and that from Commissioner Swolkień. Even if he was not tried, we have accumulated various kinds of proof, circumstantial evidence, and statements. The entire structure of the trade in young women is highly complex, as you probably know."

"Of course: there are '*gebers*,' '*fahrers*,' and '*herren*.'" She couldn't resist showing off her knowledge.

"That too, but I am thinking not so much of the division of labor as the relationships between the individual criminals." He reached for a sheet of office paper and a huge inkwell, dipped his pen in it, and began to draw a complicated diagram. "Here we have Loewenstein, or Lewicki . . . and Mrs. Dunin, lower down Sztycer. And various others. Loewenstein is a middle-ranking man. He has particular brothels under him, and in some cases, as we know, he owns them and someone runs them for him; otherwise the facility in question belongs to someone higher up, and this leech only gets a percentage. There are any number of people like Loewenstein at this level. And they do not necessarily know about each other — they probably regard each other as competitors, and have no idea that the money they rake in goes into the same coffers. Higher up, above each of them, there is another man, but we do not know how many there are at that level, or who they all are. Silberberg definitely belonged to this higher rank, he operated on an international scale, and Loewenstein was subordinate to him, as were several others. Which does not automatically mean he knew all of his . . ."

"We are talking about a secret society, if I understand correctly? As among the Carbonari?"

"You could put it like that," said Klossowitz, smiling. "Suffice it to say that the less someone knows, the safer he is, the smaller the chance of him giving anyone else away, and the inevitable result — that he will betray the entire network. They only know about their closest colleagues, their boss, and their immediate underlings."

"For certain reasons I am inclined to believe . . ." said Zofia, but suddenly broke off, stood up, went over to the window, and released the maddened fly, then casually returned to her seat. "For certain reasons, I am inclined to believe that Loewenstein was not on good terms with Silberberg. On the contrary, I think he wanted to take a terrible revenge on him. But I found no explanation in the articles I read about the Lemberg trial. Indeed, Silberberg escaped, because, as I understand, he was higher up the ladder, he had more money, greater opportunities, and he was warned . . . but Loewenstein ended up in prison. Do you think that was why he wanted revenge? Because his boss had not warned him?"

Klossowitz leaned back in his chair and gazed out of the window at the dome of a church.

"Hm, no. I don't think so, it's not enough. It is often the case that a criminal at a lower level in the hierarchy takes the blame for one who ranks higher. Of course, the higher-ranking man takes care of him and his family for as long as he is serving his sentence. That is standard practice, and it would not provide a reason for revenge. I suspect it is more likely to be about money."

"Money?" said Zofia in surprise. "But when Loewenstein came out of prison as Lewicki he bought various firms and establishments."

"Chicken feed," said Klossowitz, waving a hand. "Of piffling value. I am talking about real money. The white slave trade earns enormous sums that are pooled to form a sort of . . . criminal's bank. Spending it all at once would be suspicious, and could lead to the exposure of anyone who throws money around ostentatiously. So people like Loewenstein have their earnings kept by these criminal bankers — almost always either their own bosses, or their bosses' confidants — who multiply their capital in an entirely legal way, on the Vienna stock exchange, for instance. Silberberg took all the cash with him, including the money scraped together over the years by Loewenstein."

"Where to?"

"Just imagine, to Brazil. And immediately started doing business there on a grand scale. He had brothels in Rio de Janeiro, quite a number of them . . . apparently he controlled an entire district. Maybe even two. And all this with the money he took from here. But I still do not understand why he came back."

"He came back? To Cracow?"

"But of course. Ah, because you . . . that's curious, because it confirms your idea about revenge perfectly. He must have . . . Would you excuse me a moment?" Klossowitz got up, then stood hesitantly in the middle of the room. Finally he gathered his strength and said: "Mrs. Turbotyńska, please forgive me, but because of the court regulations I cannot leave an outsider, even one whom I particularly like and appreciate, alone with the files. I am obliged . . ."

"Please do not apologize," said Zofia, rising from her chair and moving towards the exit. "I shall wait in the corridor, it is not a problem."

"In that case," he said, following her out, then, like the steward in a monastery, he carefully locked the door and pulled on the handle twice to make sure. "I shall run to the archive at top speed, and then I will show you something!"

By the time he came back and had readmitted her to his office, the sun was so low in the sky that dank twilight had fallen outside, and only the dome of Saints Peter and Paul's church was gleaming in the reddening glow, as if someone had set a fire beneath it that was now spreading on the wind to the window's golden-hued sash bars.

"Here you are," said Klossowitz, placing on the desk a wad of documents that must have been filed in the archive recently, because on the first page the date 1895 was written in shapely script, and underneath: *Documents relating to the death by suicide of Józef Silberberg, alias José Silva.*

"Suicide!" exclaimed Zofia, and feverishly began to turn the pages. Then it suddenly occurred to her that she had heard the name before. Of course, José Silva, who had come from Lemberg, and earlier from Brazil! On the morning of the sixteenth, after that terrible night when Karolina perished. "Please tell me, could it be possible that someone . . ."

"No, it was definitely suicide, he happened to be seen from a window on the other side of Floriańska Street. Just a moment . . ." He reached for the documents and took out one of the statements. "Here we are: *Alojzy Pagaczewski, sixty-eight years old, widower of private means* . . . not relevant . . . *through the window* . . . *at the hour of* . . . Yes, here it is . . . *in a state of great agitation, apparent from his care-*

less attire and the general chaos in his hotel room, he took a revolver from a drawer, placed the barrel in his mouth, and, having fired it, fell lifeless. Straightaway, the hotel staff burst into the room ... And that we shall find in another statement, please bear with me ..." He leafed through the documents, unable to find the right one, then finally took out a sheet of paper, held it at arm's length, and read: "*Maria Zawadil, twenty-six years old, spinster, chambermaid, stated in the presence of* ... *On hearing a shot, she dropped the pile of sheets she was carrying to* ... *She knocked at the door, and when the handle gave way, she burst into the room, where she found the body lying dead* ... There was no one else in the room, no one held him at gunpoint. He shot himself in the head of his own free will."

Zofia cast an eye over the documents—the statements of a few hotel employees, the report from the postmortem performed by Dr. Albin Schwarz, who the next day had left another autopsy to the student Kurkiewicz, the transcript of the identification of the body signed by Silberberg's cousin, Jojne Apfelbaum, in short, a multitude of words and phrases, written down by various hands, no doubt including those of Cadet Ecler or Pidłypczak, provided with stamps, signatures, and reference numbers. And for a while she tried to piece it all together into a single whole. Klossowitz stood by the desk, resting his splayed fingers on it.

"So the vengeance was a success," she finally said. "Loewenstein managed to punish Silberberg for taking his money overseas. And Karolina was just a tool in his revenge."

"In what sense?"

"First the alleged matchmaker, then Wolf Sztycer, the courtship, the cakes in cafés . . . all that trouble . . ." she said, more to herself than to him. "Well, sometimes men involved in business love money more than anything in the world . . . and it prompts jealousy they would never feel because of a woman. And when someone takes it away from them, they are prepared to make some extremely unusual sacrifices to wreak their revenge, a terrible revenge." At this point her voice began to tremble, so she broke off.

Klossowitz gave her time to calm down, and then asked: "You spoke of revenge earlier. How do you know . . ."

"Oh," she said, taking a small fan from her handbag and setting it in motion; the steady movement always helped to restore her composure. "I entered the lion's den. I went to see the editor, Daszyński, who . . ."

"You went to see Daszyński!" he interrupted her. "You will never cease to astonish me!"

"Who told me in quite some detail, probably too much detail, about his political adventures, including sharing a cell with Loewenstein." Here, leaving certain matters to the magistrate's imagination, she aptly summarized the nature of the vengeance applied by the pimps within their own environment.

Klossowitz sat down at the desk, took out a large notebook, and began to jot down names and draw arrows, now deleting, now adding another person.

"And so . . ."

"And so," she continued, "he used some excuse to lure Silberberg to Dunin's establishment, and there he must have shown him that the daughter he had abandoned many years ago had met with an appalling fate. She was dishonored, perhaps before his very eyes, maybe by Loewenstein, or by Sztycer, it makes no difference . . . and from there she was to be sent to a house of ill fame in Constantinople or Rio de Janeiro."

"Well, quite, but where is the reason for killing her? Loewenstein could have wreaked vengeance on Silberberg and earned some money too."

"That I do not know. Unless . . ."

"Unless?"

"Unless the fatal thrust of the knife was not inflicted by Loewenstein, but by her own father, wishing to save her from such a life, because he knew better than anyone that it meant a long, slow death over many years."

"And in the process," said Klossowitz, raising an eyebrow, "he ruined his enemy's business deal—he didn't let him make money off his daughter. For someone who loves money that much . . ."

"Maybe, maybe," she said, shrugging. "Suffice it to say that here we have a criminal case. Even if Karolina's killer is not alive, because he died at his own hand, Loewenstein is responsible for her abduction and most likely for her ravishment. I think you have pretty serious grounds for opening a case and . . ."

Klossowitz stared hard at his notebook, as if a vision

had appeared to him there. He put the pen into a brass holder beside the inkwell, then combed his fingers through his hair.

"No, Mrs. Turbotyńska. I am not going to open an official case. I shall do it my own way. Without publicity. And I ask one thing of you: not a word to anyone. Not a word."

❧

She emerged into Grodzka Street at that lovely time of day when the sun had already disappeared and the whole sky was shimmering with a range of colors—from pink and gold in the west, through lemon yellow, willow green, and azure, to a rich dark blue, heralding the night. The black peaks of the houses and church towers were drawn against this sumptuous background like paper cutouts in a Chinese shadow theater.

As she walked—rapidly, to be on time for supper—she thought about Silberberg, a man who seemed to her entirely devoid of conscience, with skin as thick as an elephant's hide, living off cruelty to others, a cynical schemer who always landed on his feet, but who had let himself be tricked from a quite unexpected angle. So even in Karolina's terrible death there was a sort of moral, she surmised, as she walked past the long facade of Elephant House, decorated with bas reliefs of thick-skinned elephants and rhinoceroses, in that a man who had committed so much evil in his life should die of a bullet molded from the same evil; if he had not abandoned Karolina's poor mother with their baby at her breast, years later he would not have put the barrel of a revolver in his mouth . . . So even in the soul of the ultimate scoundrel a conscience lay hidden, buried deep, that told him to . . . And incidentally, those two men, battling each other with utter ruthlessness, were like a sinister version of the medieval knights who waged war with such reckless abandon! Or the armor-plated rhinoceros and the armor-plated elephant from the Renaissance bas reliefs — beasts that would never yield to one another, but would fight to the last drop of their blood, and if they did let up for a while, it was only to lick their wounds and plan an even more cruel and painful revenge. It seemed incongruent that Silberberg had not taken his daughter's death on the chin; instead of taking up the challenge like Macduff, he had shot himself in his hotel room, although he could have . . .

And then, just as she reached All Saints' Square, she suddenly stopped in her tracks and almost swooned — she only saved herself from collapsing by using her umbrella for support. Out of the blue she had realized that Loewenstein's revenge was so vicious that nothing could ever requite it; even if Silberberg had killed him, if like a Persian satrap he had killed Dunin, Sztycer, and all his underlings too, if he had burned down the brothel on Różana Street with their still-warm bodies inside, he could never have washed out the stain. Yes, he had shot himself not because Karolina had been dishonored and sold to a brothel in Constantinople; he had shot himself because it was he who had unwittingly dishonored her. The rhino's horn had ripped open the soft underbelly of the elephant; in that small house in Dębniki a drama had been enacted worthy of the cruelest plays by Shakespeare or the Greek tragedians.

CHAPTER XII

In which Mrs. Turbotyńska makes a noble resolution, Ignacy paints a detailed portrait of a sultan and describes the final hours of a deaf old woman and a clerk's widow, and Franciszka measures out plums by the bucketful, but pitiless fate mocks all plans, thanks to which Zofia finds herself in the strangest of all confessionals.

Ignacy was still asleep, gently panting away, when Zofia opened her eyes, fixed her gaze on the bedroom ceiling and considered her own conduct over the past few days. Yesterday she had been so engrossed in the inquiry that not only had she barely found time for her own domestic duties, but she had also distracted Franciszka from hers by sending her to Podgórze. At supper she had answered her husband in monosyllables as she endlessly pondered various versions of events on that terrible night last spring; once or twice she had even spoken brusquely to Ignacy, who had been sincerely worried by her absent-mindedness.

When the lace trim on her nightcap fell over one eye, she raised it by blowing hard, then made a resolution: she would devote the entire day to the house, and in particular to making jam; September was well advanced, the plums were not too juicy and were absolutely perfect for making preserves.

In Cracow every lady was famous for preserves of some kind; Countess Potocka for her rose jam, Mrs. Rydel for her apricot—apparently her recipe did not tally with any known recipe, either from Mrs. Ćwierczakiewicz, the Polish equivalent of Mrs. Beeton, or the local Cracovian ones; the fame of Madame Longchamps de Bérier's raspberry juice had spread all the way to Lemberg, a closely guarded secret that she had apparently brought to Cracow on the day of her daughter's wedding to Karol Estreicher's son, and so on, and so forth. There was gossip about adding secret spices, improving the color with dark bilberry or elderberry juice, about the proportions of sugar to fruit, and about various peculiar additives; entire wars were waged among the supporters of ladies who coated the fruit in syrup and ladies who boiled the fruit with sugar, which did cost more, but, in some people's view, preserved the fragrance better. Whereas Zofia Turbotyńska was famous for her plum conserve, the recipe for which had been a gift from her mother, Antonina Glodt, as part of her dowry.

But if this was to be a day of jam making, she would have to get up as fast as possible and goad Józia and Franciszka into performing some extraordinary labors. Preparations for making plum conserve at Peacock House were like a military campaign—first came cleaning and sterilizing the utensils with boiling water (sieves for mashing and large spoons for stirring—wooden by necessity, because metal ones made the fruit blacken and acquire a bitter aftertaste), then fetching the fruit, the little stoneware jam pots and firewood, followed by selecting, washing, and stoning the plums, before one could finally set about the actual work.

"But, Franciszka, don't forget," cried Zofia from the kitchen, as she carried out an inspection of the sieves and spoons with the gravity of Napoleon reviewing his troops before a decisive battle, "to be absolutely sure to . . ."

"Buy walnuts! Ten green ones, in their shells."

"And thirty for shelling, yes."

Because Zofia's secret was to put whole green walnuts into the conserve, which added a robust flavor; naturally, they were removed before mashing the plums through the sieves, while pieces of shelled walnut were left in the conserve, a pleasant surprise to find and bite into with a soft crunch.

Ignacy had just finished breakfast in the dining room. He had been given orders to have lunch in town and not to come home before the evening, to which he had willingly agreed, because he was fond of plum conserve, as he was of all sweetmeats; although yesterday evening Zofia had not let him read out curious items from the *Cracow Times,* now she came into the dining room specially to ask what interesting news there was to be heard in the city, Galicia, the empire, and the whole world.

"A tram ran over a deaf old lady in Wolnica Square, *a Jewish woman named Dietel Forsche, eighty years of age,"* he read, partly paraphrasing, partly quoting the newspaper. "The poor thing did not hear the signal and the driver crushed her foot. She was being led along by two small children . . ."

"My God!"

". . . but they saved their skins by running away. *The emergency service ambulancemen staunched the hemorrhage* . . . and they took her to St. Lazarus's, where Obaliński operated on her. Amputation."

"How fortunate that it was Obaliński—you are always saying what an excellent surgeon he is."

"She died after the operation," concluded Ignacy drily.

"What else is there?"

"In the City of the Emperors they are celebrating the twentieth anniversary of the accession to the throne of Sultan Abdul Hamid II. *Medium height, he perfectly represents the refined Armenian type. His face emanates forlorn sorrow, he has a wide forehead, the eyes of a mistrustful thinker with flashes of energy, a long, straight, bony nose, wide lips, prominent teeth, yellow rather than white . . ."*

"Prominent teeth," said Zofia, shaking her head.

"His hair is cropped short, his black beard is streaked with gray; he has long ears, a pale, weary complexion, fine hands that tremble nervously . . ."

"No doubt about it: opium!" said Zofia, passing judgment.

"Perhaps, perhaps, they write that in his youth he was a long way from the throne and led a life of abandon . . . *an amiable voice, posture slightly stooping.* They also write that he spends three million francs a year on stables and harnesses, seven million on palaces, thirty million on cuisine, the same amount on various caprices, thirty-five million francs on gifts and salaries, and forty million on his harem."

"You can only be pleased to have just one wife, Ignacy," she said, smiling, "who does not entail such expenses."

Ignacy chortled, consumed the last piece of a sandwich, and said: "A strange suicide in Lemberg."

"Is it suspicious?"

"No, but it must have demanded extraordinary stamina. *Maria Koitschim, widow of a railway clerk, fifty years old. She was suffering from nervous strain. After sending the maid to town for purchases she locked the door to her apartment, then, using incredible force, with the poll of an axe she dealt herself a lethal blow to the skull, which cracked under the impact, and a stream of blood spurted from under her skin."* Zofia shuddered. *"Just then one of the neighbors knocked at the door. Mrs. Koitschim still had enough* *strength to turn the key in the lock and open the door. Then she cried:* 'Schauen sie, ich bin verrückt.'"*

"It is hard to disagree."

"*And:* 'Das hab'ich mir selber gethan!'† *and fell lifeless to the floor.* Further on it says she had prepared for her suicide; in one room there was exemplary order, and in the other she had shielded the windows with pillows, *and on the bed lay a clock removed from the wall.*"

"So first she tried to hang herself?"

"How did you know?" he asked, looking up from the newspaper. "Have you read it already?"

Zofia was confused.

"No, but as she planned to commit suicide and had taken the clock from the wall, anyone might assume she wanted to hang herself on the hook that supported the clock. In many houses that is the sturdiest hook of all."

Ignacy nodded appreciatively, while it immediately occurred to Zofia that in fact a suicide of that kind was extremely suspicious. *Kill oneself with an axe blow to the head?* she thought. *Whoever heard of such a thing? On top of that a witness who appears right on time and conveniently confirms it all? Highly suspicious, indeed. But Paris is not Rome, Cracow is not Lemberg, apart from which not every mysterious death demands the attention of Zofia Turbotyńska. But what if . . .*

---

* "Look, I have gone mad." (German)

† "I did it to myself." (German)

Her thoughts were interrupted by Franciszka, who was standing on the threshold, ushering in two delivery men carrying boxes full of plums. Soon Franciszka was measuring out ten bucketfuls, because that was the capacity of the large copper cauldron usually used for the laundry, which had just been scrubbed clean by Józia. Meanwhile Zofia took some paper down from a high shelf in the larder, from which she cut out circles that she then painted with vodka; before the little pots were tightly sealed, the paper circles would be placed on top of the conserve to stop it from going bad. Then she took some flints out of a small bundle, sterilized them with boiling water, and dropped them in the cauldron — during the stirring they were in constant motion, preventing the jam from burning underneath.

The delivery men took their payment, said thank you, bowed, and disappeared through the door, as did Ignacy, who was on his way to work. Then began the great task of washing the fruit, cutting out the rotten bits while complaining that this year the plums were unusually bad and expensive, chipping pieces off a head of sugar and grinding them to a powder, and scrubbing the little stoneware pots. There was a long day in prospect.

✤

However, as everyone knows, fate can be cruel; every resolution can fall prey to temptation, and the nobler the resolution, the stronger the temptation. And thus in the very middle of the work, when they had finished pureeing the boiled plums through the wire sieves—setting the stones aside to dry, of course, to be burned later in the stoves; in such an orderly household it would never have entered anyone's mind to waste the stones from ten buckets of plums—the doorbell rang. Zofia and Józia went on mashing the fruit pulp, now with a wooden spoon, now a short whisk broom with coarse bristles, while Franciszka went to see who had come to disturb them.

At first she did not recognize the gaunt young man who asked hesitantly: "Is it here I am to ask about lodgings for a student with impeccable manners?"

She said it was a mistake, and he thrust a slip of paper into her hand, whispering: "For Mrs. Turbotyńska in person," and ran off down the stairs.

Then she remembered who he was. Cadet Ecler, but in plain clothes.

Dear Mrs. Turbotyńska,

We have apprehended and brought in some witnesses. If possible, please come to the courthouse, where the usher will escort you to the right office.

Your faithful servant,

Rajmund Klossowitz

declared the note. And thereby fate asserted itself, mocking Zofia with this message. For a short while she tried to convince herself that she had doubts, and that the duty of making sure the plum conserve had the right flavor was going to take precedence over the inquiry. But deep down from the very start she knew that minutes from now she'd be through the gateway of Peacock House at speed, hurrying off to the courthouse.

She wiped her face, which was red and damp from standing in the hot, steam-filled kitchen, then paused to gather her thoughts.

"Franciszka, could you . . ."

"Yes, madam, we'll manage," replied the girl, understanding perfectly that it was to do with Karolina.

"Don't forget . . ."

"To stir in figures of eight, yes, madam."

Zofia ran to the bedroom to wash her face, change her clothes, smarten herself up with a touch of Pompadour Milk — in short, transform herself from a housewife into a lady.

"And don't forget," she called from the hall, as she was putting on her hat, "boil it until . . ."

"I know, madam" — it was Józia who called back this time — "until the spoon leaves a visible depression."

"And the conserve coats it evenly on both sides!"

Zofia was already pressing on the door handle as she shouted this final instruction.

❧

The court usher had indeed been fully briefed; waiting for her impatiently, he jumped out of his lodge as soon as she crossed the threshold, bowed low, and escorted her to the first floor, then down a corridor to a small room and from there into a side office, where she could clearly hear someone in conversation.

"This is a special room," explained the usher in a whisper. "Please come this way."

He handed her an envelope and pointed out some small steps leading to a fairly high platform. Once she was standing on it, she could reach a brass ventilation grate, through which she could see another grate, and beyond it the next room, where Rajmund Klossowitz was interrogating a thin fellow.

". . . when exactly, sir. I know nothing. Who remembers what he was doing on one particular evening a whole year later?"

"On a holiday, Easter Monday? There are people who would remember that."

"I must have been with the family."

"With the family?" said Klossowitz doubtfully.

"If it was a holiday, I was with the family," said the man, laying a hand on his chest in a solemn gesture.

He could have been thirty, or just as well fifty—his face was entirely expressionless, with no distinguishing features whatsoever, so inconspicuous that he could easily be lost in a crowd. His complexion, eyes, hair and mustache were all a dull gray. His clothing was neither elegant nor inelegant; even from here, through the two ventilation grates, Zofia could see that his entire body was like camouflage.

"And you do not remember a new girl being brought to Mrs. Dunin's establishment?"

"I do not. It's a large place, there's often a new volunteer . . ."

"Others remember. And you would not want to come across as the type that conceals things from the forces of law and order."

"Oh, no, Mr. Magistrate, of course not," he said, using ardent words, though there was nothing in his tone or on his face to back them up—on the contrary, his voice and expression remained blank. "If others remember," he added just as calmly, "you should ask them—they clearly have a better memory."

As they were having this exchange, Zofia remembered that she was still holding the envelope; she took the letter out of it and read:

Dear Mrs. Turbotyńska,

Please take note of all the details. Perhaps something will not concur with your information about what happened or about Miss Szulc's habits. If you would like to ask any questions, please send them by means of the usher . . .

She looked up from the sheet of paper and spotted the

usher, who was standing in a corner of the room, staring at the wall with perfect indifference.

. . . and he will bring it to me without delay.

R.K.

P.S.: I am sorry we have not placed a chair on the platform, but in a sitting position you would not be able to see the interviewees' faces.

She was touched not only by the fact that Klossowitz had sent for her, thus showing his appreciation for her contribution to the inquiry and her perspicacity, but also by his concern that she would have to stand up throughout the interviews.

"So I grant you, maybe there was a girl, maybe not. They say the heart is a poor servant, but so is the memory."

Klossowitz thumped his hand on the table, causing the man to jump in his chair.

"Fancy yourself as the fine aphorist from Podgórze, do you?" he shouted angrily. "Going to do some ballet for me too, are you? That's enough. Mr. Stoczkowski," he said, addressing his legal apprentice, invisible through the grate, "take the witness to a separate room and have him wait, perhaps he will remember something. And bring in the next witness, Miss Majer."

A few moments later a woman of not very strict morals, or so she appeared, sat down on the chair.

"Mr. Magistrate," she began, before Klossowitz had said

a word, "I don't know nothing, I swear, I don't know who robbed him. He was there, he came and took advantage of the services, but who did it . . ."

"Do not try to distract me with your stories of petty theft!" he replied impatiently. "First name and surname?"

"Anna Majer."

"Age?"

"Twenty-eight."

"What were you doing on the night from the fifteenth to the sixteenth of April last year? From Easter Monday to Tuesday?"

"I was in Chrzanów, at my ma's place, please, Your Honor."

"What about the others?"

"There weren't no others at my ma's," she replied in surprise.

"Where were the other girls?"

"If I was at my ma's, and they weren't at my ma's, in Chrzanów, how should I know?" she said, gazing at him with the placid eyes of a heifer.

Klossowitz drummed his fingers on the table.

"But perhaps you talked to them on your return?"

"My return from where?"

"From Chrzanów."

"Aaah, from Chrzanów? From my ma's? No," she replied decisively, "we didn't talk. A whorehouse, with respect for your ears, Mr. Magistrate, is no place for chitchat—we're there to do hard work."

And so on, and so on. Two more people were brought in, another prostitute, this time quite haggard, coughing violently, wrapped in a thick shawl, with brightly flushed cheeks—plainly a victim of consumption, like Beetroot Mary—and then a deaf old woman who laundered the sheets and towels at the establishment on Różana Street; six times she repeated that there was no better job for a washerwoman than working for bawdy houses of superior quality, because all the bedding went to the laundry every single time, and the stains were easier to remove. But nothing emerged from any of these interviews. The apprentice was asked to take the old woman away and bring in Mrs. Dunin; meanwhile, in the empty office Klossowitz said into thin air: "Of course these interviews are of no great significance, just the first round. We shall wait for them to soften up. Later on we can use any of the details we obtain to suggest to others that we know more than we actually do, and this . . ." He broke off, because just then the apprentice came back with the owner of the brothel on Różana Street.

"First name and surname?"

"Olesia," she said coyly.

"Full first name and surname!"

"Aleksandra Dunin," she replied, as if offended.

"Age?"

"Mr. Magistrate, surely you wouldn't ask a woman her age?" she said, fluttering her eyelashes and giggling.

Klossowitz cleared his throat meaningfully.

"Thirty-five."

"In your documents it says forty-one."

"Mr. Magistrate, let's not argue about it," she said, snickering again. Zofia could see through the grate that Klossowitz's ears were going red with irritation.

"The night of Easter Monday, the fifteenth of April, to Tuesday the sixteenth of April last year."

Mrs. Dunin stared into space, as if looking for something there; briefly Zofia thought she had been spotted through the double lattice of the grate, but it was just an illusion. She took a close look at "Olesia"; here was an example of vulgar beauty, perhaps, but Zofia knew that this look of wanton abandon, and the sort of temperament written on her face—and on the rest of her body—had an effect on men. And not just on uncouth brutes, like Loewenstein, but also on better educated types, such as Engineer Bzowski, to take the most obvious example . . . She can't have been expecting the police, because her attire was for indoors rather than out, and her makeup had been very cursorily applied, though when at-risk, women accustomed to taking advantage of their good looks were always careful to show themselves to the men on whom their fate depended in their most alluring and tempting guise, aware that this was their one and only strength. But even without her most powerful weapons, Zofia couldn't deny that Mrs. Dunin presented herself in a way that could not fail to work, especially on a hot-tempered man like Klossowitz: her dark hair was pinned up, and she had a slender neck, round shoulders, and an ample bust that rippled with every genuine or feigned emotion.

"I don't know, I really don't, Mr. Magistrate," she finally began. "I'd like to help, with all my heart I wish I could, but so much time has passed, life is full of unexpected events, and one's memory is weak and misleading . . ."

"Please force it to make an effort."

"Oh dear," she said, blinking. "How can I, a feeble woman, force anything? Where am I to find the strength? Fie!"

The tips of Klossowitz's ears turned an even deeper shade of red.

"Mrs. Dunin, please bring it back to mind. Last year, the Easter holiday, Monday evening. What happened at your establishment in Dębniki?"

Meanwhile Zofia nodded to the usher and handed him some questions, hastily scribbled on the envelope.

"Ah, one of those nights of happiness and joy! We, the daughters of Venus, do not count the nights or days . . . You know how they sing: *Girls of Dębniki, Girls of Dębniki, Take a torch or a candlestick-ee, To be sure no man will squeeze you tight, As you're making your way home at night . . .*" She emitted a peal of artificial laughter. Judging by her own reactions, Zofia thought Klossowitz would lose his temper, but suddenly she realized that his ears were not going red with rage, but because Mrs. Dunin's singular charm was working on him.

She heard a knock, then a loud "Come in!" and the creak of a door; she couldn't see the usher through the grates, just his hand placing the folded envelope on the table.

"Mrs. Dunin," Klossowitz began, while unfolding the paper, "tell me please . . . *Are you familiar*"—he paused in mid-question, but overcame his hesitation and read on—"*with the problems of Leon Brand's establishment?*"

Silence reigned.

"I have heard something about it," muttered Mrs. Dunin, without fluttering her eyelashes this time.

"You have? Hmm. *Do you realize that any establishment of the kind can have similar problems?*"

"Mr. Magistrate, please do not even joke about it."

Klossowitz scratched his cheek, then said calmly: "In Dębniki, as far as I remember, there is a parish church, which means there is also a parish priest. There is a school, too, with children in it, who can be corrupted by the proximity of a house of pleasure. And after that there is awful trouble, awful. Just ask Mr. Brand. What huge financial losses he has suffered! Not only Brand is totally bankrupt, but so is the widow who lent him the capital . . ."

It was plain to see that this made a staggering impression on Mrs. Dunin; Zofia could tell that, if not gifted with a great brain, she was good with numbers, was busy calculating the risk, the budget, the rates of interest, and the loyalties.

"Aha, the night from Monday to Tuesday," she said, bursting into feigned laughter, "perhaps I do remember it after all. The end of Easter, so it does stick in the mind."

"Miss Majer was away."

"Yes. But some of the girls were at home."

"And was there someone new?"

Mrs. Dunin was reluctant again, so Klossowitz decided to help her.

"Should I ask Mr. Brand to tell you about his troubles in person? He is sure to come running on the instant; he is very eager to be of service to the police. I would advise you to oblige us in advance, that will be more profitable."

"Yes, there was one. This fellow brought her along."

"What fellow?"

"Sztycer. Wolf Sztycer."

"Lately we have been unable to find Mr. Sztycer; he must be very busy."

"He is traveling," she explained in a gloomy tone.

"Very nice, a man who is curious about the world. Does he travel far?"

"I don't know, but I wouldn't be surprised if he did."

"All right," said Klossowitz, "so what do you have to say about the new girl?"

"She was a proper crybaby, trying to cut and run, begging and pleading. That kind has to be softened up first, but there was no time for it. What can I tell you, Mr. Magistrate? You know how it is. The silly little goose, she thought she was going to be married. Well, when people are young they think life's going to change for the better, they think they're special and fate's going to smile on them . . . but with age . . ."

"What was her name?"

"If only I could remember," she said, shrugging. "She did have a name. She just had to be pretty, and a virgin, because it was a gift for Mr. Silberberg."

"A gift?" said Klossowitz, making a note.

"Yes, he liked that kind. Szlomo, that's to say Mr. Loewenstein, I mean Mr. Lewicki said he did. He liked them all, but virgins the most. Especially when they resisted." With her face almost pressed to the grate, Zofia drank in every word, but with horror; she was starting to quiver with rage and disgust. "There was some bother, as you know, but he did his thing eventually . . ."

"And was he pleased?" asked Klossowitz unemotionally.

"I have no idea. But he only went in the morning, and by then I had been asleep for hours, because we all had a bit of a party with . . . Mr. Lewicki."

"What about the girl?"

Mrs. Dunin waved a hand.

"As if I could remember every one of them. She came and she went. Mr. Lewicki must have taken her somewhere, because I didn't see her again. She's living it up abroad, bathing in champagne in Brazil perhaps, or else she's got her own establishment in Havana by now and she's raking it in. She was young and pretty, why not?"

Klossowitz turned the key in a drawer, gently slid it open, and fetched out a photograph of Karolina, taken from the Turbotyńskis' apartment during the search.

"Is this her?"

Mrs. Dunin held out a ringed hand and drew the photograph across the tabletop. She turned it to left and right.

"Yes," she replied in a soft, neutral tone.

"She does not look the type to bathe in champagne nor to . . ." Hearing a knock at the door, he broke off. The usher came into the office again and handed him a slip of paper, on the back of which Zofia had written: *Please come here for a moment.*

"I'll be back shortly. The usher will keep you company."

Moments later he stood face-to-face with Zofia, or rather facing the folds of her dress. It was impossible to whisper like that, so Zofia had to come down from the platform.

"You see, sometimes one only has to add a little pressure and they sing like canaries. One or another piece of information, a snippet from an earlier interview . . . and there you have it."

"Something else happened there, too."

"Excuse me?"

"Something else happened there," she repeated, "and she thinks we know about it. She thinks *you* know about it. She said there was bother, '*as you know.*'"

"That did come up in one of the earlier interviews. Before you arrived, one of her staff stated that Silberberg quarreled with Loewenstein, or something of the kind. We shall find out exactly what happened once we have arrested Loewenstein."

"Do you allow the witnesses to talk to one another?"

Klossowitz looked at her as if she were extremely naive.

"Of course not, that would go against the rules of the art . . ."

"Quite so, as I have heard, each of them is led to a separate cell."

"Until the interviews are at an end."

"So she had no way of finding out that you already know something. Because you did not tell her that."

For a few seconds the magistrate looked at her attentively.

"With a certain degree of caution one could indeed assume . . ."

"Please question her further. You know about it, but you want to hear her version, of course."

"It goes without saying," he whispered, then bowed and instantly vanished through the door; setting foot on the steps as quietly as she could, Zofia returned to the platform. She was so excited that not only had she forgotten all about the plum conserve, but also that she had been standing up for a good two hours.

"You mentioned there was some bother on the night in question. I'd like to hear your version of the event."

"I don't understand," said Mrs. Dunin, sounding puzzled.

"It's quite simple. People remember different details and say different things. Not everyone tells the truth. So I would be obliged . . ."

"I can tell you something," she said, tossing her head,

"but I don't think you will believe me more than your own people. That's not why you send your own man, just to hear about it afterward from someone like me."

"What man?"

Her surprise was increasingly apparent.

"Your man."

"From the courthouse?"

"From the police—that commissioner came in the middle of the night, carried out a search, spoiled most of the evening for Szlomo . . . Mr. Loewenstein . . . Lewicki. He nosed around, did some shouting, and burst into Mr. Silberberg's room."

"Commissioner?"

"Yes, what's his name," she hesitated. "Jenerak. No, Jednoróg."

Zofia had been noting down the tiniest details of the interviews throughout, but now she could not force herself to write a word, so incompatible was this idea with her understanding of the entire situation.

"Commissioner Jednoróg was at Różana Street?"

"That's right. But he left. If anyone else had shown up on such an evening the boss . . . Mr. Lewicki would have had them beaten up and thrown out, but a commissioner can do a thing or two, as you know."

"Did he talk to the girl?"

"Eh? Where would he do that? She was already in Mr. Silberberg's room by then. But once he'd gone, it all worked out. Mr. Silberberg finished doing what he had to do, then he left, except that by then, to tell the truth, I was asleep."

The interview carried on, and Zofia tried to focus on the details, but nothing else remotely interesting came up. Meanwhile, Jednoróg's visit to the house of pleasure on Różana Street, veiled in secrecy until now, set everything else in a completely different, mysterious light; it tore aside a different curtain, or sewed it up perhaps, and this puzzle would have to be properly unscrambled.

⁂

"In the first place," she began her speech to Klossowitz, "does the commissioner . . ."

"The commissioner knows nothing. Earlier on, I deliberately chose policemen who are not his subordinates to help detain the witnesses, and the matter has been kept as confidential as our procedures will allow. In any case, Jednoróg is occupied."

"Occupied?"

"Have you not heard? As a distinguished officer," he said through clenched teeth, "he has been given chief responsibility for maintaining order on the day of His Majesty's arrival, when His Majesty stops in Cracow on his way back from maneuvers. And that is a vast amount of work."

"Surely," she whispered, "surely."

They stood for a while in silence, each in their own way trying to understand the reason for the commissioner's visit to Różana Street on the night of the murder, each seeking different justifications, each attempting to connect all the facts, but none of it joined together to form a single picture. To make matters worse, Zofia had broken the promise she had made to herself to devote the entire day to domestic affairs, and not the inquiry.

"Well," she finally broke the silence, "thank you for your invitation . . . and for placing your trust in me."

"It is I who must thank you for your assistance."

"I have to go now. I am incredibly busy. Today is my day for making jam. Ten bucketfuls of plums are no small matter!"

❧

But when she got back to St. John's Street, she found the apartment filled with not only a delicious aroma, but also a despondent atmosphere. Ignacy was sitting in an armchair, looking worried, by a lamp that had not been lit, and Franciszka was standing over the plum conserve, looking equally worried.

"Ignacy, what is the matter?"

"A dreadful thing has happened. Józia is no longer working for us."

Zofia went weak at the knees, upon which Ignacy reassuringly added: "No, no, not like with Karolina. There's nothing wrong with her, I simply had to dismiss her."

She lit the lamp to take a closer look at her husband;

there were various things that occupied him in life, whether it was cycling, or dissecting the respiratory system of a turtle, but on matters to do with the servants it was always she who made the decisions.

"Ignacy?" she asked in a tone that demanded an explanation.

He sighed heavily, then, blinking as his eyes adapted to the light, he looked up at her and said: "I myself am to blame. I was not going to return, but I needed a particular article for my work which I thought I would find in the annual edition of a certain journal, rather an old one in fact, so by now it has been stored in the attic. So I came home, fetched the attic key from Franciszka, learned that Józia had gone out . . . to buy something or see to something, I cannot remember . . . then I went up to the attic, and there . . . there was Józia. Not alone."

"Not alone?"

"No. With the chimney sweep."

"Perhaps . . ." she began, though she had no idea how to continue.

"No, in an unambiguous pose."

"This is worse than a war," groaned Zofia in her customary way.

"Fortunately no one else knows about it. Apart from Franciszka."

"But Józia was from Mrs. Mikulska's agency. What awful times these are!"

She felt a migraine coming on, and decided merely to

find out if the plum conserve would have to be added to the list of today's disasters. But she soon discovered that here was the only piece of good luck amid all this misfortune — Franciszka had managed perfectly. Despite the dramatic events she had not abandoned the cauldron; she had tossed in the walnuts at the right moment and kept an eye on the temperature, nothing had stuck to the pan, and the flavor was neither too sweet nor too sour. The honor of Zofia Turbotyńska's legendary plum conserve was saved. Though unfortunately the same could not be said about the honor of the household.

Naturally, Zofia praised Franciszka, then told her to transfer the jam to the little stoneware pots. They did not talk about Józia, and only as Zofia was leaving the kitchen did she hear Franciszka say, in a tone full of contempt and outrage, but also — so she thought — suppressed envy:

"There were two chimney sweeps."

CHAPTER XIII

In which Zofia awakes with the puzzle complete, finds out about a stationary celebration, and undergoes a trial by fire from which she emerges alive — but what a life.

Some people — especially the citizens of Lemberg and Vienna, but also Cracovians who had been to either of those cities — were inclined to make disparaging remarks to the effect that Cracow was a sleepy little town; but then a great deal can happen in one's sleep. When Zofia awoke on the morning of September the twelfth, she raised the drooping frill of her nightcap from her left eye and noticed that the twin bed beside hers was empty and the sun was already high in the sky. She rang for Franciszka and learned that the clock had just struck a quarter past nine. Her first instinct was to leap out of bed, but then it occurred to her that ten minutes would not redeem her—especially as somewhere on the borders of sleeping and waking certain things had fallen into place in her mind that previously had not fitted together at all. And now she would try to remember how her semiconscious brain had tied the threads together.

But, sober and awake, her mind couldn't do it. While she had a vague idea, whether real or illusory, about why Loewenstein had abducted Karolina, she still didn't know who had murdered her or why. It would have brought Loewenstein no profit to kill the girl. Silva could have stabbed her, in a fit of passion, horrified by the act his former associate had induced him to commit—but would he have left her body there, as prey for Dunin's employees? Had Commissioner Jednoróg carried out his raid on the establishment after Karolina's death or before it? Why had he not informed anyone about it? Why had he kept it secret? What was Wolf Sztycer's role in all this? Maybe he was the one who had thrust the knife into Karolina's heart? She felt as if she knew a lot now, but at the same time she knew nothing. She felt as if she was close, but as far away as before.

She sneezed, and with a heavy sigh got out of bed. She would have to supervise the tidying in the larder, where the new pots of conserve were to be stored; she might also make some pickles for the winter, while the cucumbers were still cheap, or she might sort out her summer clothes before putting them away in the wardrobes . . . And of course she must go to Mrs. Mikulska's agency for yet another housemaid. As she was standing before the mirror in her nightshirt, wondering which housedress to put on, suddenly a completely new idea occurred to her . . . or perhaps it was the one she had dreamed about just before waking, but which had hidden itself away from her. *Yes!* she thought feverishly, *yes!* Suddenly all the pieces began to come together to form a single, complex whole. But how was she to find confirmation? Where should she seek it?

In this situation a housedress was out of the question. She would have to choose something modest, but elegant. Restrained, but not associated with the mundanity of household tasks, an austere dress of gray serge, without excessive embroidery. She hung it over the back of a chair, raised the lid of the washstand, under which a clean bowl and a jug of fresh water were waiting for her, made ready by Franciszka, and began her morning ablutions.

And yet: the inquiry was one thing, the solution another, and the house was the house. Before leaving it at half past ten she had managed to issue instructions for lunch, cast a critical eye over the shelves in the larder, and check if any of the pots topped with sealing wax had come unsealed during the night. She was already halfway down the stairs when she returned, raced into her dressing room, combed through the letter rack, and, on finding the necessary item, flew out of the apartment again like a cannonball, fired in the direction of the nearby Róża Hotel.

Hardly had she sat down to lunch, muttering something about the host of things she had to do, thus justifying her frequent absence from home of late, when she noticed that Ignacy was not only paying more attention to her than to the dishes Franciszka was serving, but also that he had a mischievous glint in his eye that she hadn't seen there for many a year; for under the professor's frock coat, as she was well aware, beat the heart of a little scamp. He was plainly struggling with himself, responding in a perfunctory way to what she was saying, while postponing the revelation of an important, happy piece of news. And the more he held back, the more impatient she became.

"What would you say, dear heart," he finally said, cutting up a lettuce leaf with his knife, "if we were to spend Wednesday evening together?"

"Is it another race?" she asked suspiciously.

"Oh, no, nothing of the kind. We shall be standing on the spot. An evening that one could call"—his eyes sparkled again—"stationary. Festive attire."

"Ignacy, you and your riddles! You know that I dislike riddles!"

"Well then, Zofia, just imagine . . ." At this point Ignacy tried to perform an ingenious maneuver, to extract something, clearly prepared in advance, from under his plate; but he did it so lamentably that the plate slid off the table and would have smashed against the floor, but with uncharacteristic dexterity he lunged and grabbed it in midair, in the process smearing sauce the length of his sleeve; then, with a mixture of embarrassment and triumph, he put the plate back on the table, wiped his sleeve with his napkin, not very carefully of course, and finally finished his sentence.

"Just imagine, on Wednesday His Majesty will be making a brief stop at the station, and we shall be able to greet him! I have the tickets!" And these very tickets, only slightly spattered with sauce, were joyfully placed on the tablecloth.

The earth could swallow up the Wawel Castle, but he would go on loving me, she thought to herself, not without pride. Then, although lately she had been preoccupied by other things entirely, she resolutely said: "You are splendid!"

He blushed and dropped his gaze like a schoolboy.

"Of course the academic senate will stand closest, the officials, the secular and church authorities, the councilors and delegates, but we too, we too, my dear Zofia, will not be far away, in ticketed places, which the press has not yet mentioned, but within my modest capacities . . . and through my acquaintances . . ."

"Ignacy, which of the university professors is as good as you are at making his other half happy? And after yesterday's disaster, too?"

"Better, my better half," he said, blushing even more.

✤

Next day, at the courthouse, on the stroke of noon, several solemn, titled gentlemen had gathered in one of the gloomy, oak-paneled offices, and were now sitting around a huge oak table. They all wore dark frock coats or dark uniforms — if not for their collars and shirt fronts shining out of the shadows, if not for their faces, on which the feeble sunlight was shining, there would have been total blackness in the room.

The first to arrive was Magistrate Klossowitz, who had invited all of them the day before "on a rather urgent and delicate matter," then Magistrate Rozmarynowicz had appeared, who had been in charge of Karolina's case — having settled in the most comfortable armchair, he was now fighting off sleep — next to arrive was the man who often stood in for him professionally, Commissioner Jednoróg, and lastly the expert on white slave trafficking, Commissioner Swolkień, and also the chief of police, Counselor Korotkiewicz, who was patently annoyed at having been dragged away from his office for some idiotic reason. The greetings were rather sluggish; they had no reason to refuse Klossowitz's polite but firm invitation, but they all suspected he had gotten some crazy idea into his head and was going to waste their precious time.

"Gentlemen," he finally began, in a voice that for him was surprisingly hesitant, "I have taken the liberty of calling our small gathering together because the circumstances seem to me exceptional. This is not just about a specific case, but also the honor of the entire police force and Cracow's entire judiciary." At this, Korotkiewicz and Rozmarynowicz quite independently gave a nervous twitch, as they did whenever anyone dared to suggest that the Cracow judiciary or the Cracow police were not perfect creatures. "I must admit that at first I approached these revelations with reserve, and yet . . . convinced by . . . well, proof, and the implications, I decided to acquaint you gentlemen with this business, too. In view of the delicacy of the matters in question I must ask you for your total discretion. Everything that will be said in here must remain strictly confidential, and the only way for it to pass beyond our company should be by means of official court proceedings."

Just then Rozmarynowicz's head fell abruptly to one side, which woke him up and forced him to cough several times to imply that he hadn't been asleep at all.

"I hope," Klossowitz continued, "you will allow the case to be presented by the person who has put the most work into it, and who has come to some striking, as well as horrifying conclusions."

"Get on with it, Magistrate," Korotkiewicz interrupted him. "It doesn't matter who presents it, as long as they do it coherently. And quickly."

"Thank you. Gentlemen? I shall merely add as a formality that the person presenting will be under the same demand for total discretion."

The only answer was an impatient affirmative noise and some throat clearing, so he smiled wanly, took two paces, and opened a side door to admit a figure into the room whom none of the assembled company was expecting to see: Zofia Turbotyńska, née Glodt.

❧

The day before, as soon as she had obtained confirmation of her theory, she had run to Klossowitz and explained it all to him, detail by detail, then she had asked him to convoke this meeting. She was not sure if she would get her way; indeed, she was striking while the iron was hot, taking advantage of the stirring moment when she had dazzled him, beguiled him with her reasoning, but he might not necessarily agree. Luckily, matters of ambition came into play here, and also a sort of equivocation: he knew that if Zofia were wrong, faint odium would fall on him as a man who had wasted everyone's afternoon because of the delusions of a mad, ridiculous harridan, but his career would not be as badly shaken as it would if he rolled out the big guns; and if she was not mistaken, the victory would be ascribed to him anyway, the glory would shower down on him for solving a case. He knew how to calculate. And she too knew that in this case the arithmetic was on her side.

Just as the day before, Zofia had chosen the gray serge dress, restrained, not brightened by any color; in it she resembled a nun in a habit, or a governess with no inclination to smile; in short, she looked like a woman who holds her own sex in contempt. Nevertheless, when she entered the room, the gentlemen were so surprised that, expecting some junior policeman or court clerk, they did not instantly stand up; the first to join Klossowitz, who was already standing, was Jednoróg, who gallantly leaped to his feet and clicked his heels, to be followed by Swolkień; Korotkiewicz got up with some effort and evident reluctance, while Rozmarynowicz merely gave a nod, without rising from his armchair.

"You will forgive me, madam," he said in a tone of surprise, "but we are in fact here for an important meeting; we are in fact waiting for the clerk, but you can in fact submit your case at the appropriate time . . ."

"Mrs. Ignacy Turbotyński," Klossowitz introduced her, "who rendered us invaluable service in solving the mystery of the murders at Helcel House three years ago."

"Yes, we remember," said Jednoróg, smiling. "An extremely interesting case."

"Now, Magistrate, surely you don't think we've come to hear gossip and chitchat . . ." said Korotkiewicz, the first to be openly indignant.

"No, on the contrary," Zofia interrupted him, "you have come for a very serious conversation, because someone in this city, and not, I am sorry to say, any of you gentlemen, has discovered the identity of a murderer."

Gradually the muttering died down, someone said "All right then" in a quiet but tetchy tone, the gentlemen sat down in their chairs, and, having refused the seat offered to her, Zofia began her lecture.

"The key to the mystery of Miss Karolina Szulc's death,

because that is the case in question, is that we are not dealing with one puzzle, but with several separate puzzles, which join together in one place and time. Moreover, three separate players are in action there, each of whom knows only part of the truth, and in accordance with this incomplete picture . . ."

"Dear lady, could we get to the crux?" Korotkiewicz interrupted her.

"You gentlemen have had a year to get to the crux," she said curtly, "and as I intend to prove, you not only got to the crux, but went far beyond the target, hitting a completely innocent bystander."

Korotkiewicz frowned, wanting to add something, but he held his tongue.

"And so let us start by saying who Karolina Szulc was. She was nobody. Just an ordinary maid working for a respectable Cracow household . . ."

"For Mrs. Turbotyńska," explained Klossowitz.

"Quite so, but it is of no significance," she replied without smiling. "She was, as they say, a love child, though it is hard to tell if the love was mutual, or if on one side it was merely the base desire of a ruthless man. Suffice it to say that he abandoned both his *sweetheart* and the fruit of their liaison, and as a result this fruit ripened in ignorance of the fact that meanwhile her father had become a wealthy man, by plying the most shameful but also one of the most lucrative trades: white slave trafficking. This man was called Józef Silberberg, and was lately known as José Silva."

Korotkiewicz glanced inquiringly at Swolkień, who affirmed it.

"Indeed, there was a trafficker of that name. We failed to convict him at the Lemberg trial, and last spring he committed suicide at the Róża Hotel . . ."

"Not just last spring," Zofia interrupted him, "but on the morning after the night of the murder. But let us not get ahead of the facts. I am sure that Commissioner Swolkień" —at this point Rozmarynowicz began to snore audibly; Klossowitz, who was sitting closest, nudged him gently— "will confirm that the power structure and financial system among the white slave traders is highly complex and opaque."

She paused, and Swolkień once again felt called on to respond.

"Indeed it is," he grunted, "one could say it has an arboreal structure: the minor employees are the twigs that grow off larger branches, which stem from boughs, and they in turn emerge from one or two trunks . . ."

"At the same time . . ." she drew him out.

"At the same time?"

"The branches and boughs do not generally know . . ."

"Ah, yes, you could put it like that. Only the closest associates know about each other, in other words the bosses and their immediate underlings, or sometimes, so to speak, two adjacent boughs . . ."

"Thank you very much. Indeed, so it was in this instance, too. The Lemberg trial, in which both of you commissioners took part, making a major contribution to its outcome, chopped off part of this mighty tree. But let us not be deceived" — Zofia stepped forward, slowly walking around the table at which they were sitting — "that the whole tree fell beneath the policeman's axe."

"Can we give the sawmill metaphors a rest?" said Korotkiewicz, bristling.

She ignored him, but she did drop the metaphor.

"Unfortunately the corruption reached the highest echelons of administrative power, and you gentlemen know as well as I do that '*Laws are like cobwebs, which catch small flies, but let hornets go free.*'"

"Dear lady!" said Rozmarynowicz indignantly. "One cannot agree. The law . . ."

"That proverb comes from the sixteenth-century poet Mikołaj Rej, but to this day it carries weight. Several fat hornets went free, and one of them flew all the way to Brazil, not just leaving his underlings to the mercy of justice, but also taking the bulk of their money with him, the cash gained from this inhuman enterprise. He was, as you know, Józef Silberberg, who in Rio de Janeiro, now named José Silva, set himself up in the business he knew best, that's to say he used the money he had brought with him to found a whole empire of brothels. Meanwhile the smaller flies . . ."

"If it's not a sawmill, it's etymology!" muttered Korotkiewicz.

"Entomology," she corrected him, not without satisfaction. "The smaller flies landed in prison, and among them was one Solomon Loewenstein, alias Lewicki, who swore a terrible revenge on Silberberg. And here begins the tragedy of Karolina Szulc, who had no idea that on the other side of the ocean, her father was building a criminal empire, but meanwhile his paternity was to determine the course of her life. Or rather: her death."

"If certain details are too sensitive, I am prepared . . ." offered Klossowitz.

"No, please have no fears," she answered him, after stopping behind Swolkień. "I am not of a timid nature. And so: we happen to know that Loewenstein had a favorite method of revenge, which was to tarnish his enemies' daughters. But this time, if I am not mistaken, he planned a truly satanic vengeance: he brought it about that . . . José Silva, by his own agency, so to speak . . . violated his own daughter."

Swolkień, Jednoróg, and Korotkiewicz fixed their gaze on her; even Rozmarynowicz showed interest, and only Klossowitz leaned back a little in his chair, with his eyes half-closed, as if watching the show for the second time, certain that nothing to be said onstage could take him by surprise.

"To win Karolina over . . . that is, Miss Szulc," she corrected herself, "he sent a man trained for the purpose, his subordinate, one Wolf Sztycer, who worked at Mrs. Dunin's brothel on Różana Street. Sztycer acted according to the standard rules: he pretended to be a well-off engineer who had fallen in love with the lovely young girl, wanted to marry her on the spot and take her with him to the New

World, where she would live a happy life in the lap of luxury. And indeed, keeping it secret from her employers, and also from her own mother, she began to meet with the alleged engineer, who took her on a long journey, all the way to Dębniki, when the right time came. And it was the right time because José Silva had arrived in Galicia. Why?"

Surprised looks answered her.

"That is a question for you, Commissioner."

Swolkień blinked, then began cautiously: "Most likely . . . he came for fresh goods?"

"Yes, very nicely put," said Zofia, praising him like a real governess. "José Silva came for fresh goods, for 'carpets from Smyrna' and 'mother-of-pearl caskets,' meaning beautiful young girls, who, in Rio de Janeiro, bought from a third party, cost considerably more than if bought on the spot, at the source, for half the price. When he heard about this journey, Loewenstein got in touch with his old boss. I am certain he did not demand the return of the money; on the contrary—he forgot all about their old dispute and showed no regret for the ten months he had spent in jail, but offered to take care of Silberberg's business in Galicia for him, and in exchange for a modest percentage he would make sure the most splendid girls were sent to the brothels in Rio. The visitor from Brazil arrived in Cracow on"—she opened her notebook—"the tenth of April, the Wednesday before Easter, and stayed at the Róża Hotel; on the thirteenth, Easter Saturday, Karolina ran off with her fiancé, who took her to Dębniki or to some other place where she was kept until

Easter Monday. That was when Loewenstein was resolved to carry out his revenge. They brought Silberberg a pure virgin, one who they knew would resist him, something that they knew that . . . in this man . . . would arouse the most ardent desire."

"I have heard of two girls being abducted out of revenge, but as for this . . . no, as I live and breathe, I have never heard of such a thing!" said Swolkień slowly, his forehead beaded with sweat.

"Hideous, hideous," Jednoróg eagerly chimed in.

Zofia turned on her heel and began to walk in the opposite direction, going back around the table, occasionally stopping behind one or another of the chairs.

"Naturally, the revenge would not have been complete if Silberberg had not found out whom he had dishonored. Loewenstein arranged a pleasant evening, the ladies and gentlemen had a drink, something to eat, enjoyed pleasant company . . . only in the small hours were those dreadful words uttered, when . . ."

Korotkiewicz interrupted her.

"Do excuse me, but I have more urgent tasks than listening to extracts from a cheap novel. Do you have any idea what investigative work involves? Believe me, it has nothing to do with tearful tales about virgins being abducted!"

"I am not presenting a novel, but the history of a certain crime," she quipped, "and my account is based on witness statements and many weeks of hard work to unravel the entire mystery!"

"Unraveling is a more appropriate occupation for a lady, I might add, than . . ."

"Counselor," said Klossowitz from the other side of the table, "I appeal to you for your patience."

"All right, be brisk about it," muttered the police chief.

"I will be brisker if you do not constantly interrupt me. Where were we? Oh yes. At dawn Silberberg found out what he had been induced to do. Shaken, he went back to his hotel room, and there, as you already know, he shot himself."

"But what about the girl? What happened to her?"

"Well," she said, flicking a speck of dust from her sleeve, "here, unfortunately, we must bring in one other person. A third player, who in this tree of white slave traders was at the same level as Silberberg, thus higher up than Loewenstein, and who drew the appropriate profits from the practice, without actually doing very much. One could even say he was paid to do nothing. Like Loewenstein, he had lost his share of the money that was taken away to Brazil, but unlike him he put cash before revenge. The third player could not resign himself to the fact that the large sums of money he had trustingly deposited in the criminals' bank had simply served to build Silva's private empire in Rio de Janeiro. And as in his devious way he is a man who believes in the power of the law, in legality, even in his own brand of what I might call *honesty,* he tried appealing to, please do not laugh, the *conscience* of his former associate . . ."

Only Klossowitz laughed, who evidently found it amusing.

"And when he discovered that Silberberg was in Galicia, actually staying in Cracow, he decided to seek the return of the debt. On that fatal evening when Loewenstein took his hideous revenge," she continued, standing behind Commissioner Jednoróg's chair, "the brothel on Różana Street was, of course, closed to clients, and two men were posted at the door to send any visitors away, if not verbally, then physically, using their fists. And yet, presumably to Loewenstein's great annoyance, the third player was allowed to enter. Because it is hard to send a police commissioner packing."

These final words, spoken with emphasis, prompted an understandable commotion; Korotkiewicz was particularly piqued, and looked around him, as if in search of someone to reject the charge at once. Only Jednoróg sat motionless, his face frozen like a death mask against the gray serge background—the dress worn by Mrs. Turbotyńska, standing behind him.

"Commissioner Stanisław Jednoróg, because that is who it was."

"Commissioner, say something!" said Korotkiewicz furiously.

"Why?" replied Jednoróg calmly. "I see no reason to question the facts. Nor do I see anything reprehensible about a policeman tailing his suspects. As you all know, Silberberg was mixed up in white slave trading, but we had failed to obtain the proof to catch him before he fled abroad. But as he had appeared in Galicia again, it was my duty to keep my finger on the pulse. As far as the fairy tale spun by this lady is concerned, I have nothing to say—I am not accustomed to defending myself against fabricated accusations."

"So why did you never mention that you were at Różana Street on the night of the murder?" asked Zofia, stopping three paces farther on, behind Swolkień, so that she could look at Jednoróg. "You were conducting the inquiry, but meanwhile . . ."

"Do forgive me," said Jednoróg, laughing. "Clearly you have no idea about the work of the police. Magistrate Rozmarynowicz was conducting the inquiry."

"We all know perfectly well . . ."

"No, madam, *we* know. *You* know nothing. You are imagining things."

"So am I imagining that you kept your presence at Różana Street a secret?"

Jednoróg raised his chin a bit, passed a hand over his face, then spoke to her as if to a naughty child: "I confess, to all those gathered here, I confess that in my conduct toward you I was guided by a certain weakness, because you are a woman, the wife of a professor, a respected person, who had suffered an understandable shock when her maid was murdered. And now I regret the mistake I made by confiding in you too much during our conversations, as a result of which you could have fantasized that you were in some way admitted to the inquiry. Meanwhile your only role in it was as a witness. The fact that I did not tell you about my visit to Różana Street does not mean that I did not mention it to the magistrate."

"Magistrate?" said Korotkiewicz, addressing Rozmarynowicz.

"For sure, for sure," came the vague response, "it must be somewhere in the files . . ."

"No, there is no mention of it in the files," replied Klossowitz calmly.

Jednoróg laughed.

"Am I to be accused of collaborating with white slave traders just because someone has failed to record my statements in the files? That has to be the most absurd piece of indirect proof I have ever come across!"

"I think our little chat is at an end," said Korotkiewicz, getting up. "We are busy people, we hold important positions, while here . . ."

"But just a moment, gentlemen," said Zofia, this time adopting the tone of a strict governess, "we are not at the halfway point yet! Surely you do not think I would have asked Magistrate Klossowitz to call this meeting if I only had flimsy circumstantial evidence at my disposal? Far from it."

"Counselor," Klossowitz's voice rang out, "I insist you hear this to the end."

Korotkiewicz hesitated, but then warily sat down again.

"So let us return to the events of that fatal night. From the statements of the owner, in fact only the ostensible owner of the brothel, Mrs. Dunin, we know that the commissioner had a short but firm exchange of remarks with Loewenstein in the hallway, then he burst into the rooms where the *honored guest* and his *gift* had been accommodated and had a quarrel with his former associate, Silberberg . . ."

"I cannot listen to this," said Jednoróg indignantly.

"Please do not whine but take it like a man!" Zofia responded, then set off on her tour of the around table again. "But I must draw your attention to a particular dependence. Loewenstein had no idea that the commissioner had ever collaborated with Silberberg; on the contrary, in his time he had been caught by Jednoróg and sent to jail for six months, so he thought it was an ordinary police raid that might additionally thwart his plans. If he had known that they were members of the same organization . . ."

"Mrs. Turbotyńska!" thundered Korotkiewicz.

". . . he would have dealt with him more boldly. But he did not know that, nor did any of his employees, because the only reason why Commissioner Jednoróg could act so efficiently and could be so helpful was that his contacts with the gang were limited to the absolute minimum. Probably only Silberberg knew to whom the criminals owed the protection of the Cracow police, and who gave them advance warning of raids by the honest Commissioner Swolkień." Sitting there with a deadly serious look on his face, Swolkień shuddered. "And only Silberberg paid him a salary, or rather dividends from the capital that kept accruing in the criminal bank. So when the two former associates began to quarrel about money behind closed doors, in hushed tones . . ."

"Balderdash, utter balderdash, there's not a word of truth in it!" roared Jednoróg.

". . . Loewenstein, Dunin, and company thought José Silva would be escorted out of the room under arrest, so the entire revenge hung by a thread, depending on whether the girl had already been violated or not. But at some point the commissioner burst into the hall and slammed the door, and that was the last they saw of him. Why? Because he had realized that they were not having a private tête-à-tête at all. Indeed, the door separated them from the hallway, and it was curtained by a thick drape that stifled every sound, as we know from Mrs. Dunin's statements, but inside the room, apart from Silberberg there was also Miss Szulc, or rather Miss Silberberg . . . I do not know how the commissioner failed to notice her; perhaps she was lying in shame amid the rumpled bedding, perhaps the light in there was too dim to see much at all, or perhaps she had shut herself in the small lavatory adjoining the bedroom, and had suddenly emerged from it . . . Perhaps on hearing the quarrel and concluding from it that the newcomer was a policeman, she came out of a corner to beg for help? That we shall never know. Karolina is dead, so is Silberberg, and the commissioner is unlikely to feel inclined to be effusive on this point."

"Would you like some more fairy tales in response to

your own? All right," said Jednoróg malevolently but in a calm tone. "I entered that room, but all I found there was the Pied Piper, handing Mr. Silva a sheep stuffed with sulfur and pitch. I trust we can regard this meeting as closed. I do not know about you gentlemen, but I have work to do. Cracow is a peaceful city, but we have quite enough crimes to keep us busy. By your leave . . ."

"Sit down, Stanisław," said Swolkień. Curtly, but so firmly that, though on his feet by now, Jednoróg sank back into his chair.

"Thank you," said Zofia, bowing to him. "So let us abandon the sheep and return to our rams. Mr. Jednoróg"—she was now standing opposite him, staring him in the eyes—"realized on the instant that his entire, elaborately crafted cover, all those years of effort to conceal the face of Mr. Hyde behind the mask of Commissioner Jekyll had gone up in smoke. As well as Silberberg, there was another person who knew his secret, an accidental, worthless female, given to Silberberg as a plaything, one of the hundreds, the thousands of girls who sail in a broad stream from all over Galicia to the bawdy houses of Constantinople, Rio de Janeiro, and New York. He understood that not only had he failed to gain a penny from his former associate, but he had dangerously exposed himself, placing in jeopardy his entire reputation, his career, his medals, his social standing and public respect. If he had stopped to think, if at the time, outside the house on Różana Street he had cooled down a bit in the night air, he would have known he had nothing to fear." Jednoróg held her gaze. "The next day, or maybe two days later, at most in a week, the dishonored girl would have shared the fate of all the rest, and the fact that she knew the Cracow commissioner's secret would have meant nothing in a Turkish brothel. But he let himself be carried away by emotion. Why? Because, gentlemen, every man is driven by some sort of desire. Some by noble wishes, others by ignoble ones. The desire for money is just as strong, and in some people stronger perhaps than the desire for flesh, which sometimes . . ."

"The proof, dear lady, the proof!" Korotkiewicz interrupted her.

Zofia leaned her hands against Magistrate Rozmarynowicz's armchair, and said: "The proof is just coming. First, the accusation." At this point she adopted an exalted tone. "I accuse your subordinate, police Commissioner Stanisław Jednoróg, of the following: on the night of the fifteenth to sixteenth of April last year he lurked under the windows of the house on Różana Street, and then, when Józef Silberberg had gone to sleep, and Loewenstein and his bully boys were drinking to celebrate the act of revenge, he helped Karolina Szulc to escape, then stabbed her to death with a knife . . . a sharp instrument . . . and threw her body into the Vistula from Dębnicki bridge. But when he found out that the river had tossed the corpse onto the shore on the Podgórze side, by means known only to himself he made sure the murder would not be investigated by the Podgórze court, but the Cracow one, which meant the Cracow police, too. Please correct me if this was not a serious breach of the legal regulations." She paused, but was met by silence. "What is more, he did everything to ensure that Magistrate Rozmarynowicz took the case, who should long ago have been enjoying a well-earned retirement . . ." Here she was expecting an objection, but Rozmarynowicz had sunk into himself, and the rest were not going to argue with the obvious. "And *de facto* took on the inquiry himself, pointing the blame at outsiders. First at Karolina Szulc's fiancé, the sand miner, but that plan failed because I interfered . . . that is, I joined in with the inquiry and pointed out the figure of the '*geber*' who had seduced the girl by passing himself off as an engineer. Seeing it wasn't going to be as easy as he thought, the commissioner decided to kill two birds with one stone. He shifted his attention to the young socialist, Maciej Czarnota, and with premeditation he exposed him to certain death at the hand of Inspector Trzeciak . . ." Swolkień nervously patted his boot leg, but kept quiet ". . . who was known for his hatred of socialists. Not only had he found the culprit and could close the inquiry, but he had also given the inspector an opportunity to shoot the activist, who was a particular thorn in his flesh. Unfortunately the '*geber*' was still wandering about Cracow, and my other servant bumped into him twice; more than that, she identified him as one Wolf Sztycer. At this point Jednoróg anonymously warned Loewenstein . . ." There was a stir at the table. "That Sztycer absolutely had to be hidden from the police, who saw him as a murderer, which could have led the guardians of the law to the truth about Miss Szulc's abduction. Naturally, Sztycer was dispatched to Constantinople or New York, and the commissioner told me the case was closed, and that Magistrate Rozmarynowicz had categorically forbidden him to reopen it."

Silence fell. Everyone pondered these words, each in his own way. Jednoróg mentally added it all up, checking to see if there was any solid *proof,* and not just *circumstantial evidence* to implicate him; Korotkiewicz was doing the same, while also estimating the potential trouble if the matter were made public, God forbid in Daszyński's newspaper; Swolkień was thinking back over all the cases in which he had cooperated with Jednoróg, and noticing certain worryingly regular occurrences, but he was well aware that the entire accusation was based on rather shaky foundations; whereas Klossowitz was waiting for the decisive thrust of the dagger. Only Rozmarynowicz belatedly said: "But I never forbade anything . . ."

"And is that all? This cock-and-bull story? That is your 'proof'?" said Jednoróg at last, laughing, with evident relief. "Oh dear, what a curious yarn we have heard, straight from the lady's colorful imagination. But this time, forgive me, gentlemen, I refuse to be subjected to further tedium." He stood up. "In normal circumstances I would sue you for slander, but I am not going to take a woman to court. I have heard that ladies with no children tend to suffer from a special kind of trouble, a kind of hysteria that can take all manner of forms, including this sort of fantasy. It is a medical fact. And so . . ."

"No, that is not all," said Zofia in an icy tone. "There is one more detail that I have not yet mentioned—the detail that completes the picture. Perhaps you remember our conversation about Mr. Bertillon's method, and Gross's manual." Swolkień raised an eyebrow in amazement. "We both complained that our police do not make proper use of the latest developments. Yet an ordinary photograph was all it took. Do you recall that charming evening? Once again, do forgive me for so absent-mindedly forgetting to send it to you." Here she reached into her pocket and brought out a piece of card, which she laid on the table.

Above the embossed name *Sebald* was a picture of three figures in festive costumes against a painted backdrop showing a ruined castle; on either side there were two men in *kontusz* coats, and in between them Zofia herself, smiling coyly from under the brim of her hat.

"People generally have a short and feeble memory. The staff at the Róża Hotel are no exception: after all, every day a large number of people make their way through several dozen rooms there, and goodness knows how many guests they have in a week, a month, or a year. And yet even a year and a half later, a person can remember something well if it is connected with a dramatic incident, and Silberberg's suicide definitely counted as one of those. As a result, his visit is still recalled in detail. And at least two of the hotel staff remember the unfortunate scene that occurred on Good Friday when José Silva, a Brazilian citizen, threw a man down the stairs, whom earlier he had invited into his room. They also remember how the Brazilian citizen screamed at him in pure Polish: 'You're not getting a cent, you schmuck, not a cent!' and also: 'Threaten me? Me? Just think what you have to lose!' They only had to be drawn out a little. And then shown the photograph, and asked if by some extraordinary chance, the mysterious man in civilian clothes was not depicted here, looking very fine in a *kontusz.* They recognized you without hesitation, Commissioner, as the man who had quarreled with Silva alias Silberberg. And so that night"—she looked Jednoróg straight in the eyes—"you swept into Mrs. Dunin's brothel in a fury: you knew it was your last chance, that Silberberg was about to leave, and then all your hopes of recovering the money would evaporate. And that is also why you reacted so *hysterically,* by killing Karolina: it was the second time that your former associate had exposed you to the risk of revealing the whole secret. At the Róża Hotel, words were spoken in public that you could easily have defended, but Karolina accidentally found out much more, and from your own lips." Addressing them all, she continued: "For your information, gentlemen, I shall add that Magistrate Klossowitz has already recorded these statements, and unfortunately this photograph will not end up in the commissioner's hands as a nice souvenir of an evening in May, because it is going in the case files as a piece of evidence."

Jednoróg was tongue-tied, as were Swolkień and Korotkiewicz. Whereas Rajmund Klossowitz was shifting his gaze from one face to another, trying to assess what impression Turbotyńska's final thrust had made on them. Plainly agitated, Korotkiewicz leaned toward Swolkień and they whispered for a while; then he stood up, bowed, and said: "Dear madam, we appreciate your contribution to the inquiry, you have undoubtedly spotted some interesting dependencies that need to be thoroughly elucidated, and the police will definitely see to it. However, it is impossible to fail to notice that the . . . accusation that you have devised . . . from various not necessarily interconnected facts, is rather fragile. It is more like a collection of observations, vague circumstantial evidence . . ."

"But, sir . . ." she protested.

"*We know* our job," he said extremely firmly. "Each of us has a series of solved cases behind him and I can assure you that our work has never relied on such casual conclusions. Pieces of evidence, deduction, yes, indeed, all these are essential things. But the court has to rely on solid proof. That sort of proof, at least so far, we cannot see. Perhaps further investigation by the designated organs will reveal something else. So thank you, Mr. Klossowitz, for calling this meeting, and, Mrs. Turbotyńska, for your story, undeniably of interest for various reasons. Goodbye."

She stood not knowing what to say. She glanced at Klossowitz, who with a barely visible flicker of his eyelids let her know that this time she should give way, so with great regret she simply said: "Thank you for sparing your time. May it prove fruitful. Goodbye."

And she walked out. First into the corridor, then out of the courthouse, and finally into Grodzka Street, into a cold, cloudy September day. Around her the city was living its life: porters were carrying goods, tradeswomen were selling things, and hackney coaches were on their way to their destinations.

EPILOGUE

The city had been beautifully prepared for the emperor's arrival. The bridges were decorated with strings of colored garlands, flaming beacons, gas lamps, and even electric lighting. All the streets running toward the railway tracks were illuminated, but especially Dietl Street where it bordered Planty Park, so that as he traveled along the viaduct through Grzegórzki, on looking down, the distinguished guest would see a river of lights—like a recreation, through the miracle of electrification, of the Vistula on the route it used to follow, before it was filled in preceding the famous visit of Their Royal Majesties over fifteen years ago. Today His Apostolic Majesty was visiting Cracow on his own. Had he wished to look up he would have seen Wawel Hill illuminated, the roofs and domes of the churches and a little farther on, the town hall tower.

He would have seen how Cracow had spent several days decorating itself with all its might, purely to show itself to him from its best side for just a few minutes. But Franz Joseph did not see the lighted bridges, or the churches, or the crowd of people heading for the viaducts and railway embankments to catch a fleeting glimpse of the train as it carried past their gracious ruler. Instead he sat hunched at a desk, on which a pile of documents towered, demanding his urgent attention: nominations for the post of general, expressions of thanks, administrative reports—in other words everything once helplessly dubbed "the barrel of the Danaids." He was bowing down to finish a letter to his dear lady friend, Katharina Schratt: *"The reception here is especially splendid, sincere, and patriotic, the ovations last a long time, but there is also the usual stream of requests that are delivered to me during every journey through this country."* Through the curtained windows the pale reflection of the lights of another Galician city fell into the imperial carriage, yet another place he was due to visit—one of the innumerable towns in this picturesque but rather wild country.

Around the station the fortunate few were gathered who, like Professor and Mrs. Turbotyńska, had managed to secure platform tickets at the town hall. The station building, recently made half a story higher and enriched with decorations, was looking very fine, but it was eclipsed by the triumphal triple arch above Lubicz Street, the middle section of which reached the second floor of the station hall. Cresting the arch there was an imperial crown with the intertwined initials *FJ* and the double-headed eagle of the Habsburgs, and above the whole construction flags fluttered on the gentle breeze, a black-and-yellow imperial one, a red-and-white one for Galicia, and a blue-and-white one for Cracow.

Ignacy was full of admiration.

"A clear sky and the beautiful blue Vistula, our city's colors, eternally united with the dynastic colors of the Habsburgs! What a stirring sight, upon my word! Don't you think, my dear?"

"Hm," coughed Zofia, straightening her black hat adorned with yellow rudbeckias, chosen at the express insistence of her husband, who was set on this color scheme, and looked around her, observing all the goings-on with a mixture of indifference and irritation.

"Look," said Ignacy, pointing, "can you see how ingeniously they have designed it?"

The arch above the street, just before the railway crossing, had turned out to have another purpose apart from glorifying the ruling house; a while ago a rotary platform for turning steam engines had been dismantled so that the street could be lowered and a tunnel built under the railway tracks; the heaps of earth and sand dug up during the preparatory work had been hidden behind a hastily erected fence, which in turn was shielded by a pillar supporting the triumphal gateway, draped in green garlands.

"We shall have a two-level crossroads," he went on, "think of that, what a miracle of technology! But I must say, I am surprised that bizarre Talowski fellow has been commissioned to build it, but never mind, the city councilors are renowned for their, er, unconventional ideas. Let us hope that he will not decorate our viaduct with spiders, scorpions, or other arthropods." Ignacy disapproved of the architect's modernist approach.

"Filth and mess have been covered up by a bunch of garlands. A mask of deception placed on top of the hideous reality. One might have expected something of the kind," said Zofia drily.

"But my dear . . ." said Ignacy, casting her a look of perplexity, but just then the chairman of the organizing committee, Dr. Weigel, called for the assembled guests to start taking their places: the generals of the Cracow garrison, the prince bishop and the clergy, the representatives of the aristocracy and nobility in their *kontusz* coats and those of the peasantry in their equally traditional *sukmana* coats, the deputies to the Council of State, the city councilors including the mayor and the deputy mayors, the vice chancellor of the university with a delegation of professors (Ignacy had not been chosen—the honor had fallen to the faculty head, Kostanecki, though to her husband's surprise, Zofia had not passed any malicious comment), the officials from all sorts of offices, and the heads of schools. And thus the entire structure of Cracow society as featured in *Czech's Calendar for the year 1896* began to wander about the carpeted platform, trying to find their assigned places among the crimson damask curtains, potted palms, and flowers, while confused members of the civic guard of honor, with blue-and-white bows pinned to their costumes, tried their best to implement Weigel's orders.

In the group of notables Zofia saw Count Starzeński, deep in conference with police chief Korotkiewicz.

"Ah, yes, Starzeński," whispered Ignacy, seeing which way his wife was looking. "Who would have expected this small town to have such an honor! Fancy the Podgórze district getting its own administration, with the count in charge." Then, when Zofia did not react, he decided to amuse her with a comical comparison. "A few days ago I read a description of the inaugural ceremony in the newspaper, and I must say, it sounds as if it didn't fall far short of the pageantry we are enjoying today." He laughed, expecting Zofia to be amused.

"Yes, that is highly probable," she said, squinting to take a closer look at Count Starzeński.

"The *Cracow Times* had expressed a very favorable opinion of him. He gave his assurance that his one and only aspiration was the good of the district and its population."

"I have heard rumors that it is his own good that is of greatest concern to him. They say he profiteers on supplying hay for the army. And lends money at high rates of interest."

"To be sure, Zofia, I would rather not believe it," said Ignacy, shaking his head, "but if it were true . . . which, as I say, I sincerely doubt, surely you do not think the governorship would entrust him with such a responsible post? The state officials in our monarchy should be men of spotless reputation, should they not?"

Zofia gave her husband a look of pity, though tempered with the affection that his good-natured naivety prompted in her. But she didn't say a word.

"I am most terribly sorry . . ." Suddenly a stick-thin redhead with a blue-and-white bow in his lapel sprang up before the Turbotyńskis.

"Cadet Ecler, I see," said Zofia, who recognized the young man instantly. But Ignacy's furrowed brow clearly implied that he did not know who this person was.

"At your service!" said the policeman, clicking his heels.

"So it is!" exclaimed Ignacy, finally remembering where he had seen the man before. "Last year, in connection with our poor Karolina! What a memory you have, Zofia! Pleasure to see you, sir."

Ecler nodded affirmatively, then tried again. "I am most terribly sorry to be so bold, but . . ."

"I see you have been delegated to the civic guard," Ignacy went on, "but how can that be, when you are a policeman? Can it be"—here he lowered his voice—"that you are here incognito, as"—he went down to a whisper—"a secret agent?"

"Indeed, Professor," said the disconcerted Ecler, "I was officially ordered to report to the civil guard, just in case . . . Naturally, it is to do with security. I was referred by the late

Commissioner Jednoróg, who was, as you probably know, one of the deputy chairmen of the organizing committee."

"We are all shocked by the terrible tragedy that befell the commissioner," Ignacy interrupted him. "Who could have imagined such a competent policeman could die cleaning his gun? What an unexpected death!"

"Quite so, who could have thought it?" said Zofia quietly.

"We owed a great debt of gratitude to the late commissioner for solving the mystery of our dear Karolina's death so splendidly," Ignacy continued. "He caught the murderer at lightning speed, sparing no efforts. Isn't that so, Zofia? Yes, yes, he was a man of distinction, unstintingly dedicated to public service. One could say he gave his life for it." Ignacy shook his head sadly. "He was the epitome of our police service; more than that, he symbolized the values that are the cornerstone of all public service in our empire. Don't you agree, my dear?" But this question too went unanswered. "It is an irretrievable loss for our city. What a pity the commissioner's funeral was held so promptly, and not at Rakowicki Cemetery, which would have been the most appropriate place, but in his wife's hometown. Unfortunately we could not attend, I am sure you understand, but I hope, more than that, I am sure today's celebration, so excellently prepared, will stand as the commissioner's legacy. And will leave behind just as positive a memory as the late Mr. Jednoróg himself."

"To be sure, Professor, thank you for your kind words,"

said Ecler, finally getting a word in. "But I must speak to you on an organizational matter . . . Mrs. Turbotyńska, would you please make your way over to the ladies' section, which is over there?" he said, pointing.

"No, young man," said Zofia in an icy tone, "I would not please. I intend to stand where I so wish, and not to be treated differently merely because I am a woman."

"But, Mrs. Turbotyńska . . ." said the young man, going red and bowing low, "I would never have made so bold . . ."

"Zofia, he meant no ill by it . . ."

"It was merely a suggestion. I am most extremely sorry if . . ."

But just then a loud shout of *"Vivat!"* rang out, roaring from the throats of the hundreds of people gathered on the platform and the thousands outside the station building. Bowing and scraping, Ecler crawled off to his designated place. Like all the men crowded on the platform, Ignacy took off his top hat and stood up straight.

As the train drove into the platform, a band of veterans began to play the national anthem. And then, in the window of a green carriage decorated with golden coats of arms, Franz Joseph the First appeared, by the Grace of God Emperor of Austria, Apostolic King of Hungary, King of Bohemia, King of Dalmatia, Croatia, Slavonia, Galicia and Lodomeria and Illyria, King of Jerusalem, etc.; Archduke of Austria; Grand Duke of Tuscany and Cracow, Duke of Lorraine, of Salzburg, Styria, Carinthia, Carniola, and of Bukovina; Grand Prince of Transylvania; Margrave of Moravia; Duke of Upper and Lower Silesia, of Modena, Parma, Piacenza, and Guastalla, of Oświęcim, Zator, and Ćeszyn, Friuli, Ragusa, and Zara; Princely Count of Habsburg and Tyrol, of Kyburg, Gorizia, and Gradisca; Prince of Trent and Brixen; Margrave of Upper and Lower Lusatia and in Istria; Count of Hohenems, Feldkirch, Bregenz, Sonnenberg, etc.; Lord of Trieste, of Cattaro, and over the Windic march; and Grand Voivode of the Voivodship of Serbia. He was wearing a general's uniform. His head was as bald as a hill in the desert, and his side whiskers were as white as a pair of snowy wings. He thanked the band with a nod, then descended the small steps carpeted in crimson velvet.

"Ah, what an imperial spring he has in his step!" whispered Ignacy.

"He stoops," observed Zofia astutely.

"What are you saying, woman?" hissed Ignacy. His graying side whiskers, representing his deep respect for His Majesty, all but quivered with rage. For the first time in ages he felt truly angry with his wife. He had gone to so much effort to get the tickets, so much bother, all in the hope of bringing her joy with places right on the platform, almost within reach of their beloved monarch. Meanwhile his good intentions were being met with nothing but asperity and remarks that were tantamount to an affront against royalty.

"I am pleased to be in my much-loved kingdom of Galicia, where so many kind hearts beat for me," said the emperor, following a welcome speech delivered by the mayor, who had assured him of the deepest affection and loyalty of the citizens of Cracow. "Indeed," he added. "I was eager to make at least a brief stop here."

He was answered by cheers.

Zofia watched it all with an irritation to which her earlier indifference had entirely given way by now. The emperor, masking his boredom quite skillfully, she had to admit, asked if "the city is rising up," if "much is being built," and so on, then various people were presented to him. Ignacy followed it all as intently as could be, while Zofia scrutinized Cracow society in disgust: here was that usurer Starzeński, there was the petty bishop Puzyna — only a near miss and Commissioner Jednoróg, glittering with medals, would have been among them too.

Did she feel satisfied? Well, she would have preferred to see Jednoróg standing before a court, demoted, publicly humiliated, and finally behind prison bars, if not on the scaffold. But she wasn't surprised that the police and the courts had chosen to settle it this way, without casting a shadow on the imperial-royal legal administration: Jednoróg had been offered an ultimatum. Either his wife and children would receive generous benefits from the state purse as the widow and fatherless children of a distinguished commissioner who had died in an unfortunate accident, or he would be tried in court, and his family would be tried by a much tougher tribunal, meaning Cracow society. Few would have made a different choice.

On the day of the memorable meeting, the police had

briskly gotten down to work. That evening at Sidoli's circus, where straight from Paris celebrated artistes were appearing, including the four Chiarini sisters on the flying trapeze and the American fire-eating Dantes brothers, several arrests were made. Those led out of the circus were Anna Blum of Thessaloniki, Ehrlich's agent from Lemberg (who allegedly recruited girls for a ladies' musical ensemble, but set requirements that they had to be beautiful and well built; Solomon Ehrlich sent them a deposit for the journey and assured their parents of *the most solicitous care*), and Szymon Lewicki alias Solomon Loewenstein, charged—as the newspaper reported on September the fifteenth—*"with the abduction and murder of Karolina Szulc, housemaid. Earlier it had been thought a workman was to blame, who was killed attempting to escape when the police tried to detain him, but clearly he had another crime on his conscience. Only root-and-branch police investigation led to the exposure of the real culprit."* Ignacy appeared to have overlooked this item, and Zofia had no intention of pointing it out to him. The trial was to begin at any time, and although she knew that neither Loewenstein nor his subordinates had killed Karolina, she believed their crime to be no less serious than murder, and was looking forward to the high sentences she was sure they would receive.

Now she watched as the emperor offered his hand to Korotkiewicz, and it occurred to her that perhaps it was better that it happened this way. The fact that she belonged to the small group that had gathered in the courthouse a few days ago, whose members were united by a pact of discretion, and that she knew how Commissioner Jednoróg's life had really ended, could open many a door for her in the future.

Meanwhile, His Majesty's twenty-minute visit was coming to an end; with tears in his eyes, whether from emotion or from straining his vision, Ignacy was staring at His Royal Baldness, while the monarch headed back to his carriage, nodding to his subjects among shouts of *"Vivat!"* Imperial Counselor and Deputy Director of Transport Zdenko Kuttig, Imperial Counselor and Inspector of Transport Hubert Husnik, Senior Controller of Transport Jan Swieczynowsky, and Stationmaster Jozafat Szczepański jointly gave the signal for the train to depart. Franz Joseph stood in the window, thanking them all for their warm welcome. As he swept the platform with his gaze, Zofia thought that for a split second he had looked straight at her, that he had picked her out of the crowd with his cold, blue, totally expressionless gaze.

ACKNOWLEDGMENTS

The authors wish to thank Tomasz Fiałkowski and Konrad Myślik for their valuable comments on details of Cracovian life, and all our other early readers for their sound advice that helped us to avoid mistakes and blunders.

In the course of writing this book we referred to a number of other works, in particular *Kaiser von Amerika* by Martin Pollack (Emperor of America, Zsolnay, Vienna 2010) and *Przestępstwa emigracyjne w Galicji 1897–1918* by Grzegorz Maria Kowalski (Émigré crimes in Galicia 1897–1918, Jagiellonian University Press, Kraków 2003).

Within the text there are a number of genuine quotations from the works of authors who should rightfully be acknowledged. These include:

- Stanisłąw Szczepanowski, who in 1888 published an

important work, *Nędza Galicyi w cyfrach i program energicznego rozwoju gospodarstwa krajowego* (The poverty of Galicia in figures and a program for the energetic development of the national economy), which opened many readers' eyes to the problems of Europe's poorest region;

- Dr. Stanisław Teofil Kurkiewicz, who from 1905 to 1906 published in Kraków his three-volume work, *Z docieków (studyów) nad życiem płciowem* (From studies of sexual life) and in 1913 another separate dictionary of unusual terms (which Tadeusz Boy-Żeleński called "kurkiewisms"), *Słownik płciowy: zbiór wyrażeń o płciowych właściwościach, przypadłościach itp.: Do użytku przy zeznawaniu przed lekarzem płciownikiem* (A wordbook of sexlore: A set of terms on sexual traits, complaints, etc., to be used in reporting to a doctor of sexlore).
- Augustyn Czarnowski, in whose book *Życie płciowe i jego znaczenie ze stanowiska zdrowotno-obyczajowego. Wedle rozmaitych źródeł zebrał i ułożył Dr Czarnowski. Wydanie drugie, dopełnione. Z licznemi rycinami* (Sexual life and its meaning from the health and moral standpoint. Collected and arranged from various sources by Dr. Czarnowski. Second edition, supplemented. With numerous prints), which was published by the Przewodnik Zdrowia ("Health Guide") publishing house in Berlin (undated but probably in 1904), we can read about the "ectodermal odor of a pure virgin,"

and how it suffers a cataleptic shock when affected by a male odor, and also about the differences in male and female attitude and about how schooling leads to degeneracy of the embryonal glands and infertility.

- Dr. Antoni Gettlich, who expressed the wisdom that women should sit at home instead of writing novellas and being bad doctors in an article entitled "Wyższe wykształcenie kobiet" (The higher education of women), in which, based on Christian culture, he argued against the idea of founding a school for girls modelled on the boys' lycée. Gettlich (whose name also appears as Getilich or Getlich) was for thirty years head of the St. Scholastica Women's Faculty School in Kraków.
- Ignacy Daszyński, who published his *Memoirs* in 1925–6.
- And finally Leon Brand, the Job of the Kraków pimps, is not an invented character, though he made his petitions more than a decade later. The documents relating to his case, including the letter from the prostitutes, are to be found in the Kraków branch of the National Archive.

Lastly, numerous quotations, including those from Robert Louis Stevenson's *Strange Case of Dr. Jekyll and Mr. Hyde,* are from the Galician press of the era, especially the Turbotyńskis' favorite newspaper, *Czas* (The Cracow Times), but also from *Nowa Reforma* (New Reform),

Gazeta Lwowska (The Lemberg Gazette), *Kurier Lwowski* (The Lemberg Courier), *Gazeta Narodowa* (The National Gazette), *Naprzód* (Forward), and *Gazeta Robotnicza* (The Workers' Gazette).

ABOUT THE AUTHOR

Maryla Szymiczkowa is the pen name of the author duo Jacek Dehnel and Piotr Tarczyński.

Jacek Dehnel is a writer, poet, and translator. He has written several novels, among them *Lala* (Oneworld, 2018) and *Saturn* (Dedalus, 2012), and his poetry collection *Aperture* was published by Zephyr Press in 2018. He writes crime fiction under the pseudonym Maryla Szymiczkowa together with husband **Piotr Tarczyński,** a translator and historian. *Mrs. Mohr Goes Missing* was their first book. They live in Warsaw.

Antonia Lloyd-Jones is a prize-winning translator of Polish literature.